Gym Class Hero

Martin Parks Kalmbach

SoTol Publishing – Toledo, OH
ISBN 978-0-9993597-0-9
Library of Congress Card Catalogue Number: 2017915209
Gym Class Hero | Kalmbach, Martin Parks
Available Formats: eBook | Paperback distribution

Dedication

For my sister and brother, mother and father, who instilled in me a love of reading, an appreciation for humor, and compassion for animals.

Chapter 1

I watched the video over and over, fifty, a hundred times. The video of Channel 47's Jackson High School Ohio state championship basketball game. I could mimic, repeat the announcers' play-by-play word for word.

"Back door layup! Got two and a foul! Jackson trails by only one with twelve seconds to play! Benny Kalkannes can tie it with a made free throw. What a comeback by the Kestrels."

I often fell asleep at night in my bed watching the recording as it repeatedly looped. I had traveled to Columbus to The Ohio State University campus with my mother and father, wearing my Junior Kestrels' red and black jersey to watch my brother Benny play in the state championship game. I idolized Benny. The starting point guard for the Jackson High School Kestrels both his junior and senior years, he had earned second team All-Ohio honors, and made first team all district and first team all-conference. Benny had taught me everything I knew about basketball. A seventh grader then, I had gone to all my brother's games since he entered high school and all I wanted in the world was to be just like him, to play basketball for the high school, for the Jackson Kestrels and lead them to the league and state championships. And that's what Benny had hoped for me, had *decided* for me.

But sometimes the train goes off the track. Events, people, emotions came into play, interfered, so the shards of a broken dream were all I held. But fate sat at the door, deciding if, when, and where it wanted to enter my life. I'd be hard pressed to tell you a defining moment, but looking back it had to have started at the beginning of my junior year. A year that taught me life lessons about relationships, trust, words, how words lose their meaning, how words are powerful, how words lead to thought and action, confidence gained, confidence lost, heartbreak and love. I'd like to say that I made all the right decisions, for myself, for my basketball team. But I can't say that. I can't say that at all.

Late summer, northern Ohio, the August evening's clouds on their ephemeral slow float from west to east. I watched their lazy shapes drifting overhead like giant white blimps, sitting with my back against the basket's stanchion on Touhey Park's concrete court, workout over, feeling the sweat in the crevices under my arms, tee-shirt damp, legs aching. The Summer Routine: Two hundred shots each night followed by fifty free throws. Keep the elbow in, follow through till the ball dropped through the basket – function follows form.

The court sounds at Touhey resonated in my ears as I went through the familiar repetitious routine: the thumping sound of the ball as I dribbled it on the cement court, scrape of shoes on concrete, the chink! of the ball hitting the chain net, plopping, catching, pausing a split second, falling to the court, reverberation of the metal backboard—clunk!—as the basket shook and swayed on bank shots.

One cloud, rorshachian in shape, billowy white with a tinge of pencil gray floated away, not content to ride with the others on their journey. Thoughts turned to the coming season, my junior year at Jackson High School. I had never gone out for the team. The coach and I didn't see eye to eye since an incident in gym class early in my freshman year, that coach now gone (losing seasons, parent complaints, school board bending). As my brother Benny, who starred on Jackson's state team five years before, told me, I had up till now only starred in my phys ed classes, sarcastically calling me a "Gym Class Hero." (Known as the best

2

three ball shooter in the school, I could rain threes, teardrops from the sky). But the last time I played organized basketball had been in eighth grade. Only a gym class hero. I was determined that that was about to change.

A morning thunderstorm greeted the new school year. The newly waxed floors of Jackson High welcomed the student body as they herded in through the glass double doors by the office and down the main hallway, dripping water from new backpacks, laughing, calling out to friends as we spotted them, many not seen since the end of last school year and the beginning of summer vacation. Walking to my locker I heard my name called from somewhere behind me, recognized it. I cocked my head, and turned to await the certain abuse headed my way.

"Kalkannes! Part the waters. Here comes the gym class hero!"

My brother's taunt had spread, a scarlet letter targeting me. My buddy K.J., K'wame Jordan, starting school's opening day with a well-placed shot to my ego. K.J., the team's starting center, wasting no time. Last year's coach, Coach Ballmer, master of the sports cliché, always referred to K.J. in the local paper and in T.V. interviews as "A force to be reckoned with." Another favorite of Coach Ballmer's, whenever a player scored a lot of points had been to say, "He had a hot hand. He was literally on fire tonight." Literally? Conjured up visions of flames shooting out of a scorching appendage. When K.J. had made the varsity as a freshman Coach Ballmer told the media that K.J. "Had a great future ahead of him." I wondered where else K.J.'s future could be - behind him? We started calling K.J. "Wreck," in deference to Coach's continual admonition of K.J. being that force that the other teams would have to reckon with. He definitely could make an impact on his basketball environment, at 6'4" and 200 pounds.

"Heard you were thinkin' about playin' this year, Stevie."

"That's crazy talk, Wreck," I said with a grin.

Even though I didn't play with the team in their summer

basketball league or show up for open gyms, word had gotten out. K.J. gave me his stern, furrowed-brow look.

"You not playin'—that's just stinkin' thinkin'. You and I both know you've got game."

K.J. poked his finger in my chest. Hard.

"You're playin'. End of discussion."

"How do I know the new guy will let me?" I said.

What had the new coach heard about me, if anything? That I was a great shooter? That I had a reputation as a loose cannon? That I had never played high school basketball?

Wreck sang out in a high-pitched voice, pleading, mocking. "Cause heeee's the new guy, Stevie. He doesn't know that you're one ca-razy person, place, or thing. You better go talk to the man. But maybe Steve-o's doubtin' his stuff, huh?"

"Maybe I will," I said. "You know me, Wreck, that I don't like to play by the rules, color within the lines. But then," I added, my arms up and out with palms up, flashing a smile indicating that I couldn't help what everybody knew, "Ain't no shame in my game. Maybe I need a little coaxing."

Another part of my game - false bravado. I didn't feel any urgency to express that point to K.J. just then.

The new coach came from the East, an older guy, been coaching since God was a boy, a stickler for hard work, commitment, good defense, discipline, and team play. A stickler. I couldn't be sure that I wanted to play for a coach who was a stickler. I had to admit that my reputation included being more than a little crazed, that I enjoyed making a spurious comment now and then. That usually didn't go over well with sticklers. My mother often told me that I had been raised by wolves, that it hadn't been a Nature vs. Nurture thing, it had been both. I decided to wait a few weeks before I talked to Coach.

The new school year took on its own rhythm. A comfortable

sameness—get up at 6:30, shower and dressed by 7:00, breakfast 7:05–7:15, the honk of Hobie Gajun's old beater Plymouth in my driveway for the short trip to JHS. Pre-school banter in the hallway, same prescribed routes to class and lunch, bang of the lockers shutting after school, the walk to the parking lot. Nights I ate dinner, played basketball at Touhey Park, walked the dog, and up in my room, mixed in some homework with ESPN, texts, tweets, e-mail and phone talk. Friday night football at the end of the week provided a welcome diversion for the autumn nights. We cheered, Jackson lost (usually a whole lot to a little bit). And on and on as late summer made way for fall.

Toward the end of October an added excitement took place—a transfer student. She became the talk of the halls and the main course topic in the lunch lines within an hour. The Senior girls, congregating at the windowed end of the cafeteria had something new to digest with their flavored water, salads, deli subs and waffle fries. A first period rumor, its wildfire spread by the runners delivering passes from the main office, fanning the flames—a new girl in school and you ought to see her—whole classrooms inquisitive—their fascination displacing the Pythagorean Theorem, Iambic Pentameter, the Laws of Motion, The War of the Roses. What's her schedule? What's she look like? Where's she from? Heard she's really hot…

Mindy was a wild child, a sixteen-year-old with the feminine wiles of a college co-ed. Her looks—dark hair, French bangs, ponytail, a tomboy, look of an innocent—belied the impish schemes that went on behind her brown eyes. The student body hadn't seen anyone like her before. A little dynamo, more than cute, a little tease, a lot devilish, a whirring left and right brained construct of sultry sweet smelling protoplasm, soon to be stirring up no small amount of trouble for Jackson's teachers, boys—the love struck—and the jealous co-eds (mostly those we referred to as "The Young and the Breastless"). All to Mindy's delight.

5

Fate had made a one-hundred-twenty pound delivery of infatuation, delivered to Jackson High School. She, for me. There could be no other reason.

I had to breathe her air.

Chapter 2

Sitting in study hall last period of the day, Indian summer had made its last trip to Jackson, warm wind wafting in through the opened windows when the end of day announcements came on, stealing us from our late afternoon reverie. My head down, turned sideways on my desk in the row nearest the windows, two minutes to go before the clock overhead the study hall monitor's desk clicked over to 2:30, dismissing us for the weekend. (I always liked to sit by the windows in any class that I could. The pull of being outside being ever present.) I had been watching the helicopters twirling down from the small copse of maple trees outside the window, caught in updrafts then falling in a swirl, riding the wind to their inevitable landing, spreading their seeds on the school's light green grassy lawn that soon would be losing its color, changing to winter's brown.

"There will be a meeting for all boys intending on trying out for basketball on Monday after school in the gym. See Coach Arnold for more information."

That weekend, on Sunday, I walked on the path through the forest of the metropark a half mile from my house. My thoughts were on basketball, whether to play or not to play. I had questions, doubts. What if I didn't make the team? After all, it had been over two years since I played competitively. What if I made the team but rarely saw the floor, relegated to being a bench sitter? Could I handle that? I pretty much had my competition figured out, who I had to be better than in order to win playing time. I thought I could beat them out, but yet … Would it be easier, simpler to not play and remain a sort of school legend, the kind talked about at class reunions twenty or thirty years later by the guys, the jocks who did play, the High School Harrys that couldn't let go of their lifetime hi-lights that culminated when they were eighteen, drinking beers, reminiscing? "You should have seen Stevie play. Man, could he shoot. We would have won the league if he had come out for the team." That would be better than making the team and being a scrub, the players put in with two minutes to play when the team led or trailed by twenty points. I walked the trails, hands in my jacket pockets, crunching leaves, thinking.

I thought about my dad, too, those thoughts turning back to my eighth grade year. Did I want to please him or aggravate him by playing or not playing? My dad had confronted my coach, Coach Wellborn, after one of the games. Lumbering down the steps then awkwardly over the bleacher seats, his face red, he came roaring up to Coach Wellborn as Mr. Wellborn collected his play board and a few stray warm-up jackets behind the bench.

"You don't know if the ball is stuffed or pumped!" my dad shouted as Coach Wellborn turned around, looking like a deer in headlights. "You run that last play for Stevie and we win! Everybody knows that Kenny can't make that shot!"

Actually, I had been the first option. I couldn't get open.

Coach Wellborn tried to tell my dad that, but Dad waved him off and stormed away, muttering, "Where do they get these guys?" My mom said he hadn't always been like that, but something about sports, especially the sports Benny and I participated in, made him a raging, opinionated know-it-all. She refused to sit with him starting with Benny's sixth grade games.

"Honey," she'd tell me, "Your dad is a good man. He wants so badly to see you and Benny do well that it drives him over the edge when he thinks you've been treated unfairly. Or what's that expression he uses? 'When my boys are getting the screws put to them.' He's a good guy, Stevie. You have to do your best to ignore him when he acts like that. He never means to hurt you."

A selective jerk. He only flamed at subjects near and dear to his heart, sports and bad drivers.

My father lived in Chicago now, re-married, a bombastic co-host of "The Tailgate Party" on WTWC 100.1, "The Windy City's Home for Sports." The past two years it had been named the most listened-to sports talk radio show in Chicagoland. He, Ken Kalkannes, hosted along with his partner Leon "Sackman" Marshall. Sackman had played defensive end for the Bears and had a more genial bent to his criticisms than my dad. One of my dad's usual on-air tirades had to do with modern players who took steroids to gain an advantage, unfair to those who didn't. His off-air tirades usually had to do with any driver in front of him who only drove the speed limit in the left lane, those in the car in front of his who dallied as lights changed to green, looking at their cell phones, and those who made left-hand turns in front of him when their turn arrow had changed to red and my dad's had changed to green. Profanities ensued in conjunction with the laying on of the horn, often accompanied by his hand's digital gestures. Those reprobates that committed my dad's litany of driving sins had become the bane of his existence along with coaches who lacked the mental capacity of gerbils.

"What is this, drive up Ken's butt day?" had been my dad's opening to a recent show.

"Do I have a bumper sticker that reads 'TAILGATERS WELCOME?' Would you run out to the parking lot and check that for me, Sackman? I could tell the color of the eyes of the guys driving behind me on Lake Shore Drive driving into work today!'"

My dad had started doing sports talk radio when he lived in Jackson, co-hosting WRSC 97.6's "The Drive" every weekday from two in the afternoon until six at night. He did the same gig in Chicago, doing his schtick for a much bigger market, larger audience now, followed religiously by guys who got amped conversing on sports, betting on games, had fantasy football and baseball teams, spent their money on their favorite team's and favorite player's gear, identified with some pro or major university team, bought everything the teams marketed—tickets, drinking glasses, jerseys, sweatshirts, ball caps, tailgating gear— all emblazoned with the name, logo, colors of whoever—the Bears, Bulls, Cubs, Sox, Northwestern, Illinois, Notre Dame, Michigan, Ohio State.

My brother had been pretty perceptive, gaining insight into these "faithful" fans from listening to them over and over on our dad's call-in show. Now we listened to him on the internet, but the guys listening in Chicago weren't any different than the guys in Jackson with buying into the marketing and trying to get some inside info so they could win their bets, their fantasy leagues. When Benny's friends came to our house to watch the Michigan-Ohio State game on a late November Saturday afternoon, wearing either their maize and blue or scarlet and gray, Benny put them in their place, more or less good naturedly.

"How much did you guys pay for your jerseys and your caps? You know that their offices of admission wouldn't touch you with a stick, but they'd gladly accept your money for tickets. It's all a marketing ploy and you guys swallow it whole. Just try sending them an application for admission. Holding up an imaginary piece of paper, Benny "read" from it.

"Here's your reply: '*To whom it concerns. Thank you for your interest in attending our university. Unfortunately your grades, ACT scores, and your parents' donor profiles don't meet our criteria at the present time. We wish you good luck in your higher education endeavors. Enclosed you will find applications for season football and basketball tickets as well as a brochure featuring our newest team wear and memorabilia, as well as a form asking for your donation to our athletic program. Please be informed that for all donations over one thousand*

10

dollars your name will be listed on the back page of the school's annual newsletter in small print.'"

My brother wore his Bowling Green State University brown jersey with orange numbers outlined in white, but he had actually attended BGSU. I didn't tell his friends about the scarlet and gray Ohio State jersey he kept in his dresser drawer.

My dad's show appealed to the demographic of men aged 25 to 49. His advertisers included sports bars, secondary ticket market sellers, gentlemen's clubs, sports book on-line betting services, auto manufacturers, divorce court lawyers, and even a jeweler— for those lucky enough to have found a mate whose idea of a romantic dinner consisted of a semi-chewable hot dog and a twenty ounce beer on a rainy cold night at Soldier Field.

The more controversy and disagreements my dad could stir up the better, anything to elicit calls and texts from listeners. My dad served up daily radio harangues about college athletes that he perceived as hired guns, pro coaches with abysmal game plans, and pointed out marketing strategies of both college and professional teams that suckered in fans, as my brother had adroitly pointed out to his friends. ("Imagine. For buying a sixty dollar ticket the Cubs are going to give you a two dollar bobblehead. I'm overwhelmed by their generosity.") My dad liked it better when the local teams lost — more for him to complain about. He routinely hung up on callers whose opinions differed from his.

Dad: "OK, Dave from Downer's Grove, give me one reason why you should drive three hours to Champaign to see Illinois get drilled by thirty points?"

Caller: "Because I went there to school. I have to support them. Besides, I get to see my old friends. It's always a fun weekend."

Dad: "YOU THINK DRIVING THREE HOURS TO SEE THAT JOKE OF A TEAM GET ROLLED BY THIRTY POINTS ON THEIR HOME FIELD IS FUN?? AND YOU PAY WHAT, FIFTY,

11

SEVENTY-FIVE BUCKS FOR THE PLEASURE?!! AND ANOTHER TWENTY BUCKS FOR PARKING AND STAND IN LINE FOR FIFTEEN MINUTES TO PAY TWENTY BUCKS MORE FOR A WATERED-DOWN COKE IN A SOUVENIR CUP AND A COLD SLICE OF CARDBOARD PIZZA? OH SURE! YOU GET TO SEE YOUR FRIENDS. WHY DON"T YOU JUST FORM A BOOK CLUB OR MEET FOR DINNER OR GO TO A PLAY ON CAMPUS? INSTEAD, YOU WANT TO SIT OUT IN BONE-CHILLING WEATHER LETTING THEIR ATHLETIC DEPARTMENT TREAT YOU LIKE JACKASSES AND TAKE YOUR MONEY? WHY DON'T YOU JUST COME OVER TO OUR STUDIO. I'LL SAVE YOU THE DRIVE AND GIVE YOU THE SAME EXPERIENCE! I'LL SHOVEL THE SNOW OFF A COUPLE PARKING PLACES IN THE PARKING LOT, BRING OUT A TV AND SOME FOLDING CHAIRS - THE COLD METAL ONES SO YOU CAN FREEZE YOUR ASS OFF JUST LIKE YOU DO ON THE BLEACHERS AT MEMORIAL STADIUM. AND I'LL GET SACKMAN TO PULL UP A CHAIR RIGHT BEHIND YOU AND PUT HIS KNEES IN YOUR BACK THE WHOLE GAME, JUST LIKE AT THE STADIUM! AND I'LL GET YA A HOT CHOCOLATE AND SOME CHIPS FOR YA OUT OF OUR VENDING MACHINE AND I'LL SIT WITH YOU, ASK YOU ABOUT THE WIFE AND KIDS, HOW'S YOUR JOB GOING AND WE'LL WATCH THE ILLINI GET DRILLED! TO MAKE IT FEEL MORE LIKE THE REAL GAME EXPERIENCE I'LL BRING A FAN OUT AND PUT IT ON YA AND THROW SNOW IN YOUR FACE EVERY FIVE MINUTES SO YOU'RE FREEZING YOUR BOLTS OFF!

Dad took a breath, came up for air and ranted on, his vocal volume knob turned up to ten, his voice getting louder as his tirade progressed.

AND TO MAKE IT EVEN GIVE YOU MORE OF THE FEEL OF BEING AT THE STADIUM I CAN SPILL A BEER ON YA,

AND PUT MY FINGER DOWN MY THROAT AND PUKE ON YOUR SHOES! AND YOU CAN USE OUR RESTROOM FOR NOTHIN,' BUT JUST LIKE AT THE STADIUM THERE WON'T BE ANY PAPER TOWELS OR TOILET PAPER LEFT FIVE MINUTES AFTER THE GAME STARTS AND YOU'LL HAVE TO WIPE YOUR HANDS ON YOUR PANTS. AND I'LL ONLY CHARGE YOU FIFTY BUCKS! AND YOU CAN GET IN YOUR CAR WHEN IT'S OVER AND BE HOME IN FIFTEEN MINUTES!"

Caller: You don't understand, I …"

CLICK. The sound of my dad hanging up on the caller.

DAD: "YES I DO UNDERSTAND! YOU"RE THE ONE LETTING THEM SHOVE THEIR WHOZIT UP YOUR WHATZIT WHILE THEY SMILE AND STICK THEIR HAND IN YOUR WALLET!

The Bears were favorite targets, easy pickins for Dad.

"What did the Bears think would happen when they traded their number one draft pick for a quarterback who pees his pants every time he sees a pass rush and takes off and runs? Tell me one time that guy stayed in the pocket against even a little pressure! THIS ISN'T HIGH SCHOOL! Who's making these decisions?! Are they letting that moron for a head coach? JUST LET THE INMATES RUN THE ASYLUM!"

I had to admit that my tendency to be sarcastic came straight from my dad. Part of his sports talk schtick also consisted of sexual expressions and innuendos that my dad and Sackman used every day to humor themselves and their like-minded audience of listeners. Much of it junior high humor. At best. (They cracked up laughing each time that the other said "boobs" or "boners.") That formula worked well for my dad's standard everyday drill. Immensely popular with young men. Women, young or old, not so much.

Between my eighth grade and ninth grade year my mom

13

divorced my dad. She had the sit-down with Benny and me where she told us that she and Dad weren't compatible anymore. My dad's diatribes had extended to more than sports and driving. His on-air persona, finding wrong with most any aspect of sports, had crept into his at-home persona. Living in Chicago now, my dad lived too far away to come to the games, but it still killed him when I didn't go out for basketball when I got to high school. Looking back, I sought his direction but resisted it. My life had turned into a fragile existence regarding playing high school sports. The complex nature of teenagers.

Although I missed the game, I embraced being spared from my dad's criticisms. At least I didn't have to hear it from the stands or at home now. The worst was when my dad would yell at me to shoot about every time I touched the ball. I'd look up at him in the stands and give him a quick head shake. Trying to run Coach's plays and follow Coach's game plan had been hard enough without dad's "recommendations" from the stands.

Dad thought the overriding idea for our coach should consist of the coach planning for me to score as many points as I could so he could tell the guys at work or at the bar how many I scored. One game, in seventh grade, the other team played a box-and-one against me and I didn't score. I think I only took two shots; their best defender denied me the ball, his whole responsibility the whole game, while the other four played zone. That led to easy shots for my teammates and we won the game, but never-the-less my dad grounded me for the weekend for not scoring.

I could still hear his voice. He targeted the refs, our coach, their coach, our players, their players, the clock and scoreboard operator, custodians, ticket takers, their fans, me.

"Don't you know what a charge is? Where did you get your ref's license?!"

Dad always picked a time when it was quiet, when there wasn't any action to deliver his condemnations. I think he thought they

14

made him seem smart or clever. He'd cup his hands to the sides of his mouth to amplify his diatribes. They resounded throughout the gym. Captain Overreaction. Prone to incendiary comments.

"Don't your kids know how to play man-to-man, Coach? Or maybe you don't know how to teach it?"

Any time I had been taken out of the game and my dad thought I had been on the bench too long he would sail his admonishment down from the stands.

"When are you going to sub, Coach? Are you trying to lose the game?"

And of course, "Shoot, Stevie, shoot! Shoot the ball, Stevie!"

My dad had been a flamer and all the school knew it. All the other parents, too. I overheard one of my teammate's father, who had gone to school with my dad, say, "The guy thinks he knows everything. When we were in school the most athletic thing he ever did was jump to a conclusion."

I constantly had to defend Dad from my teammates.

"My dad just gets excited," I told my teammates in the locker room after a game in which he assailed the usual suspects with a particularly harsh audio assault.

"His remarks just come from the top of his head."

Looking up from tying his shoes Larry "Stinky" Whippington, the buzz cut flabby third team center, said, "They more likely come from the bottom of his butt."

I couldn't argue. But as hard as my dad had been on the coaches, refs, and any and all those who constituted the opposition to his sons' talents, he reserved his harshest criticisms for Benny and me. Nightly at the dinner table, or riding in the car, or whenever a court, a ball, my dad, Benny and/or me coincided Dad picked our games apart. After one of my eighth grade games as soon as I appeared out of the locker room he grabbed my arm and yanked me out to the court to show me what I had done wrong with my shot, what grievous error I had committed, which one of Dad's list of the fundamentals of basketball I had broken. I think it might have been more for the remaining spectators, the dads and moms waiting on their sons, Dad showing them that it hadn't been *his* fault that his progeny had so many errant shots, because *Dad could teach proper shooting fundamentals to LeBron James.*

When Dad started in on Benny, Benny argued with him. And Benny also defended me, telling our dad to lay off his criticism of me. My mother had to act as policeman at the dinner table as discussions became heated, sometimes before a fork had been lifted. On the other hand, I almost always took my Dad's denunciations stoically, remaining silent for the car ride home, then went up to my room and sulked. After games that my dad deemed my efforts not worthy that necessitated his launching into a diatribe directed at me (and often my coach), he sometimes would calm down after a while and ask me if I wanted to stop for some fast food on the way home.

"Not hungry."

Not just hungry, but famished. But if you're going to sulk, by definition you can't have a double cheeseburger, fries and a shake along with a sulk. Those didn't constitute parts of an Unhappy Meal. Can't lay down a guilt trip on a satisfied full stomach provided by an adult. Against the guilt trip rules. What a relief it had been to know that if I had decided to play that he could yell all he wanted from Chicago and I wouldn't have to hear it.

An army of leaves covered the forest floor. Paper thin, ragged, jagged edges, browns blending, light to dark, taupe, tan, beige. Collective millions, lighting in piles, some orphans, born away from their browned brethren with the wind, the wind their only chance to make noise—a rustling, a skittering—on the trail walkway. Trees, the bark shades of brown and gray, some slender, some with an admirable thickness, some with smooth skin, some scaly, many standing as sentinels in their forest group, hiding their secrets of weather, winters, summers past, now mostly leafless, exposed, listening to the wind. I heard voices past and present in my mind as I walked, the decision at hand. I took a brief mental survey of my life so far. I needed basketball, but… It had to be all in or all out.

The night of the after school meeting I sat at the kitchen dinner table. Benny peppered me with questions. I deflected them, playing his cross-examination dismissively. Parry and thrust.

"How'd the meeting go? Did you talk to the coach?" Benny asked.

"Yeah, I did. Man is he old. I'll bet they don't have parts for him anymore."

"Quit bein' a smart ass! Is he going to let you go out for the team or not? I wouldn't blame him if he didn't."

"Yeah, Coach said he'd give me a chance."

"How did he say it? Do you think he's going to give an idiot like you a real chance?"

"That's exactly like he put it, Benny. Coach said, 'Stevie, I'm going to give an idiot like you a real chance.'"

Benny scrunched up his face, exasperated. Tarnishing the family name always a big deal for him.

"You're lucky if he keeps you to be the water boy."

"That would be awesome!" I said.

Benny turned away and muttered something that I didn't think sounded very brotherly.

Benny's coach, Coach Ballmer, had initially been the Golden Boy when he had a few modest winning seasons, then took a senior laden team to the state tournament. But he had limited success since that year, had become very confrontational with players and dismissive of parents' concerns as the pressure increased and ultimately had been non-renewed by the school board as the head coach. He also gave up his teaching position

17

and word had it that he relocated to New Mexico where he now taught P.E. and coached football, a sport that tolerated significantly more belittling behaviors than basketball. That train had left the station.

I made the first cut, then the second. On a Friday morning before school we stopped by Coach's office, some of us acting excited and some acting nervous, all of us anxious - and viewed the list of varsity players Coach had decided to keep on the bulletin board outside his gym class office. One was me. Taking a deep breath, I said to myself, "Here we go."

Chapter 3

Friday after school the boys that had made the team gathered for our first practice, the first official day of practice for boys basketball in Ohio, curious as to what our new coach had planned. Talking during school, most of us readied for a grueling practice in which Coach would set the tone for the season. We met in the varsity locker room. Coach told us to be there by 2:45. No one came late. Coach put one leg up on the bench in front of him, his arms crossed and addressed us.

"Fellas, take a look around you."

We looked.

"What do you see?"

"Lockers, bulletin board, the phys ed office, the clock," offered three or four of us. K.J. thought he had it.

"The team?"

"No," Coach said, bowing his head and slowly shaking it from side to side. "That's not what I'm talking about. Look over in the corner," said Coach, pointing.

We saw a couple of old jocks lying by the wall, along with two or three balls of wadded up tape, a torn t-shirt, a basketball with one of the panels of orangish brown leather coming loose, the black rubber bladder exposed, and somebody's old basketball shoes, the sole of one hanging, barely attached, no shoelaces on either.

"Now the walls...take a look at the walls."

We turned to look. The locker room walls were painted black and red, the Kestrels' colors. Painted maybe twenty years ago, the paint had peeled and cracked. On one wall, someone had decorated it with the words "The Nest" along with the Kestrels' logo, only the paint had now peeled on the bird's beak and cracked on his crest. One leg was missing, exposing the previous locker room paint, a dull color between beige and brown. One bank of the overhead lights hadn't worked since I started at Jackson and took freshman gym class. Graphic messages and poorly etched private parts pen-carved by barely pubescent boys pornographed the restroom stall walls. Unflushed pee wallowed in the urinals. Some of the guys ascribed to the theory of, "If it's yellow, let it mellow." The smell of urine and sweat lingered in the locker room air. Wads of brownish paper towels circled the base of the waste basket, the intended target not hit, the intendee neglecting to correct his miss. Coach Arnold spread his arms out, looking from one side of the locker room to the other, then directly at us.

"Boys...." He paused, then started again. "Boys, perception is reality. Don't fool yourselves. If you don't have the discipline to throw a damn paper towel in the waste basket, or flush the damn toilet, you can't play for me. We're not going to be a slip-shod outfit. This is NOT the locker room of a championship team. We're going to clean this place up, and we're going to start now."

Friday and all day Saturday we cleaned, scraped, primed and painted. Red carpeting was cut and laid on what had been a cold cement floor. Kenny Brown, a senior forward with a nice shooting touch also possessed the touch with a paint brush; a new, cartoon-like stylized kestrel now adorned the side wall, holding a basketball with his finger-like wings, replete with falcon-like eyes searching his prey, talons outstretched. (Though kestrels caught prey with their beaks, not talons. I had learned that bird factoid when we studied kestrels in fifth grade science. Solely on a needs-to-know basis. I thought briefly about informing Coach as Kenny worked but thought better of it. Maybe let that one go till later in the season.)

When we were done, Coach told us to sit down and went to his office. He brought out boxes with tee-shirts, hoodies and baseball caps, all in red and black, all with Jackson Kestrels logos.

"I don't want to see you wearing Duke, North Carolina, Ohio State, or Michigan stuff. We're a team. Have pride in YOUR team, YOUR school." Holding up a Kestrel hooded sweatshirt Coach intoned, "THIS is what we wear."

While we tried on our new gear, Coach took in the scene, offering comments—Old School comments, especially about the way we were wearing our new caps.

"K.J.! What's with turning your hat brim to ten o'clock? You'll be walking sideways."

K.J. gave Coach his sly smile as he checked his new head gear in the mirror, turning his face from one side to the other, nodding approvingly. "But that's lookin' fresh, Coach, lookin' tight." K.J. thought he was rockin' it.

Coach shook his head and sighed.

"Fellas, I'm not real big on wearing your caps like K.J. is, the angle thing, or wearin' 'em backward or the flat brim look thing that Tommy's doing, but I'm not going to fight you on it. I just wish one of you guys would wear yours like it's supposed to be worn. But at least you're wearing your own school's caps, so I guess I'll just have to be happy with that."

With that, Hobie turned his cap around, from backward to forward, making a big production out of it, curving the bill with both hands, sliding thumbs under and fingers over the brim, then on down the sides ever so slowly, putting on a show for Coach Arnold. His cap juuust right, Hobie said, "How'm I lookin', Coach?"

Everybody laughed, including Coach.

"Brown noser," I said, reaching across the bench, exchanging a fist bump with Hobie.

21

I put on my cap backward. A good look for me. Fresh. Tight.

Chapter 4

The following Monday morning not only constituted the start of boys basketball practice, but also would be the first day of the new trimester. As always, Hobie had something up his sleeve. He had corralled several classmates into fantasy baseball and football leagues, serving as the organizer and commissioner. Near the end of one of our lunch periods a week before, our lunch table denizens talked about how our fantasy football teams had been faring. Hobie sat back in his chair listening, thinking, then signaled for us to draw in closer. He had a new idea to propose.

"What if we start a Student Fantasy League? You know, like the football and baseball fantasy leagues."

We all gave him dumb looks. Not difficult for us.

"Here's what I'm thinking. Starting next trimester, next week. It's based on our students, on Jackson students' performance—their grades. How great is that? Kids you know, not some pro players in New York or Los Angeles that don't even know or care that you're alive. Everyone who plays picks two juniors besides themselves. You are on your own team. You and two other juniors. Only those who play, agree to participate in the SFL can be chosen, drafted. I doubt that Dai-Tai Ling wants to be in on this."

Ling had a 4.0 GPA in the honors program and had only been in the United States for two years, in which time she had mastered English. Many of my friends could not make that claim.

"We get twenty-five juniors and charge a hundred dollars each to own a team, so we have working capital of two thousand, five hundred dollars. We get fifty other kids to give us their grades and we'll pay them twenty bucks each, so that's a thousand we pay for their services, which leaves us with fifteen hundred bucks. The pay-out for the winner would be half, like seven hundred fifty. With the remainder we divvy it up with payouts for the rest of the top ten teams. Only core courses would count - English, Math, Science, Social Studies."

Hobie paused for a few seconds, his eyes moving, squinting, looking outward past us, thinking inward as he thought further about the details of his budding idea.

"And here's what I think: we don't go by final grades. Who wants to wait until months away, the end of the trimester, till March to know how your team is doing? We go by test grades. Whenever you have a test in any core subject you take a pic of the grade on the test and text it to me. Or maybe you could send it in a group text to everyone. I'll have to think about that. We'll have the draft on Sunday night before the trimester starts on Monday. You can either be there in person or we'll send group texts on who's been selected and who's left. We'll have a blind draw to set the draft order. Then we'll reverse that order for the second round. I'll need everybody's schedules by the middle of next week, say, Wednesday, so I can copy them off and get them to everyone."

Kyle Mahoney asked why we needed everyone's schedule.

"Don't you want to know what teachers they'll have? Say Susie and Phyllis are both taking American History, but Susie has Mr. Gravesend who if you're lucky you'll get a 'C' because he's such a hard grader, but if you have Mrs. Uncapher you can sleep every day in class, turn in homework late for full credit, get to correct all your tests till you get a passing grade and you'll end up with an 'A' or a 'B'. Just like wanting to know the team's schedule for the running backs you choose for your fantasy football team. If they have a weak schedule the running back you drafted is probably going to run for more yards. And I wouldn't just pick your friends to be on your team if you want to win, unless they're all brainiacs. Use your money with discretion when you draft your students."

Hobie was on a roll, ideas rapidly spurting out of his cerebral cortex, one after another as he excitedly detailed them for the edification of our assembled lunch bunch. We had trouble listening that fast. But no stopping him now. We had become conditioned to hearing Hobie's stratagems over the years. Mostly we respected Hobie and his ideas. Mostly.

"Remember that everybody's test scores have the same weight. Jimmy Joe Imbecile's 47% on his Geometry test counts just as much as Maddy May Brilliantine's 98% in Anatomy. We could have kids submit their past grades to me by subject so I could send them to everyone, but that's really too much work. But I'll probably ask for your and their GPA's. You'll have to do your own investigations, scouting reports, talk among yourselves. That will be important. Did the kid you're going to draft just get a job, a girl friend, boy friend, are his parents about to get a divorce or are they supportive? Are they prone to illness and could miss a lot of days? Did they suddenly become party animals? These all could be important nuances to factor in."

The gears in our brains started to grind. This...this had possibilities.

"So we go by percentage, what your student has as an average in all core classes combined. Again, we're not going to include Art or foreign languages or Wood Shop. Honors program grades count the same as the regular classes. I'm not doing all that weighted grade stuff."

Kyle sunk back in his chair when Hobie said that. Kyle's only A's since 6th grade had come in Wood Shop. There'd be no feeding frenzy to select Kyle for anyone's team. Not likely that he'd be selected until only crumbs were left.

"At first I thought that you could pick anybody *but* yourself, but then I thought that if the administration called me in to explain, I could say that the Student Fantasy League serves as an incentive to do well, and also for our classmates on our teams to do well. Maybe we'd study together, have pride in our team, that kind of thing and they'd buy it. Actually you'll have two teams—*your* team, the team you draft and yourself, and you'll be on somebody else's team that drafts you."

"So…maybe you'd want to share your winnings with your teammates, maybe depending on how well they performed on their tests?" I asked.

"That's up to you. You could be a generous owner or a tightwad owner. Up to you. You could have team bonding activities or not even talk to your 'players.' Hobie signaled air quotes when he said 'players.' You can be an owner who shares and cares or a complete jerk who complains about your guys' performances. All up to you. And remember, you're on somebody else's team, too, so they're going to want you to knock out those A's."

Then I asked Hobie, "But would the administrators buy into the money being exchanged? I can't see them going for that."

"I've thought of that. First we have to tell everybody that they're sworn to secrecy…but yeah, it might leak out that we're each doling out a hundred bucks to play. But we have fantasy football and baseball leagues that kids in school have organized, not just mine, and as long as all money is exchanged outside school they don't seem to care. Some of the teachers, especially the coaches, ask me how my team's doing. And everybody would be joining the SFL willingly. I guess we'll find out."

"They might care if we feed answers to our teammates if we take a test earlier in the day, like 1st period, that they're going to take 4th period."

"You have that anyway. It's not like that doesn't happen. Good teachers will change the order of the questions or even have different questions. Some are wise to that, some teachers don't care."

"OK, so we draft our teams," I said, "And we have this big incentive to do well, get good grades so our team will win the big money. I'll have to think about how to play defense. Some ideas are coming to mind...hall taunting, giving misleading information about the test, late night phone calls to prevent a good night's sleep..."

Hobie put his head down, hands on top.

"OK, so in the info I send out you'll have to sign an oath of good sportsmanship otherwise you're kicked out, and all monies are forfeited. Sheesh."

So, Sunday night before the second trimester started, before the opening day of basketball practice, we met at Hobie's house and drafted our teams for the Student Fantasy League, the SFL. We had to cut it off at twenty-five kids who wanted to own a team. More had wanted to. My team, besides me, consisted of Owen Murphy, a nervous little kid with glasses and a high-pitched voice who seemed physically and socially two years behind everyone else, and raced through the halls with his head down in a hurry to get to class but had a solid 3.5 GPA (though he had Mr. Gravesend for American History I felt confident about this pick because teachers loved Owen.), and my second and final choice, well, out of who had been left on the board—Jimmy "Smalls" Belinsky, he of the 1.6 GPA, he of video game prowess, he of prodigious girth, he being a lunch-time compadre of mine. I figured I could give Smalls pep talks and study tips at lunch, or maybe get into full-scale heated arguments when I'd confront Smalls about screwing up my team's place in the standings by getting a 22% on his skeletal system test. That would liven up the cafeteria conversation anyway. Name for my team: *Aberrant Academians*. And so the Student Fantasy League came into existence.

Chapter 5

Monday morning. November 2nd. 5:45 AM. Coach Arnold had told us at our first team meeting that in the pre-season we'd be practicing before school AND after school. That cut a few wannabees from trying out right away. That and we all got the gist at the meeting that playing for Coach Arnold wouldn't be any picnic. The vibe he gave off did not fit in the touchy-feely category.

I went to bed at eight o'clock the night before, not wanting to be late to the first practice, but slept little, anxious and excited. I wanted to prove myself right from the get-go to Coach Arnold.

Coach Arnold came as advertised, old school, hard-wired, demanding, our best efforts not going without criticism. A slap on the butt and an occasional "attaboy" his highest compliments, delivered sparingly. But I bought into it. I played with a fervor. Defense, defense, defense. The first week we hardly touched a ball except to work on our defensive skills and rebounding. Tail down, arms out — "Wide defense is good defense!" Coach's mantra. "Point the toe, step and slide, turn 'em, beat 'em to a spot!" Coach's terminology, his vision, becoming ours.

Coach Arnold had chosen for his staff varsity assistant Tucker Pettaway, junior varsity coach, Luke Kopastynski, and freshman coach Tyrell South. Coach Pettaway had a commanding presence, a now thickset man with a deep voice that often resonated off the bleachers when he loudly demanded we give more effort. Also our school dean—in charge of discipline.

Mississippi born and bred, from Greenville, Mr. Pettaway had gotten a basketball scholarship to Marshall University in West

Virginia where he played power forward for three years for the Thundering Herd. He then served two years in the Army before turning to a teaching career after returning to school and finishing his bachelor's degree in education. Coach Pettaway initially taught auto mechanics at a couple small high schools near the Ohio River. He had grown up on a farm, learned from his father how to fix farm equipment, and, as a young teacher he coached football, basketball and track. What he didn't learn from his father about autos and engines he learned in the motor pool in the Army, repairing Jeeps, Abrams tanks, and light armored personnel carriers.

After meeting his wife-to-be Lucille in grad classes at Ohio State where they were studying to be guidance counselors, Coach Pettaway gravitated north with Lucille to Sandusky to be near her parents. Soon after the Jackson school district advertised for a high school guidance counselor and Coach Pettaway filled the bill. After a year of counseling he became the dean at Jackson, our new dean this year, and also joined the staff of the newly hired Coach Arnold.

In spite of Coach Pettaway's largess and authoritative voice, "booming" voice might be a better term, students liked him. He used Southern expressions or ones he heard in the Army, often tinged with humor to get his points across. Sometimes he used lines from blues songs he learned in Mississippi. He'd sing a couple lines or a stanza to us with his baritone voice at practice or on the bus home from away games when we won.

Goin' down that Highway 61
From Memphis to Mississippi
That road do run
Down through the Delta
With my Tennessee gal
We goin' to have us some fun

When the cafeteria lunch ladies would ask Coach Pettaway what he'd like as he slid his tray down the lunch counter rails, he'd sometimes say, sighing heavily, "Just some peace, love, and understanding." And he'd laugh that deep chuckle that started from his button-popping stomach, drawing smiles from the students patiently waiting in line behind him along with the briefly entertained lunch ladies, ladles and scoops paused in-hand.

When Coach Pettaway heard Mindy in the second floor hallway make a snide remark to a freshman girl a few days after she had transferred to JHS - something about what the freshman co-ed was wearing that met Mindy's disapproval, he waved her over and said,

"Girl, what may be your name?"

Mindy told him. "Mindy Derosiers, Sir."

Mr. Pettaway delayed his reprobation for a few seconds, arms folded, eyeing Mindy, then said, "Girl, you just ain't walkin' right."

Mindy, eyes big, looking up at Coach Pettaway towering, looking down at Mindy, said, "What do you mean Mr. Pettaway?"

"You know what I mean, Mindy. We don't cotton to that. Check yourself before you wreck yourself."

And he cocked his head at Mindy, peering at her with one eye, the other raised in anticipation waiting for her to accede to his advice. A brief stalemate.

Then Mindy, her eyes downcast, admitted, "You're right Mr. Pettaway."

"That's my girl. Now you all go on and have a great day."

A coy expression briefly crossed Mindy's face as she swaggered back across the hallway, liking that she had her girlfriends' total attention.

Coach Kopastynski, or "Coach Luke" as we called him, a

former Kestrel, had played college basketball briefly for Bowling Green State University, but quit after his sophomore season when it became apparent that neither a starting role for the Falcons nor an NBA career looked to be in the works. Someone else would have to be the Chicago Bulls' first round draft pick. Coach Luke, like my brother Benny, subbed in the Jackson school district, Benny at the junior high and Luke at the high school while they waited their turn to be hired to the faculty full-time. Both also worked at the Crow Bar in Jackson's downtown part-time as bartenders and waiters. Freshman coach South came straight out of college, Ohio University, hired to coach basketball and be our new ninth grade algebra teacher. Staff in place for the four month calendar event called Ohio high school basketball season.

Chapter 6

As Thanksgiving approached we witnessed a new phenomena in town. People standing on street corners had been popping up at the main intersections, near the mall and around the courthouse. Some asked for donations for the homeless, for church groups to send kids to camps, for veterans. Others held signs telling drivers to smile because God loves them. Some proselytized, wanting the return of prayer in schools or to join the new mega church in town, some demanded religious freedom, others implored the separation of church and state. Still more protested, against the building of a new box store, pet stores that bought dogs from puppy mills, state issues by number that raised the minimum wage or dismantled rights of union workers. A lone signman—actually a young signwoman—wearing a blue peacoat and a pink knit hat held hers aloft, gripping a wooden pole, standing on the same corner, the northwest corner of the courthouse square, day after day. Her message consisted of a plea, words imploring people to consider their actions toward other humans. The sign read: *We're In This Together*.

I wondered if words on a sign could prompt and propel people's thoughts, spur people to action, commit them to acting upon their new found logic. Could the spoken word, or words read coming from others elicit fervent responses, generating a blind faith, or did we have to arrive at our conclusions on our own? What, how, when, and why communication was delivered to us...the key had to be in there somewhere. Wasn't what we understood based on our experiences, what we perceived to be true based on our understanding? I decided that I needed to delve more into my thinking process to decipher the power words had on me.

Our starting line-up after our last pre-season scrimmage had become K.J. Jordan at center, our captain, wiry strong with mad hops, had been on varsity since he was a freshman. (K.J. asked us to stop calling him "Wreck." He thought it unsophisticated, a reflection of the old coach's often crude, clichéd, simple utterances to the media, unencumbered by the thought process. "Wreck" didn't fit with K.J.'s new self-persona, he told us, that of a dignified, self-assured, stylish sophisticate. He had been elected senior class president at the end of last school year; a man for all the people, he told us, from citizen high to citizen low. K.J. had taken to wearing sport coats and nicely pressed slacks and sweaters to school.) Tommy Hurlburt, a squatty body, would start at power forward, Kenny Brown at small forward, a slasher, a guy who could take almost any defender on a dribble drive to the hoop, Jose' Jimenez, quicker than heck and a ball-handling fool would be at point guard, and me at the shooting guard. K.J. and Kenny were seniors, Jose' and I juniors, and Tommy a sophomore.

I had beaten out my best buddy, Hobie Gajun, also a junior, at the 2 guard after the first scrimmage, but Hobie still got plenty of PT—playing time—backing up both Jose' and me. Hobie, one of Coach's favorites because of his constant hustle, always had his motor runnin', diving for loose balls, taking charges, a rat terrier on defense. The coaches had named Tommy as a starter the day before our first game. A surprise starter, a sophomore, only 5'9" but a space eater, a round mound, baby fat slabbing his lower stomach, arms, chubby cheeks. But when he posted he couldn't be budged, and had surprising agility for someone of his build, deceiving quickness when he made his post moves, a good passer and voracious rebounder. He tended to get in foul trouble which

33

drew a salvo of Coach's invectives during the film sessions in Coach's classroom.

"Tommy," Coach would say, watching Tommy mug yet another opponent with his whack-a-mole defense, "That would get you five to ten years in Leavenworth if you did that on the streets." And we'd bite our lips to keep from laughing as Tommy would slink down in his seat, attempting the impossible, trying to become invisible to Coach.

Whenever I wasn't playing basketball my thoughts turned to Mindy. That isn't entirely true…my thoughts often turned to her even when I was playing. I eyed and spied her frequently when the cheerleaders and varsity boys' basketball practices coincided in the gym, and during the junior varsity boys' games (she almost didn't make the cut though, despite her beguiling spunk and athleticism because of a few demerits for tardies, a result of too much socializing in the halls, a few for sarcastic remarks that delivered direct hits on her faculty targets.). I changed my routes to class between periods to catch a glimpse of her, trying to make eye contact, trying not to. I had learned, memorized her schedule by the end of her first day, as had many of my male classmates who entertained the same fantasy I had. I asked to use the hall pass in every class, taking a route that would take me by Mindy's classes, hoping the teacher had left the door open, Mindy seated in view. Though my interest was piquing I couldn't be too obvious, less she see me. Piquing, but no peeking. I lay awake at night thinking of scenarios, what I would say when we finally met.

Chapter 7

Junior English. Our teacher, Matt O'Donnell, a former seventies hippie, or so he told us, and one of Jackson's most popular. After waiting for the class to get situated in our seats Mr. O'Donnell, in his usual professional attire of dress shirt, neatly pressed slacks and colorful tie, countered with a man-bun along with a small earring on his left earlobe, stood at the podium at the front of the class.

"Today we begin our poetry unit with the sonnet. How many of you have heard of Petrarch, the Father of the Sonnet?"

No hands went up. Petrarch, an unknown, a non-entity to the inhabitants of English College Prep IIIA, Room 116, 1st Period, Jackson High School. Petrarch might well be offended. That was of no concern to us.

"Could anyone tell me what a sonnet is?"

Carolyn Fisk leaned a little way forward on her desk and tentatively put her hand part-way up, arm bent at the elbow, afraid to totally commit an answer that might well be wrong.

"Yes, Carolyn?"

"It's a poem thing."

"Yes. It is a poem thing. Could you elaborate on that, Carolyn?"

Carolyn thought for about twenty seconds. We waited. Mr. O'Donnell waited.

"Ummm…" Carolyn searched for her brain's synapses to make an internet connection to her cerebral cortex for the recollection of what consisted a sonnet. Her gray matter's cursor kept spinning…and spinning. Error message 404. File not found.

"No. I got nothin.'"

Carolyn shook her head. Carolyn had come back to the pack. We awaited the next question.

"Who knows what unrequited love is?"

No hands went up. The odds of Mr. O'Donnell getting a right answer now appeared about to be the same as his chances at winning the Ohio Lottery Megamillions two weeks in a row. Maybe less.

Mr. O'Donnell peered out at the class, row by row, at a room full of sleepy eyed students. He closed his eyes and pretended to snore, deep-throated. Then, feigning acting startled, pretended to awaken, stretched his arms overhead and yawned.

"Maybe we should just drop the subject. And the object and the predicate," Mr. O'Donnell said to no one in particular, a joke for himself.

Again seeing no reaction Mr. O'Donnell turned to Maggie Kilberry, his anointed red-haired freckle-faced confidante who sat to the immediate left of the lectern, put a hand to the side of his face to seemingly keep us from hearing what he was saying. In a hushed voice, a for-us-to-overhear loud hushed voice, he said to Maggie,

"We could deadhead 'em. You know, what they do to flowers. Cut off their heads, their blossoms, so they grow back bigger and better. Maybe if we cut off their heads"—Mr. O'Donnell nodded in our direction—"their brains will grow back bigger and better."

Maggie giggled.

Mr. O'Donnell looked down briefly at his notes, then darted his eyes up over the top of his reading glasses attached by a chain around his neck, hoping for reaction to his joke, but observed that we hadn't the slightest idea what he had referred to. He sighed heavily and continued on, like Diogenes carrying his lamp in the daylight, looking for an honest man, surveying his audience, looking for any sign of anyone understanding anything he talked

36

about. Getting none, blank faces giving no sign of acknowledgement, he soldiered on. Instead of cajoling and nurturing us to want to discover the information on our own volition, for our own enjoyment, the thought occurred to Mr. O'Donnell that we resembled clams that he had to pry open and force knowledge into.

"Petrarch was an Italian. You do have an idea where Italy is, right?"

This time Mr. O'Donnell didn't look for our reaction. A few nodded their heads, a few hands went up. They could locate Italy on a world map, or thought they could.

"Petrarch fell in love with a young woman by the name of Laura de Noves on Good Friday in April, 1347, when he first saw her in his church in Avignon. Avignon being a part of Italy then, but now it's part of France. The French captured it in the 1800s. On that Good Friday Laura entered the church, it appeared to Petrarch, in a golden glow."

Mr. O'Donnell spread his arms out and up, moving them from overhead to his sides to show how the glow encompassed Laura.

"Her blonde hair seemed to be illuminated by the sunlight streaming in through the stain glass windows. Love struck, Petrarch composed and sent 365 sonnets to her. Sonnets, you know, the poem thing. She never replied to a single one. Laura's husband being a nobleman, an important dude, man about town, she didn't think it proper. She died twenty-one years later of the bubonic plague, also on a Good Friday. Legend has it that when her body was exhumed years later her hands clutched Petrarch's sonnets to her bosom. What can we learn from this? One is that it's a good thing for Laura that Petrarch didn't have text messaging. He'd have been arrested for stalking for sure."

I never understood the concept of stalking, didn't understand the rules. If you wait for someone outside her house or apartment for say, three hours, and they never come home, does that count as a stalk? If you go to her workplace but she called in sick that day, is that a stalk? And say you're lying back on your couch, watching a game or a movie. You've got your drink, your bowl of snacks, shoes off, feet up, and you look in your planner and you see that you have written: "Desdemona—Stalking 10PM-12AM." Crap! Now you've got to put your shoes back on, forget the snacks, head out into the cold night and you don't even know if Desdemona is where she's supposed to be for you to perform your stalkage. If you'd ask me, I'd tell you that it takes waaay too much dedication and determination to be a good stalker, not to mention that you'd have to have a lot of disposable time on your hands to be dedicated to stalking. When would you watch your shows?

Mr. O'Donnell continued on with the story of Petrarch and Laura.

"Petrarch's sonnets are probably in every English textbook today. Isn't it funny that they're called "text" books? They should have the hashtags #Sonnets#Petrarch#Laura#Stalking under their titles."

We laughed. We kinda got it.

"The other thing you need to know is that the sonnet is considered one of the most beautiful forms of poetry with their quatrains and couplets. A guy named William Shakespeare also wrote them, as well as another Englishman, Edmund Spenser and even Dante. Don't worry if you know little about them. They don't know much about you, either."

We read a poem of Petrarch's in class, from a series of sonnets he wrote to Laura called the Canonziere. I tried not to show any emotional response. I couldn't help but think of Mindy. Would I be like Petrarch to her, my love unrequited, like his? Mr. O'Donnell told us it had been said about Petrarch's sonnets that they were written "For a woman he would never know, for a woman he could never have, he should change the world forever."

> *It was on that day when the sun's ray*
> *was darkened in pity for its Maker,*
> *that I was captured, and did not defend myself,*
> *because your lovely eyes had bound me, Lady.*
> *It did not seem to me to be a time to guard myself*
> *against Love's blows: so I went on*
> *confident, unsuspecting; from that, my troubles*
> *started, amongst the public sorrows.*
> *Love discovered me all weaponless,*
> *and opened the way to the heart through the eyes,*
> *which are made the passageways and doors of tears:*
> *so that it seems to me it does him little honor*
> *to wound me with his arrow, in that state,*
> *he not showing his bow at all to you who are armed.*

The strategy: I knew a friend of Mindy's, a blonde on the cheerleader squad named Robin. One of those girls who we referred to as "wholesome," Robin grew up a farm girl, member of the 4-H Club, USDA approved, about twenty pounds overweight, but a pretty rounded face, great dimples, bubbly, with straight shoulder cut blonde hair that that she parted on the right side, her hair angling, bangs sweeping down over her left eye. After she finished a cheer Robin continually pushed away her bangs, along with attempts trying to blow them out of her eyes. I milked Robin for tidbits about Mindy. One she had told me the day before, that Mindy liked poetry, that she often wrote poems in her spiral. That night in my room I composed a poem to Mindy, my Petrarch to her Laura, and screwing my courage to the sticking place (I think Shakespeare said that, but I don't think his reference had intended to be toward budding teenage hormonal desires), and dropped it into a slot of one of the louvered vents in her locker after practice the next day. Temporary insanity. I plead guilty as charged.

A Heartbreak Unheard

Night time tears
Begin their tug
At my heartstrings
I went out into the night
Seeking solace from the light of ancients
Hoping the night time sky would answer my cry
Face turned upward, pleading at the enveloping canopy
Of darkness
Howling her name at the moon
Wailing, sailing, skyward, a missive at the moonbeams
Riding my soulfelt plaint at the constellations
Bouncing from star to star,
On a mournful, searching celestial journey
For all the cosmic matter to consider a matter
My tearful concern bouncing off beams of moonlight
Riding its way high across the hemispheres
The sound of her name the stars' delight
Sailing further away
My soul's angst, my tears, fears
Unanswered this night

I had always been a decent writer. Probably due to my mother teaching us to read at a tender age. But this, this had been a complete gamble. Going for the touchdown with the ball on your own one yard line with a long pass on first down. A Hail Mary heave. Or more apt, a Hail Mindy heave.

Teenage communique. A missive from Mindy. Heading to lunch the next day Robin handed me a folded note.

"Liked your poem, Stevie. Thanks! Would U like to meet me by my locker after practice tonight? I'll wait for you."

Signed "Mindy."

She liked it!

I hadn't been at all certain that I had the social skills, the sophistication or experience that a guy needed to date a girl like Mindy. The needle wavered at about two or three on the Likert Scale. I'd have to rely on my naivety. It's part of my charm, I wistfully thought. Ready or not…You may turn your test over and begin.

We talked for about an hour, sitting on the hall floor hard tile. (Mindy's locker being No. 259 — second floor where the Sophomores were assigned, in the Science wing, among a bank of beige lockers, between the stairway and a biology classroom, on the east side of the hall.) I had gotten there first, and after a few minutes, wondering if she'd show, sat down on the hallway floor with my back against her locker. A minute later Mindy came up the stairs to my left, gym bag over her shoulder, saw me, our gazes quickly locking, her face lighting up.

"Scootch," Mindy said. She gave me a hip and butt check as she sat down, shoving me slightly to my right so that we sat side-by-side. Our bodies both sweaty—I think "glistening" is the term for girls—from our practices. Mindy had her Kestrels' red cheer warm-up top on, her name embroidered in red on the left chest over a white megaphone, the Kestrel bird in black outlined in red and white on the right. Gray sweatpants and red tennis shoes completed her practice ensemble. Sometimes her arm touched mine—her right, my left. Even through my Jackson hoodie it gave me goose bumps. I hoped that she couldn't tell that my heart was racing.

"I'll tell you about me then you tell me about yourself," Mindy said. "And you can ask me anything. I usually tell the truth."

With that, Mindy told me she had come to Jackson from Milwaukee. Her dad made big-time money as a highly successful pharmaceutical salesman and had been transferred here as his

41

company had expanded to the Ohio area. Mom not in the picture anymore. An artist, she had left her dad for another artist. Mindy hadn't seen her mom in more than two years and only kept in touch through her mom's sporadic phone calls and cards on Mindy's birthday and Christmas. Mindy said she had many of her mom's traits, though.

"My last name is Desrosiers. Pronounced *Deh-rose-eee-ay* in France but we say *De-ROSE-zhers* here. It means 'from the roses' in French. My first name means 'love' in German."

Mindy looked in my eyes for a reaction. I looked in hers, wondering what she wanted my reaction to be.

"I'm German by engineering but French by design. That's what my mom always told me. She said we have artistic talent and an artist's temperament like the French but that we can be stubborn like Germans and have to always get our way."

Looking back, maybe that should have been a red flag. But my cerebral cortex had been subtlely sabotaged by my libido, illogical thoughts trumping, clobbering, stomping on, obliterating my logical thoughts. Mindy could have told me she had been raised on a cannabalism diet and worshipped a sun devil and I wouldn't have cared. I probably would have considered it adorable.

We had a bond. I hardly ever saw my dad anymore. He lived in Chicago with his new wife now. My mom, an attorney, an assistant prosecutor for the city, supported my brother and me. Slender, blonde, pretty and smart. Made me proud to be her son. (Except when she power walked through the neighborhood, her arms alternately swinging three pound weights in synchronicity, one arm, up, other down, like an old-fashioned Oklahoma oil derrick digging at the soil. Benny asked her, "Mom, can't you just go to the gym like other moms instead of doing that dork walking? It's kinda embarrassing." But Mom said she liked to walk in the neighborhood, the social aspect, and gave us ten minutes worth of encounters about elderly neighbors she stopped to give a hug to, neighbors she learned had new jobs, daughters expecting a baby, grandchildren updates. Benny replied with a sigh and an eyebrow-raised fake smile, "Well OK then ...").

Mindy pulled her knees up to her chest and went on.

"My mom's crazy, though. She drives, like, a hundred miles an hour. We had an accident when I was seven years old when she almost drove off the road around a curve and swerved back and hit another car almost head-on that was coming at us. I fractured my skull in two places. My mom broke her cheek from the air bag but she mostly was OK. I had been asleep in the back seat and had unhooked my seat belt and got thrown out of the car. I remember looking up, lying in a field and cows were looking down at me and I heard sirens. I was in the hospital for like, two months. It happened in October and I had to miss the rest of the school year and had to take second grade over. That's why I'm sixteen and only a sophomore. I'm a May baby. I'll be seventeen before school's out."

As we finished giving each other our bios, Mindy said she liked Jackson so far but why were so many of the girls in the high school so unfriendly?

"They're all so snarky except for most of the girls I cheer with. I asked this one girl in social studies that sits in from of me for a piece of paper and you wouldn't believe what she said to me. Two words. Something that is physically impossible for me to do. But the guys have been really nice."

"Beats me," I said. I remembered my dad playing an Eagles song about the new kid in town.

"They're very tribal. They don't like outsiders. I think it's just that they see you as an invasive species. You're kinda like the new flower taking over their garden. They're weedy and needy."

Mindy gave a sly Mona Lisa smile. She was well aware of the impact she had been having and liking it, on me and the school. She played with the strands of her hair as we talked, stretching and twirling them. Then she looked directly in my eyes and asked if I wanted to go out with her after our game tomorrow tonight.

Mindy edged toward me, keeping her gaze eye to eye, and whispered, "There's a definite risk that we could have a good time."

After a pause she added, "We'd have a bunch of fun. And fun is one of my favorite F words."

"I'll have to see what the guys are doing."

That's all I could come up with. Lame. My brain raced at about a thousand RPMs, my firewall gone. I wanted so badly to go out with Mindy, of course, but hesitant to leave my teammates. The Honor Code. Don't leave your team. Respect the Shield. Band of Brothers. The razing they would give me. An unwritten rule: You hung with your teammates after the game.

"If they want to go where the cheerleaders go, we can do that."

Mindy put her hands on her hips, like women do when they're not totally pleased with the answer you just gave and expect you to change it. Immediately.

"Don't go *if'n me*, Stevie!"

I told Mindy I'd try to find out tonight and let her know. She put her hand up to her ear in a semi-fist, thumb and pinky finger extended, the universal "Call me" sign.

"Call me, you big jerk," she said, laughing.

I nodded, heart pounding, hopes up.

Chapter 8

We started the season rolling, winning all of our scrimmages easily, gaining confidence in Coach Arnold's system heading into our opener at home against Port Monroe. I hit three threes in a row in the second quarter to break the game open. My junior class brethren in the bleacher's student section, my homies, my peeps, threw up both arms with every three pointer I shot with their hands forming the '3 goggles' sign, thumb and forefinger touching, forming the goggles over their eyes, the last three fingers straight up indicating a three-pointer. My confidence soared. An affirmation of my ability every time the ball touched nothin' but the bottom of the net, the scoreboard ringing up three more points for the Kestrels.

Besides hitting three-pointers with ease I had opened the season hitting all my free throws. Twenty-six for twenty-six. Teams had trouble guarding me tight to take away the three. If they did, I drove, and either scored or dumped the ball to K.J. or Tommy for an easy layup or got fouled which resulted in an automatic two points as from the free throw line. I.could.not.miss. Twenty-six free throws, three short of the school record twenty-nine, set by my brother five years before. I had the stroke down. Coach Arnold gave us out of bounds plays that would get the ball to me at the end of any close game. He told the team he wanted the ball in my hands when the opponents fouled to stop the clock at the end of games. Get the ball to the best foul shooter.

"Some guys," Coach told us in practice, "Can make their free throws at any time except, *except when the game is on the line.*

45

Stevie's our guy… right now."

Coach didn't give out that many compliments. He made sure to qualify his statement. *Right now.* Coach then turned his head and looked at me. I feigned humility.

We easily dispatched the visitors, 77-57.

After our win against Port Monroe, a perennially weak league opponent, we faced powerhouse Midlothian High, the Tarblooders, last year's league champion the next night, the Saturday before Thanksgiving. Coach Arnold told us it would be our first real test. We sat on the bench in the locker room, wiping away the sweat from the pre-game warm-up. Coach's demeanor more agitated, animated than usual; he wanted us to feel his sense of urgency.

"Well, boys, this is what we practice for. I expect every one of you to know your responsibilities, your role, run your plays as we practiced and help your teammates on defense."

He made me nervous. I bent over, head partway down but looking up, lest Coach thought I wasn't making eye contact. One of his rules for a man to live by. You must make eye contact, along with "Have a firm handshake, not a handful of worms." Coach squeezed his ever-present rolled-up program at both ends. I hoped he wouldn't single me out. He eyed us, one by one, up and down the bench, his eyes meeting ours, his glare challenging. A brief thought appeared from somewhere, nowhere, that he was trying to bully us with coachspeak, imploring his will to become our will. Coach finally spoke. The words came out slow...and stressed.

"Boys...we have to hunker down. This isn't war, but close."

"What do you mean by hunker?" I asked Coach.

He exploded. I hunkered.

In the pre-game lay-up line Hobie, having spotted Mindy and me in the hall, and as guys are wont to do, started the grief-giving.

46

"How's the new sweet smelling girlfriend, Stevie?"

"Just test drivin' her, Hobie. Need to check under the hood. I'll get back to you. "

"What do you think the shelf life is on dating her? I think she's gone with two guys already since she transferred here. I'll bet she left a debris field of ex-boyfriends when she left Milwaukee. Findings based on observable quantitative analysis. Not subject to provisos, stipulations, or limitations. Proceed at your own risk. Risk may entail considerable investment of time and money. Be advised that failure to secure privacy and personal data and breaches in security may result in catastrophic effects for the investor."

"You vastly underestimate my appeal to the fairer sex, Hobie. Previous carbon-dating timetables do not apply to yours truly."

"Good luck with *that*," Hobie said as he took the pass, swung the ball hip-to-hip and drove toward the basket.

The first half was supposed to be a test, but testament would be a better word for how we played. We were flawless. Led by fourteen, 36-22 at the half. Walking to our locker room, Hobie made a sizzling noise—"Szzzzzzz"—poking then quickly withdrawing his pointer finger on my right bicep, shaking his finger, seemingly burnt because of my red hot shooting— four first half threes along with hitting all three of my free throws. Tied with Benny for the school record for consecutive made free throws. It would be no problem breaking the record on my next attempt. I sneaked a peak at Mindy. Red and black Kestrels' cheer outfit, white and black saddle shoes, red ribbons in her hair, sitting in the first row of the stands with the other JV cheerleaders while we headed into the locker room, got a smile and a wave. Good fortune had started last night; a few of the guys had talked with the cheerleaders and agreed to head to Lonnie's Pizza Place together after the game. The stars were aligning on my planet, or so I thought.

There's a reason why basketball is played with two halves. We played as bad in the second as we played well in the first. With twelve seconds to go and down one, 53-52, a Tarblooder fouled me, a desperate hack on my arm as he tried to get around a backscreen set by K.J. on a three as I drifted off his pick. My thoughts went back to my summer free throw routine. Wipe the sweat off my hands by touching my socks, shorts, get the ball from the ref, take three dribbles, swish. You gotta stick the landing, Benny always told me, using his gymnastics analogy, seal the deal. Although my dad tried to take credit for teaching me how to shoot, Benny had been the one who I learned proper technique and my free throw shooting routine from. And now I was positioned to break his record and bring us a victory on top of it. Only the first bounced around on the rim, looked as if it was down, then came out. Stunned. I couldn't believe it. Second one, slight to the right. My mind in panic mode, trying to figure out what I done wrong. Third—clank. A Midlothian rebound, a foul, a last second desperation heave by Hobie from over half court veered wide left and the Tarblooders celebrated at half court. The basketball gods, fickle again in their adoration. Loved us in the first half, left us in the second half.

Teammates consoled me on the way to the locker room. When we heard the coaches enter all became deathly quiet. Coach Arnold started in mildly. He still had his program in his hand, tapping it against his thigh. The more he talked the more intense the taps became.

"The first half we played with focus. But games are two halves, fellas. We have to learn that lesson. Some individuals thought the game was over at half-time."

Then Coach started to heat up. Ten minutes into his talk Coach Arnold was apoplectic.

"Is that what a team with any integrity does?! What do we always tell you? You play like you practice, and those of you who dog it in the drills

and when we scrimmage are the ones who killed us tonight. You let down your team, your teammates and coaches, your family and our fans. Winning is a verification of your moral fiber, your internal makeup, your fortitude. Some of you came up lacking in those categories tonight and I'm not going to stand for it!"

The assistant coaches, eyes big, acted as if they were viewing a madman. Then just as quickly as Coach began his tirade, he stopped. With a clenched fist wave of his program across his chest, his red face gave us one more shot. "Aw, hell, boys." Coach trudged into his office, slamming the door behind him for effect.

Hair wet, equipment bag slung over my shoulder I exited the locker room, looking for Mindy. And I found her. Mindy, arms around K.J. in the darkened gym, his around hers, consoling each other, gently rocking back and forth. I must have stared at them for over a minute. Then quietly I headed for the red lighted exit sign at the end of the gym and out to the corridor.

Love's labors—lost. High school, my school.

I refused the offers of well-meaning teammates to go out after the game, deciding to make the mile walk home alone in the cold night, to punish myself, a figurative self-flagellation, a spiral of shame. I decided not to listen to my iPod. I wanted to deprive myself of all things pleasing, all things good. Undeserving, not worthy. My self-esteem had taken two hits in a manner of minutes. As I started down the walkway from the field house, as if on cue, it started to rain. Looking up at the street lamps, I saw the drops coming faster, propelling through the glow of a lamp's globe on a downward slant, in sheets now. The wind blew. Small tree branches snapped, scurried across the sidewalk in the darkness, going somewhere fast, on their own agenda. I leaned into the cold wind, the pelting rain, collar up, ski cap pulled down over my ears. It was a little wild on the continent tonight, just right for my journey in self-pity.

Chapter 9

Saturday morning. Sleep had been restless, sporadic last night. I turned, then tossed (Why do we always have to toss, THEN turn when we can't sleep?) the visions swirling in my mind of misdirected free throws, Mindy and K.J. hugging, my brain's neurotransmitters short-circuiting, setting off startling alarms in my dream state. During the game I hadn't heard the disappointed home crowd's dismay—"ohhhhh"—coming from the stands as each foul shot missed the mark, but in my dreams my head filled, resonated with the sounds as my brain remembered the sensations of the crowd noise, my classmates' shouts and cheerleaders' disbelieving exhortations. My waking senses mixed with scenes of a slow motion movie of Mindy and K.J. What a drop in my emotional bucket. I rolled over on my stomach, pulled the covers over my head, wrapped the pillow around my ears, eyes closed, hoping the visions would go away. I had looked up at the stands to my brother immediately after the final buzzer sounded. He had his head down, slowly shaking it from side to side.

I heard my cell phone vibrate. Pushing my pillow away I checked my messages. I had gotten a few late last night from friends, teammates and one from my dad. The teammates' were meant to cheer me, but up in my bedroom I had been firm on wrapping my interest in Sports Center and tuning out my world. My dad's: **Benny just texted me about your free throws, how you blew the game. What the hell is wrong with you?** What a jerk. I wished that he'd just leave me alone. What the hell was

51

wrong with *him. And Benny!* You'd think that family would be supportive. I shut off the phone. I expected that this incoming text would be more of the same—teammates telling me to forget it, they had my back or God forbid, another from my father. But looking at the screen, it displayed a puzzling message. No name and I didn't recognize the number. A one sentence text. It read: **I can help you**. And underneath: the name Alison Johnson.

I hardly knew Alison. A senior, not in my circle of friends, though she was in my Food and Fitness class. Perplexed, I tried to think of how and why she wanted to help me. I don't think I had ever noticed her at a game before. Was she referring to basketball? Alison had a lanky build, dimples, and tight curly light brown hair which she parted in the middle, framing her face, the curls cascading down to her shoulders. With her dusky skin she looked to me to be bi-racial. Alison usually wore jeans and sandals, a black turtleneck or tie-dyed tee shirts. Sometimes she had a red bandana tied around her knee, and two or three rings on her tawny-colored fingers. A peace symbol with flowers adorned her backpack, a pink badge affixed that read, 'Girrrlz Rock!' She looked and acted more mature than the other senior girls. She knew she knew things the others didn't.

Often as I entered the Food and Fitness classroom Alison and Mrs. Gordon talked by Mrs. Gordon's desk; usually they both were smiling, laughing. Alison was really into the class, wanting to know about ingredients that made up the foods for the menus Mrs. Gordon gave us to make; how many calories, were the ingredients organic, was the produce from a local supplier, how much sodium and MSGs each contained. Not the stuff that teen-age boys worried about.

And, I recalled that Alison practiced yoga, that when we went up to the wresting mats above the phys ed offices in the auxiliary gym on the day that Mrs. Gordon introduced us to yoga that Alison had been really into it, eyes closed, her long legs crossed in the lotus position, looking meditative while we, the boys, rolled our eyes and sheepishly tried to imitate the movements Mrs. Gordon showed us, Downward Dog, Crocodile, Cobra, the Cat and the Cow, Child's Pose. Alison did them effortlessly. When Mrs. Gordon complimented her, Alison said she took yoga classes at the Y and the community college.

In short, Alison's path hadn't touched my orbit. Her interests, her maturity, her friends, all from another galaxy. I thought the stars would go blue before I'd ever do yoga willingly. I didn't know it at the time, but Alison's text was about to change my world as I knew it.

As I showered I thought about what I would text back. I thought about approaching Alison in Food and Fitness. My mind jetted ahead to Monday, what would I say. I had a vision of myself nervously trying to be cool, sidling up to Alison—viewer discretion advised—trying to get the words off my tongue. "Did you, uh, text me?"

I stayed in the shower a long time. The warm water soothing as I tried to seek some sort of semblance with my life, seeking direction. But as I sought answers, only more questions filled my mind. Dressing provided some relief; putting on my favorite clothes—t-shirt, blue jeans, hoodie, basketball shoes—clothes that were my old friends providing comfort. Still pensive, thinking about Alison's message, thinking about Mindy, thinking about missed free throws, thinking about letting Benny down, my food for thought suddenly became overpowered by a thought for food. Sunday morning breakfast called. I headed downstairs, en route to the kitchen, where I would show no mercy on the oatmeal, on the eggs, on the toast.

Chapter 10

First period Monday morning as I sat in Geometry class Miss Genovese started by saying, "Good morning. Hope you had a good weekend. We're beginning the new unit today."

"Awww."

Low, disgruntled sighs emanated up and down the aisles. A few slunk back in their seats, kicked out their feet frontward from under their student desks. Miss Genovesee pretended not to hear the faint protestations.

Miss Genovesee wore her pink sweater today, buttoned almost to the top over a white blouse and deep pink skirt, her dark brunette hair pinned up (all she needed were black and white saddle shoes, mouse ears and she'd be an Annette Funicello, 50s era, Mickey Mouse Club look-a-like who I had seen on the retro television channel on Jackson's cable). I wondered if she dated anyone, and if she did, did they talk about geometry, about school, and did she talk about her students—about me—to her BF?

My mind wandered from Miss G. to Robin, Mindy's best friend who sat up front. Robin actually understood the purpose of high school. She tried to learn as much as she could in every class, a model student. Unlike Robin, to the rest of the class starting a new unit sounded like nothing but work. Dead ahead. But Robin beamed, looked giddy. Bounced a little in her seat. Eagerly attuned to devour Miss Genovesee's theorems and postulates.

"It's the unit on right triangles, right, Miss G? I've really been looking forward to this! Can my row go to the board first?"

I stared at Robin. The whole class stared at Robin. To have that much interest in learning a subject that we thought we most likely would never use. And difficult to learn on top of it. And eager to do so. Only one conclusion came to mind. She must have a mutant gene.

Ms. Genovesee handed out the note sheets, with Robin's help, of course. Contrary to Robin, I, on the other hand, gave the impression of being an often disinterested student. When teachers called me out on my disinterest, I appeared to be interested in their interest about my disinterest and promised I'd try to do better. I almost always agreed with them; as a result, they liked me. Most of the time as the end of a trimester neared my scholastic endeavors faded. A planned obsolescence. At the beginning I did all assignments, read everything assigned, novels, chapters, handouts, stayed after class, volunteered to lead groups, raised my hand first to answer discussion questions. Teachers associated my name with their top students. Toward the middle of the trimester I slacked off a little, still answering the initial questions teachers put out to the class, then taking the rest of the period off, doing most of the reading, still doing almost all assignments, but not all, to completion. Teachers still maintained a favorable view of me, my performance. By the end of the trimester my academic metabolism had ebbed, effort lax, modus operandi reduced to being barely awake in class, sometimes head down, or slouched back in my chair, hood on my hoodie up, book bag not opened a half hour into the period. Sometimes I did fall asleep, head lying sideways resting on my arm, a small pooling of drool dribbled from mouth to cheek to arm to desk. Teachers rarely questioned me, thinking maybe something was wrong at home, and they didn't want to get into that. That's what guidance counselors were for.

I felt the urge to make an unsolicited remark.

"We're just cogs in the machine, Miss G. Whatever you think is

55

in our best interest."

Miss Genovesee looked up from the podium at me, contemplated an answer, then dismissed it. No time to waste. This being her time to shine. A new theorem awaited its unveiling at her trained hand, readied to bring geometrical enlightenment to the great unwashed innocent math minds seated before her.

Miss Genovesee began detailing the Pythagorean Theorem for us, referring to it as "Geometry's Most Elegant Theorem."

"A squared plus B squared equals C squared. True for every right triangle. Mathematicians have reveled in its complex simplicity for centuries."

Miss G. had alerted us last thing in class on Friday as we crammed our notebooks into our backpacks and jammed pens into pockets right before the bell that we would be taking up the Pythagorean Theorem on Monday. Sunday night in my room I had Googled Pythagoras and found 1) He was a vegetarian 2) His followers came up with the theorem and he claimed credit for it. Followers. Pythagoras: glory grabber. Who knew? Made me wonder about the others we had learned about in our Roman & Greek Mythology, English Lit and Psychology classes— Archimedes, Beowulf, Sophocles, Plato, Hercules. We never heard a word about Mrs. Archimedes, Mrs. Beowulf, Mrs. Sophocles, Mrs. Plato, or Mrs. Hercules. They were never given any due while their famous hubbies glommed on to all the credit for some new philosophy or heroic adventure. Didn't those guys have day jobs like everyone else? If they didn't, their wives must have supported their husbands, their "work," by scrubbing the steps of the Parthenon or sweeping the aisles of the Coliseum. At that I drifted back to class happenings. But one thought occurred when I turned back from dazing out the window to Miss Genovesee, my chin resting on both balled up fists, looking attentive. If there was Roman and Greek mythology, was there also American Mythology? I pondered that for a while Miss Genovesee drew

56

another triangle on the whiteboard and zestfully talked about familiar right triangles. I knew about familiar triangles. Right now the long and short sides were K.J. and Mindy, I was the hypotenuse and though it was familiar, nothing was right about it.

Chapter 11

Miss Genovesee continued to gleefully labor on the board, using her ruler to draw triangles to scale and labeling their measurements on each side. My mind drifted back to basketball, then to Alison's message. Next period I would see her in Food and Fitness. Mondays we cooked, so we'd be out of our seats. That strengthened the chance for me to say something to Alison about her text. But what would I say? I thought about that as I put pencil to paper. I solved right triangles with sides of 3-4-5, 8-15-17, and 7-24-25. I liked the solidarity of math, the certainty that the rules never changed. Learn 'em, and they would apply the rest of your life. A sense of permanency. Not exactly a human attribute, at least when it came to relationships, to girl friends.

Miss Genovesee waxed and waned in her presentation, the waning caused by a few students challenged by trying to identify the hypotenuse, the short leg or the long leg, not being able to discern the sixty degree angle from a thirty, puzzled as to which constituted a forty-five and ninety for that matter. When her presentation finished, satisfied that most of her students could at least detect a triangle from a square, certain that Pythagoras would have been proud of her presentation, Miss G. asked the class,

"Are there any more questions before I assign the homework?"

I raised my hand.

"Miss Genovesee," I paused before I asked my question, making certain I had her's and the classes' attention.

" Was math discovered, or was it invented?"

Miss G. frowned, then bit her lower lip, creased her eyebrows, turned her head to one side looking perplexed, started to answer, then stopped. My classmates turned to look at me, some with puzzled facial expressions, others blank, a few with smirks. Those were the ones familiar with me, the ones that knew about my spurious comment making. I responded to my fans with an open-armed gesture, mouthing the words, "What? What?" as if I didn't know.

Miss Genovesee looked as if she had been hit by an asteroid (it appeared to me), her brain cells spinning as she pondered. She turned her attention back to the class and said, dismissing my question.

"Page 114, do the odds, except skip number 9. Be sure to draw the diagrams."

Then she closed her book, went to her desk and sat down, blinked her eyes a few times, and looked up at the clock.

Chapter 12

Third period. Food and Fitness. An elective class with both juniors and seniors. Would the mystery behind Alison's text soon be known? Consorting through the hall on the way to class, Hobie came alongside.

"Hey Stevie, Two questions. First what happened with you and Mindy? I thought you guys were going together. You're like a Mayfly. Emerge from your cocoon, wake up, meet, mate, lay eggs and die in 48 hours. But you only lasted about 24. And how hard is practice gonna be today? Coach wasn't very happy Friday."

I eyed Hobie for a second, giving him the stink-eye.

"Thanks for reminding me," I said.

What happened with me and Mindy? Heck if I know. I had had only one girlfriend, for two weeks in junior high. Ginny Burgermeister. In the spring, eighth grade year. Being more interested in sports than girls, and Ginny, much more mature than I had been, as every single girl on earth is at that age than the boys are, soon figured that out. That concept had only recently occurred to me. As such, I hadn't had any action since my eighth grade picnic. Ginny might remember it differently. In all actuality I admit to not having emerged. Still in the larva stage, in my cocoon.

I slugged Hobie in the arm then promptly took off, pinballing through the clogged hall to Food and Fitness.

I eyed Alison talking with her friends on the other side of the room as I entered the classroom. Thinking about what I would do, I slid into my seat and put my book bag on the floor. I still hadn't made a plan; would she come up to me/should I approach her/should I ignore her text or text her back, and if I did, what should I say. I decided to just wait, wait and see what played out. (When it came to talking to girls, making the first contact, my brain often turned to guacamole. I had no go-to move. Basketball, yes. Girls, no.) Mrs. Gordon interrupted my thoughts.

"Today we're going to work on our Thanksgiving recipes. We'll be using the same recipes for Christmas—excuse me—I should call them 'holiday recipes'—we respect all faiths here," and she gave us a reassuring nod. "We'll be cooking a little today and all period tomorrow for our dinner Wednesday. Wednesday remember to come here instead of going to the cafeteria for lunch. We'll be working in groups. I have a sheet I'm giving you with your group and what dishes you'll be preparing, the recipes and directions."

Row by row Mrs. Gordon passed out our assignments, our fates. Number one concern always "Who's in my group, any of my friends?" And two, "Whatever I have to do, I hope it won't make my brain implode."

"Everybody will begin their preparations tomorrow, but groups with foods that take longer prep time can start practicing their preparations today. Refer to the directions on your sheets. You'll have to decide who's doing what. We want this to be good—we'll have visitors. The principal, some teachers and maybe some school board members will be dropping by. I know you'll all do a great job. I don't want any squabbling or quibbling. No Squabblers or Quibblers."

She shook her index finger at us, a mild but stern warning.

"Let's get started. Remember to follow the directions checklist and you'll be fine. I know I'm going to be so proud of you."

Mrs. Gordon put her hands on her hips and gave us a big smile that looked a little fake to me. I figured she thought she should be concerned about a few of us taking this as seriously as we should.

But she should have remembered that we were teenagers and we're talking about food here. What could possibly go wrong?

A hand raised in the back. Sandy Appelbaum had a question about Mrs. Gordon's evaluation of our preparations.

"Will there be valuable prizes?"

Mrs. Gordon shook her head slowly.

"Nooo. But it will be for a grade, and of course, remember we always have pride in what we do when we make something for others."

Sandy replied, "We'd rather have valuable prizes."

I liked that. I wished I had said it.

I found my name on the hand-out, our names listed in groupings of four next to the dish to be prepared, appetizers, main dish, side dishes, desserts. My name appeared with another guy and two girls, in the group preparing the main dish, turkey with stuffing. I looked at the other three names that I would be working with. Josephine Jimenez was one. She went by 'Josie'. A member of the girls basketball team, a twin to our boys' point guard Jose', lean, with kinda buff arms. Not that she could bench press a Buick, but she had good definition. Down side—Josie's demeanor—more than slightly moody. Sometimes I wondered who had the job of poking her with a stick when she awoke every morning to get her irritated. The other guy listed besides me was Kyle Mahoney, a member of my lunch crew. A long-haired headbanger, drummer in a band, always wore black t-shirts with band names—today's was *Nine Inch Nails*—a guy who didn't take things too seriously except for his music, always joking around, party trained. And the third member of my group: Alison Johnson.

Before we started I had a question to ask.

"Mrs. Gordon, what's the difference between dressing and stuffing?"

Mrs. Gordon didn't take the bait. She nipped that conversation in the bud.

"Just follow the directions, Stevie. You can call it whatever you want. But generally, dressing is cooked outside the bird, stuffing cooked inside. If you live south of the Mason-Dixon Line, it's almost always called dressing."

I sulked for about six seconds, my effort to get attention, one-upmanship foiled. She knew the answer. Advantage Mrs. Gordon.

My group met at one of the big tables in the front of the room near Mrs. Gordon's desk. I pushed myself up out of my seat and walked over, Alison's text in mind and wondered if she would say anything to me right away, later on, never, only unless I brought it up? But as I walked over I saw Alison approach Mrs. Gordon. Mrs. Gordon had her fingers rolled in a ball under her chin, looking down as she listened to Alison, a doubtful look on her face, looking like Rodin's "The Thinker." Alison appeared to be pleading a case, animated, about the dish she had been assigned? Or her group? Me?

We waited. Kyle sat back and gave a smirky smile at Josie, who deeply sighed, arms folded and said,

"Can't we just get started? What is she talking about that she thinks is so important? She thinks she can get whatever she wants. Did Alison have a big glass of suck-up sauce for breakfast?"

They both turned to me as if I had the answer. Shrugging my shoulders, I gave Kyle and Josie a quizzical look. We saw Mrs. Gordon nodding her head up and down, agreeing with Alison, the conversation continuing, Alison looking excited. Josie, with no little amount of sarcasm leaned toward us and said,

"What's she doing now, trying to win Best In Show? Or maybe 'I'd like to thank the Academy.'"

Josie laughed, too emphatically if you asked me, at her own jokes.

A minute later Alison came on a bounce back to our table,

making a cha-ching fist along with a big smile and a "Yes!"

"Guys! Mrs. Gordon said we can make a veggie turkey!"

Excited, gesturing, her arms extended, Alison displayed an invisible turkey.

"She said we have to make a real one, but we can make a vegetarian turkey, too, a Veggie-Turkey! I always wanted to do this! They're advertised as being gobblicious!"

This pronouncement of Alison's led to us leaning forward, Josie and me with our arms still folded, looking dubious, Josie mouthing "What the…?" and Kyle, eyebrows arched, a smiley smirk on his face, hands outstretched on the desk, liking the surprise. Alison continued,

"It's a turkey, but it's made of tofu and soy. No turkey has to die! It's a mock meat!"

Josie and I gave each other a side glance. Tofu not being on the list of ingested food items in our lives so far. Kyle's head wobbled side-to-side, still smiling. But that pretty much had been Kyle's reaction to anything you told him since he was a toddler.

I had known that Alison had a reputation as an animal rights activist, had seen some of her Facebook postings on my friends' Facebook. I can't say her actions surprised me. We leaned back in our chairs and listened.

"This will be sooo great!" Alison continued. "Hey, how about if Stevie and I make the veggie turkey, and," giving Josie a hopeful look, "you and Kyle make the real turkey? And we can help each other when need be!"

Josie straightened up, gave another dramatic audible sigh, and looking away from Alison, said, "Whatever."

I turned to Kyle and said, "You know, we just may have a case of conflicting personalities. Mahoney and Kalkannes ready at your service. Diagnosing personality disorders since ten minutes ago. No problem too big or too small. Satisfaction guaranteed or your money back. Thirty days same as cash. We service all makes and models. Accept no substitute. Call anytime, day or night. Operators on duty. Past performance not necessarily indicative of future results. Not available in all areas. Some restrictions may apply. Residency requirements in effect. Not suitable for all ages. Not to be combined with other offers."

Kyle did the thing where he raises his eyebrows and smiles at the same time. We sat back and enjoyed the show, Kyle nudging me with his elbow.

"Look."

Kyle's sentences often began and ended on the same word.

Josie's eyes flashed darts at Alison. Alison looked back at her once, then again, then down at the handout, her mind trying to figure out what she had done to offend Josie.

Alison started to say something to Josie, then reading Josie's face still staring at her, looked downward again and mouthed a few words we couldn't hear.

Josie bent forward toward Alison.

"What did you say? If you've got something to say to me, say it so I can hear you."

"I was just wondering why you would cop an attitude…"

Just at that point Mrs. Gordon sensed some negativity in the room and clapped her hands.

"Let's go, let's go. No time to waste. Let's get started."

Following the directions Mrs. Gordon gave us, the dual turkey making started off rather well, considering that a cat fight might have broken out at any moment. The only blip happened when Alison bravely went over to Kyle and Josie's station to check on their progress, and I heard Josie say, "You don't have to check on us. You're not my mother!" But a few minutes later Josie came to our station carrying a smoking pan and asked Alison a question, something about making the stuffing, about whether the onions and the celery looked sautéed enough. The picture of the ones on the recipe displayed a golden yellow color when done from the butter that was added. Josie's onions and celery were tinged with black. More than tinged. Crusted might be a better word. A crusted black. Alison's response—very gentle, and well, motherly. Peering down at the remnants of Josie's cooking experiment, Alison said,

"You might want to start over. I'm sure those are good, but they might be a little too, um, crunchy."

Josie looked down at the charred remains of her creation in the smoldering pan she carried.

"Yeah, that's what I thought, too. Thanks."

World War III averted. I looked over. Kyle, standing, back to us, a pencil in each hand, drummed the desk to the head-banger beat in his head. Josie still stared at the skillet, now fizzling. I made a mental note of the location of the fire extinguisher in the room.

Chapter 13

"Please clean up your stations," Mrs. Gordon directed the class with ten minutes to go in the period. Alison and I hadn't had much to do other than look up the preparations on the internet as we needed to get the ingredients for the veggie turkey, the tofu, soy, cane sugar, starch and a few others which Alison said she would get that night, that Mama Johnson would gladly buy them for us. (Mrs. Gordon told us that as the department chairwoman for Family and Consumer Sciences her budget didn't allow for two turkeys, veggie or not, and that we would have to buy the necessary ingredients ourselves. Alison looked to me, and I readily agreed.)

As we washed down the table (preparing recipes, cooking or not, as a health precaution we did this at the end of every class), Alison asked me, "Did you get my text?"

With most girls, talking with them for the first time I'd be a little nervous, but Alison had a way of distilling that process, making others feel comfortable (well, except for the noted Josie episode).

Alison started, "I came to your game the other night. I don't know much about basketball, but I think I could help you on your foul shots."

"I'm listening," I said with a puzzled look. I had never heard that Alison had an interest in sports, or played on any of our school teams.

"I think it's your brain and your breathing."

"I kinda think it's my form and my follow through," I replied, my bicep and forearm on my right arm forming an "L", pushing an imaginary ball up and out over my right eye, reaching, following through with my hand and fingers pantomiming my free throw form, shooting at an imaginary basket.

"You may think that, but I'm sure you have proper form. You practice all the time, right?" Alison continued talking, explaining further as she scrubbed the table.

"Remember what Mrs. Gordon talked about when we did yoga up on the mats, about being in the moment, about breathing in and out, what she called being in the spaces in-between?"

I'm sure I looked pensive. I stopped scrubbing, started thinking. "Yeah, I remember, but I'm not sure I get all that. I always take a deep breath when I get to the free throw line. I have a routine. It always worked in the past."

Alison thought about that, looked up, and wiping her hands on a paper towel, said, "But that didn't help you Friday did it?"

"Nooo. But the game was on the line, and the crowd...I just choked."

"That's what I'm talking about! It's your state of mind, what we call 'mindfulness.' Why don't you come to yoga with me this week, give it a try. I really think the thought process that goes into yoga will help you."

The bell rang. I pondered for a few seconds, then asked, "When and where is it?"

"Tomorrow, Tuesday nights at the Y. Seven forty-five. Let me know tomorrow."

I nodded, interested, apprehensive. Alison put on her backpack, smiled at me and gave a small wiggle wave with her fingers to Mrs. Gordon as she made her way out of class.

We practiced after school tomorrow, so I could go, although dubious that yoga could help. But I wanted to believe Alison. Heck, I just wanted to make my free throws.

Chapter 14

At practice after school on Monday Coach gathered the team together at mid-court before we started practice. Usually Coach Arnold's gave us snippets of the day's practice plan and went over scouting reports. He told us that we'd be watching tape of some of Friday's game after practice. Coach, somewhat of a dinosaur, always said "tape" instead of "the video" or "the recording." I would have liked to have informed him that Beta and VHS had died a slow death, but demurred. For now anyway, considering my performance on Friday. Why scratch the bear? Coach got right to what had been on his mind since the scoreboard clock read 0.00 on Saturday night. No surprise there. We already knew. Could see it coming, hoped it wouldn't, but it came anyway. It being Coach's critical assessment of our play. We called "it" criticism. He called "it" coaching.

Coach shook his head and said, "Boys, we can't let this happen again. Losing a fourteen point lead at the half because we were so, so *content* with ourselves." He then launched into a repeat of his after game locker room talk from Friday, although he left out the profanity. If I thought I had a long weekend thinking about how we, I, lost the game, it had to have been even tougher on the coach and his staff. I'm thinking they watched the game video about, oh, five or six times. When Coach had us watch the game recordings he would point out a mistake—loudly, his teeth gritting, almost crying, a dagger to his heart—and single out the perpetrator and break down the turnover, errant pass, or missed shot, bad fundamentals or poor choice of a shot, pass, or dribble. Then he'd hit rewind, we'd look at it again and he'd yell at the offender once more.

"Hobie! How can you expect K.J. to make a good post move after you pass the ball at his feet? How many times have I told you to hit his target hand? Use a ball fake first, read the defense then make the proper pass. The bounce pass would have worked there! And K.J., keep your shoulders square to the passer! Use your arm bars, keep 'em up, fight off those guys. You had twenty pounds and three inches on that guy defending you and he owned you in the second half! You can't chicken fight down there! Claim the lane! These are all things we've told you every day in practice. Geeez!"

He went on. And on. Coach's glasses were misting, his cheeks turning red as he ran his fingers through his gray-white hair, what was left of it, more mussed than usual, exasperated. Many of us looked down at the floor, especially the guilty parties responsible for causing Coach's angst.

Coach simulated a defensive stance, his arms extended outward, bending his old knees as much as he could. I thought he was about to cry. What we did—or didn't do—obviously reflected on his integrity, as a coach, as a human being. That's the message that I got.

"And your defense in the second half! What was that? Or I should say lack of defense?! Didn't ya learn about Newton's Laws of Motion? Objects in motion tend to stay in motion. Objects at rest tend to stay at rest? I never saw so many guys play defense flat-footed. You might as well have had red flags and yelled, 'Ole' when you let them drive right past you! Isn't that what the matadors or toreadors or whatever they're called do? Get in a stance, would ya?!!"

Coach took his glasses off and wiped the sweat from his nose on the right sleeve of his white coaches' polo shirt with the Kestrels' logo.

Coach Arnold could easily have been a Roman general, back in the day, a red plume on top of his gold helmet, exhorting his troops to defend Rome against the Gauls. His sword pointing in the air, leading his legions, "Defense, boys, defense!" He would have been right in his element.

I dreaded the after practice film session, thinking what Coach would say about the missed free throws. I listened as he spoke, occasionally looking up, but mostly had my head down. I knew that more than anyone else that the culpability for the crime pretty much rested with me.

"Boys, one play…one play could define your season, your high school career, good or bad. You have to play with a sense of urgency. And you have to have discipline. I've heard all about how you lost games last year despite having so much talent due to taking bad shots at inopportune times, not taking care of the ball in critical situations, not willing to give it your all on defense. All we—myself, Coach Pettaway and Coach Luke—all we can do is prepare you best we can. If you do what we tell you, you WILL be successful. But the main message I need to give you today is that you need to be made of sterner stuff."

A morgue-like atmosphere hung over practice as we started. Afraid to say anything, afraid to make a mistake. But the coaches, surprisingly upbeat. Snag in the road they said.

"Sometimes it takes a while to season the gumbo. Sometimes you have to break a few eggs to make an omelet," Coach Pettaway told us.

They clapped and whistled at every good thing we did, exhorting us. We did full court fast break lay-up drills with a rebounder passing to an outlet near the sideline, the outlet (everyone was a point guard in this drill) on a speed dribble to center court and then to the top of the circle, hitting the sprinting rebounder who filled the outside lane going in for a lay-up. We had to make 32 in two minutes and when we did the coaches

71

clapped and shouted praise. Practice started and continued well to our astonishment. Humming along, surprisingly in normal mode, the green light on.

At the end of practice we divided up into partners for free throw shooting. We played a game called "Iron and Cotton." If you made a perfect swish, hitting nothing but the net, your team received two points. If your foul shot hit the rim, the orange metal, and went in, one point. On a miss you had to subtract two points from your team's score. Each player shot ten foul shots. My partner, Jamey, swished his first two foul shots perfectly. My turn. I could feel the coaches' eyes on me as I shot. Something I had found so easy before had become so difficult. I think I had the yips - my shot herky jerky, not fluid as it used to be. Each coach came over to offer advice after each one of my misses, usually with their arms folded, speaking in a low voice, trying to be helpful.

"Keep your elbow in." "Finish up on your toes." "Follow through till the ball goes in the basket."

Coach Arnold finally lost a little patience on my fourth straight miss.

"Damn it, Stevie. You have to make 'em pay for fouling you. It's an attitude as much as anything."

I nodded several times. Jamey and I did our sprints along with the other pairs who finished behind the winners, Kenny and Hobie. Coach called us to the half-court circle, told us he'd see us tomorrow after school, that he was canceling the film session, and gave me a look. I could see him listing "Stevie's free throws" to his To-Do list. A thing broken. A thing that needed fixing. A thing that kept him awake at night.

Chapter 15

In Tuesday's food and Fitness class Alison and I proceeded to make our veggie turkey. Alison took this on with a serious determination. Me, a little less so. I started to laugh when after adding the ingredients our veggie turkey looked like a nondescript gelatinous gooey glob. We stepped back and took a look. I stifled a snicker; I knew the importance of our cooking project to Alison. She went right back to work with her latex-gloved hands working away, molding and sculpting. Alison appeared to know what she was doing. She always appeared to know what she was doing, had a palpable confidence about her. Her self-esteem had to be about a ninety-nine on a hundred point scale. Mine? About a fifty-six. I often stumbled, faked my way through. Trying to do my part to help, I provided moral support through a few useless suggestions as I walked around the table, inspecting the veggie bird from different angles, as if peering at a work of art in Michelangelo's studio.

"Looks good from this side… Might need a little more, uh, stuff on the tail end… I think it's going well, don't you?"

To each helpful comment Alison replied, "Uh huh."

Yep. WE were doing great. Us. Alison and me. Our team.

I looked over at Josie's and Kyle's station. Kyle worked on the stuffing, Josie having turned over the job to him. Josie had one hand on her hip, looking amused as Kyle stirred the contents in a mixing bowl, much of which appeared to be permanently glued to his spatula, Kyle trying to shake it off, the stuffing taking flight onto his shirt, his pants, the floor, the table counter top. (Today's t-shirt—Black. Ozzy Osbourne. *Crazy Train*.) Josie caught my eye, left hand still on her hip, thumb on her right hand pointing out, doing a sideways get-a-load-of-this gesture at Kyle. She laughed as Kyle mixed some, shook the spatula some, mixed some, shook the spatula some.

"Untouched by human hands," Josie said for my benefit as she laughed at her own funny.

And to think she had done so well herself with the celery and onion cooking conflagration. I gave her a slight side-to-side head shake, glad that I had been paired with Alison instead of Miss Demeanor.

With only a few minutes to spare in class before the bell, I have to say our visual veggie turkey looked impressive. With a little imagination, it appeared bird-like, sans feathers. Alison looked pleased.

"What do you think, Stevie?"

"I think the culinary arts are my new calling," I said, crediting myself for Alison's creation.

"No one could have handed the spatula to me any better than you did, Stevie."

I bowed.

"Thank you. I'll be autographing copies of my new cookbook after class."

Even though the master chef I had become, apprehension set in about the taste test at Wednesday's luncheon, how the critics would rate our veggie cuisine. Four stars? A thumbs up? Or would it be something ventured, nothing gained? I hoped not for Alison's sake.

Chapter 16

Tuesday night I met Alison at the community college which shared their recreational facilities with the local YMCA. She secured a visitor pass for me at the front desk and we headed in, climbing the stairs to the second floor studio. Alison was carrying her yoga mat; she told me that there were extras along the wall that I could use where we went in. We walked past the elliptical machines. Some overweight members of our species as well as those athletic and toned pedaling away, eyes on television screens, some with ear buds piping inspirational exercise music into their ear canals. We entered the studio. A few of the devotees had laid their yoga mats on the floor, water bottles nearby, and were taking off overcoats, sweatshirts, and boots, revealing their yoga outfits. Alison introduced me to the instructor, Joanie, while more of the class streamed in.

"Welcome to our class, Stevie," Joanie said after I signed the sign-in sheet. "I hope you enjoy it. Is this your first time doing yoga?"

"Other than at the high school once or twice in Food and Fitness. I'm really just a rookie."

"Just relax and you'll be fine. That's the key."

It seemed to be about three women or girls to every guy. Most of the women wore proper yoga clothes, while the men were mostly in t-shirts and gym shorts. Alison wore black yoga pants and a salmon colored sleeveless top, the upper back hollowed out semi-circular so that I could see her shoulder blades. Along with black leggings that seemed to be the popular yoga outfit for the women.

After welcoming me Joanie invited me to take a mat from the stacked pile and told me to place it wherever I liked. Alison had put her mat down next to Joanie's in the middle of the room and waved at me to come next to her, but I retreated to the rear of the studio room. Joanie turned the lights out, and turned on the golden rope lighting that ringed the studio floor. A wall length mirror graced one side of the room so that we could see ourselves, correct our positioning. The other side of the room featured an equally large window, showing a panorama of the campus, a canopy of treetops, walkways partially illuminated in a dark yellow glow, some of the college buildings alit and alive, others seemingly lifeless in the cold of winter. Stars sparkled overhead. Most of the class of about fifteen were busily stretching, while others sat cross-legged, eyes closed, getting in the mood.

Joanie began class by tapping a tiny silver bell, to bring our attention to her.

"Welcome. Are we ready? How's everybody doing tonight? Is it warm enough in here?"

She received reassuring nods.

"For anyone new tonight I want to let you know that I always give you a safe alternative to any of the poses, stretches, movements that we do. You can always return to Child's Pose at any time you'd like. We're not here for competition or judgment."

Joanie then put on new age music, creating a soothing background for our aural senses.

"Let's start on all fours. Are we ready? Place your starfish hands on the mat."

She paused, waiting for all of us to assume the positioning with our hands and knees on the mat's surface. In her soft voice she led us in a series of movements and stretches called the Vinyasa Series.

"Flow at your own pattern and pace," said Joanie. "If you wish you may return to Child's Pose at any time."

Child's Pose was a welcoming position with our forehead on the mat, on our knees, back extended comfortably upward, tail back, arms outstretched frontward. The series started gently then progressively became more demanding. Joanie guided us from Downward Dog - tails up, the tail being our human fulcrum point, head down, palms and toes touching our soft rubbery mats to plank position - which I had known as push-up position - lowering down slowly down - the Crocodile, then curling toes under, pushing our chest and head up, arms straight on the mat - the Cobra, back up to Downward Dog. And so it went as our movements coincided with the repetitive rhythmic of the synchronized harmony of the music, our muscles stretching, straining slightly, from positions our bodies enjoyed to movements challenging the sinews of our arms, shoulders, biceps, triceps, quads, calfs and achilles. We paid attention to our breathing as Joanie advised, inhaling going into a pose, exhaling coming out. I watched the others each time we began a new series, self conscious. But I soon realized that the others were into their movements, in tune only with their own universes. Meditative. We went from down on the mat to standing.

A momentary respite for our muscles as Joanie suggested we shake our legs out and rotate our ankles, asking " How's everybody doing?" Then, "Let's start with Warrior One. Place your back foot at a 45 degree angle, firmly into the mat, bend the front knee, hips facing forward, arms outstretch overhead, bent at the elbows."

Warrior One flowed into Warrior Two, turning our arms straight out in front, straight back behind us with a twist of our trunks. Balance, I was learning, was the key. With Warrior Two we were slightly doing a forward lunge. It would be a while before I could commit my movements to muscle memory instead of having to watch, think about my body's motions and poses. But I liked it. As class approached the end, we lay on our backs on our mats.

Joanie instructed: "Taking all the muscles in your feet, your toes, your ankles, your legs, your quadriceps, your fanny, your stomach, your chest, squeeze them so tightly, so tightly, so tightly," her voice rising, "now relax." Deep breaths. "Now taking your neck, your head, your jaw muscles, your eyes, your forehead, squeeze so tightly, so tightly, so tightly. Now relax."

We finished by squeezing our shoulders, biceps, arms, fists, fingers. A final sighing, deep exhale.

"You've released all the tension in your body. You're so relaxed now, your body is in a totally relaxed state. Let's prepare for final relaxation."

We lay flat on our backs, the Corpse Pose, eyes closed, in a semi-conscious state, the new age music softly, naturally aiding the mind's mood as we breathed in, breathed out. About ten minutes later the soft dinging of the bell brought us out of our somnambulant trances. We finished with a few shoulder and neck, fingers and hand stretches sitting upright on our mats. Class ended with Joanie taking her right hand overhead, then down to meet her left in a prayer position, saying,

"We always end by saying 'The spirit within me honors the spirit within you.'" And she and we bowed to each other.

"Namaste."

I didn't want the session to end. I felt calm, relaxed, at peace. Yoga. Body, mind, spirit.

Chapter 17

The highly anticipated Food and Fitness Holiday Feast Day started at 10:45, the start of third period, readied with thanks to Mrs. Gordon for staying late after school Tuesday and coming in before school Wednesday to check the food preps and providing some TLC as needed to the side dishes, including much needed surgery to Kyle and Josie's. Our assistant principal, Phil Kleindienst, sampled the veggie turkey on his plastic plate as I came in during our lunch period. Alison stood off to the side, her hands together, up and under her chin as if praying. I think Mr. Kleindienst had been tipped off by Mrs. Gordon that Alison created the culinary brainchild on his plate.

"Mmmm…this is quite, this is really…um, really….edible. What did you use for the, what do you call it? Texture?"

Alison told him, a little hesitantly, "Wheat gluten. Do you like it?"

"You know, I do, Alison. I wasn't sure what to expect, but it's actually quite tasty. Nice touch with the mushroom gravy, too."

Alison pointed at me.

"Stevie thought of that."

I shook my head.

"Yep. When you're talking your foodstuffs, victuals, sustenance, I get inspired, Mr. Kleindienst. Kidspiration."

Mr. Kleindienst took another bite, gave another "mmm" - I think that was mostly for Alison's benefit, then started working on his green bean casserole and mashed potatoes.

Third period we had spent setting up for the staff, students and visitors. Mrs. Gordon had the food ready in warmers. The aromas tantalized; I wanted to pull up my chair to the buffet and dig in but that would probably constitute a dining faux pas. Mrs. Gordon told us "Visitors first." It wasn't as if I could actually get to the buffet, anyway. Some of the more rotund female faculty, along with the principal, Mrs. Huffington, were forming a blockade around the table with their tugboat-like derrieres, maneuvering into position as if the buffet table was a barge they were tying up to. The Denver Broncos' offensive line had nothing on them. I'd describe Mrs. Huffington's build as two giant volleyballs, one atop the another. I couldn't discern if she had a distinct fulcrum point between where the top of her torso met the bottom half. I became distracted by the largess of her kankles. Her shoes had to have been taking a severe downward beating. I wondered if there would be anything left when the ladies consummated their foraging. Their goal seemed to be to eat anything that wouldn't eat them. Kyle and I stood off to the side, in line with the others in our class, holding our plates and plastic ware, looking like the sad children from Botswana pictured in the TV ads appealing for donations. I hoped someone would sponsor me.

Josie munched on a banana and chips at a desk on the other side of the room against a wall.

"I wouldn't eat that stuff if I were you guys," she said to Kyle and me. "It looks so gross. And the veggie turkey - you couldn't pay me enough to eat that Frankenfood."

Kyle lifted his plate to his mouth and pretended to chomp a chunk out of it.

I said to Josie, patting Kyle on the back, "My boy here is a food connoisseur, an epicurean, known to frequent the finest of fast food dining establishments in the tri-state area. He's given two thumbs up to our bountiful banquet feastings."

Josie wrinkled her nose, scowled, and tossed the banana skin into the trash. "Adolescents," she hissed at us.

Kyle and I bumped fists. She had us pegged.

The tugboats had parted the buffet, seeking port to place down their accumulated hauls. Mrs. Huffington, the last to leave, smiled at us as she manhandled two biscuits onto her already overcrowded plate, pushing the corn and cream cheese into her green bean casserole, and after one last lustful look over the buffet, waddled in the wake of her dining mates. Kyle and I, like scavenging crows, descended on the remnants left behind.

Chapter 18

Stevie, Want 2 meet me and my friend Jillian @ mall food court 4 lunch @ 1:00? After practice on Friday, on Thanksgiving break I checked my cell phone. A text from Alison. Food court? Sure. I texted her back. **CU then and there.**

I'd like to say that I'd pick them up, but I had no wheels. My mom said maybe for my seventeenth birthday in March. Benny had gotten an athletic grant-in-aid to Catawba Community College where he had played point guard for two years; he had been recruited by some four year schools, Tiffin, Kenyon, Capital, to play and further his education but they would only give him a partial scholarship; Mom would have to pay the rest. She gave Benny a choice. She'd pay the tuition so Benny could further his athletic career at one of the expensive private schools or he could attend state schools Kent, Toledo or Bowling Green and she'd buy him a car. Benny chose Bowling Green and the wheels.

Hobie gave me a ride. The girls sat on the bench by the food court entrance, checking their cell phones.

"Hey Alison."

Alison introduced me to her friend Jillian, and told me she and Jillian had been best friends since second grade at Firelands Grade School. Alison and I sat at a table in the food court at the mall with Jillian. I nursed a chocolate shake, the only thing Alison allowed me to order on my own. Lunch consisted of a salad with apple pieces and walnuts in place of my usual Colossal Burger—at Alison's strong suggestion. In line ahead of Alison and Jillian at the mall burger restaurant, Nemo's, I had ordered what I usually ordered, a Colossal burger, two patties with cheese, loaded with onions, tomato, lettuce, bacon, and pickle. I always figured that I burned up whatever calories it contained in about the first fifteen minutes of practice. Not that I worried about it. A tug on my shoulder.

"Steven!" Alison said.

Actually her look said it.

"You're going to eat *that*?"

"Absoltively," I said, pondering what size order of fries I wanted, the gargantuan or the elephantine size.

The girl behind the counter waited. I waited. For Alison to pick out what I should order. Alison perused the fine print at the bottom of the menu gathering the ingredients and calories information. Looking up, she gave the Nemo's counter person a shake of her head, nullifying my order. The counter girl had seen this before when five year olds ordered ice cream while their parents were looking up at the menu overhead behind the counter. Alison pointed to a salad with apples and walnuts with a vinaigrette dressing, tapping the picture with her index finger. A vinaigrette dressing?

"Sure," I said meekly. "I couldn't decide between the salad and the gigundo-burger the size of my head. They look equally tantalizing."

Alison leaned sideways on the counter and looked at me.

"You have so much to learn."

The counter girl took Alison's and Jillian's order, gave me a tight smile and a quick upraised eyebrows look; *Wimp*! is what it said, and placed our orders. She gave us each a cup for our ice waters.

After filling our stomachs at the food court Jillian suggested we go for a walk at the metropark.

"Let's go on an adventure," she said. Everything with Alison and Jillian had to have an aspect of fun.

"We like going to the park. And we love liking things. We're enthusiasts. And we can walk off our lunch. I feel kind of bloated. And, we can wear our cool new wraparound sunglasses!"

Leaving the mall, an overcast gray late November sky loomed overhead with an occasional drizzle of rain on our faces, but I didn't want to spoil Jillian's fun. Far be it for me to tell someone that their new funglasses weren't necessary.

I looked at her.

"And we can walk off those twenty-seven calories in the salads. Right?"

A head shake and a semi-dramatic deep sigh from Alison.

We stopped at Food City before going to the metropark. We needed snacks to fuel our walk. Healthy snacks, of course, Alison said. Trail mix, raisins, apples, bananas. We'd stop at a drive through for coffee and hot chocolate.

I knew that Kyle worked there. Sometimes he bagged for the cashiers, sometimes he stocked shelves. I spotted Kyle in the pet food aisle. He had a shopping cart with items that shoppers had picked out then later decided they didn't want, abandoning them in store locations remote from where they had been picked off the shelves, or at the check-out when they had second thoughts or not enough money for their purchase. Kyle's cart contained cereal boxes, greeting cards, bug spray, cake mix, cans of beef stew, twelve packs of pop, ketchup, laundry detergent and a huge bag of dog food that Kyle was hoisting from the cart and putting back in its proper shelf space. Additional random items peaked out from underneath the detritus, waiting to be re-stocked.

"Hey Kyle! Workin' hard! Keepin' our economy goin'. Good man you are, Kyle Mahoney."

"Yep. Got the orphans, the go-backs. Takin' 'em back to their homes."

"That brings a tear to my eye, K-Man. Always looking out for those in need."

"That's the kind of guy I am."

We laughed as Kyle gave a mirthful smile. Instrumentals of soft rock songs from the 80s played from overhead speakers throughout the store, ostensibly to put the shoppers in a tranquil, happy shopping mood, interrupted only by a request for employee number one hundred thirty-seven to clean up a spill on aisle nine.

Picking a 20 ounce can of peaches out of his cart, he showed it to us. "Found this bad boy in with the dog food. Mmm-hmmm. That's some mighty good eatin' there, if you're a vegetarian St. Bernard."

A shopper, a guy slowly butt-walking his cart came down our aisle, leaning both his elbows on the blue plastic cart handle, pushing us to the side out of his path. Alison and Jillian dramatically splayed themselves, arms out, backs against the shelves, terrified looks on their faces. Butt-Walker gave them a slight sneery look and without so much as an "excuse me" continued down the aisle, forcing Kyle to obediently move his orphans, side squeaking his cart to make room for Butt-Walker.

Jillian fake wiped the fake sweat off her forehead, and grimacing, said, "Whew. *That* was a close one."

Alison furiously nodded her head up and down, looking scared, playing along.

"I thought we were goners."

Crisis averted, I continued our conversation with Kyle, who had the peach can tucked under his arm, looking for other intruders lurking between and behind and beyond the cans of dog food displayed in their proper habitat.

"I have to say that I like the way you look out for the canines, Kyle, extricating that can from the kibble and dog food cans. In fact, just watching you work I'd say you have to be one of Food City's most valued employees. Hard-working, conscientious, dependable, appropriately dressed. I take back some of those things I said about you. You're a credit to your gender. I think I'm going to get emotional."

Kyle gave us an Elvis "Thankyouverymuch."

"One question, Kyle. We're looking for trail mix and raisins. What aisle?"

"Beats me," said Kyle, shrugging his shoulders. "Maybe aisle three. Maybe not. I dunno."

"I thought you were supposed to know where everything is. How can you take the go-backs back when you don't know where the go-backs go?"

Kyle liked the rhythm of what I just said, mouthed "How can you know where the go-backs go" and tapped out the beat with his fingers on the cart handle.

"I just walk around with the cart until I find the right aisle. No one seems to care. My boss, Buddy, one of the assistant managers, told me not to kill the job. I get more hours in that way. Helps Kyle's bottom line. Last paycheck was forty-four bucks. I'm going for fifty this week."

"But aren't you a stocker, too? Aren't stockers supposed to know where everything goes?"

Kyle reached into the cart and picked up a puzzle magazine.

"Supposed to" are the key words there," he said. "They give me a cart or a palette back in the stock room and somebody pushes me in the right direction. They gave me women's hygiene products, cold cream, body wash, hair color, all that stuff one of my first nights. I think it was some kind of joke they were playing on me. Took me about four hours to shelve one cart. I was busy reading the backs of the packages and the spray cans. I learned more that night than I ever did from my dad about women. Did you know that there's make-up that senses a woman's skin tone and turns it into the right color shade of foundation? I didn't know what foundation was. I'm in the know, now. And did you know there're tampons with anti-gravity capillary action? I don't know how that's done, though. I think each one has a tiny warp

86

drive in them. I always heard that something strange happened to girls once a month, but I really didn't know anything about periods, period. No idea that women's bodies were leaky and troublesome. What you can learn about the fairer sex just by reading the back side of the packaging of women's hygiene products."

Alison and Jillian listened, both narrowing their eyes, frowning, not knowing if Kyle was telling the truth or putting them on. Kyle put the puzzle magazine back in the cart, and said, "What's another word meaning gobsmacked?"

"I know you were in my health class, Kyle," Jillian said. "Don't you remember Mr. Swoboda going over the menstrual cycle?"

"I must have been absent that day. Did he hand out notes? I don't remember getting any."

"Thanks for that revelation, Kyle," I said. "But you don't know where the raisins are? It seems I might have overrated you, your performance and compassion for fulfilling the needs of the valued Food City shopper."

"Working is what's overrated," Kyle said, examining a box of macaroni and cheese he lifted out of his cart. "I gotta try this stuff. Looks nutritious, yet filling. A taste treat. And only seventy-nine cents."

Alison, Jillian and I gathered around Kyle, leaning over to read the small print on the back: cooking instructions, ingredients and percentages of daily nutrition requirements.

"A meal in a box, man. What will they think of next?" he said.

Alison made some remark about gluten, Jillian nodding.

"I'm thinking this would go good with a 32 ounce root beer," said Kyle as he rubbed his stomach.

"I know what I'm eatin' tonight."

Looking at me - as if I were to blame because Kyle was my friend - Alison just shook her head. Then she turned back to Kyle.

"Kyle, I've never heard you talk this much. You hardly say a word in Food and Fitness."

"This is my out of school persona. It's all about pleasing the customer here at Food City. For minimum wage I'll do a complete personality change to ensure the happiness of our Food City patrons. It's company policy. I read it in the brochure they gave us when I had my interview."

"That you'd be a corporate shill just so that we can have an enjoyable experience shopping for our consumables, and for minimum wage. That's commendable. There is hope for the youth of America," I offered.

Kyle eyed me, taking his gaze off the box of macaroni.

"When you put it that way….."

He didn't finish the thought. Tossing the macaroni back in the cart, Kyle started trotting away, looking over his shoulder at us.

"Hey, I gotta go. That's my clean-up. I'm employee one hundred thirty-seven."

Kyle flipped his employee badge up with his thumb, indicating that it, indeed, read Food City Employee number 137.

"I've got aisles five through twelve. I hope it isn't mayonnaise."

Alison yelled after Kyle.

"Astounded."

Kyle abruptly stopped and turned back toward us.

"What?"

"Astounded. That's another word for gobsmacked."

Kyle nodded, then finished jogging past the pet food, and turned right, out of site, his exploration of what caused that pesky spill in aisle nine about to begin.

Alison and Jillian and I headed out of the Food City parking lot fortified with our bounty of healthy snacks - no thanks to Kyle - with Alison at the wheel. We had lost Jillian for a few minutes as

Alison inspected the ingredients on the trail mix package. But we spotted Jilly Bean—as Alison often referred to her—in the produce section when we went looking for her.

"Can't forget these guys, guys," Jillian said, possessing three bananas.

"Fructose, glucose, sucrose, and fiber, all in their own container. Yellow packages of energy. And they also contain tryptophan. Know what tryptophan is, Stevie, what it does?"

"Nope," I confessed.

Jillian brandished two of the bananas at me, the other holstered in her right jeans pants pocket, accusingly testing my banana knowledge. I put my hands up. She had me out-gunned, or out-bananaed.

"Tryptophan changes the protein in your body into serotonin. Know what serotonin does?"

"Nope."

I noped her again. Oh-for-two on my yellow elongated curvy botanical berry edible facts.

"It reduces tension, makes you happy, less depressed." Jillian did a little dance, a shimmy, a happy dance that a banana-induced state would do for you.

"And do you know, Steven, about the beneficial properties of a banana peel?"

"They're making non-slip ones now?"

"No, silly."

Oh-for-three.

"You can put them on bug bites and bruises because they have healing properties, and if you rub your teeth with a banana peel every other day they'll make your teeth brighter."

Who knew? I left Food City enlightened, thanking Jillian for the peel spiel. Did the other fruits laying innocently in their bins have powers I was unaware of? I would never throw another banana peel away again. I decided to eat a banana before every game from now on as part of my pre-game ritual. My new formula: Yoga plus Tryptophan equals Made Free Throws.

Chapter 19

Fall had been uncharacteristically warm in our part of the northern climes. Flora still clung to many of the branches of the deciduous trees and fauna went about their winter-preparing activity. As we entered the park a rabbit hopped onto the pavement in front of us and stopped. Alison braked and opened her window.

"Hey bunny honey, watch your cotton tail. You don't want to get hit. That would spoil your whole day."

A couple bounces to the grass on the other side of the road and the rabbit assumed a rabbit pose, hunched, watching, either celebrating his or her random dash-hop to the other side, or wondering why a large creature head had just admonished him—or her—for the path it had taken in his—or her—own park. The bunny noshed on something appetizing like dead grass, nose twitching, an eye on us.

Jillian turned around from the front seat (she had claimed it with an exclamation of "Shotgun!" as we walked to the car in the Food City parking lot) and asked me, "Do you know Alison's idea on what you should do if you hit a rabbit or a squirrel or any animal, furry or sans fur, with your car?"

My mind tried to picture a non-furry small animal. A skink? But I couldn't recall what a skink looked like. A lizard maybe. I think I remembered from my Bible school days that Adam, he of the famous Adam and Eve had given the animals their names. Adam must have possessed a sense of humor to name an animal a skink. The genesis of skinkdom.

"Hunh-uh. What's her theory? I take it that Alison is rodent friendly?"

Alison's head nodded yes as she drove slowly through the park, looking for a primo parking space.

"Very. Bunnies, squirrels, skunks, woodchucks, chipmunks, hamsters, gerbils."

Alison nodded to the affirmative, verifying.

Alison and Jillian both sported their military, cadet style caps with bedazzling pins on the sides. Looking bedazzled was in. A and J and my mom liked wearing glittery, sparkly, bejeweled pins on their shirts, jeans, headwear, and purses. While Alison had thick light brown curly hair, Jillian's hair shone shiny black, thin and braided. Both wore black hoodies and jeans. Their hoodies' enscriptions read what I took to be from biblical scripture, Alison's stating, "Ask the Animals, and They Will Teach You. Ask the Birds of the Air, and They Will Tell You. Job 12:7-10." and Jillian's, "Speak Up For Those That Cannot Speak For Themselves. Proverbs 31:8-9." Both of their hoodies had silk screen images of birds and forest creatures under the texts. I put that in my memory data bank, to ask about their hoodies later.

Alison detailed "Well, if you hit a squirrel, say it's dead, OK, you should erect a little memorial by the side of the road like humans do when someone's killed in an accident. And you should put a photo of it on a poster, unless, of course, the squirrel's face is smushed beyond recognition, in which case a generic photo of the same rodent species would be acceptable."

"Should you put flowers around it on a monthly basis?" I asked, thinking that somehow contributed to the conversation.

"No. Don't be silly. But you would have a self-imposed fine of fifty dollars. Part of that would be to pay for the memorial, and the rest would be to pay for nuts or pumpkin seeds or acorns, or whatever the rodent you hit eats. It would go to his family. Now you probably won't know what family is his unless it's a neighborhood squirrel, let's say, and even then you probably can't identify all of them by sight, so you may have to do a search - find his loved ones in the forest."

I tried to follow the Alison commemorative deceased rodent plan. I didn't think in my entire existence that I could positively identify the identity by sight any of the individual rodentia that I shared my living environment with.

"What if you find a nearby squirrel but you're not sure if the nearby squirrel is related to the squirrel you hit?"

"DNA testing may be necessary to link the obliterated squirrel with his squirrel clan. You may have to live trap them. You have to supply your own gloves."

I leaned my head between Alison and Jillian's seats, head down, listening as Jillian explained the insurance policy for rodents.

"We were thinking originally that you should create an obituary for it—I mean her or him—and get it in the paper, but then we thought that was going too far."

"You mean you don't think the other stuff is going too far? I mean, traipsing through the forest, interviewing squirrels at random to see if all their flesh and blood is accounted for? I can imagine that conversation. Would I get one of those "We regret to inform you" scripts? I don't think I could tell them that I did it, that I ran over Uncle Bob. I'd tell them that I just happened to come across his carcass, and that if there's anything I can do… I can imagine a squirrel staring at me at the entrance to their den, on their haunches, paws together, and saying, 'Chuckie? They got Chuckie?!!' And I'd sigh and say, 'Yeah… On I-280. It wasn't pretty. Flatter than a pancake. From all reports he was out squirreling away - pardon my language, nuts for you guys for the winter. Tried to cross the highway for unknown reasons, reasons known only to Chuck. You have my condolences.'"

"Going too far?" Alison said. "Well, we just think it's not right that we take over animals' environments, their habitats and they have to suffer when they were here first. They've got just as much right to be here as we do. And if you're at least a little attentive you can see the little guys when they're going to make a Kamikaze dash across the street. People drive too fast, anyway, and they do it because they're not disciplined, go to bed too late because they're watching some stupid reality TV show and then they get up late, have to hurry to get to work on time and go through red lights and cause accidents or race through neighborhoods and hit innocent little animals, and they just keep on going."

That made sense. We got out of Alison's car, our discussion continuing.

"But we love animals, all of them," added Jillian. "You ought to see Alison in the summer right after a thunderstorm. She looks on the sidewalks for worms. You know, when it's broiling out. When she finds one she picks them up and puts them in the grass so they won't cook on the sidewalk when the sun comes out. She calls them 'Frybabies.' Now I do it too. And we are always careful not to step on the bug children when we hike in the park and walk on the sidewalks."

I pondered these concepts as we walked, Jillian to my left, Alison to my right. Alison slowly twirled a yellow and orange maple leaf she had picked off the path, examining the veins that radiated from the stem. Jillian carried her cell phone, headphones around her neck, multi-tasking, watching and talking and texting, taking snapshots of the fauna and flora and Alison and me as we mugged for her camera. Both girls still wore their cool new sunglasses.

"Would you guys be serious just for a second?" Said Jillian.

Alison and I then leaned together, arms folded, with the most serious of serious faces, pouty lips, frowny furrowed eyebrows.

"That's so random," Jillian said, shaking her head.

"Random," a favorite word of Jillian's. She fit it into the

conversation every five minutes or so. I think her definition of random was random, whatever definition she wanted to think it meant at the moment. Sometimes you just had friends like that.

Alison and Jillian both had curious minds. They liked words, liked to use new words they picked up. They sometimes made words up. And they liked to dress alike, not exactly fashonistas, but teen semi-hipsters. At the moment they favored headbands and pony tails. I'll bet they had seventeen different colors of hairbands between them. They were a good look for both. And another thing; they liked to share the newest trivia they had learned, much of it from the environmental science class they took together.

"Do you know how far Monarch butterflies fly when they migrate?" asked Alison.

She really didn't expect me to know. I think she'd have been disappointed if I did. She wanted to tell me, for me to be surprised, surprised that they traveled so far, surprised that she knew. I played the foil for her information, and Jillian's, showing my sheer wonderment face.

"They can go 265 miles in a day! They go to Mexico, where they hang out in the winter. Longest migration of any insect."

Alison flapped her "wings," elbows out, to demonstrate. I nodded in semi-amazement, imitating Alison with my own wing flaps.

Jillian jumped in.

"Do you know that all the water we have now is all the water we ever had? It's the water cycle. Precipitation, transpiration, condensation, evaporation. The water that's coursing through your body, that you pee out? It well may have been drunk out of a long ago lake that no longer exists and peed out through a Tyrannosaurus Rex's kidneys four millions years ago."

Alison's turn.

"We're citizen scientists. Mrs. Schlagheck told us about them.

Anybody can be one. We have a rain barrel at my house and we measure rainfall and snow amounts and then report the results to other high schools and even to the community college and to Channel 47. Every once in a while they'll mention my name when I text them with how much rain or snow fell at my house. And we're into Cli-Fi, too."

"You're into what?" I asked.

"Climate fiction. Stories about the catastrophes that will result if Earth keeps heating up. And some of them have hero scientists, like climatologists and oceanographers that come up with ideas to save the earth. But people shouldn't go on doing what they're doing with carbon emissions and dumping toxic waste into the ocean and lakes because they think, 'Oh, some scientist will think of a solution. It'll be OK.' They say that if climate change continues that the level of Lake Erie will be significantly reduced. That will really harm the life of the creatures that live along the shore and add to more algal blooming. We may have a dead lake sometime in our lifetime if we don't start to change how we live. But the cli-fi books are fun to read and they make you think, and want to do something to help."

Jillian tag-teamed in.

"And we go to the marsh and the wetlands at the Ottawa Wildlife Refuge by Lake Erie in May for the Biggest Week In American Birding and report on the birds we see. It's when the warblers fly up from South America and Panama and Costa Rica and they have to stop and rest and re-fuel. Lake Erie's right on their flight path. It's so cool. There's birders from all over the world that come to see them. We take our binoculars and our bird books and try to identify the little guys. We try to imitate the warblers' calls."

Alison turned to me.

"Do you know what a warbler's calls are called?"

"Warbles? Chirps? Cheeps?" I guessed.

"Nope. They're called zips, jeets, and chips. Their calls are googlable. There's even an app for warbler calls."

Jillian and Alison both pursed their lips and warbled. Or something akin to warbling. Each made trilling, tweeting, quavering noises. Mixed in with whistling wheezes and laughing snorts and snerks.

"We're not very good yet," Jillian said. "Last year was the first time we went. My dad took us. I think we drove him nuts on the way home with our bird calls. But you've got to have some self-control if you're a warbler watcher. You can get 'warbler neck' from looking up for a long period of time. Very painful."

Alison and Jillian both demonstrated warbler watching for me, looking up, craning their necks, hands holding imaginary binoculars.

"So," I asked, " do the warblers get 'people neck,' you know, from looking down at the people looking up at them?"

Jillian dismissed my question.

"No known reported cases."

We walked on. I didn't think that my thoughts and A and J's thoughts intertwined. Further evidence immediately followed with an Alison inquiry.

"Do you know that euglenas are tiny creatures that are found in both fresh and salt water and are both heterotrophs and autotrophs? They're neither plant nor animal. They're both. They can use chlorophyll or they can eat stuff they find in the water by surrounding it and engulfing it."

I wished I had engulfed more particles at the food court.

Jillian continued as the conversation moved from air to sea.

"Do you know that tunicates are these tiny sea creatures that are tube-shaped and have a sieve in them, and when water comes in the trap food particles and oxygen, then squirt out the rest of the water?" Jillian made a squooshing noise, pushing in the sides of both her cheeks with her index fingers.

"They're called 'sea squirts.' They look like little roundish-ovalish tubes with a hole in their tops. You can find them on docks, rocks, and the undersides of piers and boats. Alison and I saw some at the lake, on the pier. It was so funny! Alison was on her stomach at the edge of the pier with her head over the edge peering underneath. Uh, that play on words was intended. Get it? Peering underneath the pier? - the boardwalk you walk on and looking intently for the tunicates. I couldn't see her head. I held on to her feet so she wouldn't fall in."

"Yeah. I get it, I get it. I'm visualizing."

"Anyway, some old guy came walking by and asked what she was looking for and Alison said, 'sea squirts.' We both starting laughing so hard. The guy just looked at us, then shook his head and walked away."

"Did you see any?"

"Oh yeah. Alison saw a whole little colony of them. I looked, too. They were different colors. We wanted to take some home and put them in the aquarium my little brother has, but we weren't sure if they'd live very long that way. It would be so cool to say when people asked, 'What pets do you have?' you could say, 'I have a dog, two cats, and a pod of sea squirts.' And how cool would it be to watch them squoosh the water out of the tops of their heads?"

Jillian continued.

"Know what my mom called me the other day? She said since I gave up eating meat but still eat fish that I'm a 'vegequarian.' You know, that I just eat what's in an aquarium. But I think the right term is pescatarian for someone who only eats fish."

Her tone suddenly became very serious.

"I'm trying to become an ovo-lacto vegetarian."

"A what? Sounds painful."

"An ovo-lacto vegetarian. Like Alison. Not eat any cows, pigs or chickens, but still consume dairy products. Eggs, cheese, milk.

Ovo comes from the Latin word meaning egg and lacto means milk. Don't use your stomach for an animal graveyard. Then the next goal is to become vegan. Spare the animals, shut down the slaughterhouses, share the earth. End the animal holocaust."

Alison repeated Jillian's words.

"Spare and share. Likable verbs."

We neared a clearing, thin groupings of icy stalks peeking out from a snow covered winter meadow, the taller protruding grasses brown now, with their ice coverings, bent to the east from the prevailing west winds. Our appearance sent a flock of Snow Buntings sailing skyward.

After a few minutes Alison's thought process about likable verbs evolved to the verb world in general.

"Why isn't the word verb a verb? It would just seem right if it was."

"Transitive or intransitive?" I asked her.

"Definitely transitive. Those kind of verbs get around, always looking for action. They can be very verbal, and be very, very aggressive."

"Why are they so aggressive? Maybe those verbs are too tense."

Alison's paean to transitive verbs continued, ignoring my wordplay.

"Like, you could say, 'Don't be verbin' me.' Or, 'Are you staying home tonight or do you want to go out verbin'.' It's the new age syntax, verbs dominating other forms of speech, throwing modesty aside, verbs showing hubris, verbs newly empowered, dominating adjectives, adverbs, nouns, prepositions. Intransitive verbs are out, verboten. Passe'. They've been shown the door. "

I asked, "Can I quote you verbatim? Use your verbiage? You're quite verbose, you know."

"Sure. Word for word, verb for verb."

Walking on, I cautioned Alison.

"But don't you fear roaming gangs of transitive verbs, using

99

their influence to convert innocent synonyms to join them, without rhyme, reason, or proper sentence structure? Unregulated they'd undoubtedly want to create their own biome. 'If you're not transitive, no admittance. Don't even think about it.' Jack-booted transitive verbs. And I think you're forgetting something."

"What's that?" asked Alison, re-wrapping her scarf under her chin.

"Direct objects. Transitive verbs can't go it alone. They need their D.O.'s. They're addicts. The transitives aren't anywhere near as tough as you might think."

"Well, I'm sure there are some, the tough guy transitives, the rogue verbs, the mas macho ones that try to go it alone. Verbs are gender neutral, stoic, not like some of those needy nouns that feel they have to specify their sex. And don't even get me started on pronouns."

"I don't think how tough they are matters," I mansplained. The Grammar Police will have them arrested on the spot if they're caught without their direct objects. The transitional verbs have to have their D.O.'s on them at all times."

Alison said she saw my point, but that she still considered the transitives vastly underrated and that they aren't going to take it anymore.

"Talk about underrated, not being appreciated," I said. "How about the articles of speech? Imagine being stuck in life as an 'a' or a 'the.'"

Alison turned to me, agreeing and said, "And they're important little guys. What could we do without them? Grunt? Maybe we can be their publicity agents! Get them their props!"

"Count me in. I'll get right on it."

Immediately I had a campaign slogan.

"How about "A' and 'The' - Don't leave home without them.'"

That drew an Alison smile. Jillian shook her head, but she, too, smiled. Jillian had been studying an ant on a mission on her side of the path as Alison and I discussed the mission of verbs.

"Did you know that ants are very nationalistic? I read that. They'll die for their colony. They're team players. And know what else? When their colony needs to be moved the ants vote on where the new one should be."

"I thought I saw an ant back there wearing an 'I voted today' sticker," I said.

Jillian gave me The Look.

"Hey," I said, "I'm not anti-ant. Or pro-ant. I'm ant ambivalent. I'm decidedly, clearly, strongly adamant about being ambivalent regarding ants. It's the antithesis of taking a stance either way."

Unfazed by my reply, Jillian continued.

"Do you know that the word for ant in Latin is *formica*? Do you know the name of the acid that they make, you know, why it stings when they bite you?"

I thought for a second.

"Ant acid? Like when your stomach is upset? Ants invented antacids?"

Jillian gave me a backhanded *whap*.

"No, it's formic acid."

"There must be an antibody for that, " I said, flinching in case Jillian continued her whap-attack.

I hadn't imagined having older girls, seniors, as my friends. A new experience. Very cool. I think they looked upon me as some exotic find they had made, like a seashell that was different from all the others that they found on the beach. Our new-found friendship was mutualistic. Alison and Jillian always bubbled with excitement as they told me about their love for animals. I had to admit that I liked their passion. I thought for a while they were just being silly, seeing if I would bite. But the longer they went on, the more convinced I became that they were sincere. As we walked through the woods up the path through the pine forest I, too, looked for scuttling bugs in the event their route took them on a collision course with the three of us.

"Maybe the park rangers could put up bug crossing signs. That and tiny yellow flashing traffic lights about a centimeter off the ground at the crossings for the centipedes and their bug brethren to caution them of impending doom from the booted, sneakered, cross-trainered and running-shoed joggers, power walkers, amblers and strollers. Signs posted: Scuttle Bug Crossing. WARNING: BIPEDS DO NOT STOP. CROSS AT YOUR OWN RISK. And the signs would show the adult bugs holding their bug children's hands, or legs or antennas as they crossed, making certain that their bug tads had a safe crossing. Or maybe a crushed cartoon bug lying on his back with x's over his eyes and his cartoon tongue sticking out, dead as a door nail."

Alison and Jillian rolled their eyes. Could I help it if I was taking their thinking to a another level? Jillian gave me a slight shove on the shoulder, knowing that I was making fun of her's and Alison's ideas. I made an off-balance pretend stagger, then looked down and gasped in horror as I bent and faked picking up a crushed six legger. The girls both peered, mouths open, aghast as I opened my hand to reveal—my hand. No bug to mourn. The bug populace unharmed.

Jillian pulled her hoodie up, the air getting chillier, our cheeks redder. On cue, Alison pulled hers up, too. Shadows spread across the park, the sun low on the western horizon. The day's last sunlight spliced through tree branches losing their vestiges of autumn leaves. We were finishing our walk on the two mile long looping trail, over the suspension bridge of the cold creek water and up the path, the forest becoming quiet at dusk except for the deer on their habitual slow stop-and-go twi-light migration to the other side of the park where they would bed down for the night. We walked slowly, enjoying the peacefulness of the park, having the feeling we were alone, but that the parks' inhabitants knew we were there, waiting for us to leave before they could get started on their night's activities. Walking by, kicking up loose stones on the path we became aware of a metropark intruders' maxim: Sometimes we watched the deer, sometimes the deer watched us.

Chapter 20

Leading up to Christmas break we had won three of our four games, winning all our league games but losing to non-league North Treadway Memorial. North Treadway had been one of those "perennial powerhouses" for years, a big fish, a Division IV school in a league with all smaller, DV schools located in east central farm country, near the Indiana border. But they were good. On the other hand, what else was there to do but play basketball at a country school? Their school didn't even field a football team, its enrollment being so small. Our record stood at 6 and 2 after defeating non-league opponents Hull Prairie and Muscatine 52-42 and 70-31, league member Sun Prairie 47-37 and the loss at North Treadway 61-44. A three-way tie at the top. Us, Upper Sandusky and Midlothian all at 4 and 1.

Chapter 21

Wednesday, December 18th. Our last school day before Christmas break. The band director approached us in the hall where we congregated before school while getting ready for our morning classes, pulling books and notebooks from our lockers.

"Which one of you is Kyle Mahoney?"

Kyle swirled his head, his half smile showing, puzzled.

"That is I, Sir."

The band director, Mr. Hoolihan, paused a few seconds. I think he had hoped Kyle would be a little more clean cut instead of a kid with unkempt shaggy hair and chin stubble wearing a *Guns 'N' Roses* t-shirt. Mr. Hoolihan ruled the marching band with an iron fist. He wanted nothing to interfere with his goal of getting the band to qualify for the State competition every year. The male band members were not allowed to have any facial hair, the boys had to have their hair above their ears, the girls not to have hair below their shoulders, no visible tattoos and certainly no dreadlocks or corn rows for either sex.

The marching band practiced three nights a week, from six to nine PM in the Fall besides the football games on Friday nights and competitions on Saturdays. Mr. Hoolihan thought the football games were held for the sake of his band to perform. Often he showed his irritation at crowd members who would start making their way down the aisles of the home side bleachers to go to the concession stand or restroom at the beginning of halftime. That showed complete disregard for Mr. Hoolihan and his band. He would turn his head while directing the performance from the podium on his exalted band director tower, still waving his baton, to survey how many people, and who they were, that had left their seats while the trumpets, flutes, percussion, cymbals, and tubas shattered the night air with their night's production. And the football coaches had a certain disdain for Mr. Hoolihan's direction of the band; in the last few minutes of close games when most schools' bands played the fight song at every opportunity to spur on their team and keep the crowd fired up, since he considered them a show band, not solely an adjunct of the football team, Mr. Hoolihan would have the Jackson band break out with the theme from *Oklahoma!* He must have continually wondered how that could have failed to get the crowd whooped into a frenzy.

Though Mr. Hoolihan relaxed the rules for the winter pep band, by that time many of the band members came up with any excuse not to play to get away from Mr. Hoolihan.

"Kyle, we're in need of a drummer for the pep band. Our two drummers from marching band are both on the hockey team and they couldn't commit to pep band. They'd have to miss too many games. I asked them if they knew anybody in the school who played the drums and they said you. I hope you'd like to give it a try, otherwise I have to drum, and I can't really conduct and drum at the same time."

Kyle closed his locker slowly, thinking, pulling on his combination lock after he snapped the lock shut and turned back to Mr. Hoolihan.

"Cosmic. I'm gamey."

Mr. Hoolihan looked over at me, needing an interpreter.

"I think that's a yes. He's a jokester. But he's harmless. Smelly, but harmless."

"We usually practice twice a week, then once a week later on toward the end of basketball season, and play at most of the home games, both boys and girls. Most important is that you learn the

National Anthem and the fight song. The others, the rock classics, like 'Hey Baby,' 'Swingtown,' you may already know. And you'll get a Jackson High pep band knit shirt with your name embroidered over the pocket."

"Sweet," said Kyle.

"Practice this week is tomorrow at noon in the band room, girls game Friday night. Can you make those?"

Kyle flashed the OK sign with thumb and forefinger.

"Yep."

"Then I'll see you tomorrow at noon. Just knock on the outside door that leads to the band room and somebody will let you in. The drum kit is brand new. Just got it this year. I think you'll like it."

"Stellar."

Mr. Hoolihan and Kyle shook hands. Kyle Mahoney. Pep band member. The first club, sport, or organization he had belonged to since being in the Jackson Public School System, unless being a crossing guard in sixth grade counted. A teacher thought that being a crossing guard would teach Kyle much needed responsibility. But that experiment only lasted a week before a school bus driver reported Kyle for looking down reading a comic book while waving second graders across the street in front of her oncoming bus.

In Kyle's defense he did admit his error when the littluns scrambled back to the curb while the bus driver laid on the horn and slammed on the brakes.

"My bad," Kyle told the wee ones, then went back to reading his comic. A one page memo went into Kyle's file in the guidance office detailing the incident, noting the date and time, and that Kyle had been instructed to turn in his crossing guard belt and badge.

Chapter 22

Excited for Christmas break, a good mood prevailed at practice, coaches included, as we readied for our holiday tournament to be held the Friday and Saturday after Christmas. The team headed into the locker room after practice, sweaty, laughing, spirits high. Tommy had forgotten his practice jersey, having left it on the bleachers. He had gotten up from the bench and run out to the gym to get it, wanting to get back to the locker room before Coach started with the after practice talk. No sense getting on Coach's bad side, no matter how slight the transgression, by being late. Coach had said he wanted to go over the Christmas break practice schedule with us.

We could hear Tommy coming, clomping in his basketball shoes, accelerating, his footsteps hurried, pulling open the locker room door then taking a right turn into the varsity locker room. A too-fast right turn. Barreling in, his reversible jersey in hand, Tommy tripped over a gym bag, did a dance step on one leg trying to avoid hitting the bench with his knee, tripped again and did a header into a locker behind us and sat down. We sat partly amused, partly concerned at the human tornado we had witnessed. Coach Arnold stopped in mid-sentence, mouth open, disbelieving what he had just seen.

"Pump the brakes, Big Fella," Coach Pettaway bellowed.

We laughed as Tommy rubbed his head, sitting on the floor by the locker. We assessed the damage. Bump on the noggin, collateral damage in the form of a strawberry on the left knee.

"Man down!" Jose' hollered.

"Is the locker OK?" said Jamey Watson, one of the back-up forwards. Because of his lightweight stick figure build, pool noodle arms, looks and disposition—ears as large as satellite dishes, big black-rimmed glasses held by a strap around the back of his head, buzz cut and goofy harmless demeanor, and by far our tallest player since sixth grade basketball elementary school, Jamey wore the nickname we had bestowed on him—"Tower of Power." We laughed again.

My turn.

"This is why we can't have nice things!"

"Notify the next of skin!" Hobie yelled.

A sophomore back-up guard, Willard "Punky" Schmidt chipped in, piling on the abuse, cupping his hands together to his mouth to P.A. his announcement.

"Crash in Turn 2. The yellow caution flag is out. Call the Waaaaambulance."

We laughed harder, leaning over, holding our stomachs. But then Tommy turned his head toward us, and we saw blood running down the left side of his face, coming from a gash near the corner of his left eye, curving underneath. Uh-oh. Coach Arnold clambered over the bench toward Tommy.

"Somebody get me a towel and go get Mike!"

Mike Swoboda, our trainer. Since I was the closest to the door I sprinted out of the locker room, across the gym floor, running right through the girls' practice that had just begun and into the trainers' room. Mike was taping an ankle when I came in hollering for him. Quickly I told him of Tommy's crash and burn. Mike grabbed his medical kit and latex gloves and followed me, trotting back across the gym floor. Running ahead of him, I held open the locker room door where I could see Coach Arnold holding the towel against Tommy's head, the towel streaked with wet crimson from the gusher of blood that had emanated from the wound. Tommy was subdued, trying to put on a brave face, but grimacing. The locker room quieted, all eyes on Mr. Swoboda as he cleaned Tommy's cut and applied a butter-fly band-aid to it.

"Gonna need some stitches, Tommy. I'd say quite a few. And you should have the orbital bone x-rayed. I don't think it's broken, but better get it checked just in case. Is anybody home that can come get you and take you to the emergency room?"

Tommy said his dad should be home from work, and asked Kenny Brown to get his cell phone out of Tommy's Kestrels gym bag so he could call. We listened as Tommy asked his dad to come get him, telling him he had cut his eye and that he had bled pretty good. Tommy held a towel over his left eye. Next we heard a pause. We all thought the same thing—his dad asking how it happened.

"Uh, no, it was after practice Dad, in the locker room."

Another pause. Another question from Dad.

"No, I wasn't fooling around, Dad. I wasn't horsing around. I tripped. I lost my balance. I was running into the locker room...Yes Dad? I forgot my jersey and then...Yes, Dad? I know I shouldn't have...but I tripped when I was coming through the door and I didn't want to hit my knee on the bench, and I tripped again...and Dad? No, I wasn't messing around, honest Dad."

Some of us, well, I think all of us, choked back laughter, trying to muffle it with a cough, at first only a few small snickers sneaking out. Then Coach Arnold gave us the look, the look that says "Don't say it," but that triggered our funny bones. Our history with Tommy, he being the corpulent baby of the team, Coach picking on him on the court at practice as the newbie, at film sessions as Coach's way of showing how much he cared about Tommy—alternating anguish and fondness, frustration and reluctant admiration, knowing how good Tommy could be, if only, *if only Tommy would devote his life to basketball, if only Tommy would care as much as Coach did, and why, why wouldn't he? Why wouldn't all his players? Why?* Coach's fatherly touch with Tommy set Tommy apart from the rest of us. An unexpected starter, he had been nursed along through Coach Arnold's coaching and cajoling. Tommy's talent had been appreciated by all of us. No doubt whatsoever that he contributed to our success. But Tommy had so much to learn. Wide-eyed, a sophomoric sophomore, his questions and "pronouncements" amused and astonished us. Back in November on the Tuesday before Thanksgiving at the end of practice team huddle Coach reminded us we'd practice noon to two on Wednesday as we didn't have school, then asked,

"Anyone have anything to add for the good of the order?"

Tommy raised his hand rather hesitantly.

"I don't think I can come tomorrow, Coach."

Coach folded his arms.

"I'm listening."

"I have a job I have to do," Tommy said.

"Go on."

"Well, the day before Thanksgiving my mom always needs me."

"Because ....?" Coach prodded.

"Because my job is to taste-test my mom's Thanksgiving dishes."

Coach and the rest of us listened, all ears and eyes on Tommy.

"We divide it up, my brothers and me."

Tommy's two brothers, one a year older, the other a year younger than Tommy both had his same bulky stature. They played football, wrestled, and threw the discus and shot-put on the track team. Burly men.

Tommy went on to say that Mama Hurlburt adjudicated the dividing of the taste-testing duties in the early afternoon. Quantities were limited. The boys lobbied for who got to taste what. Without prompting Tommy went through the list.

"Corn with cream cheese. Green bean casserole. Stuffing with mushroom gravy. Sweet potatoes with brown sugar. Redskin potatoes. Kidney bean salad. Pumpkin and apple pie."

As he ran through the list Tommy closed his eyes, lifted his practice jersey and rubbed his stomach.

The players and coaches had stood, listening mirthfully as Tommy mentioned one-by-one the items he would be sampling the next day, the reason why he had to miss practice. What a rookie. But, the coaches and players resolved Tommy's issue by agreeing to start practice an hour early, in time to get Tommy home in time to Mama Hurlburt's kitchen for the annual taste-testing.

The laugh track started anew hearing Tommy's explanation to Dad Hurlburt. Cracking up, we started in again reliving Tommy's pratfall. "Tripped!" "Face plant!" "Kaboom!" A few did their slow motion re-enactments of the derailment, imitating with academy award winning performances The Trip, The Fall, The Crash, The Aftermath. Never underestimate the lack of maturity of the teenage boy. Accept no substitute.

Coach finally got us calmed down. He said he'd talk to us at the beginning of practice tomorrow, that if Tommy had to miss any games he'd have to think about the line-up. Some of us waited with Coach and Tommy for his father to come and told Tommy to text us later with the damages. When he lowered the towel we inspected his eye, cheek, and eyelid. Closed, swollen, blood pooling, reddish trending to purple. Impressive. He'd have to do one-eyed texting.

Just when we had started to play well, the last half of the Midlothian game notwithstanding, heading into the holiday break with our Christmas tournament coming up in a week. What could Tommy be thinking now; he had won a starting position on the varsity by working his butt off, and now this, at Christmas time. For Tommy and the team—what else did the fates have in store for us this season. But for now, God rest ye, merry gentlemen, let nothing you dismay.

Chapter 23

We had always celebrated Christmas—the fam and I—at our house. Last year, as in all years, grandpas and grandmas, aunts and uncles, cousins stopped over. My dad and his new wife came at the invitation of my mom and shared a drink with the other adults. As in years past, starting two weeks before, Benny and I helped Mama Kalkannes as she cooked and cleaned, wrapped packages and sent Christmas cards. We put up the tree, always a real one, a Scotch pine—none of those artificial trees for us—and put on the decorations, the Christmas lights, ornaments, and tinsel. Benny always had his special ornaments that only he could put on. God forbid I would even touch one of his ordained favorites when I got the others out of their nest eggs in the ornament box. Mom advised from the kitchen, wearing her Christmasy green and red apron as she kept an eye on a fresh batch of cookies in the oven, the smell penetrating the living room. We drank hot chocolate (Mom an egg nog), the TV tuned to a Christmas special. I think I had eaten two pounds of her chunky chocolate Christmas cookies in the last week. But that paled compared to how many Benny ate. He'd disappear into the kitchen while we were watching a game and reappear with two in each hand, one in his mouth and a couple more wrapped in a napkin under his arm.

"How nice of you, Ben. Thanks."

A look from Benny that said Get A Grip.

"Never mind, never mind. I'll get my own," I said, standing up, my voice rising an octave higher, acknowledging that my request had been totally out of the question, pie-in-the-sky.

Without turning his attention away from the Cavaliers and Lakers game on TV Benny yelled at me over his shoulder as I headed to the kitchen.

"Bring me a glass of milk. Get a new glass, would ya, not the one I used for orange juice."

My turn for the Get A Grip look. But I quickly decided, in the spirit of the season, to put the hostilities aside, and being the good little brother, brought him his cow juice in his preferred vessel. Plopping back down on the sofa—Benny always claimed the recliner—he said it came under the Eldest Child Rules—I gave an audible sigh. Benny gave no reaction. I wondered if Benny had thought about what he planned to get me for Christmas, if the fact that his condemnation of my basketball season so far would affect the price of the present he'd buy for me. He *had* to get me something so he wouldn't meet Mom's disapproval, wouldn't he?

After we attended the late church service on Christmas Eve the three of us, Mom, Benny and I, sat by the fireplace in the living room (an unspoken truce called to cease hostilities and not to aggravate our mother). The house smelled of Christmas, a potpourri of pine cones, evergreen and cinnamon, and a comforting aroma of burning wood permeated the living room from the crackling logs in the fireplace. Decorated for Christmas in reds, greens, golds and silvers, the staircase and the living room entryway were adorned with hunter green garlands and wreaths with red holly berries. Christmas cards lined the top of the fireplace mantel.

We sipped our hot ciders spiced with nutmeg, eating Christmas cookies, watching the snow fall through the living room picture window, listening to Christmas carols. Peaches, our beagle at my feet, alternately snoozing and begging, her brown eyes pleading for a piece of cookie. Candles flickering on the fireplace mantle, lights twinkling on the tree and green, red, gold, and blue minis strung above the doorway arches were the only lights we had on, the Christmas spirit sinking in, washing over us, catching the simulated starry aura when the tinsel shimmered on the tree from the fireplace heat.

An old black and white Christmas movie from the 50s played on TV, but we had the sound turned all the way down, having seen it a dozen times at least and knew every line, preferring to listen to the Christmas music. Comfy on the couch, sunk into the cushions I counted my blessings, taking a drink of cider and feeling the warmth traveling inside me, thought about my life in its current state. My dad leaving still bothered me, but the stress level had gone way down since he left. Warm, safe, relaxed, with my small family, feeling the renewed faith the season brings, excited for tomorrow, Christmas day, excited and thankful for what the basketball season had brought thus far. Christmas Eve - my favorite night of the year.

Chapter 24

Holiday tournament game day. When we came into the locker room for our one o'clock walk-through we saw the tournament champion caps. White dome, red brim, emblazoned with "Lonnie's Pizzeria" on the side, a ball going through a net on the front with the words "Holiday Classic Champions" in boxes that our athletic director Mr. Goldsbee had left that would go to the winning team. An added incentive. Jackson hadn't won its own holiday tournament in seven years, even losing the year the team with Benny went to state. But then, some of the best teams in the state were invited yearly to the tournament, and they came because they were treated well, with team dinners, coaches' and players' gifts like tee-shirts, gym bags, drinking glasses, and team dinners, at Lonnie's of course.

The tournament's official name, the one no one ever called it, was the Lonnie's Pizza North Coast Holiday Classic. Sportswriters, sportscasters, fans, players, coaches referred to it as the Jackson Holiday Tournament. The tournament always drew big crowds, along with media coverage from the local TV station, WJAX Channel 47, and our town newspaper, *The Jackson Courier-Times*.

Mr. Goldsbee had been interviewed by the sports anchor for Channel 47 the night before. The Sports Guy asked Mr. Goldsbee what to expect from this year's tournament field. Mr. Goldsbee had an annoying habit of repeating the initial question anyone asked him, then answering it followed by asking himself more questions out loud. He liked to hear the sound of his own voice.

"What do we expect out of this year's tournament field? I expect that it's going to be a very competitive tournament, that the winner will have to play their best basketball, be on the top of their game each night to win the championship."

"And what can the fans expect? Four great high school basketball games from four great teams representing four great high schools. Annually, our tournament is the best holiday tourney in the state and this year is no exception. Mobey Tech, St. Bernard's, Indian Lake - all great teams."

Mr. Goldsbee lacked mentioning St. Bernard's credentials, their 1 and 5 record, and also Indian Lake's 2 and 4. Minor details.

He continued.

"Am I forgetting us? No, Coach Arnold and Coach Pettaway have done a tremendous job with our team this year. They have the kids believing in themselves that they can compete night in and night out with any team in the state."

Mr. Goldsbee, prone to hyperbole. Lots of it. Really, really prone.

"And who do we have to thank? Our wonderful sponsor, Lonnie's Pizzeria, of course."

I had seen Mr. Goldsbee at Lonnie's on occasion, drinking at the bar with his coterie of buddies, many of them members of Jackson's booster club. I wondered if he'd get a free drink or two from Lonnie for mentioning Lonnie's place on the sports report. The sports reporter held his microphone out for Mr. Goldsbee's answer to his initial question, and occasionally looked down at his notes in his other hand, and seemed to want to get one of his own questions in, but Mr. Goldsbee didn't come up for air. No chance for Sports Guy to get a word in. The realization came to him after Mr. Goldsbee asked himself a third question.

Sports Guy's producer waved, giving him the "Cut" sign, slashing an index finger across his neck. Mr. Goldsbee rolled on, in the middle of asking himself another question when Sports

Guy had to pull the plug.

"And what kind of turnout do we expect? From what I'm hearing…"

We never did hear what Mr. Goldsbee was hearing because the camera shifted to a close up of Sports Guy saying, "And that's it for the preview of the Jackson High Holiday Tournament starting tomorrow."

The camera faded away with Mr. Goldsbee trying to make one last point, looking directly at the camera, leaning in front of Sports Guy pointing at it, loudly saying, "Brought to you by Lonnie's Pizzeria!"

We easily won our first Holiday tournament game by defeating St. Bernard's Academy from Cleveland 68-40. A festive mood filled the gym. Mr. Kleindienst did have to warn our students once about taunting the St. Bernard parochial students when our public school kids chanted, "God loves us for free!"

The only suspense came from seeing if the bench warmers would score. Gary Vergiels, scoreless this season in varsity games (he started on the JVs but dressed one quarter for varsity) had a wide open bunny with ten seconds to go. The starting five and top subs stood and waved our towels, rooting on our teammates that ordinarily saw little action.

"Give it to Gary! He's open! Give to Gary!"

Gary trailed St. Bernard's offense as they headed upcourt, cherry-picking. (Their nickname: the "Scotties." Go figure. But everyone, even the sports section writers, referred to them as "the Bernies.") Jason Watson picked off a long upcourt St. Bernard pass, then fired a perfectly thrown long one-bounce pass to Gary, driving in for the lay-up. But Gary put the ball up too hard off the glass and it hit the front rim and bounced out.

"Ohhhhh." The student section had so much wanted to go crazy when Gary scored. We snapped our towels at the bench and cussed just a little —'Damn!'—but we laughed and grinned as the

119

seconds blinked off the clock, Gary holding his hands on the top of his head, elbows out, chagrined as the final buzzer sounded. We went through the post-game little league handshake line, actually the low five line now, slapping hands down low, with the St. Bernie's players.

"Good game, good game, good game, good game, good game...."

We gave their coaches actual handshakes, out of respect. As the custom dictated.

We expected that Coach would tell us we played OK, but we had to play better in tomorrow night's game or we would have no chance.

"Fellas, I liked the effort tonight. I thought we lost a little intensity in the second half. Instead of Intensity with a capital 'I' it was more like intensity with a small 'i.' That won't get it tomorrow night. We'll need thirty-two full minutes tomorrow. Coach Pettaway—anything to add?"

"Man, I was rootin' so hard for you, Gary. But don't get your daubers down. You get another opportunity, you take the shot, son. Don't be shy. The meek shall inherit the earth."

I raised my hand.

"Coach Pettaway? If the meek inherit the earth, wouldn't they no longer be considered meek? All the meeks would be high-fiving each other, doing chest bumps. Wouldn't they then be meekless, all full of themselves after all that inheriting?"

Some of my teammates looked down, smiling, amused. Others looked up, awaiting Coach P.'s answer.

"Let's us just win tomorrow, Stevie, then we'll have us a talk about all this inheriting and how to be humble about it when we do."

"Gotcha, Coach."

Coach Arnold scratched his head.

"I don't know about all that, Stevie, Coach Pettaway. But let's get changed and go watch the next game, boys. We play the winner tomorrow night."

We huddled, put our hands together, yelled, "One, Two, Three, Team!" and headed for the showers. While I peeled my jersey off another thought hit me. What are daubers, and if sometimes we let them get down, can we also get them up? Do daubers sometimes linger somewhere in the middle in their dauberness, not interested in going up or down? Very mysterious, these daubers. And did they only come in multiples? Could a person possess just one dauber? Fairly certain they were intangible, not things but thoughts, but not totally certain.

A good night at The Nest. I thought Benny would be waiting outside the locker room to congratulate me when I came out, but only Mom greeted me, with a hug and a "Good game, Honey." Benny had already left, headed to the bar.

Chapter 25

In the inner sanctum of our locker room Coach Arnold and Coach Pettaway went over the scouting report for the championship game. Our opponent, Mobey Vocational and Technical School, commonly referenced in the sports pages as Mobey Tech. An all-boys school. Nickname: The Craftsmen (but also known as The Techsters). Their logo intended to intimidate: a muscled guy with big biceps wearing a hardhat and a tool belt, carrying a wrench and a drill, a sneer on his face.

Coach Arnold read their starters' info from his scouting report, and told us who would be assigned to guard who when we played man-to-man. We all had a rooting interest in who Coach decided to guard Quinton Chones. Some, the gamers, rooted, salivated to be given the opportunity to guard him, some others rooted that their assignment consisted of not being in the same zip code come game time as the manimal known as Quinton Chones. Chones, last season's Ohio's Division IV Player-of-the-Year as a junior, had transferred to Mobey Tech from a private boys academy in Columbus. Rumors flowed as to the where, what, why, and how. Did Mobey's administrators or alumni offer his dad a high paying job, did Chones get in some kind of trouble in Columbus, did he have academic difficulties? Regardless, he was our problem now, all six feet, eight inches and two-hundred and forty-five pounds.

"Kenny, I'm giving Quinton Chones to you. I think your quickness will bother him. But you gotta play defense *before* he gets the ball, not after he catches it. Don't let him get it. He can't score if he doesn't have it. His shooting range is about a slam dunk. He hardly ever shoots from over three feet and I doubt he shoots over twenty percent when he gets the ball anywhere away from the basket. But you let him catch it on the block and he makes ninety percent of those. Once he gets position on you it'll be like guarding an anvil. He'll make you look silly. Don't let him back you down with that big butt of his. What do we always tell post players? On offense keep your feet still when you're posting. On defense keep your feet moving when you're denying the post. Get around him, overplay him, have your arm up where he puts his arm, don't let him pin you and don't worry about helping out with anyone else's man. K.J. can help you from behind. His guy, Scarborough, number forty, is 6'4" but he only averages four or five points a game. He's mostly there for rebounding in their offense."

Ordinarily Tommy guarded the power forwards and K.J. the centers, but since Tommy wouldn't be playing, Coach Arnold chose Kenny, the small forward, to guard Chones, front him, in Coach Arnold's game plan to sandwich Chones. Jason backed up Tommy and would start in Tommy's place. Jason, he all of a hundred and forty pounds, a low-calorie power forward. But K.J. kept shaking his head. He wanted to guard Chones.

"I can handle him. I'm tough, Coach," said K.J. "I lead the thug life."

"You?!!" I gave K.J. a look of incredulity. "The thug life?!! You're thug lite! You have perfect diction and a 3.9 GPA and got a 32 on your ACT. You have an acceptance letter from Princeton! And no tats. You don't meet the criteria. You're not in the club."

Coach Arnold, scouting report in hand, with Chone's name and tendencies outlined in red, peered at K.J. for about ten seconds, briefly contemplating K.J.'s immodest proposal, then delivered his decision.

"Kenny will take him, K.J. We appreciate your offer."

K.J. considered making more of a case for himself. He wanted to appeal Coach's decision, lobby for a new trial. I think that's why he started a response with, "But…" But I cut him off.

"You better see your union steward and file a complaint."

K.J. gave me a look that told me to shut up, and looked back at Coach. Coach had turned his back and had already started on the guard match-ups. The verdict was in with no chance of an appeal. I think Coach heard my remark and decided that this, again had not been a time for humor and he moved on without comment (though Coach Pettaway, chewing his gum, arms folded, locked eyes with me for a second).

More strategizing from the coaches. Offense. Coach Arnold passed out two sheets of stapled offensive diagrams with new options on the plays from our 2-1-2 offense that used two guards, a center and two forwards.

"Chones is probably going to guard you on defense, K.J. We're going to move you away from the basket tonight. Play the high post instead of low post. Let's draw Chones away from the basket so he can't block shots and get all the rebounds."

Coach Pettaway chipped in.

"Not gonna be a Block Party for Mr. Chones tonight."

Coach Arnold added, "If you do get the ball down low, give him a head fake or two before you put it up. Get Chones to leave his feet, then make your move and he'll foul you."

"I don't think that's possible, Coach Arnold," I chipped in.

"What?" Coach wondered why I questioned his logic.

"It's pretty much physically impossible to leave your feet unless maybe they're bolted to your ankles and somehow a very potent force causes a separation of the feet from the ankle joints."

Coach looked down at his notes as I dispersed my thoughts.

"Don't want to be rude Stevie, but it's just a saying and I really need you and the team to concentrate on the game plan. We don't have a lot of time to get through this."

If Coach wanted to repeat anatomical impossibilities, far be it from me to stop him. I thought about Chones, wondered what he was doing right now, at this moment, in class, in the gym, walking the halls at Mobey Tech. His personage, two-hundred forty plus pounds, made of atoms, sinew, flesh, muscles, calcium, water, bones and blood would occupy my thoughts, my team's thoughts, our coaches' thoughts for much of that season, a body whose brain matter and bodily components would be plotting to make our bodies, our thoughts, our moods, our lives miserable.

Coach Arnold continued.

"If he wants to stay under the basket instead of coming out to guard you, fine. We'll keep giving the ball to you at the high post and you can shoot fifteen footers on him all night. If he comes up to guard you that'll open the driving lanes for Kenny and the guards."

Coach then launched into a story about some mastodon center that his team had played against in pre-historic days, about 1972, for which the same strategy had worked. When he finished the way-back time machine flashback, Coach asked if anyone had any questions.

My opening. "Was that when they got the ball out of the peach basket after every basket?"

"Stevie, it was slightly after that. You might think I'm the guy that invented the game when I nailed the peach basket to the wall of the YMCA but you'd be mistaken. That was James Naismith. I just held the ladder for him."

We didn't know at first whether to laugh or not. Coach appeared serious. We looked at Coach Pettaway, standing to the right of Coach Arnold. He had his head down, a hand over his eyes, trying to contain himself on his throat-catching snickers.

After a momentary silence Jose' finally said, "Oh I get it, Coach. That's a joke, right?"

And we all laughed, nervously at first, looked to see if anyone else was laughing, then harder as Coach Pettaway could contain himself no longer, and let loose, head back with a deep, loud-laughing belly-burst that could probably be heard through the locker room door out into the lobby. Coach Arnold smiling, proud of himself. He had connected with his team, his boys, and felt they were ready to play.

That morning Alison and Jillian had come over a few minutes before I had to leave for practice. I had just come in the house from taking the wheelie bins filled with Christmas residue, boxes to be recycled, trash consisting of wrappings, used paper plates and holiday greeting cards that weren't keepers out to the curb for garbage pick-up day. As I put on my letter jacket the door bell rang. I thought Hobie at first, but then, he usually honked. The girls stood on the porch, in high spirits as always. They had an idea and couldn't wait to tell me.

"Stevie, we decided we're going to be your fan club, your posse. We're going to make signs and bring them to the game, like 'Got Kalkannes? We do!' and we're going to make like a newspaper front page for your team. Jillian can take the photos of you and maybe some of the other guys shooting baskets at your game. Is that what it's called, shooting baskets? That doesn't sound right—and dribbling the ball and I can copy 'em and paste 'em and post 'em on sheets that we'll put up all over school on game days. I can do it in yearbook class. Mrs. Donofrio will let me. Do you think Coach Arnold will care?"

"Why don't you two talk to him first. I think he'll want more of the team thing, not just me."

"And we have another idea."

Jillian carried a small plastic drug store bag. She produced a bottle of hair gel from inside, holding it up for me to see the label.

"We think you'd look great with spiky hair. The gel has polymers. When you put the gel on, they wrap around your hairs

126

and bind them together. When the gel dries, the polymers shrink and pull the hairs really tight together. And we could die your hair black on the sides and red on the top. You know, with temporary hair dye, the kind that washes out. Get the spirit, Stevie!"

Laughing, Alison pulled out two boxes of hair dye from the bag.

Jillian continued, trying to talk me into their plan.

"We can do it right now. It only takes a minute."

"Uh, let me think about that one. I'm not sure if that'd be a good look for me, and you know, Coach Arnold is kind of old-fashioned. I don't think he'd like it if I showed up with jacked-up hair. I might get in his dog house."

Alison uh-huhed me, but she wasn't giving in.

"We thought at first that a Mohawk would be what you should wear, but then we thought, no, just a Fro-hawk, with only the front part spikey. You gotta do it, Stevie. It's, it's like it would be part of your new baller image. It would be so *you*. And how about if we all get temporary henna tattoos, like tribal arm bands? How cool would that be?!"

I took the gel and the dye, thanked the girls and told them I would think about it. Spikey hair and tribal tats. I had never thought about my "image" before. And Alison called it a *baller* image. I had to admit that the idea had no small appeal. Sometimes a guy likes attention.

Chapter 26

The consolation game over, stretching and game plan talk by the coaches ended, the twenty minute warm-up clock started. As our pep band trumpeted our fight song we exited the locker room on the run, splitting into two groups, the first player going to the right, next player to the left, slapping hands when we passed underneath the basket at the far end of the court, each line flowing into our shooter and rebounder layup lines on our half-court.

Mobey Tech followed suit, their team led by their co-captains carrying basketballs, their warm-up tops in black with "Mobey Tech" scrawled in gold script with a tail coming off the last letter veering left under the school name, the mascot name "Craftsmen" embedded. Our whole team had their eyes on their first player as he jogged by us, a man-child, a house. Quinton Chones. He looked to be thirty years old with a five o'clock shadow, hulking shoulders, and sculpted body. I thought that he was balding a little, too.

"How would you like to guard *THAT*?" Hobie asked me as we eyeballed Chones.

"I gotta give K.J. props for asking to take him. And God help Kenny. He's gonna need it. He better get a helmet."

"God yes. Hide the women and children. Chones' a grown-ass man. That land mass has tilted the court down toward their end. I'd rather give up my man card than guard *him*. If you need me I'll be doing some loin girding in the locker room."

The cheerleaders didn't act as daunted. They hadn't received a copy of the scouting report. As the students filed in the cheerleaders started their first cheer of the night, questioning the student body's attentiveness and readiness.

Ready? OK!
How's it feel to be a Kestrel?
How's it feel to be way up HERE?
(Pushing their hands up twice, exulting, high to the sky)
How's it feel to be a Craftsman?
(Shimmying down, pushing arms down alternately, hands, palms descending to the floor.)
How's it feel to be way down low?
(Dropping their voices a couple octaves to gutturally accent just how abysmally low a place a Craftsman inhabited on the measure of all things real or imagined.)

A couple minutes into our warm-up I saw Alison and Jillian come dancing in on the light red rubbery runners, the lengthy mats that protected the gym floor from the season's mud and snow, running from the lobby to the bleachers. Laughing, each carried a sign in their hand with my photo that they had cut out from the sports section from a game earlier this season. They had the photo blown up and pasted on their signs. "Got Kalkannes?" over the photo, "We Do!" underneath. The girls wore men's hats, fedoras, Alison's white with a black hatband, Jillian's black with a white hatband, along with pink framed lensless glasses and hot pink tennis shoes with their black crew neck sweaters and jeans. Their hair sported newly dyed strands of red streaks with red tips all around on the ends. A and J, girls with a game plan and game ready. Each wore a red scarf that hung down to their waists, hipsterish.

"Stevie, look!" Jillian yelled, standing in front of the bleachers by the entrance, as if I could possibly miss her and Alison.

Jillian held up her sign for me to see, giggling. She knew she had caught my eye. A pre-game passing drill with Toby came to a standstill. Two hand overhead pass, chest pass, bounce pass. In theory. As I read Jillian's sign Hobie's pass winged by my head and thumped against the second row of bleacher seats, almost nailing Coach Arnold. He and Coach Pettaway looked over. I gave them a furtive look, eyes darting at them then quickly away. I retrieved the ball, acting nonplussed, looking at Hobie. He had turned to scan the stands behind him to see what I was looking at, why his pass had almost bonked me in the forehead. Coach Arnold and Coach Pettaway both eyed me, both with arms crossed, talking with each other, probably about me, and probably not in a good way. I wondered if they had noticed my gelled hair. Luckily, at that moment, the Mobey Tech coach came over, passing the scorer's table to our bench to chat with our coaches, and took their attention away from me. Focus, Stevie, focus. Let the record show that Stevie would not be distracted by two high-spirited feminine members of his budding fan club.

Warm-ups over, the team stood near center court in a line perpendicular to our bench for the national anthem. Our pep band played a passing version, preceded by Kyle's a little too long drum roll. We stood respectively, hands behind our backs, looking upward. I resisted looking at A and J, my gaze upon the stars and stripes and league team pennants hanging overhead from our gym's A-frame ceiling supported by large red-pink colored iron girders, a flag hanging for each of the schools in our league, the Lake Erie North Coast Athletic League, in their school colors with their mascots' logos adorned: Crane Creek Egrets (Black & White), Deshler Dreadnaughts (Maroon & Gold), Grafton Gryphons (Forest Green & Blue), Lower Sandusky Cormorants (Aqua Marine & Purple), Midlothian Tarblooders (Red & Black), Port Monroe Sailors (Navy Blue & Silver), Sun Prairie Fighting Prairie Dogs (Scarlet & Gray), and ours, Jackson Kestrels (Black & Red).

Introductions followed. Coach Arnold looked up at Chones as they shook hands and with his other hand gave Chones a pat on a huge bicep with his program. As we walked out to the center circle for the opening jump ball, the pep band blared our fight song, followed by a piercing call of a bird of prey, an eagle shriek from the public address system that resounded throughout the gym. Actually, a kestrel's cry sounded more like *Ke-Ke-Ke*. The audio visual guy—probably a kid working in the AV department—who programmed the sound board apparently didn't think a *Ke-Ke-Ke* would send a mortifying shiver through the oppositions' players and fans.

Chones proved to be unstoppable. Defensive strategy be damned. He scored on their first four possessions, in the low post just above the right block, muscling Kenny out of his way, K.J. not able to do anything but put his arms straight up from behind once Chones received the pass. The Techsters ran three different man-to-man offenses, all with the first option being to get the ball to Chones. Block-to-block cross screens - little for big, hi-low post action for lob passes from Scarborough, and guards coming up the lane from the block to back screen for Chones, freeing him going to the basket to receive a pass from the wing.

Coach Arnold called a time-out three and a half minutes into the game. The Craftsmen led, 12-2.

"I'm getting pretty damn tired of hearing 'Basket by Chones.'"

Coach stared at Kenny. Kenny countered, palms out.

"But Coach, I'm getting screened right and left. Then he does that split-seal move where he puts his leg between my feet, spins around with that huge butt of his and knocks me back about three feet. And he pins my arm against his body. I can't do nothin'."

"Anything," I said. "You can't do *anything*."

I shouldn't have drawn attention to myself. Coach waved his program at me.

"How many times are you going to let your guy pass the ball right by you into the post, Kalkannes? *How many*?! Why do you think we do those pressure the passer drills? I suppose you think

131

it's all up to Kenny to stop that guy. It's a team game if you didn't know it, Kalkannes."

Coach, I hated to admit, was right. All my teammates looked at me. Looking away I wiped the sweat away from my face with a towel as the horn sounded, summoning us back to play.

Coach Arnold with a final instruction.

"K.J. You've got Chones. Kenny take Scarborough. And let's go to Blue press when we score.

We came out of the time-out more intense. And when we scored we picked up three-quarter court - our 2-2-1 press we called "Blue" - with the intention of hassling their guards, making them turn the ball over or at least making them start their offense from farther away, or making their bigs handle the ball away from the basket, creating problems for the Craftsmen. Down 18-7 at the end of the quarter we had cut the lead to 28-21 with three minutes to play in the half. Off an out of bounds play under their basket, Chones powered the ball in and drew a foul from K.J., his third.

Shaking his head side to side, Chones wagged his index finger at K.J., signaling *No No No - You're not stopping me.*

K.J. had been called for two previous fouls on Chones, one when he was helping Kenny on defense from behind when Scarborough threw a lob pass to Chones underneath and K.J.'s arm got tangled with Chones', and another on an offensive foul when he drove into Chones, who didn't budge.

Coach shot up off the bench, giving his usual sign of displeasure, the wave of his program, at one of the refs, a tall thin guy.

"What are you calling! That's either a foul on their guy or maybe a travel, but a *charge?* Are you kidding me?!!"

Tall Thin Ref eyed Coach, putting a hand on his whistle, the signal that another fusillade from Coach would result in Coach being T'd up, a technical foul.

Coach called another T.O. Coach Pettaway got to K.J. first.

"No excuses, K.J. Remember what we taught you. Keep your feet moving on defense, keep your feet still when posting on offense. If you keep an arm's length away and keep your feet moving you can get around him on defense and he can't seal you, and put your arm up where he puts his target arm to make it harder for a lob pass to get through to him. And on offense look to give Chones head fakes and go around him. You can't go vertical on that guy. Go horizontal, go around him."

K.J. listened patiently, desperate to hear something, anything, that would help. He looked a little more uncertain than the K.J. who spouted off at practice, the one saying he would claim World Domination over Quinton Chones.

I'd have to concur with the coaches, that reading K.J.'s face now, his boasting certainly could be considered unjustified braggadocio, depending, of course, on who was doing the considering.

With the score 34-26 and ten seconds to go in the half, Kenny drove from the left wing, got by his man, hooking the defender's arm with his elbow to gain an edge, a step, a technique that refs never called, then skied over Chones and banked the ball in. From the radio broadcast behind the scorer's table:

"A stop and a pop by Brown. IT's GOOD! IT's GOOD! What a drive by Kenny Brown! Here come the Kestrels!"

Our crowd had been nervously watching, more groaning than cheering, and thinking that Kenny was on the verge of a three-point play, burst into their loudest cheering of the game, shouting, clapping, fist pumps and fist bumps. The cheerleaders needed little prompting.

Are we in it?
Well I guess!
Victory, Victory, JHS!

Then, a late whistle. The ref who whistled the foul, a pudgy dark-haired guy that had to keep tucking his black-and-white striped shirt in as he moved sloth-like up and down the court, walked toward the scorer's table.

"Offensive foul. White number thirty-two, hooking."

He gave his referee's signal, using their mechanics, for a hook, making a tugging motion pulling an imaginary stick toward his stomach. Only his signal was one used in the National Hockey League, not Ohio high school basketball.

Coach Arnold jumped off the bench.

"What!? Hooking? You're kidding, right? This isn't hockey. You weren't even in the right position to see it. You *obviously* have never played this game!"

The *obviously* went right to the ref's manhood. Accusing me of never having played? is what we could tell he was thinking by the look he gave Coach. He formed a quick "T" with his hands.

"Technical foul on the Jackson bench! Two shots and the gray team's ball out of bounds," he told the scorekeeper, leaning over the scoring table and pointing at Coach Arnold. Coach Arnold stood with tightened fists on hips, staring back, then gave a dismissing program wave at Pudgy Ref. Looking exasperated, sweat forming above his eyebrows, Coach turned to our bench, explaining his plaint to an agreeing Coach Pettaway.

Our scorekeeper, jayvee player Tyrone Lattimore's dad, gave the ref a dubious look before he marked the technical in the scorebook. Tall Thin Ref at the far end held the basketball, spit-shined black referee shoes, every dark black hair in place, waiting for the technical foul to be administered. Pudgy Ref waddled over to Mobey Tech's bench to notify their coach to choose a player to shoot the free throws. Our crowd's attitude quickly changed. It sounded as the Roman Coliseum must have, calling for Pudgy Ref's blood. Booing cascaded to the rafters, fans' hands cupped around their moths, jeers louder and louder as their point guard, Belisario, Mobey Tech's best free throw shooter, drilled two perfect foul shots.

From a box formation sideline out-of-bounds set opposite the scorer's table, the Craftsmen's throw-in went to the right corner to their number 21 who had run the baseline off Chones' screen under the basket. Guarding my man near the top of the circle, I quickly realized there was no backside help on Chones who had parked yet again on the right block, clearing K.J. away with the strength of his forearm. The lob pass came from number 21 over K.J.'s head. I dove down and whacked at the ball as Chones started his power lay-up. To Chones, it seemed as if a mosquito had touched his arm. I could hear the radio play-by-play announcer yell, *"A HOOP AND A HARM!IT'S CHONES AGAIN!"* That ended the first half scoring. 41-26 Mobey Tech. A hammering. A bloodbath. A smackdown. An ass kicking.

On the way to the locker room K.J. crossed paths with Chones. I heard him say something to K.J. and K.J. say something back.

'What'd he say to you?" I asked K.J., coming up alongside him as he pulled open the door to the locker room.

"He said, 'You assholes are weak.'"

"What'd you say back to him?"

"I complimented him on his efforts in the first half, wished him well for the second half, and extended a holiday greeting. WHAT DO YOU THINK I SAID?!!"

"A personal suggestion as to what he might do during half-time?"

K.J. smirked.

"Yeah, something like that."

The coaches gathered in the corner of our locker room, Coach Arnold and Coach Pettaway talking strategy, Coach Kopastynski grim-faced looking at the stats on the clipboard. We sat on the bench, hushed, discouraged. Could the coaches possibly think of a way to stop that battleship disguised as number 44? No yelling, no theatrics from Coach Arnold or Coach Pettaway when they finally addressed the team. Coach Arnold began slowly.

"We're going to try something we haven't done yet this year. We're going to the 1-2-2 zone that we practiced but haven't used in a game yet. That'll give us more help on the backside, take away the lob passes to 44. It should help with pressure on the passers, too."

Coach Pettaway chimed in, "And you probably won't have to get through any screens since they'll be running their zone offense. When Coach and I scouted them they didn't show any screening action in their zone O."

His back to us diagramming the defense, the X's, with a black marker on the whiteboard, Coach Arnold added, turning his head,

"You perimeter guys, you guys play the snot out of the ball, pressure the passers, make it hard for them to get it into 44. Do a better job than you did in the first half."

He drew a small "O"—O symbolizing the offensive guy with the ball on the wing trying to pass the ball into Chones, and a huge X representing our defensive player. That would make it easy to keep the ball out of the post if our perimeter defenders, as Coach depicted them, were the size of Godzilla with wingspans of condors. I wanted to point out to Coach that his drawing misrepresented the actual sizes of the participants, was not drawn to scale, and did not accurately depict the event he intended to portray. Objects not as large as they appeared. I thought better of it.

"When your man doesn't have the ball, sag toward the post so you can discourage a pass or double the ball when it does go into Chones. Triple team him if you're close. We'll give up the outside shot if he kicks it back out. Hell, we'll have a parade if he kicks it back out. Wings have to rebound on the backside. That means

136

Kenny and Stevie. You're probably going to have to box out Chones or Scarborough. I know that's a load. Jose', you're playing the point and you go away on perimeter shots to help the wings on rebounds. Stick with Blue press to slow up the guards, make them pass it up instead of dribble it up. Maybe they'll make some mistakes. Look for your traps at midcourt and the corners. Let's get within ten points by the end of the third quarter and we'll go from there."

Coach Pettaway said he had one more thing. He went to the whiteboard and wrote the word "Impossible" in big letters. He then turned to us and said, "How many of you think it's impossible to come back and win this game?" Of course no one raised their hand. Mine might have gone up just a little, imperceptibly. But then Coach Pettaway, marker in hand, turned back to the board, broke apart the letters m and p and put an apostrophe after the I. "Now what does it spell, fellas? *I'm possible.* The impossible isn't always if you believe in yourself, fellas."

By the time we came out of the locker room halftime intermission had wound down to 1:45 left on the clock. We only had a minute to shoot before Coach would call us over for a few brief reminders before the second half started. I took a pass from one or our ball boys and was about to launch a practice three pointer when K.J. signaled, waving with both arms, calling the team to the foul line.

"This is embarrassing. I'm going to play as hard as I can for the next sixteen minutes. Let's play like lunatics. Take a look at 'em down on their end."

We turned to look. The Craftsmen were half-heartedly warming up for the 2nd half, acting if the game was all but over. Chones stood at the three point line, launching three-pointers, air-balling one after another as his teammates laughed. Their demeanor looked much different from their first half warm-up. However, Chones looked big as ever.

The Craftsmen had the ball out on the side to start the second half, the arrow on the scorer's table pointing toward our defensive end, signaling Mobey Tech's ball.

The ball came inbounds, their point guard, number 21 bringing it up, their coaches yelling that we were in a zone. 21 fed it to number 35 on the left wing who looked for Chones coming across the key. I played the snot out of the ball, as instructed. 35 faked a pass low and tried to pass high, by my ear. I got a few fingers on it, grabbed the loose ball and fed a long pass to Jose' up court for a lay-up. We jumped into the 2-2-1 press. 21—I think his name was Corky—turned, started to dribble and instead of giving him room to dribble as I had done in the first half, jumped him and he traveled. On the inbound I came off a double screen, turned, caught the pass from Kenny, and locked and loaded, having turned my shoulders square to the basket, hit a three from about 21 feet. 41-31. Next possession Chones caught the ball in his usual habitat, but we doubled him immediately front and back, Jason and K.J. having sandwiched him. He dropped his shoulder and drove K.J. back about five feet and with a two foot take-off, deposited the ball in the basket with a vicious dunk, then stood over K.J. and stared down at him. A whistle. Tall Thin Ref pointing at Chones, other arm with his hand behind his head signaling an offensive foul. Number three on Chones. K.J., arising from the floor after being a human sacrifice, yelled in Chones' face. Chones pushed him away. K.J. stumbled, caught his balance and went back at Chones. I quickly stepped in between them, with my hands to K.J.'s chest and a look that said *"If you value your nose being located in the same place it is now, walk away."* K.J. snarled over his shoulder at Chones as I separated him from Chones' reach, ushering K.J. away, Chones laughing at K.J.

Mobey Tech's coach vaulted off the bench.

"What are you calling? What did he do? He didn't do anything he didn't do in the first half!"

Tall Thin Ref ran by the Craftsmen's bench on the way up court and demonstrated the lowering-the-shoulder move Chones had made when he plowed into K.J. Mobey's coach waved him off with both arms, yelling, "No way!"

On our next possession we fed K.J. in the post on the right side. Chones had been playing behind K.J., bodying K.J. off the block so that K.J. would have to shoot over Chones' outstretched arms from three or four feet away instead of shooting an easy turn-and-bank off the corner of the square of the backboard from a foot away. This time K.J. turned to the middle, elbows out protecting the ball, and gave Chones a head fake as if he were going up for a jumper. Chones straightened up, arms high. K.J. quickly swung the ball to his right hip, crossed his left leg over Chones' with a long, low step - an up-and-under move - exploded on his takeoff and laid the ball in the basket as Chones arm came down across K.J.'s. Foul number four on 44!

"And one!" K.J. yelled.

Chones slammed the ball to the floor, but caught it with both hands before it bounced over his head.

"That's BS," he muttered loudly, as he turned away from Pudgy Ref, putting his hands on his knees, pulling on his shorts, a profuse sweat soaking his jersey. Tall Thin ref, a dozen feet away, eyed him, looked as if he might T up Chones, but then holding the ball, backed away under the basket as the teams lined up for the free throw. Pudgy Ref ambled over, pushing his black and white striped shirt back in his pants, one finger up signaling one free throw. Tall Thin Ref bounced the ball underhand to him. Bouncing it once more out of habit, with both hands, making sure that the ball hadn't become deflated in the last minute, Pudgy Ref checked to see that the teams had lined up properly, as if that duty had escaped the attention of Tall Thin Ref, and handed the ball to K.J. saying, 'One shot, fellas. Play the miss." Pudgy Ref's black toupee remained in place, for the record. I double-checked. For

139

the record.

K.J. drilled the free throw. 41-34, Craftsmen.

Old Mo, momentum, began changing. Our bench was up, swinging their towels in the air. Mobey Tech called time out as the pep band played our fight song, the pep band director waving his baton, cheerleaders exhorting the student section. We could hear the Craftsmen's coach giving his team a tongue-lashing in their huddle.

"You're playing scared! Someone besides Quinton is going to have to step up. How about if we try to get the ball reversed against their zone instead of dribbling through it! And one pass and a shot when we get it over half court? Are you serious? You're better than this!"

Their coach's harsh critiquing firing up his team, along with K.J. drawing HIS fourth foul, resulted in a back-and-forth game into the middle of the fourth quarter. The Craftsmen led 48-44 at the end of the third quarter. The game had slowed to a crawl, with both teams using eight or ten passes each time down, probing the defense. Every possession painful with the leading scorer for each team on the bench. They had figured out that I was the only outside threat we had, and switched on all the screens. I couldn't get open, hardly touched the ball. The Mobey Tech defense shut down Kenny's drive, everybody dropping to help position every time he caught the ball and swung it side to side, hip-to-hip, looking to drive by his defensive man and get to the basket. Jason acted afraid to shoot, looked nervous, immediately passing the ball back out when he caught it near the basket. Coach had subbed Hobie, all 5'7" of him, for K.J., so we were really on the small side. We went to our motion offense, passing and cutting, reversing the ball, trying to back door our defenders, looking to break somebody open, but the Craftsmen knew the pattern and kept shutting us down, one possession after another.

Coach Arnold took a knee in front of the bench, giving us his wisdom for the fourth quarter as we gulped from our water bottles.

"Keep working guys, keep working. You're doing great on defense. They only got seven points that quarter. Somebody's going to have to step up for us. Jose', don't be afraid to shoot. You hit four threes in a row when we scrimmaged the other day. They're playing off you. Jason and Hobie, take one if you're open. Kenny, since they're shutting your drive off with help from Stevie's man, look for Stevie when you drive. Penetrate and pitch. And you guys keep setting drift screens, the back screens, for Stevie."

Coach Pettaway took me aside.

"Stevie, this could be your time. Be ready, son."

I looked at Coach P. and slowly nodded, taking in his words.

Yeah, maybe it would be my time. I'd wanted so much to rescind the damage for the Midlothian debacle.

With a little over four minutes to go we trailed 55-52. Coach Arnold conferred with Coach Pettaway about when to send K.J. back into the game. Mobey Tech's coach watched the clock, wondering the same, when to put Chones back in. As long as he had the lead and K.J. was on the bench he was nervously OK with also keeping Chones on the bench. We were working hard on defense but couldn't sustain any momentum with our offense. We trailed by only four points, but it seemed like a dozen, points being so hard to come by.

Our ball after I snagged a rebound off a Craftsmen's miss on a twelve footer. Outlet pass to Jose' who zigzagged through their defense, drove to the basket and tried to lay it in with an underhand layup under Scarborough's attempted block. The ball shot off the underside of the rim, almost decapitating their number 35, and bounced out of bounds. Coach Arnold winced. At least it was our ball. 3:44 to play. Coach Arnold summoned for K.J. As K.J. ran to the scorer's table we looked down to see if Chones would be coming back in also. Not yet.

We looked to Coach for the out-of-bounds call. He signaled an "O," for Old. Coach said it was the oldest inbound play in the history of basketball. Box formation. Kenny took the ball out, K.J. in front of him on the left block, Jamey Watson on the right block. Jose' situated himself at the left elbow, me at the right elbow. Kenny slapped the ball and checked his first option as K.J. screens across for Jamey. Up top Jose' screened for me coming across trying to get open for a three, then popped to the top as a safety valve. The Craftmen's low defenders switched men. But that was what Kenny was looking for; K.J. reversed pivoted, sealed the defender on his back, fended him off, caught Kenny's bounce pass, went up strong and scored. We sprinted back on defense. The scoreboard read 55-54, Mobey Tech.

Coach Arnold waved us back with both hands, not wanting the press, not wanting to give Mobey Tech an easy chance to score if they broke it.

"We need a stop. C'mon guys! Hands up, hands up!"

Chones ran to the scorer's table to report back in. Two minutes remained in regulation. The Mobey Tech coach stood, lightly bouncing on his tip toes, turning over in his mind whether to take a time-out to put Chones back in, or since he was ahead, letting the clock keep winding down as the Craftsmen stalled, taking the air out of the ball. We stood in our 1-2-2 while the Craftsmen's guards played catch. The clock wound down to 1:30, then 1:00 to go. We kept looking at the bench for instructions from Coach Arnold on when to come out of our half-court zone to either play man-to-man or try to spring a trap. Coach kept gesturing, pushing a palms down sign, for us to stay just as we were. With forty-five seconds to go our fans in the home stands yelled suggestions.

"Get out on them! Pressure the ball! Foul 'em! Foul 'em!"

With thirty seconds Mobey's coach signaled for a time-out. Chones came back in.

Coach Arnold waved at us to hustle over to our bench.

"OK, guys. Here's what we're going to do. We're going to our 12 Black, the half-court trap. Match-up, disguise it as a man, get close to whoever's in your area. When the pass comes in, trap it. If the ball comes out go for the steal. We don't get it, foul. Doesn't matter who. 21 is their best foul shooter, and 33 their worst, but we can't worry about that now. Any jump balls we have the arrow."

Number 33, their inbounder, took the ball out near the Craftsmen's bench. The ball came into 21, Corky Belisario, their point guard. Jose' pressured him near half court. 21 kept pivoting, hoping to get fouled, dismissed the thought, then started his dribble. Their offense spread out, in a 2-1-2 shape. Kenny came out to trap when 21 dribbled. Jose', playing sideways, forced 21 back toward Kenny on the right sideline, pinning him. 21 hit 33 with a sharp chess pass in the corner. K.J. came out on him with his hands up. But 33 drove around K.J., looking to skip a pass cross-court. He hit number 11, their 2-guard, who skipped a diagonal pass right back to 33 under the basket. 33 squared his hips and anticipating K.J. trying to block his shot, went for the power lay-up. The ball hit glass, then rim, then came out. Chones went strong for the rebound. I checked him. A minnow boxing out a whale. A whistle as Chones leaned over my back and tipped the ball in.

"Wheeeeet!"

Both referees had blown their whistles. They immediately conferred at half court, Thin Ref covering his mouth as he talked, Pudgy Ref listening, then doing the same, seemingly agreeing with Thin Ref. Which would it be, a basket and a foul on me or an over-the-back call on Chones? Thin Ref walked to the scorer's table. He loudly announced the call, and indicated with his fingers the offending player's number.

"Foul on gray number 44. Over the back. Number 22 white will

143

be at the line."

Number 22 white. My number.

Two seconds remained on the Lonnie's Pizzeria scoreboard clock. Disbelief from the Mobey Tech bench and fans. Chones looked down at his number, trying to comprehend that his jersey had the number 44 on it, the number called for a foul. We walked to the other end, as a cacophony of sounds swirled from the crowd.

From the Craftsmen's fans: "Terrible call! Terrible! You can't call that! You homers! Refs shouldn't decide the game!

And from ours: "C'mon Stevie! You can do it! You can do it!"

A calmness came over me. The spaces in between. I visualized the ball going in the basket. Everyone in their spots on the free throw lane. The ref wiped the sweat off the ball, gripped it with both hands, his index fingers pointing out indicating that I had a 1-and-1, make the first, get a second, and told the players along the lane to play the miss. A split second before he handed me the ball Mobey Tech's coach yelled at the refs, stomped to be heard, his hands forming a "T" for time out.

"Time out! Time out! Time out!"

The referee underneath the basket, Pudgy Ref, saw him, did his fastest semi-shuffle out just as I reached for the ball, blew his whistle, pointed at the visitors' bench, and yelled.

"Time out, Gray!"

Coach Arnold went over the strategy.

"After Stevie makes these, all they can do is launch a long one. Jason, you'll stay back and don't let anything over your head. Jose', you, too. Make 21 go back toward his basket to get the inbound pass."

Coach looked at K.J. and Kenny.

"Expect a rebound but don't get in the lane early. Run your "X" game." Coach made an "X" with both index fingers crossing.

Coach Pettaway gripped my arm as we broke the huddle and

winked at me. Hobie patted me hard on the back.

"You CAN do this, Buddy."

I peeked at Alison in the front row across from our bench. Her Stevie sign against her leg, she stood, along with all the student section. She had her hands clasped, eyes closed, cheeks slowly blowing in and out. Jillian leaned against her, her face tucked into Alison's shoulder, face sideways, barely able to watch.

I tensed, then relaxed my fists and forearms and blew my own cheeks in and out. The time was at hand. The Jackson student body counted on me.

The referee repeated his instructions and put the basketball in my hands. Joanie's introductory yoga words went through my head. "We're not here for competition or judgment." But that's what we were here for, right here, right now, competition and judgment. An intangible object held my fate, my team's fate. I let my mind numb and took the shot, feeling the grain as it left my fingers, arcing its way toward the orange rim, the white net, the square outlined on the glass backboard. The ball decided to hit the rim and bounce almost straight up. K.J. x-ed with Kenny. K.J's long arms extended over a phalanx of jumping players, grabbed the ball, and knocked it off the backboard and in as the horn sounded. The numbers clicked over…. 54 to 55 to 56 in red for the home team on the scoreboard as the refs ran off the court, their coach frantically taking a short sprint after them yelling, an arm pointing down at the other end where his player had been called for an infraction of the rules and disqualified a short few minutes ago.

"Hey! Hey! What about the over-the-back! What about over the back!"

Us - dog pile! Or more precisely a pile of birds - a cast, a cauldron, a kettle of Kestrels heaped on K.J. as he pounded the floor and yelled, "Yeah! Yeah! Yeah!" Rather repetitious but appropriate considering the circumstances. Our students surrounded us, yelling, whooping, pounding any player they saw between the shoulder blades.

Trophy presentation. Championship caps. Not even upset at missing my free throw I rocked my cap along with my teammates, yelling, congratulating each other. Compliments came from the coaches on my box out.

The team streamed into the locker room, exchanging hard high fives and jump bumps, hip-to-hip, amidst celebratory shouts. Mr. Pettaway, last in line, closed the door to the outside world and let go with "Great Goobley Woobey, boys! Never a doubt, never a doubt! We had them all the way!"

K.J. shouted, "That was a miracle whipping, Coach!"

That got a smile from Coach Arnold, who said, "Maybe not a miracle and maybe not a whipping, but I think you boys came of age tonight."

Coach Arnold talked briefly, congratulating us, then turned us loose. Music boomed in locker room, an old CD Coach Pettaway had brought in for us. He swore by the Philly Sound.

"The best music ever made, boys," he had told us. "The Stylistics, Spinners, O'Jays, TSOP. Soul 70s music. Al Green, the Commodores, the Grand Master of Funk—Bootsy Collins, Harold McFadden—*Ain't No Stoppin' Us Now*. Soul Train! The best show ever, fellas!"

We had bought into it, The Sound of Philadelphia and Bootsy filling the locker room after wins.

"Push your hands in the air!" said Coach Pettaway, doing just that, his shirt coming out revealing his prodigious stomach, sweat beading on his forehead in the post-game celebration as we gave it up to the funk music coming from Coach P's boom box. And we did just that. Gave it up to The Funk, Hands In the Air. Our confidence soared. We all, all of us, thought that there ain't no stoppin' us now. We're on the move.

Chapter 27

Two texts showed up on my phone after I left the locker room. A text from Benny that read: **Good win, but if U played better defense and passed the ball more you'd have won a lot easier.** I thought that Benny just didn't get it. He still had his point guard mentality, of passing, distributing the ball for assists, whereas my role primarily consisted of shooting and scoring. And no doubt my defense was nowhere near as good as his had been. The two years I didn't play hadn't helped my defensive ability. I texted him back:

Since when R U my coach? Fun Fact: We won and that's all that counts!

The other: a text from Kyle. His garage band, Rabbits In the Living Room, would be performing at one of the other band member's garage Saturday night. I had the honor of being invited. The band's text Kyle copied and sent read:

Rabbits In the Living Room performing this Saturday in concert at Jake Twitchell's house - 914 North Sherman Ave. 8:30. Free!!!! Come one, Come all! Snacks, Hot Chocolate and Hot Cider provided! Please - No alcohol.

Kyle would be performing live, in the flesh, with the rest of the Rabbits. Alison and Jillian schmoozed with the hangers-on outside the locker room - parents, girlfriends, classmate buddies, little brothers and sisters running around the gym, the custodial staff. They could, and did, talk to anyone without fear or reservation. A and J, as I had begun to refer to them as, had ended talking with the Hurlburts, offering their well-wishes and sympathy for Tommy's mishap when I approached, holding out my cell for them to see Kyle's text that he had received from Jake Twitchell and forwarded to me.

"We're in!" shouted Alison.

Jillian sensed another adventure, nodded whole-heartedly, 'Yepper!" and did a little head bob and shoulder shake, followed with an "Uh-huh! Uh-huh!"

Upcoming, straight ahead, Saturday night. A fun time to be had by all. A festive affair, a festivity. Rabbits In the Living Room would be expanding their habitat to Rabbits In the Garage. Rabbits In the Living Room, made up of Kyle Mahoney, Jake Twitchell, who went to the community college, Jake's younger brother Kai and Kai's friend Darby Senna, both sophomores at Jackson. Jake had started the band about six months ago after playing in four other short-lived garage bands in high school and college—Loose Gravel, Presumed Innocent, Just Words, and A Casual Acquaintance. Jake played lead guitar and sang lead vocals, Kai played the electronic keyboard, Darby bass guitar. They both backed up Jake on vocals. The drummer and non-vocalist—Kyle Mahoney.

Chapter 28

Signs in the Twitchell's front yard directed us around to the back, a rabbit photo and a hand with a pointed finger showing the way. RABBITS IN THE LR! THIS WAY! When we got to Jake's we found that the band's jam session would be held not in their garage but in back of his parents' house in a large octagon shaped pole barn twenty-five yards to the rear of the house. About thirty kids stood around drinking hot chocolate, gloved fingers wrapped around paper cups and sipping steaming apple cider from thermos cooler jugs that Jake's mom and dad kept refilling, alongside a table with boxes of donuts. I went for the glazed donuts before Alison could issue a health warning to me and stuffed one in my cheeks.

The band warmed up, Kai checking the connections for his combination organ and synthesizer, the notes oscillating on wavelengths first shrill, then diving down to lower chords deep and rich. Kyle thunked his drumsticks on the drums, first a slow thump-thump-thump, building up to a series of faster drum rolls, banging the symbols, looking as straight-faced and serious as Kyle could, knowing eyes were upon him. All business. Jake checked the small sound machine, adjusting dials on the amp, hitting lower then higher chords on his guitar which I felt as much as heard, stinging notes, riffing slightly recognizable stanzas. Darby fingered fuzzy low-toned notes down then up then back down the scale that resonated through my body. They warmed up their instruments. I warmed up my listening.

Hobie tapped me on the shoulder.

"Isn't that Josie sitting behind Kyle?"

I looked. As God is my witness, yes, it was Josie sitting in a folding metal chair a few feet behind Kyle. Kyle and Josie? A match made in, in… Food and Fitness?

I stared dumbfounded. Hobie addressed the situation, his voice intense.

"This cannot be. My sensibilities are offended. Those two together? Attention must be paid. We must counsel that boy, make him understand the perils of getting too close to that feral cat referred to as Josie."

"You have sensibilities?" I asked Hobie as we continued to stare, with the same astonishment as if we were looking at a two-headed snake.

"I have sensibilities," Hobie said in defensive mode. "One or two they think. Last time they tested me. However, the results were inconclusive."

"I saw Kyle at her locker the other day after school talking to her. He had his hand on top of Josie's locker door, like they were friends, but I just figured it had something to do with their Food and Fitness assignment. This happened right under our noses, right before us, Hobie, and we didn't realize what was happening. Kyle has a thing for Josie? Do you think Josie made the first move? Guys have been killed by friendly fire, you know."

Hobie, still staring, nodded repeatedly, slowly.

"When do you suppose she started acting like she does. So pissy."

I pretended to deep think, rubbing my chin.

"When the sperm met the egg."

"But that might not prove true in theory because look at her brother. Jose's an agreeable dude. He must have gotten the good demeanor genes. I can't believe that Jose' and Josie are the offspring of the same parents. Something cataclysmic must have happened to Josie's DNA when she sprang off."

"I'll bet if you check Josie's Punnett Square, under the demeanor trait column would be two recessive letters. Small d, small d. Personality deficiency. Could you imagine if she ever reproduces? Stop guards must be put in place."

"But they're dominant small d's. Geneticists are confounded. I heard that one of them got bitten when he got too close to a Petrie dish containing one of her cheek swabs."

"Maybe it's not genetic. Maybe the girl just has issues."

"Why don't you ask her?"

"Sure, Hobie. I'll casually approach the she-woman. I'm sure if I ask her if she has issues, she'll take it to mean in a good way. I'd have to wear a hazmat suit for my self-protection. I think Josie came with a manual attached to her that says to keep an assured clear distance. The potential for serious injury will ensue if directions are not followed. Poor Kyle. His early warning system must not have activated. He obviously didn't read the warnings in the small print that came with her. We have to schedule a therapy session-slash-pity party for him at the earliest opportunity."

I made a downward slashing diagonal motion with my index finger.

Hobie, agreed, and said, "All girls are cute, and she's cuter than most, but I wouldn't touch her with a pair of tongs. She carries a high level of toxicity. The EPA should be called in. She'll be leading Kyle around like a dog in a few days. You watch, he'll be wearing a collar."

"Medusa was cute, too, when she was the same age."

Hobie turned to face me.

"Operation Separation. We have to get to Kyle before he gets love struck by that untamed shrew. We might have to send him away for a while, change his name, get him in a witness protection program."

"Yes. Protect the innocent, the guileless, the unsuspecting. It's for his own good."

We looked back over at Kyle, who had finished warming up, a towel over his shoulder. He laughed as Josie said something in his ear, then we watched in horror as they kissed and laughed again.

"Shield thy eyes, Hobart. May they be plucked out by harpies rather than to witness such a troublesome vision."

Hobart shielded, with both hands. I did the same.

"Are they done yet?"

"I'll dare to check," I said, spreading my fingers ever-so-slightly.   Josie had gotten Kyle some cider in a paper cup and held it up to his mouth, Kyle opening wide, Josie tipping, poring as if giving a drink of water to a plant. Cider dribbled down Kyle's chin, but Josie wiped it away with her hand and kissed him where it had moistened Kyle's teen goatee chin stubble.

We viewed this transgression in pseudo-horror. Hobie grabbed my arm with both of his as I turned away, an arm across my eyes. Hobie started to sob quietly.

"Kyle," he said, "We hardly knew ye."

"Hobart, we'll continue to scrutinize this abject abomination that so disgusts us. Maybe some good will come of it. Maybe it will become our cause, saving naive young men from ill-tempered temptresses. Kyle's tale will be a cause celebre'. We'll wear black ribbons with RITLR on them on Sweetest Day to bring attention to the pitfalls of falling for those vultures who prey on our gender. We'll pause to reflect upon those of us who have fallen for their devious seductive devices."

Hobie slowly surveyed the assembled guests, mostly our classmates, but a few I didn't recognize, from other high schools probably, or maybe from the junior college.

"Don't they all understand the gravity of the situation? Josie and Kyle just kissed! Lips upon lips. They're witness to the contributing of the delinquency of a minor."

"Uh, there're both minors," I said. "Neither of them are

eighteen. That may not come under the category of a punishable offense, although Kyle is bereft of logic at this juncture. He would be deemed incompetent to stand trial if it comes to that. Temporary, well, intermittent insanity."

"The state should make statutes just for Josie. We need to petition the legislature."

"Yeah. Probably so. Kyle's outkicked his coverage. His learning curve has used up all its bendy parts. We can't help him now. He's on his own. But then, he, as we all do, has free will. Life, liberty, and the pursuit of happiness. See the Constitution for more information."

We considered Kyle's situation for about ten more seconds, then I asked Hobie,

"Is Kyle a victim of fate or his own actions?"

Hobie put a finger to each temple, squeezed his eyes shut, using his psychic abilities to divine an answer. I awaited his revelation in marveled wonderment. What seemed like a minute passed before Hobie opened his eyes, a startled look on his face, shook his head to bring him back to earth from whatever hypnotic state he had been in that had divulged the answer, and after a dramatic pause announced, "I pick both A and B."

"Huh." I said, and nodded, agreeing.

Such weighty matters we had been called upon to consider. We had taken the task with the seriousness required, with all due diligence, and the answer had been revealed. It reminded me of the method of using a stick to divine where water is located beneath the ground, only instead of a stick we used Hobie. Hobie had led us to the answer. But the problem of extracting Kyle from Josie remained, for now, unsolved.

"Hot chocolate?"

Hobie pointed his head sideways at the vat.

"Don't mind if I do," I said, our attention mindlessly and instantly diverted from Kyle's hots for Josie to hot cocoa.

Jake's dad had been bringing out jugs of hot cider and hot chocolate from the house. Slim, wire-rimmed glasses, graying hair tied back in a pony tail, he wore a brown tweed jacket over a Steely Dan tee-shirt, jeans and low cut boots, a constant bemused look on his face.

"Hey Mr. T," I said as he sat the jug down on one of the folding tables. "The Dan." I pointed at his tee-shirt and threw a few lines from a Dan song at him, *Deacon Blues,* and we said the chorus lines together, then awkwardly congratulated ourselves, though Mr. T started high fiving me as I attempted a fist bump. Then he fist bumped as I was going up top. We finally shook hands and laughed, looking around to see if anyone had been watching us. Never take for granted that adults know the drill.

Seeing that Alison and Jillian still stood talking with her friends in the corner under a neon craft beer sign that Jake's dad put up on the wall, I picked a pink frosted doughnut from an opened box. One with multi-colored sprinkles. Finished it in under a minute. A swig of hot cider washed it down as I lingered near the table, standing close but not hovering, not wanting to be accused of being a hoverer. I figured two arm lengths away would take me out of that category, and eased slightly back, bumping into Sandy Appelbaum. Sandy turned to see who had interrupted the conversation she had been engrossed in with three or four of her friends. I think they had been discussing their boots, as Sandy and the other girls looked down, inspecting the footgear of a girl they were looped around, a tall girl wearing black ski bib overalls over her dark maroon sweater and a maroon, gray and white knit tasseled ski hat with ear flaps. I didn't know her, but she looked toasty in her winter garb. Sandy reached out and hooked my arm, acknowledging my presence, pulling me toward her but looking back, not wanting to miss any of the dissection of the look of Miss Apres-Ski's boots. I heard "so fuzzy!" "cushy," "darling," "love the buckles!" "warm *and* waterproof," "infinitely, totally thoroughly cool," through the din in the garage. I waited until the discussion subsided, not wanting to interrupt such an important fashion critique.

"Hey Sandy."

"Hey Stevie. Have any donuts yet? Are they good?"

I wondered if any remnants were on my face of the previously consumed doughnuts, giving Sandy a hint that I had already sampled.

"That's the rumor. Let's try one, shall we?"

Two steps back from whence I came, I lifted a nearly full box, and offered them to Sandy's group, accepting thank-yous as if I had made them myself, then extracting the last one, a jelly-filled pastry calling my name before setting the empty box back down.

Sandy and I doughnut-bumped our treats. Down the hatch. Yum.

Jake took the microphone, guitar in hand.

"Hey guys. Thanks for coming. Have some cider, some hot chocolate, some cookies and doughnuts. Gotta thank Mom and Pops for those."

We turned and applauded Mom and Pops standing at the back of the garage. Mom held a fresh batch of chocolate chip cookies, right out of the oven, her oven mitten still on. Mom equally hip to Pops, thin-faced like Jake, long grayish-blonde hair, granny glasses, looking hippie-ish, beige tunic over a dark green turtleneck adorned with a long turquoise necklace, jeans and black boots. She placed the cookies on the table and gave a waist-high little smiley wave when Jake acknowledged her and Pops. Pops put his hands in his jeans pockets, closed mouth smile and nodded. I got the feeling they were proud of their sons, that they approved of their sons' musical aspirations.

The crowd of kids had swelled to about fifty or sixty, almost filling the pole barn, some standing in globular clusters and others in pairs, milling around, all having donned winter gear - colorful bomber hats with earflaps, vests over hoodies, warm wool sweaters, turtlenecks, scarves, leg warmers, knee length jackets, thick mittens and gloves. And one girl with ski bib overalls. The garage thermometer needle wavered between fifty two and fifty-five degrees. Those standing near the fire emanating from the rusty dark red fifty-five gallon burn barrel by the open garage door warmed their hands, their breaths showing in the frigid night air then evaporating. I looked around, checking for Alison and Jillian and found them in back of the garage to the left of the band's set-up by a warm air vent. Jillian's arms and hands were animated, her fists pumping up and down as she entertained her sometime boyfriend T-Roy who graduated last year from Jackson, and Alison and K.J. K.J.? Alison and K.J.? Hobie had left me to greet his girlfriend Piper who arrived with a few of her classmates from the small country day high school right outside the Jackson town limits, in Jackson Heights. I tried not to stare, but K.J. had both his arms around Alison, holding her tight against him from behind, Alison clutching his hands as they both laughed at Jillian's antics. I heard Alison laughingly say, "Jilly Bean, you're such a dork!" It occurred to me as I stood by myself, hands in my coat pockets, alone in a crowd, that all my friends had paired up. All but me. I wanted a girlfriend like everyone else I told myself again.

Chapter 29

"Let's get ready to rock!" Jake let go with a guitar riff getting the assembled throng's attention, conversations stopping, an anticipated exciting time afoot.

"Dudes and dudesses, hope you enjoy the show! Let's turn this mother out!"

They launched into their first number, a cover of Guns and Roses' *Welcome to the Jungle*. Jake closed his eyes as he played and sang, his Telecaster guitar slung low along his hips, his singing more of a screaming primeval sound. The windows rattled, the rafters shook. We loved it. Kyle hammered with both sticks on the drum heads, punishing, pummeling, pounding, the beat energizing, captivating, the crowd rocking, some dancing in pairs, some alone, some in groups, some dancing with frenzied histrionics, some in slow motion, many mouthing the words. Alison and Jillian head bobbed with the beat, extending necks and chins frontward then back, like in sync sea gulls. A few minutes later they added long-arm clapping, mouths open, agape, feigning rock star adulation until Jillian cracked up laughing, and acting dizzy, grabbed Alison with one arm around her waist and held Alison's forearm, looking wobbly. While the band pounded on in the din of the garage Jillian and Alison collapsed to the floor, arms around in each other in a prolonged series of giggle fits. Girl fun.

Jake and his brother Kai came from a multi-culti family of mixed religions, Jewish and Buddhist. Made them in essence Jude-Budes. Their dad, Walter converted from Catholicism to

Buddhism in his twenties after a Peace Corp commitment in Thailand. Soon after returning to the states Walter married Roberta Schlisserfitz, now Roberta Schlisserfitz-Twitchell, a Jewish girl he met at a coffeehouse concert. Jake and Kai's musical upbringing consisted mostly of listening to their parents' Klezmer and Tibetan flute music. But their tastes gravitated to heavy rock when they transferred from the Montessori school to the Jackson public schools in grade school. The ball game ended for the boys' dulcimers and flutes when they found their dad's collection of 70s and 80s rock LPs in the attic. Roberta came home one afternoon to the sound of Grand Funk Railroad and instantly recognized that it didn't have a Yiddish sound to it. Walter, sitting on the couch having flashbacks reading the LP liner notes, looked up at Roberta, a twinkle in his eyes, adjusted his wire rim glasses and shrugged. Roberta put the groceries on the kitchen counter, walked over to Walter and sat down next to him, taking the LP from his hands. She turned over the album to look at the cover and sighed at the sight of Mark Farner, thinking back to one of her first dates with Walter when they drove to Toledo to see Blue Oyster Cult, Bob Seger, REO Speedwagon, Sammy Hagar and Grand Funk Railroad at the Toledo Speedway Jam. They sat on the couch for an hour while the boys played imaginary instruments, air guitars and drums, listening to *We're an American Band, The Loco-Motion, and Foot Stompin' Music.* Walter took the boys to the music store the next day and signed them up for guitar and keyboard lessons.

Alison and Jillian, up and rockin' it now, with their left hands on left hips, right arms extended, right hands waving back and forth in the air with the continued detonation of the beat. Jake had introduced the number.

"OK, guys, we're gonna play one of our own, one Darby and I wrote. It's called, 'We Ain't Waitin' Another Day.'"

It started slowly, the lyrics Jake singing having to do with the usual teenage angst due to impatience. Impatience predictably turned to rage as the volume from the drums, bass, and guitars amped up. The eruption of sound didn't allow for my ears to discern the reason for the sudden mood swing-raging in the lyrics. Seeing the Twitchell's four bedroom house, how well off they were, maybe it could have been that the boys didn't get their milk money one day for school? But I, too, joined in the chorus as did all the garage gang.

"Get, get outa the waaaaa-aaaay! We ain't waitin' anotha daaaaa-aaay!"

Catchy. We didn't exactly sound like the Mormon Tabernacle Choir, but hey, yelling the lyrics to rock anthems doesn't require formal training. I never did figure out what it was that we wanted and weren't going to wait another day for.

The Rabbits played on, the amps booming, bass amplified, the drum's explosion of sound, extended guitar riffs, Darby's fingers hitting the frets with an urgency, Jake attacking the Telecaster's power chords, bending, shaping, altering notes, fret end pointed at a forty-five degree angle, Jake's face contorted, grimacing, sweating. The Rabbits ranged through the heavy metal color wheel with covers of *Black Sabbath, Deep Purple,* and *Blue Cheer.*

I excused my way to the rear and circled around the back perimeter of the garage crowd, a slow centrifugal force pulling me as I moved along an arc a few feet at a time. No one seemed to notice me. The show ended with a final burst from Kyle, bashing the cymbals, drilling the drumhead, and bamming the bass pedal. An appreciative crowd whistled, hooted, clapped. I could envision the Rabbits ascending from garage band to bar band in short order.

I left with two contrary feelings, pumped with adrenalin from the show, but feeling sorry for myself because it seemed everyone had a girlfriend or boyfriend but me. I waited by Alison's car as she said goodnight to K.J. and Jillian to her college guy. They came quick-walking and giggling from the back, down the driveway, Alison with car keys in hand. Revved up by the show, revved from the interaction with their BFs. On the way home they chatted about their guys and upcoming plans. I sat in the backseat and pouted.

Finally noticing my silence, Jillian asked,

"Stevie, why so quiet? Didn't you think the Rabbits sounded great?"

"Sure. A lot better than I thought they would."

Jillian had turned so she could see my face. Girls always had to see your face when they talked with you. Guys, with friends, not an issue. I often talked with Hobie off and on all day at school and couldn't tell you what he had been wearing if you asked. Girls could give you a top-to-bottom review and assessment of what clothing, accessories, and make-up their friends and non-friends had worn to school on a daily basis.

"So what's the matter? Be honest."

"Nothing big. Just wish I had a girlfriend. We've had this talk before. The Mindy thing has kinda bothered me."

No one said anything for a minute. Jillian spoke first.

"More about Stevie's perceived inadequacies, after sports and weather."

Alison glanced back at Jillian, then at me, turned back to keep her eyes on the street and gave me her thoughts.

"The trouble you have with girls, Stevie, is as we've talked before, you put them into two categories. They're either too good for you or not good enough. And if they do go with you want to find something wrong with them, because of your low self-esteem. If they go with you, you think then they're not good enough because if they were, why would they go with you? The ones who won't date you, that just contributes to your lack of self-esteem. You judge yourself by what you *think* others - girls and guys, think of you. You have to get over that. You can't keep judging yourself by what you think others think of you. Celebrate your *you-ness*. Don't get me wrong, you and everyone else should try to better yourselves. That would make you and anyone else more appealing, and you should adhere to societal values. You have to take a shower and comb your hair now and then, be able to carry a conversation, and have a sense of humor and display a modicum of intelligence. Well, that all helps. But being your friend I'm telling you you're good-looking enough and you're smart enough and appealing enough the way you are. You have very pleasant features and some girl or girls will be attracted to you. It'll happen. That's all I have to say about that. Other than quit feeling sorry for yourself."

Alison pulled into my driveway a few seconds after ending her diagnosis of my problem and personality issues and dropped me off. I got out without saying anything, but then made a motion for her to roll down her window.

"Thanks, Alison. Really. That helps. Gives me a lot to think about. And I think you're right about everything you said."

"No charge, Stevie," Alison said as she powered her window up, Jillian leaning over to give me a little goodbye wave with her fingertips as she said, "Sorry, Stevie. We love you."

Chapter 30

My mother always encouraged us to make New Year's resolutions, always suggesting that we make ones that would make us better people, to help others and to help ourselves. So I made two. 1) Drink more water 2) Not to be so judgmental. I decided to start the un-judging with Josie. The search for her redeeming qualities would commence upon our return to school after the Christmas break.

Chapter 31

Practice had been good since the holiday tournament win. We had a week between games, and so the coaches thought it a good idea to bring in the alumni to scrimmage us one of the days. The alumni included, of course, my brother Benny. The coaches knew enough to not let us guard each other. Coach Pettaway waved Benny and me over as we finished warm-ups. They sensed internecine warfare had a likely chance of occurring.

"Fellas, I don't want you two guarding each other. I've heard the stories. I don't think the Jackson rescue squad would appreciate us calling them over because of an altercation between the two of you. That would be counter-productive to what we're trying to accomplish with this scrimmage. We want everyone to play hard and have fun, and respect that we're all part of the Kestrel family, alumni and current players alike."

I shook my head in agreement.

"Uh-huh. Got it, Coach."

But Benny, not having to worry, his playing days over, put up a mild protest.

"But Coach, Stevie's been talking smack all year. I think a little humblin' might make him show the proper respect for yours truly and the other guys, speaking for the alumni."

Coach Pettaway listened, but I could see he didn't go along with Benny's line of thinking.

"Sorry, Benny. I respect your competitiveness, but I'm turning down your request. As my grandmama would tell me, 'It just be's that way sometimes.' You can guard Jose'. That'll keep you busy enough trying to keep up with him."

Good decision by Coach Pettaway. As he said, the rivalry between my brother and me bordered on legendary. We played the scrimmage with a running clock. Close at first, we eventually wore them out. Too many of the alumni considered beer one of the basic food groupings, and had slaked, then over-slaked their thirst at the Crow Bar until it closed at 2:30 AM after a short practice the night before. They struggled to get up and down the floor in the second half. Four or five made frequent trips to the restroom, waving for subs as they exited the floor. We won easily. Bragging rights to the junior Kalkannes.

Chapter 32

I found A and J at their hangout, The Coffee Ground, on 2nd Street near the community college. I hadn't heard from Alison and/or Jillian in the five days since the garage band performance, so I went looking for them. Mom had the day off and let me have her car, the one Benny and I referred to as the Suburban Assault Vehicle. Since girls travel in pairs I knew if I found one, I'd find the other. I could have texted them, but I liked the vague ambiguity, happenstance of just happening to stop in at the same time and place they had. Of course, they could be with their guy friends, too. That would, using a word I heard a hundred times a day at school — suck.

On my way there my phone buzzed, a text coming in. Stopped at a light, I checked the message. A selfie. Mindy in a swim suit on a beach on the Gulf of Mexico. The message. **Just me. Miss you!**

I guessed right, seeing Alison's car parked against the curb in front of the coffee shop. But first I texted Mindy back.

"Hey. What's up? How's F-L-A?"

"Great. @ beach every day. Working on my tan. I'm a heliotrope! On varsity cheer now! Cindy Baumholtz kicked off b/c caught drinking @ a party. CU soon?"

Decision making time. I put down my phone. I had three choices, the way I saw it 1) Total evisceration of my pride. Give it up like nothing had ever happened and go back to dating the hottest, most fickle girl in the school 2) Tell Mindy we'd "have a talk," to discuss our relationship like two mature people. Sometime during, before or after the talk would be when I gave in. 3) Like a guy with strong moral fiber tell Mindy that there wasn't a chance in h-e-double hockey sticks that we'd get back together after the stunt she had pulled on me after the game with the Tarblooders. I decided to wait on texting her back, to get Alison's and Jillian's take on what I should do first.

I pretended not to notice A and J when I walked in. They sat at one of the raised rectangular tables by the window next to the front entrance, having an animated discussion, leaning across the table, talking fast but listening to each other's points. Lots of nodding along with sips of their lattes. They took up two of the four high backed chairs. Boyfriend-less. I wandered over after getting my coffee— a shameless pumpkin spice—looking around, pretending not to see them, with all the nonchalance I could muster. Alison looked up, realized it was me, then looked back at Jillian and made a last comment. Jillian had her back to me, turned and she and Alison both said overlapping Hey Stevie's.

"Hi guys. Mind if I sit with you? How are the besties doin'?"

The casual approach. I couldn't wait to find a way to segue into my Mindy dilemma.

Alison answered.

"You know, girl talk. About our men. And some other stuff, like if we should get our hair cut. How are you, Mr. Kalkannes?"

"I'm good…good…good," I said.

Jillian said, "Did you ever notice that when you ask someone how they are and they answer 'good,' the more times they say 'good' the less good they are?"

"Very insightful, Ms. Jillian. But we can talk about that later. How are you guys?"

"We're good. I mean, Good! Just talking about, you know, weighty topics. Men, our hair, random stuff."

Alison added, "You forgot World Hunger. Honest to God we were talking about that. About how if the world would go veggie we could feed everyone."

I sat back and frowned, evaluating their hair and hair decision for a few moments, then leaned forward, scanning back and forth, looking at Alison's hair then Jillian's. I thought it best to weigh in, help with a resolution on the hair quandary before diverting the flow of the conversation to the quagmire Mindy had put my brain in. Solving world hunger would have to wait until I resolved my Mindy situation.

Alison had braided her hair all the way around the top, the "Dutch Crown" look. Jillian had braided hers in the back so it hung down, a single braid over her shoulder to one side.

"Know what I think?"

Jillian smiled at Alison with a "This ought to be good" look and said, "Sure.

Give us a man's opinion. Let's have it."

"Keep the boyfriends, keep the hair. The braids look crisp. Think you could do mine?"

Alison caught a small giggle coming up and said, "Maybe corn rows."

"Yeah! Let me think about that. The Allen Iverson look. 'Practice?? Are you talkin' about praaaactice?'"

I gave them the oft-repeated line from the famed Iverson interview. Neither Alison or Jillian had inherent knowledge of NBA players past or present, so I had to give them the context for my Iverson impersonation. They looked somewhat humored. Time to mention Mindy. They both took a sip of their coffees as I switched subjects.

"I need some help, guys."

I showed them the texts Mindy had sent.

Both peered at the screen, reading Mindy's messages and viewing the swimsuit photo of her on the beach. Jillian remarked,

"Well, she wins the swimsuit competition. Now let's see how she fares with the talent contest."

Alison said, "Seriously, follow your heart. Stevie, if she means that much to you, give her another chance. If you don't, how will you ever know if it would work out?"

I took in Alison's words, then shifted my eyes to Jillian's. Jillian had her head down, listening to Alison. They rarely disagreed, usually coming to a consensus after a round of girl talk, but not this time.

"I'd like to see you man up, Stevie. I don't know her, just know who she is.

And of course I've heard talk about her, and have seen her flirt with some of the senior guys. But if you go right back to her...well, good luck with that. Why would she change how she acts toward you?"

"Maybe she finally realizes what she's missing?" I said, eyebrows raised, hoping that Jillian would agree.

Jillian patted my hand. "Sure, Stevie. I'm sure that's it. She came to her senses walking the beach in Florida in her bikini showing off for the college boys. Just keep telling yourself that."

Alison gave a mild doubting look at Jillian.

"Maaaybe you're right. But think about it. Think about what she'd be losing. He's cute, has a hot bod, he's funny, he's kind of a deep thinker, kind of, he's a basketball star, he's not in love with himself like a lot of guys are—well maybe a little when he talks about basketball, but he is thoughtful. And he's working on being non-judgmental. And he writes poetry. What other guy does that that you know?"

I looked the other way, pretending not to hear while they discussed the dynamics of my personal likeability quotient. Deciding my rating on the Stevie-O-Meter. Where would the needle land on the scale of one to ten?

"I am kind of a big deal around here," I said. "You may have seen my work." They both laughed.

"But think about Mindy's personality," said Jillian, turning her cup in her hands as she spoke.

"From what I hear she's self-absorbed, thinks she's *all that*—entitled, privileged. She knows she's hot, she likes to be the center of attention, and she doesn't mind causing some trouble if that's what it takes. And she has, from what I've heard, a history of bouncing from guy to guy. The Law of Diminishing Returns. She always needs something more, somebody more. Goods and services. Supply and demand. Mindy operates in a free market economy as far as boyfriends go. Are you meeting her needs on a continual basis? You are kinda of a big deal when it comes to basketball, but what else ya got? Besides your handsome adolescent face, cool guy demeanor, wicked sense of humor and two rockin' older women you hang with?"

Alison turned back to look at me.

"You've got to take all that into consideration, Stevie. We don't want to see you get hurt. And you know her better than we do. But if you think she's going to change her ways just for you, I think not. You have to decide if what you're giving is worth what you're getting."

"Yeah. The Gordian Knot," I said, citing a reference from the Greek mythology course I had taken, referring to a problem with a seemingly unsolvable solution. "A conundrum. It's not like I'll lose any sleep over it or anything."

With that, we finished our coffees and got up to leave, my problem still problematical.

"Girls," I mock snarled.

"Guys," they rebutted in unison.

We left the coffee shop, teenage minds pondering teenage thoughts.

Chapter 33

The day after Christmas break ended we all, kids and teachers, struggled to get back into the school routine. Getting up at 6:30 after two weeks of staying up late, leisurely awakening at nine, ten or eleven, getting up only to throw yourself on the couch to watch TV after eating breakfast, those days now past. A sleepy school populace dragged themselves through the first day back to school. We trudged down the hall past the guidance office to lunch after morning classes, warehoused, sheeple, en masse, our bodies' actions dictated by the clock, by the spaces we inhabited from 7:45 to 2:30, biorhythms disturbed, passing classmates with the same zombie-like first-day-back looks on their faces, doppelgängers returning to class.

At lunch I sat with my Junior classmates. My group had appropriated about five round tables in an area adjacent to the seniors' tables at the beginning of the trimester at the cafeteria's far end. One table between the juniors and seniors served as a demilitarized zone, where juniors and seniors could sit together. Very rarely did anyone break the unwritten rules of the student cafeteria. Punishments consisted of, but were not limited to, having the elder classmates talk about you in a disparaging manner, snide remarks, and get-a-clue looks. Sophomores ate at the other end near the entrance where the display cases demarcated the hallway from the cafeteria, and freshmen sat, lunched, made noises, laughed at stupid stuff, threw food at each other, and generally acted like their squirrelly, immature selves, sequestered next to the sophomores where teachers on cafeteria

171

duty could keep an eye on them.

The unwritten rules permitted discretionary visitations from the frosh and sophs to our junior and senior end, allowing visits to the guys' tables if the visitor happened to be an especially cute girl. The rules also stated that if an upperclassman met with a lower class brother or sister it had to be in the middle, the neutral zone. Probably little Johnny or Susie wanting to borrow money for a giant cookie from the snack bar or asking for a ride home. Only social visitations allowed. Others keep out.

Sometimes the cafeteria lunch lines stretched out so that an underclassman stood only a few feet from our table. The deli line, next to the snack counter, abutted the senior tables by about ten feet and on days featuring nachos or sandwich wraps, students came hustling into the lengthening line that reached to our junior tables, the kids shoving, jockeying for position. Sometimes a freshman, thrown out of line by his elder classmates, flung over a chair, landed by, or on our table. Proper cafeteria decorum dictated that we straighten him up, give him a pat on the chest and like a too-small fish, throw him back. After all, we had been there too.

I sat down next to Hobie and our usual Junior lunch buddies, Kyle, Phil Cox, who everybody called "Philco," Eddie King, AKA known as "Eddie king," Jimmy "Smalls" Belinsky—weight three hundred, three oh five, expanding by the day, and Smalls' girlfriend Kayellen Laberdee. About all I knew about Kayellen is that she worked in the library, mostly at the desk by the entrance and would scan the bar code on your books when you checked them out. If anyone not having their book checked tried to sneak out the library's exit door, activating the sensor beep, Kayellen would immediately take the offensive, springing into action, grabbing the black hot-line phone to the office and report the absconder.

"We have a runner!"

The pursuit would be on, hall monitors summoned, book bags of hall walkers examined, restrooms inspected, teachers asked to check their hall pass logs. Nabbed offenders taken by their ear to the office, a hall monitor returning the book to its flock, a grand entrance entering the library, book held aloft as if it had been the Holy Grail, serving as a warning for all those assembled researching, homework doing, pleasure reading gathered at the library's tables and computers, a message for anyone who had even a fleeting thought that they could get away with pilfering a Jackson High School periodical, book of fiction or non.

Kayellen possessed another talent besides manning the bar code scanner. Given any opportunity in school and out, she checked her cell phone mega times per minute at an alacrity here-to-fore unknown, scrolling the screen at a remarkable, implausible speed, thumbs and fingers in an enviable, blurring, dextrous display of manual dexterity. Her fingers received and delivered texts in nanoseconds. Many of her classmates possessed admirable, though lesser, textability skills, but Kayellen's flew off the charts, her texting prowess nonpareil, legendary.

Eddie King backed up Jose' at point guard, but also played three quarters JV (you were allowed to play five quarters a night, so he had two remaining in case Jose' got into foul trouble or suffered an injury). Eddie had two brothers at the high school, Albert and Freddy. We also had two other Eddie's in the Junior class, so to avoid confusion— "Which King are you talking about? Which Eddie are you talking about?" Eddie had conglomerated his names. Some of us accented the Eddie, some of us King, voice rising in pitch. EddieKING! Eddie often referred to himself in the third person - only he pronounced "King" as "Kang," as in, "Eddiekang, he ain't goin' for that." Eddieking normally didn't say much, but would insert a line here and there that ranked high on the entertainment index, worthy of repeating whenever and wherever the guys gathered. We imitated his syntax, which

Eddieking seemed to enjoy, made him officially one of our prime dudes. "I be Eddiekang," became a fan favorite that Eddie used whenever he accomplished any noteworthy act, like scoring and getting fouled on a corkscrew drive to the basket in practice or getting a decent grade on a big test. We appropriated his catchphrase.

Hobie: "What did you get on your Chem test?"

Me: "93. I be Eddiekang."

Hobie banking in a twenty-five foot three pointer at the end of a quarter in a practice scrimmage:

Me: "Woah, Dude."

Hobie: "I be Eddiekang."

And the first time Hobie saw me talking with Mindy in the hall.

Hobie: "You move with alacrity, my man. I think you hit the mama lode."

Me: "I be Eddiekang."

Kyle's hair appeared unusually kempt today, as opposed to unkempt, probably at Josie's urging. Well, Josie's insistence. Well, Josie probably combed it for him. Kyle and I both brown bagged it. My mom still made my lunch for me. I told her many times that I should be doing that at my age but she said she enjoyed doing it. And yeah, she did put in little notes for me occasionally, a show of a mother's love for her son. Aware that most moms stopped with the lunch notes when their kids reached fourth grade, I made sure I pocketed those right away before my tablemates noticed.

"Hope you're having a great day, Honey!" "Do your best today, Stevie!" But she also would write notes with quotes she had read, sometimes biblical, sometimes philosophical. I unfurled today's: "Even youths grow tired and weary, and young men stumble and fall; but those who hope in the Lord will renew their strength. They will soar on wings like eagles; they will run and not grow weary, they will walk and not be faint." When I got home I'd add it to the collection I kept in my dresser drawer. Never know when Mom would have an inquisition as to if I had read them.

Philco and Smalls and I bantered about Kyle and the Rabbits' performance. Eddieking leaned back in his chair, eyes closed, listening to his head phones, head slightly moving to a rap song beat.

"Man, you guys rocked. They're talking about you guys in all my classes," Philco said as he inspected the mozzarella sticks on his food tray.

Tuesday's lunch menu always featured mozzarella sticks with marinara sauce. Six elongated crispy, crusty fried brown gooey cheesy globs stared up at Philco from their white cardboard basket. A cafeteria favorite when paired with mashed potatoes. Per federal and state child nutrition guidelines the cafeteria server ladies also plopped a required veggie - green beans, broccoli, cauliflower, carrots - into one of the food tray compartments. These generally completed their lives in futility, shunned, uneaten in their journey from farm to supplier to school to plate waste to rubber trash tub to garbage truck to landfill.

I eyed Phil's red-orange plastic cafeteria tray. Some jokester had written "Vacuum Butt" on it with a black permanent marker. I didn't know the meaning of "vacuum butt" but hoped I'd never have one or be one. Sounded painful and embarrassing. I briefly thought about the jokester's thought process as he graffittied the tray, wondering if he - had to be a he - knew his tray defacing would be the butt of jokes for future students, a running joke about posteriors for cafeteria posterity.

Kyle nodded at Phil's remark, enjoying his new-found celebrity status. Smalls already had attacked his lunch, having stuffed a big bite of a baloney and mayo sandwich into his mouth, shaking his head, agreeing, cheeks enlarged. Smalls corroborated Phil's approval of Rabbits In the Living Room, adding something that sounded like "Crat snide fone, Kawl," his words muffled by his mouthful. I stared at him for a moment, trying to decipher the quasi-words that had emanated from Smalls' mouth. Kyle nodded, looking inside his brown paper lunch bag. Apparently Kyle spoke, or at least understood, mufflage, Smalls' preferred lunchtime language of communication. Kyle asked what I had today.

"Peanut butter and jelly. The no mix good stuff PB and blueberry preserves on multi-grain wheat bread. Green and red peppers in a baggie with dill dip. Apple slices. And a homemade oatmeal raisin cookie that Mama Kalkannes made."

I held up the clear baggies for Kyle to take a look, to verify the foodstuffs I possessed. All to be sloshed down with a half-pint brown carton of fat-free chocolate milk with a smiling cow on the side. I had decided to go veggie for at least a week, Alison's influence, of course. My mom approved. I eyed Kyle's brown bag.

"What's you got?"

Kyle showed me his sandwich, holding it up for my scrutiny. Some yellow thin cardboardy substance on white bread.

"An ungrilled cheese."

"That's some mighty good cuisine you got there."

Pointing at the accoutrements accompanying the ungrilled cheese sandwich I asked Kyle what else Dad Mahoney had packed for him. Kyle's dad, a sometime pipe fitter at the oil production plant on the east side of Jackson, made Kyle's lunch along with his own every morning.

"Famous Dave's barbecued potato chips, and a monstrous energy drink. And an orange. Want it? I don't eat oranges. Why did my dad put it in there? My family doesn't eat fruit."

"I'll pass for now, but thanks."

Kyle launched his orange toward the waste barrel five feet away from our table. It landed atop lunch period A's residue from their trays and lunch bags - small containers of applesauce, half eaten sandwiches, pizza crusts, brown bags with potato chip stains.

I hadn't talked with Kyle since the garage band concert. Josie had asked if I would change seats with her in Food and Fitness that morning so she could sit next to Kyle. I said I didn't mind as long as Mrs. Gordon approved. Somehow Josie convinced Mrs. G. that the move would be a good one, that she could help Kyle with the worksheets that Mrs G. routinely gave us. Five minutes into class I looked across the room to their table. They both stifled giggles, pinky touching, giving each other footies under the table. "Oh, this is a good idea," I had said to myself. After finishing a green pepper with a crunch, a swallow, and a swig of milk I said to Kyle,

"Looks like things are going good with you and Josephine. That she asked to move her seat next to yours to further your educational advancement. What a selfless act. Mother Teresa has nothing on her."

Smalls gulped down a bite and said, "Wait! What's this? You're going with who?!!"

I had seen Smalls at the Rabbits' garage gig, keeping the boxes of donuts busy, and standing near the rear under the open garage door. Smalls never wore a coat, to my knowledge. Usually bare-armed, came to school in shorts until the temperature dropped to near zero. Smalls' RITLR concert attire consisted of a triple X sized t-shirt, overalls, work boots with undone laces and a winter bomber hat with upturned fleece flaps. One of those big guys whose temps always ran hot. Smalls must not have witnessed the Kyle and Josie puppy love festings. Some of us hadn't been so lucky.

"Whom, it's whom, not who and it's Josie."

"She's more a what than a who, or a whom! She'll eat you alive, Kyle. Literally, figuratively. Both of those. You've heard of female praying mantises eating their mates, right?"

Kyle scratched his head with both hands.

"How can you stand all that girl's sarcasm?"

"Josie gets me. And she has these cute nicknames she gives me."

Phil asked, "Don't Josie and Jose' have two older sisters?"

"Yep. Nikayla and Morena," I said. "They're sweeties."

Smalls breathed deeply, audibly.

"I know that Jose' is a good guy, but I think Daddy Jimenez should have ceased begetting when the begatting was good."

We pondered, ate, pondered.

Philco leaned over to Smalls. "You just got crossed off their wedding guest list."

After a minute I asked Kyle, "By the way, what was it she called you after class when we were walking out?"

"Her little idiot savant."

"How charming. Doesn't that hurt your self esteem?"

"I find it cute, thank you."

Between bites of the second half of my sandwich I asked, "What do you call her?"

"My tweetheart."

Smalls, Philco and I did a collective groan. Kayellen looked up, briefly stretched her fingers twice, frowned and looked back down at her cell phone and resumed thumbing through her text messages and websites. Eddieking frowned along with Kayellen.

"That girl ain't right. Sumpin' wrong with that child."

Kyle ignored Eddieking.

"I'm not sure about the chemistry between us, but there sure is lot of biology and anatomy. And I like her geography. Good topography."

I put down my sandwich. I threw an imaginary penalty flag in the air.

"Excessive use of personal details. Fifteen yards from the point of the foul. That's way, way too much information. Off the grid. Unacceptable in a communal setting. Disturbing."

Kyle lowered his head to the edge of the yellow substance sticking out, lifted up the top slice of bread, probed the cheese with his finger and replied with a grinning mono-syllable.

"Yup."

We digested Kyle's comments along with our lunches. Actually, I had to be happy for Kyle because Josie made him happy, but also a little concerned because of what he ate for lunch. Day after day Kyle ate bag-packed crapola. Kyle had told us from time to time about his home life. It could be described as turbulent, unsettled. His mom and dad drank too much, smoked too much, fought too much. Dad had been laid off frequently, mom worked for minimum wage at a retirement home. They stayed up too late, watched television to the wee hours, and their rented house in such poor shape that Kyle said he wasn't allowed to have his friends over. But Kyle wore a daily happy face to school.

When Kyle finished the examination of his cheese sandwich I asked, "Kyle, do you ever ask your dad to give you something, something, a little more healthy and appetizing for lunch?"

"I don't like to complain. My dad always says 'Don't complain, don't explain.' We qualify for the reduced price lunch program, but my dad says that's too embarrassing and he wouldn't sign the form."

"Well, if it was me I think I'd forge his signature. And I'd take your lunch back home tonight and I *would* complain. Give your dad some feedback."

Kayellen, without looking up from her phone, said, "Feedback. Literally and figuratively. Tangible and intangible."

We had to think about that one. You could see our brains whirring, stuck in neutral. The girl had a quick mind. She tolerated us, the mental sloths, sitting with her for God knows what reason.

"Good one, Kayellen," finally said Smalls. "I get it. *Feed*, like in *food*."

179

Smalls offered Kayellen a fist bump. But that meant a cessation of her texting. Kayellen offered an elbow for Smalls to bump. Smalls lightly knuckle-bumped his girlfriend's elbow.

"I take what I can get," he sighed.

We knew who wore the pants in that relationship.

I made a mental note to ask Mom for an extra baggie of veggies for Kyle. Maybe not kale for Kyle, but broccoli, celery and carrots with dill dip. Kyle's taste buds and digestive system had been duly warned, the battle to be waged every forthcoming school day during Lunch B.

Halfway through lunch Hobie wandered back from the snack bar to our table, turned a chair around backward and sat down, carrying a figure-eight soft pretzel and a small paper cup of cream cheese. His attention had been directed at Cheyenne Gilchrist, a senior marketing ed student who worked the snack counter during A and B lunch periods.

"Honing in on Cheyenne, are you?" I asked Hobie.

"Nooo. Well maybe. Yes."

"So you're a honer."

"No. Definitely not. Well maybe. Yes."

"What about Piper? I thought you guys were pretty tight."

"We are. But Cheyenne's got something Piper doesn't have."

"Pretzels?"

"More than that. I like Piper because she's kind of innocent. One of those rich kid private school girls who's really shy around guys because she's gone to all girl schools all her life. Cheyenne's like eighteen going on twenty-two. She works two jobs, has a fantasy football team, and tells dirty jokes. They're complete opposites. She asked me to go to the Valentine dance thing next month with her."

"So let me get this right. You have two girlfriends now."

"Yeah. I guess I do."

Two more than I had.

Philco threw in a comment. "Spin and win."

Hobie continued, "And as luck would have it, Piper's going skiing that weekend with her family. I'm golden."

"For now," said Smalls.

"What is this, man, rutting season?" added Eddieking.

"Listen carefully. Our menu has recently changed," I said.

We all looked at Hobie. Even Kayellen looked up from her cell phone, her texting fingers overheated, slightly smoking. None of us said anything else, just four owl-eyes looks staring at Hobie.

Hobie grinned and said, "I'm only seventeen. How do I know what make and model is best for me unless I do a little sampling? I always swipe right."

Kayellen, texting again — Breaking News!— most certainly to her friends about Hobie's infidelity, commented, "Disgusting. Guys are just...disgusting."

Smalls didn't say anything, but pointed a finger at himself, incredulous, deploying his air bags, mouthing the question, "Me?"

After all, he thought he had passed Kayellen's field test for dependability.

Philco kicked back in his chair, looking around the cafeteria hoping for aberrant entertaining behavior and added, "Guilty until proven innocent. Due process a fleeting dream for those of us of the philandering male gender. Myself, I take the Alford Plea."

Eddieking, headphones around his neck, offered,

"A man gonna do what a man gonna do."

Smalls, Philco, and I looked at each other. Either extremely pithy or extremely stupid what Eddieking had said, we weren't sure. Then we nodded together, pursing our lips, eyebrows raised. Pithiness prevailed.

The cafeteria monitor, the new ninth grade algebra teacher and freshman boys basketball coach, Tyrell South, duly and dully read the usual impersonal lunch period ending instructions into a microphone at the snack bar.

"Clean up your tables. Throw the trash in the receptacles. Water bottles, cans, plastic in the recycling bins. Put your trays back in the stacks. Push your chairs in then you can leave. Everybody have a great day."

We cleaned up our table, pushed in our chairs, pitched our trash into the receptacles, energy drink and water bottles in the recycling, put our trays back in the stacks and trooped off to class. Have a great day? Maybe. I remembered not to be judgmental and blame the day for any indiscretions.

Chapter 34

Still wanting sleep I slow-motioned up the stairs to my locker the following day, a Tuesday morning. Back from Florida, awaiting me—Miss Derosiers. Arms folded, fingers around her elbows, and a smile. Looking great. Me: disheveled, hair being its unruly self. Basketball shoes: untied. Khakis: wrinkled. Sweater: old, brownish yellow, hole under one arm. Also wrinkled. I looked at her with a dumb look. Shouldn't there be an advance notice? I hadn't seen Mindy in school yesterday. She and Dad Derosiers must have flown back home last night.

"Were you ever going to text me back?"

"Had to think about it. I thought you and K.J. had something going."

I stood looking at her, thumbs hooked around the straps on my backpack.

"No, silly. Why didn't you go to Lonnie's after your game? I thought we were meeting there but you didn't show up."

I turned away, started dialing the combination on my locker, thinking what to say. Mindy moved closer. Whatever numbers I dialed had no connection whatsoever with my combination.

"When I saw you and K.J. in the gym, well, I thought, you know..."

"We're just friends. I was consoling him."

Consoling. So that's what she called it. I think I needed the consoling more than K.J.

She touched my arm with one finger.

"Can we go out this weekend? We'll have fun, I promise. A

good time, a *very* good time, will be had by all."

She squeezed my arm then put her index finger on my lips to shush me as I turned toward her and started to respond.

"Don't say no. Just text me later. You know you want to."

I watched her walk down the hall. I knew I wanted to.

"Are you going back with her?"

I jumped as Hobie had walked up and stood right behind me.

"Didn't see ya, bro."

"You looked a little, a wee bit preoccupied. And now you're post occupied. She's got you around her pinky finger. Why's your face all red?"

"She asked me to go out with her this weekend."

"You seem a little nervous about that."

"Maybe."

Kyle walked up, giving me a puzzled look and said to Hobie, "The dude's looking a little sketchy this A.M."

"He's going to go out with Mindy again. The boy's a mite flustered. She just got up close and personal with him. In fact, I can still smell her."

Hobie pulled on the arm of my sweater, thumbing the shoulder toward Kyle.

"Have a smell."

Kyle sniffed.

"Ya. Nice."

"Alright, guys," I said. "It's just a date."

Kyle looked at Hobie. Hobie looked at Kyle. Both smirking.

"What?" I asked.

Hobie put his hand on my shoulder.

"Brother, a date with Mindy…is not 'just' a date."

He looked down, searching for words, found them.

"You know that she's a mind messer. Your brain is awash with Oxytocin. The love drug. You can't think normally. She makes you stupid. Being in her presence, just thinking about being with

184

Mindy may cause you to experience nausea, cramps, excessive sweating, shortness of breath, hyperventilating, weight loss, sleep deprivation, excessive urination, loss of ability to articulate thoughts, stammering, decreases in judgment, insight, reliability and impulse control."

Kyle nodded.

"Yeah. All that."

I kept dialing my locker combination, spinning the lock as Hobie detailed the contingencies I might face. The combination escaped me. Hoisting my backpack without the stuff I needed for first period I sloughed off to class, but headed in the wrong direction. Hobie caught my arm, turned me around and as he gave me a slight shove in the right direction, said, "You'll be all right. Or not."

Chapter 35

The season played on, with our team gaining confidence. Tommy returned from the DL, scarred literally but not figuratively. Coach gave Tommy his starting position back after two practices. Jason took it well, telling Coach, "Whatever I can do to help the team." My thinking was sort of along those lines: Whatever I can do to help the team—as long as I start.

The girls' team had started out strong also, winning eight of their first ten. It became a kind of competition between us and the girls to see who would have the better record. I pretended not to care, though when Josie sent verbal potshots my way when we lost it irritated me.

"*Really* nice game last night, Stevie," she'd say, the remark dripping with sarcasm.

Josie and I had sparred since junior high. Since I hadn't played the past two years I had more-or-less dried up as one of her sources of derision. But the hiatus had ended when I went back to playing this year. Josie thrived on getting under my skin. She had other targets, too, male and female, adults and adolescents, but I seemed to be her featured prey. When we met the Sunday night for the draft for Hobie's Student Fantasy League Josie's cunning reached its epitome.

Hobie announced each draft pick as if he were the NFL commissioner. While I looked at my sheet of remaining students, studying who I should take in the second round, my attention quickly diverted to astonishment.

"With her first round pick, Josie Jimenez chooses Stevie Kalkannes."

Stunned, I looked over at Josie sitting on the couch next to Kyle. She slapped her knee and laughed so hard she had tears streaming out of her eyes.

"She can't do that, Hobie!" I yelled in desperation.

"She can and she did. Nothing you can do about it."

That nefarious, scheming mammal. She knew I couldn't do anything to hurt her chances of winning by sandbagging my tests, because, well, these would be my grades we're talking about. I'd be sabotaging my own grades for the purpose of seeing her team lose. Plus my grades counted for my team, too. She had me. On days that I had a test that Josie knew about—she had Mr. O'Donnell as I did—when she'd see me Josie would say,

"Do your best on your test today, Stevie. Countin' on ya."

I usually hit her with a comeback that fell a little short.

"Shut up."

I remember thinking that Josie would be someone I'd read about in the papers several years from now on the lamb, someone who embezzled millions and disappeared without a trace. Always scheming. Always looking for an edge. Not only wanting to win but wanting to embarrass.

When it came down to the dregs of the draft choices, Kyle's name along with five or six others remained on the board. Certainly Josie would choose her BF with her last pick to complete her team. Nope, she had said. Didn't want to put too much pressure on the boy. She knew Kyle would be a liability to her chance at winning. Her team name: the Serpent's Teeth. She liked the Shakespearean phrase "How sharper than a serpent's tooth it is to have a thankless child." Fitting.

The girls had a home game against Holland Wednesday, a non-league team the girls considered a big rival because of the tight

187

games they had played the last few years. Holland had won most of those, and had advanced far into the state tournament, to the district finals and regionals on a yearly basis. As we ended practice and the custodians flipped the switch to activate the bleachers accordian-like slow motion expansion from the walls, the guys talked about going to the game. The girls drew about a hundred or two hundred a game on weeknights, double that when they played on a Friday or Saturday night. We—the guys— usually came close to the gym capacity of fifteen hundred, especially against league schools. I liked going to the girls' games. My buddies and I could spread out, lean back, joke around, sometimes try to get under the skin of one of the opponents' girls, especially those who displayed fine genetics and/or athletic prowess.

"Hobester, will you be attending tonight's encounter between our beloved Kestrel girls basketball team and the Blue Zippers of Holland High School?" I asked Hobie as we stood by our locker room door. "Good seats still available, but I hear they're going fast."

"I'll check to see if I can get a ticket on Stub Hub," Hobie said, wiping away sweat on his face with his practice jersey, watching the bleachers mechanically conveying themselves outward as the side baskets droned up to the ceiling's edge.

Hobie and I planted ourselves in the second row across from the girls' bench, popcorn and soft drinks in hand. At the boys' game the students all stood from tip-off to game's end. At the girls' games we—especially the boys basketball players—laid back in the hard plastic bleacher seats, aloof, giving the appearance of doing the girls a favor by being there. But sometime during the first quarter I had a startling revelation. Something I hadn't really realized before. Just how good a player Josie was. She flew up and down the court. Sleek. With grace. Fluid. Turbo-charged. She weaved and water-bugged her way around and through the opponents, the ball like a string on her fingers, at Josie's acrobatic command. Saw the game develop. Made the right moves, the right decisions. All the time.

Why hadn't I noticed this before? Probably because I, like my buddies, didn't give the girls their due, this being *only* a girls basketball game. At times it looked as if the other team played five-against-one, all five players guarding Josie. Her Kestrel teammates had wide open shots but couldn't seem to hit any. Our girls' talent level nowhere near compared with the Blue Zippers'—except for Josie. The other starters, Cristina, Delavan, Genesis, and Harmony, averaged about twenty points a game among them. As Josie said, although their shooting range extended to about fifteen feet away from the basket, their making range only extended to about five feet. Josie provided the other twenty-five to thirty a game. On average.

On defense Josie pestered Holland's point guard so badly, stealing the ball from her and forcing her into turnover after turnover, traveling and making bad passes, that their coach had to take her out of the game. Twice Josie faked as if she had been headed upcourt after she scored, her back to Holland's in-bounder, only to turn and quickly dart in to steal the inbound pass and score. And what quick hands she had, flicking dribbles off their guards' hands, off their legs and out-of-bounds. I had seen Hobie do that in a boys' game occasionally, but Josie did it several times to the Holland girls. It got so that when whoever Josie guarded received a pass, they immediately passed it to a teammate so they would avoid Josie's intensive pressure. Their large center tried to set screens on Josie near half court but Josie, arms extended, moving her legs and feet with quickness, sensed the screens, got skinny—a term coaches use—and around them. Two illegal, "moving" screens were called on the Zippers' center before their coach, a young athletic woman with short cropped dark hair and sharp facial features, went to having two guards

189

bring the ball up, then when Josie surprised them with run-and-jump double teams their coach had a forward bring up the ball, with some success.

The game came down to the final minute. Josie had been fouled with six seconds to go and with her girls down by one point, went to the line for two free throws. She calmly sunk them both, then playing safety, her range sideline-to-sideline, stole a long pass from a Zipper girl to seal the win. For the game Josie had shot eleven free throws, made eleven free throws. And added twenty-seven points, six steals, five rebounds and five assists. All in a night's work for Josie.

After the game I hung around with Hobie and the girls' new fan, Kyle, waiting for them to emerge from their locker room. I stood at the back of those waiting, maintaining my cool, looking as dispassionate as I could while the girls accepted the well wishes of their fans, friends, and family. Their coach, Mrs. Trubee, walked by and gave Josie a big squeezy hug as Josie gave a tight-lipped happy, not wanting-it-to-look-too-egotistical smile. She saved those for me. As the group broke up, as Kyle and Josie started heading toward the exit—Kyle carrying Josie's equipment bag—I had to ask Josie something. I forced myself to get Josie's attention.

"Josie, what do you think about right before you shoot your free throws?"

"Does that mean you're congratulating me?"

"Sure. Whatever you want it to mean. Just tell me."

A sly smile came across her face. She knew she would now be one-up in our gamesmanship contest. Not that we kept score, but I knew that Josie knew this could be a time she could really connect with a verbal shot, diss me and dismiss my request. But she chose the high road and let me in on her secret to success.

"I sing happy birthday to myself."

"You   do   what?"

"I sing happy birthday to myself. My birthday is my favorite day of the whole year. I want to be happy when I shoot foul shots. And since I almost always make them it makes me happy when I go to the line."

I couldn't even speak. I had no comeback. I had nothin'. None of the coaches I ever had mentioned singing a happy song to yourself when you went to the free throw line. They always talked about taking a deep breath, relaxing and good fundamentals. The yoga mindset hadn't quite taken hold yet. I hadn't made the total commitment, the transition from letting go of the old behavior patterns, hadn't developed the calm mind that yoga promised if I would have only wholly believed in its mindfulness tenets. In the studio's dark tranquil atmosphere I had begun feeling confident, visualizing my body's movements, my mood relaxed. In a packed field house under the lights I couldn't shut out the crowd, the significance of the make or miss. I stared at Josie with as dumb a look as my face could show. Josie then sang Happy Birthday to herself, just in case I didn't know the lyrics. Her face beamed as she sang. Kyle nodded along happily.

Happy Birthday to Me
Happy Birthday to Me
Happy Birthday to Josie
Happy Birthday to Me

"That's just so, so stupid. Who told you to do that?" I said when Josie finished.

"Nobody. I just came up with it on my own. It works, doesn't it?"

Hands in my Kestrels letter jacket pockets, I sighed heavily.

"Yeah, I guess it does. What about when you miss? Do you still sing Happy Birthday?"

"I change when I miss till I make one again. But unlike *you, I* hardly ever miss - as you know."

Verbal jab landed.

"OK, I'll bite. What do you sing then, when you miss?"

"Lefty loosey, righty tighty. I say that twice to myself to correct all the technicalities that go into my shot. Reminds me to keep my elbow in with my right hand under the ball, and to hold the ball loose—or is it loosely, I forget—with my left hand on the side of the ball with my fingers pointed up."

"I don't think they're called 'technicalities.' I think you mean techniques, or more correctly, fundamentals."

"It works doesn't it? Not like your technicalities do."

"Correlation doesn't always imply causation."

"English, please."

"You can't tell me that singing some stupid song or a simple-minded phrase causes you to make your free throws."

"They do and it does. You seem to lack the credentials at the present time to be telling *anyone* how to make their free throws."

Hobie, overhearing the conversation while waiting to give me a ride home said, "The language game is so to say something unpredictable. I mean, it is not based on grounds. It is not reasonable or unreasonable. It is there—like our life. That's a quote from Wittgenstein."

Oh, that clears things up for me, I thought.

After taking Kyle by the hand, Josie turned back to me.

"If they ain't hatin', you ain't poppin'."

Ouch. A kidney punch followed by a right cross. A technical knockout, a TKO. A dollop of sarcasm added to a dose of criticism. Kyle shrugged his shoulders, looking puzzled, but nodding as Josie gave the tip of her index finger a quick lick and flicked it in my direction. Chalk another one up for Josie.

Chapter 36

We hit the halfway mark in the season in a tie with Midlothian, both of us with 6 and 1 league records. Upper Sandusky fell to third place after getting upset by Sun Prairie. The Prairie Dogs had been playing better, with three sophomores in their starting line-up. A road trip to Sun Prairie, the longest one we'd take in the regular season, loomed at schedule's end. The coaches warned us about looking ahead. But we all knew the schedule, and heck, the coaches had even put up the school athletic teams' poster on the bulletin board in the locker room (with a Lonnie's Pizzeria ad and a photo of a grinning Lonnie at the bottom), and we couldn't fail to notice that we played at Midlothian at the end of the week. But next up, the Deshler Dreadnaughts.

Deshler High School had seen better days. Their school had been built around 1910. A dark-bricked building with high arching windows, it looked like a World War I airplane hangar from outside. Foreboding aged brick turrets looked down at us from the roof. Deshler had been a perennial bottom dweller in our league since I could remember. We even used to pound them in junior high. But this night, a sleeting, drizzling Tuesday in late January proved to be different.

The coaches prepared us as usual, Coach Arnold warning us that Deshler could probably beat the Boston Celtics three out of five. Their top scorer, Dwayne Hickey, only averaged eight and a half points a game. They played a packed in zone defense and prayed the other team had a bad shooting night. Pulling up to the school in our bus I became immediately depressed. Letter jackets tugged over our heads with one hand to ward off the rain, the other clutching our black and red equipment bags, we walked in through the large heavy wooden doors down a dimly lit hallway, over threadbare carpeting to the gym. I don't think any of the team photos in the display cases pictured anyone still alive. One caught my eye. A black and white framed photo, guys wearing what looked like white tank tops with an Old English D on the front, and shorts that only went halfway to the knee posed standing around a trophy, the player in the middle holding what looked more like a medicine ball than a basketball with "1929 County Champs" brush-painted in white on the ball. They must have been deadly with the two-hand set shots. Their last championship, I wondered?

We sat through the first half of the JV game, watching the Dreadnaught junior varsity struggle to get the ball past half court. The Dreadnaught players looked dejected three minutes into the game, getting pummeled by our junior varsity 12-0. We half-listened to our coaches in the pre-game locker room talk, and went mindlessly through our warm-up routine. The Dreadnaughts' coach must have given his team a heck of a long pre-game speech. Five minutes into the twenty minutes between games he still hadn't brought his team out on the court. The Dreadnaught cheerleaders, looking expectantly toward the door at the end of the gym that led down the worn steps to the Dreadnaught locker room began chanting.

Where's our Dreadnaughts
Where's our team?
Down in the locker room
Pickin' up steam!

Ten minutes passed on the clock. Still no Dreadnaughts. Going through our shooting drills we had a hard time paying attention, our eyes continually glancing toward the end of the gym, checking for the Dreadnaughts' appearance. We looked over at Coach Arnold. He just shrugged his shoulders and gave us a puzzled look. A ploy by Deshler to get us off our game? A buzz could be heard in the stands, shaking of heads, men in farmers' hats, plaid shirts and jeans standing in the bleachers with their hands in their pockets, talking, occasionally gesturing toward Deshler's bench and entrance to the gym as the clock wound down to game time.

Hobie, as had been our ritual all year, had gone in front of me in the lay-up and shooting line. After we both rebounded for teammates' jump shots in the opposite line and had jogged over to the shooting line, Hobie turned to me.

"What the heck is going on? Why aren't they warming up?"

"Maybe we should send out an APB to try to find them."

"A what?"

"All Points Bulletin, like the Highway Patrol does. Put up road blocks. Activate the spike strips on the nearest highway. Check the outgoing flights. Bring in the search dogs. Alert the news stations. More information as it becomes available."

The Deshler band played "We Will Rock You" as their students shouted 'Rock You!' at the appointed time.

"I think they're just messin' with us," said Hobie. Trying to get our minds off our game. Tryin' to get into our heads."

"Ya think?"

"I'm sure of it. What a dastardly, diabolical, heinous, vile, evil tactic. Underhanded. Shameful. Contemptible. We'll give no quarter. They'll be squirming, pleading. Leniency will not be shown. We'll eat their livers."

"I don't think there's any rule that says you have to warm up. Maybe they won't be sweaty. That Hickey dude really oozes sweat. His sweat glands should sue for time and a half pay. Didn't you guard him a little in our last game? First minute of the game

195

we were next to each other on the lane on a free throw and he tried to step in front of me. Slimed me with his arm. Got his DNA all over me. Refs shouldn't allow that. Should be a rule."

I imitated a referee making the sliming call.

"Number twelve! Excessive sliming!"

And then flicked away imaginary excessive sweat from my arms and called a technical, alternately pointing, one arm in the air to signal a foul, then smelling and flicking away imaginary sweat from my forearm.

We found out later that Deshler had gone through their warm-ups in the small practice gym at the other end of the school, one that even pre-dated the dungeon-like gym they played in now. I recalled playing in it in junior high. Cracked floorboards, arching block glass windows at the south end, overhead a running track that likely hadn't been used since one of the world wars, an old scoreboard hanging down from a railing at the north end on which the hands of a clock spun slowly around counting down the time in the quarters, the score numbers under "Home" and "Visitor" ceasing to work long ago, replaced by flip-cards with home score in green, visitors in red used by a manager at the scorer's table to keep the tally. Dimly lit, birds flew in through cracks in the roof, nested in the corners among the ancient ductwork. And that's where the Dreadnaughts' varsity had warmed up, then raced through the hallways down to the main gym, making their entrance with thirty seconds to go in warm-ups, thirty seconds after the buzzer sounded with one minute to bring the teams to their benches to ready for introductions. Indeed this had been a strategy by their coach, Buzzy Highwater, to distract us, to maybe give his team an early advantage, and conceivably steal a win that would make their miserable season more tolerable, give Buzzy something, anything, good to talk about at their end of year team awards night.

Well, Deshler got their wish. We had a bad shooting night. I missed my first four shots, two threes, a pull up jumper and a driving lay-up, made a three, then missed two more, then got whistled for traveling. I followed that hi-light by throwing a pass to Kenny on the wing, who had cut backdoor when I thought he wouldn't. Turned into two points when Hickey intercepted and went down and laid it in and I fouled him from behind. Thirty seconds later I fouled him again when I let him drive around me, bumping him with my hip. Not my best half. We trailed 28-16 and coach read us the riot act at the intermission.

"You guys got yourself in this hole, now get yourselves out. One pass and a shot just about every time down. Is that how you beat a zone? I think we reversed the ball three times the whole half. Is that what we practiced? K.J. and Tommy — you guys might want to think about moving on offense, not burying yourselves on the baseline. You know what to do, cut to the open spots, go to the short corner and mid-post. Jose', Kenny, Stevie, what happened to penetrate and pitch? We're two for twelve on threes. Whatever you're doin,' it ain't workin'. And Stevie, are you interested in playing any defense tonight? Hickey has thirteen of their points. You're making him first team all-league in one half."

I couldn't argue. I began my psyching myself up process. Dwayne Hickey was going to be in for a rude awakening in the second half. No way he'd get to the basket on me. I'd frustrate him, get a hand on his passes, a hand in his face every time he shot. An attitude adjustment in place, we took the court with a minute to go for a few shots (I nailed both threes I took from the left side, giving me a shot of confidence), then trotted over to the bench.

"Work the ball, fellas, work the ball," counseled Coach Arnold.

And we did. Going inside out, K.J. passed back out to Jose' for a three at the point, then threw a diagonal pass to Kenny when the double team came and Kenny got to the basket on a dribble drive, drew the foul and converted for a three point play. 28-21. I face guarded Hickey, denying him the ball on Deshler's first two possessions of the second half. Confidence growing, our defense had thrown up roadblocks to the Dreadnaughts' patterned offense. Hickey's not going to get the ball, much less a good look at the basket the whole half, I told myself. But then, *Bam!* Their big forward drilled me on a down screen trying to free Hickey. A moving pick. An illegal screen. Their forward had extended his forearms and sent me sailing as I tried to get around him.

Then The Call:

"Foul on Red number 22." My number.

The ref, a short guy with Napoleonic little man tendencies, made a pushing motion, clasping his fingers under and around his right wrist and making an exaggerated shoving movement with his right palm, then bowlegged away with a smug look, thinking he had made the correct call, demonstrated the correct mechanics right out of the official referees' handbook. There was no way! Coach Arnold and Coach Pettaway were always telling us to keep our arms out, away from our bodies (The "Wide Defense Is Good Defense Theory"). That made it much harder for an opponent to screen you.

I pointed at myself and said, rather loud, in Little Napoleon's direction, "ME? ARE YOU KIDDING?!!"

I think he might have T'd me up, but his attention had been quickly diverted by Coach Arnold angrily waving his program in the ref's direction and yelling. I stood staring, unbelieving. Then I saw Hobie heading for the scorer's table, check in, and head in my direction. Shaking my head no in the diminutive ref's direction, I jogged to the bench, slapping Hobie's hand on his way in. Coach Arnold seethed, transferring his wrath from the ref to me.

"Just not your night, Stevie. Yeah it's a crappy call, but you can't be yelling at the ref. Let me handle that. Have a seat."

The ref's call infused our team with determination, made us mad. Hobie dogged Hickey, and our defense stiffened. The offense got back on track, but not full force. Deshler kept double teaming our posts when they caught the ball on the block, and our perimeter shots missed more often than they hit their mark. Deshler clung to their lead. Meanwhile, I sat.

With four minutes to go Kenny stole an inbounds pass when Coach slapped on our full court press after Tommy made the second of a two shot free throw. Kenny laid the ball in, cutting the Dreadnaughts' lead to four, 42-38. After a few more nerve-wracking possessions by each team and time-outs for strategy, we still trailed, but had cut the lead to one. Two opportunities to grab the lead went awry, one with a minute ten to go when K.J. missed a wide-open power lay-up, coming down with a backside offensive rebound, then powering it up too hard as it sailed off the other side of the rim with a minute five to go, then Jose' missing a contested lay-up after a steal when we double-teamed Hickey at half-court and Jose' stole Hickey's pass out of the trap (the refs missing a Dreadnaught body foul, pushing Jose' off balance).

With twenty seconds to go the Dreadnaughts bled the clock, played keep-away, stalling with their one point lead, 48-47. But Hobie, playing Hickey insanely tight, slapped the ball off Hickey's leg and out of bounds, the ball shooting over the end line in our half of the court. So we had to go the length of the court to get a shot, a shot to win. Coach Arnold signaled a time-out to draw up our Hail Mary play. The players in the game sat on the bench, directly in front of Coach Arnold, on one knee, talking and diagramming a play on his playboard. Those of us not in the game formed a semi-circle around Coach's back, watching the X's and O's, our offense against their defense, that he drew on the board. I caught some of what Coach told the team, but not all.

Their pep band pumped out their fight song out at a deafening pitch. Their students, yelling, exhorting their team to pull the upset, stood behind us all the way up to the top of the bleachers of the fortress-like gym. The high-arched windows fogged above the top row. Winter jackets that the kids had flung hung wrapped around the pipes, the plumbing that ran atop the gym from the wall, perpendicular to the iron girders that edged the old concrete bleacher, partially blocking the view of spectators that sat behind them.

Since I wasn't involved in the desperation play Coach was drawing up, my eyes wandered to Mindy across the way. She was mouthing something at me, I think about where she would be after the game when we got back to Jackson. I mouthed back a "Where?" I had twisted around, my back to Coach's last instructions.

As we put our hands together for our huddle break - "Team!," Coach suddenly turned to me and said, "You take it out, Stevie. Get in there. Go in for Hobie."

Coach grabbed me by my arm and launched me toward the scorer's table. Taking my warm-up off up over my head, I sprinted to the scorekeeper to report in. I think Coach wanted me to take the ball out because of my baseball prowess. I played a pretty good third base last spring for the Kestrels JV team, a position where a good arm is a requirement.

Jogging back toward the end line, the referee holding the ball to give to me, I cupped my hands and in a loud whisper said to Jamey Watson, sitting at the end of the bench, "Who am I looking for?" Jamey, leaning forward in anticipation of the last chance play, thinking just maybe we'd pull off a repeat of the Duke/Christian Laettner miracle heave-and-shoot buzzer beater against Kentucky in the 1992 NCAA tournament, looked at me, a brief disbelief across his face. Stevie doesn't know what the play is!

Pointing down court with the index finger on his right hand, he yelled, "To K.J.! Throw it long!"

OK, I got it. I windmilled my arm a time two while our players positioned themselves for the last play. Coach Pettaway yelled, trying to get my attention.

"Stevie! Make sure it gets there! Don't leave it short!"

K.J. stood, leaning over, hands on his knees looking at me, down court under our basket to the left. I thought that he probably would be getting a screen across from Tommy, a block to block screen to free him as soon as I launched the ball. It would have to be about an 80 foot toss, and be right on the money for K.J. to have a chance for the catch-and-shoot. I backed up as far as I could get to the wall, but made certain I had room for my arm to extend back to make the baseball pass. Dexter put their tallest player on me, on the ball, a guy stork-like, a stick, with his arms raised high. My pass would have to have some serious arc to get over his hands.

The throw would be a "spot" throw in; I had to heave the ball from where it had gone out of bounds; I couldn't run the baseline to shed The Stork. And the ceiling in their old gym had a lengthy net hoisted up to the ceiling width-wise, one they dropped down to split the gym in two when they had gym class, boys on one side, girls on the other. The net hung down a few feet, protruding from the ceiling. My throw would have to be perfect. The ref remind me I couldn't move, blew his whistle and handed me the ball.

Cocking my right arm back, left foot forward, body turned sideways like an NFL quarterback, the ball left my hand intended for where K.J. would be headed. Only K.J. moved toward half court to set a back screen for Kenny as Tommy curled to the top of the key in case the pass fell short. My eyes watched in disbelief, my brain instant-analyzing, a nano second insta-thought realizing I had made a grievous error. I had made the pass too soon, and to the wrong locale. I watched as it sailed to the right when it should have gone to the left side of the basket.

There would be no heroics on this particular night. A cruise missile, the ball hit half way up the wall, knocking down a

Deshler maroon and gold pennant, emblazoned on it a basketball with "1956 Tri-State League Champions." The ball dropped to the floor, bounced five or six times, then rolled across the floor to the bleachers. I sunk to a deep knee bend position, unbelieving, staring at it for a few seconds, trying to shift the blame from operator error to the evil ball, the evil ball with bad intentions that derailed my heroic effort. I put my fists over my ears to shut out the throaty roar of the Deshler fans. The lead referee at the other end retrieved the ball from a spectator, a twelve year old chubby kid with red cheeks in a maroon and gold Dreadnaught hoodie who held it high aloft, a prized trophy, shouting, "Wooooo! Woooo!" His twelve year old miscreant buddies - they of the junior high set who stomped their feet and yelled at our players during warm-ups and when we shot free throws, pounded chubby red-cheeked boy on the back.

The buzzer sounded for a sub; Hobie ran in and motioned for me to come out. Coach glared at me, arms crossed. I put my hands out to the sides, palms up, affecting a quizzical look as if to say, "I don't know what went wrong." I went to the end of the bench and put my head down, studying the popcorn that had been dropped and scattered underneath the bleachers.

Jamey said in my ear, "I was trying to tell you that K.J. was going to set a pick for Kenny."

"Yeah," I said with a sigh. If only I knew then what I know now the thought that filled my head. After the low hand slaps going through the line with the Dreadnaughts who tried hard to suppress their euphoric smiles we descended the stairs down into the dark catacomb-like tunnel which housed the ancient locker rooms. We sat waiting for the coaches as steam burped and belched from the radiator, wafting up toward pipes wrapped in electrical tape. One of banks of the overhead florescent lights flickered, another whole bank sat dead. One that did fully function, near the locker room door, seemed out of place in its brightness among the relics, the aged lockers, benches, and posts.

Coach Pettaway took the lead this time, Coach Arnold in back of him, head down, arms folded, glasses off in one hand, listening, looking exasperated.

"Boys, you get what you deserve in this world. Some catfish think they'll never get caught, but know what? They do. We— Coach Arnold, Coach Luke and I just talked and we decided that this one's on us. We didn't prepare you for this game like we should have. Sometimes the predator gets captured by the prey. But because we say we didn't do our job, well, that don't— doesn't—absolve you of not doing your job. The coaches, we are not your adversary. We're in this together. We all need to do our jobs if we're going to win this thing. That's all I've got to say. Coach?"

Coach Arnold put on his glasses, then took them off, and wiped them out of habit, out of frustration, out of a need to think about what he wanted to say.

"Boys, I agree with everything Coach Pettaway says. I take responsibility. I'm the head coach. I'm the one who has the final say on the game plan, the practice plan, who plays and who doesn't. Lots of season to go, fellas. But I'll be damned if I'm going to let this happen again."

Sitting, watching the coaches talk I felt guilt, that I had caused our defeat more than anyone else. Maybe it should have all-consumed me, but sitting on the old, cracked plastic chairs in their crappy locker room I mostly thought about checking my text messages, wondering where the guys, where Mindy wanted to head when we got back to school, what we would get to eat. I needed to compartmentalize my thoughts better, but sometimes my thoughts didn't think the same way.

Chapter 37

Mr. O'Donnell waved me over. The day after I played wall ball on the last second play I received a pass from the office in Mr. O'Donnell's class. Mr. O'Donnell always joked around with the students running passes from the office. Sometimes he'd open the classroom door and give them Lurch's "You rang?" or if he was in the back of the room and one of the students would get up to open the door when the runner knocked, he'd say, "Don't answer that! They're hall people. Don't you understand?! They're not like us!" As if they were aliens or swamp creatures.

Once you got Mr. O'Donnell's humor it was funny—he WAS funny—and most kids did. Halloween day Mr. O'Donnell had walked to the front of the room with his English Literature book in hand, put it on the podium and leafed through it, looking for the starting place for the short story the class would be assigned to read and discuss that day. Then he looked up and smiled at the class with huge false fake teeth with fangs. I mean, what can you say. Kinda scary-funny. A girl or two jumped, one then sighing, putting her hand over her heart and took a deep breath. We stared while Mr. O'Donnell fake teeth-smiled the room, but then we laughed. I think a lot of what Mr. O'Donnell did had a subtle message. That day we started reading "The Murders In the Rue Morgue." I think he intended a macabre connection between the fake teeth and Poe's writing, to get us on edge. Definitely edgy. So Mr. O'Donnell.

Mr. O'Donnell read the name on the pass and brought it to my desk. Handing it to me he said in a German army officer's World

War II bad movie accent,

"Vhy are zay callink you down to zee office? Vhat did dey tink you do? You von't tell zem anytink! Name, zee rank, unt zee serial noomba. Zat is it! Dey vill tell you to get in zee bus and to ask no questions! You vill do vat dey say, but tell them nothink! Ya vol?" I smiled and nodded as I looked to see who it was from. Dean Pettaway. Coach Pettaway. I wondered whether he wanted to talk about basketball or discipline. Had a teacher written me up? Thinking I had done nothing to deserve demerits, but I did get back to geometry class a few minutes late that morning from an assembly we had about drugs, this the annual Drug Awareness Week with daily announcements about the damage we could do to our young minds, culminating in a Friday assembly in the auditorium. A speaker gave the history of his drug filled crazed binges as a no-account lowlife who had finally seen the light. The usual think-before-doing-drugs-just-say-no talk that we had listened to since fifth grade. Late getting back because I had been talking to Mindy, I tried to nonchalant it coming into Geometry class. Miss Genovesee hadn't said anything, though she had already started class. She had given me a brief look, one of those that let me know that she knew that I knew that she knew I was tardy but she wanted to get on with class.

Inside the main office I waited at the counter. Somebody's mom held a brown bag lunch as Ms. Schnitzel, the front office secretary-slash-attendance officer, looked up the student's schedule and promised mama that her son or daughter would have their lunch delivered to them because God forbid they might be hungry for two more hours before they got home from school.

When it was my turn Ms. Schnitzel gave me a nondescript look, one that I couldn't figure out the meaning (did she think I got called down because I had been a bad kid?) and pointed to Mr. Pettaway's office down the hall around and behind her desk.

"Come in, brother man," Mr. Pettaway said when he saw me

standing at the open doorway. "Have a sit down."

Mr. Pettaway sat behind his desk, reading glasses on, peering down at what looked like someone's school suspension papers. As he signed off on some scofflaw school rule breaker who would be spending the next three days in the in-school suspension room, I glanced at the photos displayed on his office walls. A family portrait pictured Mr. Pettaway with his wife and their two children, one a girl and one a boy. The boy, Martin, went to our junior high. I heard Mr. Pettaway tell a teacher that he named his son after Martin Luther King, and that he and his wife named their daughter - a sixth grader and a heck of a volleyball player already - after Rosa Parks. Another one pictured a photo of a green clad team with a young African-American man wearing number 55 in the middle of the back row. Mr. Pettaway when he played basketball for Marshall University. Non-smiling, with an afro and long sideburns, arms crossed over his chest, as were all his teammates in the back while the front row kneeled, one leg out - the right leg - left knee on the floor - with their right arms across the legs. No smiles there, either. Many of the white guys had shoulder-length long hair, some had beards, while the black guys sported 'fros and mustaches, fu manchus. It looked as if their goal had been to have an intimidating picture of no-nonsense hard guys that could cause some mayhem.

On the shelf behind his desk Mr. Pettaway had an autographed Ohio State team football and another photo of him pictured with a large man I thought I recognized as one of OSU's Heisman Trophy winners, both wearing golf shirts, Ohio State caps, holding golf clubs in one hand, arms around each other, laughing. Buddies. Alongside the photos Mr. Pettaway displayed his framed bachelor's and master's degree diplomas.

Mr. Pettaway put the papers in front of him to the side. Besides suspension paperwork they contained tardy slips, teacher discipline referrals, and demerit logs. He took off his glasses, set them on his desk rather deliberately, clasped his hands together in front of him on his desk, as if he was weighing his words and started the conversation. I liked Coach Pettaway. I was a little fearful of Dean Pettaway. I should have summoned my union rep to come with me.

"Stevie, I'm putting on my coach's hat here."

Coach pretended to put an invisible hat on his head, mimicking the hat-putting-on procedure with one hand in front of his forehead tugging down, the other hand in back of head helping.

"Stevie, here's what I want to tell you, my take on what happened at the end of the game last night." I nodded.

"It wasn't that your pass hit against the wall. I'm not concerned about that, about the physical aspect. Well, maybe a little. What I'm much more concerned about is that you didn't know what the play was, where the ball was supposed to go. I notice a lot during a game, more than you would think. I saw your body language at the end of the bench after you were taken out of the game, after you figured out that you weren't going back in. I'd say that, from my observation, that you lost interest in the game, the team, that you were pretty much only thinking about yourself and why the coaches wouldn't put you back in. If I'm wrong, tell me."

"No, that pretty much sums it up, Coach."

"You know, Stevie, teams are built on trust. Your coaches, your teammates trust you to do your best, in games, at practice, and even when you're on the bench. When you're on the bench....what do you think is the role of players when they're on the bench? Sometimes it's to get a breather, especially if you're a starter, but otherwise what's your role on the bench?"

I thought for a minute. I think I knew the answer he expected. I thought how to put it in words, words Coach P. would like.

"I ought to be watching the game trying to help my teammates, especially the one that went in for me, that's playing my position. Like when the other team subs, who they should be guarding and if they're running the plays right, if they aren't I can give them a shout, tell 'em what they should be doing."

Coach P. agreed, saying, "That's right, that's right."

I finished, hoping I had given Coach what he wanted to know. But then he hit me with the essay question at the end of the test.

"What would you say was your attitude when you sat at the end of the bench last night? And one thing, after each time out when Coach Arnold didn't put you back in, when you realized you probably weren't going to play the rest of the night you distanced yourself more and more from the coaches, moving all the way to the end with the JV kids. Am I right? Is that what we expected from you?"

"No, Coach."

"So how would you describe your attitude at the end of the game when you didn't know what play we were running when Coach Arnold put you back in?"

"Selfish, Coach. Feeling sorry for myself. I let my team down, I know that. I had an 'It's all about me' attitude."

Coach Pettaway looked down as I talked, listening, and had picked his reading glasses back up, lightly tapping them on the desk in front of him.

"Why didn't you know what the play was, Stevie, who we were running it for, what your options were?"

I sighed.

"I didn't pay attention when Coach Arnold drew up the play. I was trying to communicate with Mindy, trying to find out where she was going after the game. We haven't been talking much lately. I didn't think there was any chance I was going back in the game. I feel so badly, Coach. It's not a good excuse. I let the team down."

Coach nodded.

"I'm glad to hear that, Stevie. You owned up to it. Only blamed yourself. You don't want to know what Coach Arnold had to say in our coaches' meeting after the game. He was ready to throw you under the bus, move you to second string or maybe down to the junior varsity for a while. This is only a game, high school basketball is, but we put a lot of time and effort into it. We have certain, certain values we try to teach along with skills. Stuff you know, like team play, being a good teammate. What goes along with that is trust. I think you've broken your teammates' trust as well as the coaches', Stevie. Often it's difficult summoning trust when you want it. You're going to have to earn it back. To not have my team's trust, man, I'd rather drink muddy water and sleep in a hollow log. You can apologize to 'em, say you're sorry, but if you don't mean it, don't *show* them, then those are just weasel words. You're a smart guy, Stevie. You'll figure it out. You'll have to wait until practice to find out what Coach has decided about whether you're still a starter. Anything else you want to tell me?"

I decided a mea culpa had to be the best course of action, to throw myself on the mercy of the court.

"I bear all responsibility, Coach. I understand that whatever the consequences are, I deserve them. I'll do my best to win yours and Mr. Arnold's and my teammates' trust back. Thanks for the talk, Coach."

But Coach Pettaway wasn't finished. He stood up from behind his desk, came around, faced me and put a hand on my shoulder.

"You know Stevie, all relationships, the good ones, are built on trust. Not only your team, but your family, your girlfriend, your neighbors. My neighbors trust me to keep my yard up, to not play loud music at two A.M. and I trust them to do the same. Mrs. Huffington counts on me to come to work and do my job everyday like I'm supposed to, even if I was up late. Some days I'm so tired from my head to the bottoms of my feets, but your bosses don't want excuses, they want results. If I had a bad day in the office—you know that being the dean I don't always deal with the premier clientele of our student body—if I had the most miserablest of days Coach Arnold and all the players still trust me to do my job. You have to compartmentalize, do your best at whatever it is you're doing now. And your classmates when you're working together, like doing a project with them, you trust them to do their part and they trust you to do yours. What happens if you don't do your part when you're doing a group project for a class, Stevie?

"We'd probably get a really low grade, or else someone may have to do my part as well as their own."

"That's right. Then what happens to the trust the kids in your group had with you?"

"I'm sure it wouldn't be very good."

Mr. Pettaway agreed, voicing an 'Mmm-hmm,'" then asked,

"What happens to your reputation as far as them wanting to work with you in the future?"

"They wouldn't want to work with me, wouldn't want me to be in their group. I'd be an outcast, a pariah, an undesirable, persona non grata."

I thought those had been the right answers, what he wanted me to say. I hoped the questions wouldn't get harder.

Mr. Pettaway paused for a half minute, debating whether to ask me a question on his mind.

"Maybe it's none of my business, Stevie, and you don't have to tell me, but how are things going with you and Mindy?"

"I'm never sure, Coach. One day she acts like my girlfriend, the next day she doesn't. The funny thing about the game is that she never showed up after we had that talk, whisper, whatever in the last few minutes. Didn't text me back after the game. And then today she tells me she didn't see my text. I know she did. She always has to have it on her own terms, what's best for Mindy. Hobie calls her a 'crazy little minx.' "

"Maybe you're throwin' your love on her just a little too

210

strong."

"Yeah. Maybe. It seems like a game sometimes that she's playing. Kind of like she might want to date other guys, but she wants to make sure I'm always there for her. But if I ignore her for a few days, don't see her at her locker, don't call or text her, she calls me, texts me, and when she sees me at school, she tells me she misses me."

Coach Pettaway sighed. "She probably does. You don't miss your water until your well runs dry. Let me tell you my story with the wife. Believe me, I love that big-legged woman, but there were times in our relationship, early on, when we were at Ohio State when I couldn't be sure if Lucille loved me or not, wanted to stay with me or not. We had to talk it out, share our feelings. Not an easy thing for us guys. But at your age, Stevie, be careful about going all in. Sometimes the hunter gets captured by the game. While maybe you think that's a good thing right now, you might want to have another think later on. It worked out good for me, but… "

Coach Pettaway put his arms out, a quizzical look on his face.

I thought about what Coach Pettaway said. Something about dating the hottest girl in school though, well, I wasn't going to walk away from that, at least right now.

"Seems to me, Stevie, that Mindy's smart enough not to burn her bridges behind."

When he said *burn* it sounded like *boyn*. That Mississippi upbringing. Took me a few seconds to figure out what he meant.

"One more thing. And this relates to your team, to Mindy, how she treats you, you treat her, to your life in general. You can say that you'll be more trustworthy, but until you do it, people aren't going to believe you until you actually come through. Your character is determined not by what you say you're going to do, but by what you actually do."

"Your teachers trust that you'll do your assignments, keep up

211

with the reading they assign, that you'll study so that you get the most of the class and better yourself. Ultimately that's our goal as a school system. We trust that after you graduate you'll be a trustworthy, contributing member of the community."

Nodding, agreeing, I said, "Gainfully employed. Not be a burden to my family. Or become one of the outcasts of society."

"That's the idea. Either you're a team player or you're not. You can't pick and choose. There's a saying that sports don't build your character as much as they reveal it. You're the same person on the court as you are off it. If you're selfish off the court, then you're probably the player that doesn't like to share the ball, always wants the accolades."

Coach Pettaway pronounced it *accoo-lades*. I started to correct him, thought better about it, then said, "I understand Coach. It won't happen again."

"And here's a question for you. Don't answer right now. I want you to think about it. Would you rather score twenty a game, be first team all-state and your team finishes fourth or fifth in the league, or would you rather your team wins the league championship and you score five points a game? You know what most parents would say. But you're a part of this team, YOUR team."

Coach Pettaway pointed at me when he said "YOUR." Then he added, "Think about it. Are you a team player? My grandmama would say, "Either you is or you isn't.""

"I'll give it some thought, Coach. I see your point. I'm sure you're right."

"So I can tell Coach Arnold we're on the same page?"

"We are, Coach."

"You're all in?"

"I'm all in."

In truth, maybe seventy-five percent in. I thought that the coaches should have put me back in earlier. Hadn't been real happy that they had given up on me.

"Put it in the vice, Stevie."

We shook hands. His huge right hand swallowed mine, his left hand giving a sign of approval of my responses as he squeezed my right shoulder.

"Stevie, you can get bitter or you can get better. You picks your choice."

"I'll get better. Promise. See you at practice, Coach. And thanks."

Coach Pettaway stood at the door's opening, watching me leave, walk through the main office and out into the hallway. I heard Ms. Schnitzel asking Mr. Pettaway how it went as the main office door gently closed.

"Just leading horses to water. Just leading horses to water."

Walking back to Mr. O'Donnell's class at the end of the long first floor hallway I contemplated the conversation with Mr. Pettaway. I had mixed emotions. I had busted my butt all season, then made just one mistake. Yeah, it was a big mistake and I regretted it, but that the coaches thought I hadn't been a team player rankled me.

Kids hard at work on an assignment when I entered the room, Mr. O'Donnell glanced up at me from a computer where he had been assisting students when I entered. I handed him my signed office pass.

"The handouts are on the table."

Mr. O'Donnell gestured at the table at the back of the room.

I read through them. The handout stated the topic assigned, the rubric—five paragraphs including a thesis statement, three body paragraphs with supporting logical ideas, details and examples, and a concluding paragraph, how many references we needed, when the rough draft and final drafts were due. The topic: a Description essay, part of the new English Common Core curriculum. We were to choose a word we wanted to describe, with Mr. O'Donnell's approval.

I wrote down the word I chose and took it over to Mr. O'Donnell.

He took my paper in his hands, immediately handed it back to me and said, "That will work."

The word I chose—Trust. I think Mr. Pettaway had already written my paper for me.

Chapter 38

The next day my English class met in the library per instructions from Mr. O'Donnell, ostensibly to work on our research papers. But first we had to suffer through an introductory talk from the head librarian, Mrs. Frothburnt. She and her underlings (see Laberdee, Kayellen) ruled the library with an iron fist. I highly suspected that Mrs. Frothburnt had Gestapo training as part of her Library Science degree.

The librarian, AKA Judith Frothburnt, waited for us to be seated at the large rear section of the library that was used for presentations. We sorted out who we wanted to sit with as Mrs. Frothburnt waited impatiently. As the chatter subsided and most of us looked up in her direction, one table off to her right hadn't quite gotten the message that they needed to. As we learned in first grade—zip it, lock it, and throw away the key. Tabitha Schultz, Kylie Hempstead, and Paris Lillo chatted on, drawing everyone's attention, including a glowering Head Librarian. Kylie, suddenly looking like a stunned deer in the headlights, shushed Paris, Paris letting out a too-loud, "What?," not getting it, followed by a giggle, her face turning red. Tabitha leaned her head forward, hand over her eyes, not wanting to look, not wanting to see her classmates' glares nor the scowl of *der fueher*. Mrs. Frothburnt put down her materials with a clunk on the table beside her.

"You girls at that table. Come up here. Bring your student IDs."

The girls dug through their purses, picked out their IDs, shoved back their chairs, ignored the few under-their-breath comments from a few boys and summarily made the trip up the aisle to The

Court of Mrs. Frothburnt. Mrs. Frothburnt snatched each ID out of their hands and wrote down their names and student numbers on The List. The girls hung their heads in shame. When she finished Mrs. Frothburnt handed back the IDs, pausing to check the ID photo with each girl's face. No one would dare show her a fake ID. No one. Mrs. Frothburnt then waved the girls back to their seats. The Walk of Shame.

"Don't waste my time again, girls."

Mrs. Frothburnt wore a blue dress that extended down to her ankles. A round white collar, Pilgrim-style, surrounded her neck. Something a third grader might wear to church. Brown hair tied in a bun, glasses with brown speckled frames. Mrs. Frothburnt— thirty-five going on sixty.

"I regret the delay, students. Some of us that are present value their library time and care to hear my presentation. Obviously, others do not. But let's get started, shall we? I'm Mrs. Frothburnt (there was a MISTER Frothburnt? Holy cow...) the Director of the Jackson City Schools Educational Technology and Media Services Center. I'll be giving you vital information and whatnot on writing your term papers. But first I'd like to familiarize you with what we have to offer. Over and to your left are the periodicals, the newspapers, journals and whatnot."

Sitting at a table with three of my classmates at the back, I shuffled the handouts we had been given on library protocol and raised my hand.

"How often do the periodicals come in?"

I had noticed that the latest Sports Illustrated in the magazine racks was months old.

"They come in periodically."

That answer had my brain swirling. Did she really say that?

And then, "What's your name, young man?"

"Kip. Kip Longfellow."

Mr. O'Donnell peered over his glasses at me as several in the class snickered at their tables.

Mrs. Frothburnt rubbed her hands in front of her, possibly a little anxiety kicking in at the breach in her planned talk. But more likely a little perturbed.

"Well, Kip, after they arrive in the mail—and we receive them later than you would at home because being a school we pay a lower postage rate so it takes longer. Once we get them our library workers sort them, along with the new books that need to be shelved, enter them into the databases on the library website, then place them in the appropriate bins, stacks, racks, and whatnot. It does take some days, a good amount of time to get everything in its proper place. Does that answer your question, Kip?"

"It's Flip, not Kip, but I just wonder why it's November and the most current Sports Illustrated you have on the magazine rack is the opening day baseball issue from March."

Mrs. Frothburnt bit her lip and looked at Mr. O'Donnell. Mr. O'Donnell said, "Flip, we need to move along." Mrs. Frothburnt gave an enthusiastic nod to Mr. O'Donnell, then slowly moved her eyes to me, lingering a second before resuming.

"If you'd refer to the handouts that have been provided to you, please turn to page two, to the section on accessing the search tools for your papers. Notice the list of search engines that is probably much longer than you have used before. You'll be able to find information and whatnot on topics that you can't find on Google."

She held up her copy, pointing to the section we were to follow, waiting for the laggards to catch up and turn their handouts to page two.

"If you'll continue down past the search engines and the kinds of information and whatnot each provides, you'll see the section on how to log in with your own password. Use the first three numbers of your school ID student number, the first initial of your first and last name, in lower case, then after that it will ask for a

217

password of eight letters or less, containing one number and one mark like an asterisk or an exclamation mark or whatnot. Your password can be anything that's not considered a profanity or anything not suitable for school. It can be a pet, your favorite sport, a nickname or whatnot."

That was it. I couldn't take another "whatnot." I raised my hand again.

"What's whatnot, Mrs. Frothburnt?

"What?"

"Whatnot. Not 'what.' What it is or isn't? What is whatnot?"

"It's everything related to what you're talking about. It excludes some things, not others."

"Even what it's not?"

"Yes and no."

Mrs. Frothburnt paused, then continued.

"It's...kind of vague but it's not. It includes what's likely to include but excludes what isn't likely. So it's not what isn't but more what it is—likely to include, that is."

"How am I to decide? So you're saying whatnot is inclusive and exclusive then."

"You could say that."

"I just did."

"Does that clear up what whatnot is and isn't?"

"Of course not. Whatever."

"You don't have to get snippy, Kip."

"It's Flip, if you remember, and I'm just seeking some clarity on your use of the English language."

Mrs. Froshburnt's eyes shot darts at me and she muttered something about her having to "suffer fools," then locked them on Mr. O'Donnell.

Mr. O'Donnell motioned for me to come with him to a lounge chair around the corner from the presentation area by the ferns, the relaxed reading area in front of the large window overlooking an outdoor eating area used in warm weather by the library staff.

"Stay here until she's finished talking. And Stevie, quit acting like Stevie. You know what I'm talking about."

I did and I said I would, satisfied that a salvo had been fired at Mrs. Frothburnt's rhetoric, her pomposity, her impatience, and her whatnot.

Chapter 39

"Whew. Two tests tomorrow. One I'm really worried about. What time do you get done with basketball practice tonight?"

After school I had met Mindy at her locker, loading books into her backpack. I waited patiently as she hoisted the load, two textbooks weighing about as much as a small child. I helped adjusting the straps as Mindy shouldered the backpack into place.

"Should be done at six. Schedule says four-to-six."

"I've got this geography test. I studied all last night. I can remember most of the lakes and most of the rivers, but the mountain ranges, I just can't remember which one's which, which one's where."

Geographically challenged. I wondered how a kid that had been to or flown over almost every lake, river, canyon, desert, hill and mountain range in the continental United States with her well-to-do sales rep dad would have so much of a problem.

"What's in it for me?" I asked, smiling and looking away.

"Depends. Depends on what grade I get. The higher the grade the more grateful I'll be."

Mindy gave me her devilish look-to-the-side look, eyebrows uplifted, plying and playing me. She looked back, catching my eyes catching her eyes, as she knew she would.

"My dad will ground me if I get anything lower than a "B" on my grade card. He'll have a cow."

I pretended to ponder whether I'd help her or not. And whether I wanted to prevent the impending history-making improbable man-cow homo sapien-bovine birth.

Mindy added, "I'll be *extremely* grateful."

"*Extremely* grateful? That's just short of a presidential handshake."

She moved closer, looking up at me, her chin a few inches from mine.

"I'll think of something you'll like. Deal?"

"Quid pro quo. I like it. Deal."

"What's quid…quidproco?

"Quid. Pro. Quo." I enunciated the Latin slowly, carefully.

Mindy said, "And that means…what?"

"It's a legal term lawyers use. My mom uses them all the time with Benny and me, like if you guys clean up the kitchen or your bedrooms we'll have pizza tonight. It means if you do something for me, I'll do something for you."

Mindy took this in somewhat thoughtfully, but quickly shifted the language to her favor.

"We can quid pro quo, Mr. Kalkannes. We can quid each other as amateurs or pros, your choice. And remember, what is said in the library stays in the library."

And she put her chin up to mine, a few inches away, eyebrows raised. No fair.

Our eyes looking into each other's, we shook hands. Seven, eight, nine slow shakes.

Her's fit perfectly in mine.

I met Mindy at the library a few blocks from my house. A new convertible with a license plate that read "MNDYSU," a Jackson High School parking permit hanging off the rear view mirror, it occupied the visitor parking space nearest the entrance. Walking in through the library's foyer my radar scanner spotted Mindy sitting at a table by the back window, her notes, laptop, papers, books and markers spread out in front of her. Mindy looked up, smiled and winked. Her motioning crooked index finger beckoned for me to join her. Patting the seat next to her, Mindy said in a quiet voice, "Come here, Big Boy."

I looked behind me, over my shoulder, feigning surprise, then pointed at my chest.

"You mean me?"

"Yes, you, silly."

Mindy had a master map of the United States and a couple blank U.S. maps on the table in front of her.

"I think there's only a couple lakes and rivers I can't remember. But the mountains, those stupid mountains. I stayed up until two o'clock last night studying."

I shook my head. "If you studied long you studied wrong."

"Then help me."

"OK, Brown Eyes, I'll point to the mountain range and you tell me which one it is. Are you an auditory learner? Maybe when you hear yourself say the name you'll better remember."

I pointed to the Ozarks, in Arkansas.

"Ummm… the Adirondacks?"

"Not unless they moved them."

"Did you try mnemonics or any memory techniques? You know, like if you had to remember the Great Lakes you'd use H-O-M-E-S—Huron, Ontario, Michigan, Erie and St. Clair. Then you could chunk sections of the country, Northeast, Southeast, Midwest, like that. Or, look for small identifiers. Ozarks has an "ark" in them just as Arkansas does."

We spent an hour and a half going over Mindy's map. I think I pinpointed her trouble in memorizing the material. She had to check her incoming texts every two minutes. Some she commented on, some not. The nots were the ones that concerned me.

She laughed after looking at one.

I asked her, "What's so funny?"

"It's, he's, Barry, he's nothing. Just nothing."

I nodded with a half frown.

As we walked out to the parking lot I decided to ask her about going to the forthcoming Valentine's Day dance. The odds as I viewed them: 50/50.

I asked. Mindy replied, a little slowly, placidly, going through the rolodex in her mind, thinking if going to the dance might make her miss something more important.

"Yeah. Yeah, I guess. That should be fun."

"Don't get *too* excited," I said.

"I had to think about my stupid dad. You know how he is. I had to think about if he had stuff planned for us. He actually puts a calendar on my door with nights marked off where I have to do all this stuff with him. I never get a whole weekend to do what I want. Sunday nights I have to go study and no TV, cell phone, anything. He makes me sit in the kitchen while he watches *his* programs. I have to tell him if I need to Google any information for what I'm studying. What am I, *ten years old*? He even checks my cell to see if I texted anybody. And I told you that he's a salesman and he travels and sometimes is gone overnight? He texts me, like, twelve times from the time school's out until eleven o'clock when we *Skype.*"

Mindy rolled her eyes when she said Skype. Skyping with her dad obviously something she'd like to skip.

"And God forbid If I did get a grade below a B. He'd never let me out of the house except to go to school. I think he actually likes to ground me. I'd be cheering for you guys from my house instead of the gym. He says he's trying to keep me out of trouble but I think he's a control freak. That's what caused my mom to leave him. Sometimes he marks off Saturday night for me to go to dinner with him with some of his business buddies and their wives and girlfriends. It's sooo boring. I wish he'd get a girlfriend."

I immediately thought *Hey, my mom's available*, then mentally slapped my face. The scenarios THAT would bring up.

Shakespeare would salivate at writing a play about it. Thanks but no thanks.

For the first time, I felt sorry for Mindy. I knew her dad didn't let her have the freedom most kids had. She never went into detail before, just told me that her dad had plans for her. I saw her maybe one night a week other than at basketball games and school. Besides cheer practice she had gymnastics practice, church on Sunday mornings and Wednesday nights, and volunteered — her dad signed her up — to read to underprivileged little kids at the library on many of her "free" nights. With homework that left little time for Mindy to get in trouble, outside school anyway. I thought maybe that's why she acted like she did, all the attention seeking, the desire to create drama with her teachers and classmates because of her discipline obsessive dad. Drama had the effect of dopamine to her, a reward for her wired brain. And like a drug, Mindy needed more and more to get the attention, the high she sought. I probably should have avoided dating this girl, I thought to myself so many times. However my thinking always concluded with *"But she's so so damn hot!"*

Chapter 40

The classroom hi-light of the week occurred Friday morning. Before class, out in the hall Sandy Applebaum told a group of four or five of us that she had seen Mrs. Gordon, a divorcee, at the movies with a guy Sandy assumed to be Mrs. Gordon's boyfriend. Sandy eagerly went into the graphic details. Sandy talked fast, wanting to impart all the explicit details before the bell rang for class.

"I went to the Fair Oaks Mall last night with Analise Romanoff to see the new Jennifer Anniston movie. We sat about five rows behind Mrs. Gordon and the guy that must be her boyfriend. Not a bad looking guy but fat cheeks and kinda heavy, like Mrs. Gordon. I wonder if she thinks he's a hunk? He had on a black sports coat, white shirt and a tie, loosened like he just got off work."

Sandy loosened an imaginary tie around her neck, in case we didn't comprehend the loosened tie concept. Apparently Sandy thought this loosened tie business had some big implications, portended something eventful, a foreshadowing.

"He had short brown hair and glasses, Mrs. Gordon wore a turquoise sweater with an orange scarf and had make-up on, some rouge and mascara and reddish lipstick, more make-up than she wears to school."

Sandy put imaginary rouge on both her cheeks. She had our total attention.

"About halfway through the movie the guy put his arm around Mrs. Gordon and she moved over in her seat closer to him and

225

said something in his ear and they both laughed. By the end of the movie they had their heads together."

Three or four more kids joined the circle around Sandy, including Josie and Kyle and a couple of Sandy's friends who had a class across the hall.

"When the movie ended we kind of ducked down so Mrs. Gordon wouldn't see us."

Sandy ducked down, eyes big, shoulders hunched, showing us how one would duck down when the situation called for it.

"They left right away. We kind of blended in with the people going out, like ten, no twenty feet behind them. He still had his arm around her."

Sandy demonstrated how you would put your arm around someone by putting her arm around Alicia Kaye Appelwhite, a friend from the class across the hall. Sandy walked Alicia Kaye to the classroom door, her arm tight around Alicia Kaye's waist. AK fulfilled her role of pretending she was Mrs. Gordon by putting her head on Sandy's shoulder, who played the role of Mrs. Gordon's boyfriend. The acting couldn't be considered anything but tight, an accurate portrayal. Then Sandy turned and said to us, "Like that." We didn't know quite what to think, other than maybe a teacher shouldn't be displaying such lascivious behavior in public. Or that teachers should even be out in public.

The bell began to ring and we hustled in. Mrs. Gordon rearranged stacks of papers at the front of the room, then looked around, taking attendance.

"Sorry I didn't get your tests graded last night. I had planned to, but I never got to them. Just too tired last night. I'm sorry. I promise to grade them over the weekend and get them back to you Monday."

Josie raised her hand.

"Since you're tired, Mrs. Gordon, maybe we could just have a study hall today."

"Oh, I don't think so, Josie. We have to start the new chapter on shopping for our field trip to the mall next Friday."

"Oh. Well, since you're so tired it made me wonder why. I just wondered if you had an S.O. with your S.O. last night."

"A what?"

Mrs. Gordon, not comprehending, tried to repeat what Josie had asked, mouthing the words to herself. An S.O.... a what with a what...? Mrs. Gordon shook her head, seeking explanation.

"A sleepover with your significant other."

The class didn't know whether to laugh or not, whether Mrs. Gordon would take Josie's remarks jokingly or as a disrespectful challenge to her authority.

"Go Josie. Go see Mr. Pettaway. Out. Now."

"Alright, I'm going, I'm going," Josie said as she grabbed her backpack. Josie didn't need to be told the way to Mr. Pettaway's office.

"But aren't you acting just a little *prickly* today, Mrs. Gordon?"

The class turned their eyes back and forth between Josie and Mrs. Gordon, as spectators at a tennis match do as the ball is volleyed back and forth over the net. I briefly thought about giving Josie polite applause - as is done at a tennis match for a good shot - for her particularly taunting remarks. She had set up Mrs. Gordon perfectly with a lob followed by a vicious backhand.

"Out! Now!"

"Alright, alright."

On her way out Josie turned back and added a parting shot.

"I heard your boyfriend is a hunk."

Mrs. Gordon, simmering, waited for Josie to leave, then picked up the room phone to call Mr. Pettaway. Mrs. Gordon stood partway out in the hall as we tried to listen to what she said. We couldn't make out every word, but we knew one indisputable fact. She saw it as a disrespectful challenge to her authority.

Chapter 41

Friday night we dispatched Midlothian with ease. After the Deshler debacle the coaches had put the team through the two hardest practices of the year. Coach Pettaway told us that the coaches had decided that they'd been too easy on us, and he added, "That stuff about resting your legs the day before a game, that's all a state of mind. You think that way, you're just fattening frogs for snakes."

We nodded as if we understood the reference. But Madame Fortune had smiled on us. Because of a fight in their last game, against Upper Sandusky four Tarblooders, including three starters, had been suspended for the game against us and their next game, a non-league one. It had been a real donnybrook, with several fans getting involved also. The *Jackson Courier-Times* ran an article about the game and fight, stating that the origins had gone back to a summer league game in which several players from both teams had gotten into it in the parking lot after the game. The four guilty parties sat behind the bench - not able to play but nattily attired in shirt and tie. We made eye contact with them as we warmed up at their end. One or two nodded, others gave us a nondescript look.

"Shouldn't they be wearing orange jump suits?" I asked Hobie. "Shackled to each other maybe?"

"Depends."

"On what?"

"Whether they lawyered up. They could have been suspended for the rest of the year, kicked off the team. Made to give up their first new-born child."

"If you know the name of a good attorney, let me know. Might need one myself some day."

"That'd be your mom."

"Oh, that's right. Sometimes I forget she's a lawyer. Not many can make chocolate chip cookies like she can. A disarming tactic for an assistant prosecutor."

"Problems with the IRS? Facing a foreclosure notice? The bank about to repossess your car? Your cellmate shanked in Club Fed and they pinned it on you? Don't face it alone. Call 1-800-MamaKal."

"Shank you very much for the mama props, Hobie."

"No dispensation was provided for this information. It may not be disseminated for the public without the express written consent of Major League Baseball."

We showed no pity for Midlothian. We ran off to a 19-6 lead at the end of the first quarter and took the subdued home crowd out of the game. 62-39 had been the final. Back tied for first.

Sunday late afternoon I picked up Alison and Jillian in my mom's SUV, accompanied by our dogs who socialized in the back, tails wagging, posturing, paws on one another's head like wrestlers, play growls, with Alison and Jillian refereeing. At the park Alison's dog Pickles, a tan Cairn terrier, sped-walked down the trail on his retractable lead, anxious to see what lay ahead, his little legs in constant footfall, or pawfall, motion on his linear expedition while Jillian's golden retriever Clumber wanted to meet and greet every person and dog heading the other direction as they passed. My tri-colored beagle Peaches did what beagles do, beagling her way down the trail, nose down checking scents, tail up and wagging side-to-side, doing tree and trail inspections with an occasional whimper when she found an especially appealing one. Sometimes we humans walked side-by-side, sometimes we spread out with twenty or thirty feet between us depending on our dogs' proclivities.

When Peaches and Pickles stopped to sniff at the same tree, Jillian, quizzed me. I had started to pick up that Jillian thought of walking at the park as more than simply exercise or an enjoyable nature experience for the senses, but as 1) A tutorial in which she sought to impart recently gleaned knowledge about a hodgepodge of subjects, including but not exclusive of, science, vocabulary, God, religious tenets, animal and human behavior, diet and fashion 2) An opportunity to interrogate me that usually displayed my lack of depth of knowledge of all of the afore-mentioned.

"OK, Stevie, when you hear the phrase 'It's raining,' what is 'it'? The sky? No. You wouldn't say the sky is raining. The weather? The weather is raining? Nope. The atmosphere? Nunh-Uh. The climate?"

She shook her head at each negative pronouncement, and looked at me and said, "So what is 'it'?"

I looked back at Jillian, trying to decide how much I cared.

She continued.

"According to Webster's, 'it' is used as an expletive subject of an impersonal verb that expresses a simple condition or an action without implied reference to an agent about the weather."

"You're right about raining being impersonal," I said. "Rain has no interest whatsoever in what I'm doing when it decides to be its intransitive self. Never asks. Never considers my opinion, my feelings, what I'm doing, what I want to do, or what I am wont to do."

I said *wont* with an inflection for Jillian's benefit.

"Same with snow. And some girls I know."

I continued, Jillian looking at me quizzically.

"I'd rather that it only snowed on weekdays so we wouldn't have school, but noo. Snow is only concerned about itself. And that stuff about no two snowdrops are identical, how would they know? Couldn't there be identical twin snowdrops?"

"Well, Stevie, research shows that about a septillion snowflakes fall every year, and each one has about a quintillion molecules. So it IS possible that two could be alike. And did you know that the biggest snowflakes form at the highest altitudes where it's the coldest? They're called dendrites and look like the pretty ones you see on Christmas cards. When meteorologists know how big the flakes are going to be they can make more accurate predictions on how much snow will fall."

The weather. It had been a mild start to winter but now it had changed. Snow fell, ice forming, roads bad. We watched the weather reports nightly, especially interested in how many inches of snow predicted. TV stations interviewed the Ohio Department of Transportation (ODOT) spokesperson ad infinitum. The interview always included a reporter standing out in the elements looking skyward, falling snow descending in his or her face before or after showing scenes of snowplows and salt piles at the ready. Newspaper articles cited the snow amounts daily as Jackson closed in on monthly record snow amounts. City snowplow operators ready to work twelve hour days clearing the roads. Students excited at the thought of school being canceled the next day. Girls did snow dances, wore their pjs inside-out for luck as Mrs. Gordon told them she and her friends did when they were kids. We watched the weather map on TV, the snow coming in from Indiana across the border, gathering strength. Fort Wayne had been hit with ten inches, Indianapolis seven and a half. A southwesterly flow expected to continue, spreading eight to twelve inches throughout northern Ohio overnight into the next day. Cell phones buzzing as texts flew back and forth with the latest weather updates.

As Jillian and I walked and talked the dogs frolicked, sniffed particularly appealing ground, bush and tree smells and marked their territories, the snow clouds looking more ominous. Alison and Pickles came walking back and joined us. Alison looked upward, the tie-chords on her knit hat loose. Not having brought my gloves, I pulled my jacket sleeves down as far as I could over my hands, one hand in a pocket, the other clutching Peaches' leash. What had I been thinking, not to bring my gloves? Or wear my winter jacket? Or my knit hat? I soldiered on. I thought the imminent snow had Alison's interest but something else crossed her mind.

"When you get to Heaven will your parents be the age when they died, and you'll be the age when you died, so that you might be older than your parents? Or will there always be the same separation in ages as how old you were when they died? It would be weird if I'm, say, 85 when I die and I go to Heaven and my parents are like, in their 70's. Or will I go backwards, and be the age I am when they die?"

I said, adding nothing to the conversation, that I had never thought about it, but I guessed that you wouldn't be older than your parents.

Alison thought for a minute, and when Pickles stopped to smell the base of a pine tree, said, "I think both, and that you and your parents will be at all stages of your lives, from when you were little till you were old, and you'll see your parents when they were little, and sometimes you'll be old together, sometimes young together, and sometimes you'll be a baby and they'll be your young parents, then you'll be grown up and they'll be older, the same difference in age that we know on earth. But it will waver, like maybe a dream, but it will be wonderful. It'll be all good. And all your pets will be there. They say your pets in Heaven will come running over the Rainbow Bridge to greet you when you enter Heaven."

Jillian and I both said together, "I like that."

We walked on, now looking up at the towering pines in the pine forest.

Since both Alison and Jillian seemed to be deeper thinkers than I am, and had a better understanding of the Bible, of religion, of faith, I asked them a question.

"Why do you think God lets bad things happen to good people?"

Alison fielded that one.

"Because of the original sin. It's from the Old Testament. When Adam disobeyed God in the Garden of Eden that made us mortal, like all of humanity had sinned, like it the choice all of us made, eating the apple, not just Adam's, so that when we die, our mortal bodies die, but that we can go to Heaven through our good deeds. We were born with free will. God gave us that, to choose between doing good and doing evil. That's just the Cliff Notes version, Stevie."

"I know most of that. But I always have wondered, since going to Bible school, why God didn't make us all perfect, so there would be no sin, so we'd all live happily ever after. No killing, no wars, no poverty. Why did he make us his ant farm?"

"No one can truly answer that," Alison said. "You have to decide what to believe. Look around us, at the forest, how wonderful nature is. Would an angry god make this?"

"I'd like to think not. But I've heard that some of the Founding Fathers were Deists. Do you know what those are?"

Alison said she thought she knew, but for me to tell her.

"They're people who believe God made the world, our universe, then left, walked away. They believed we're on our own with taking care of it."

Jillian, listening intently, said, "I don't like that. I think God's everywhere, in Heaven, on earth, everywhere."

"Do you picture God as sitting on a Golden throne high above us, wearing a long beard, in Heaven looking down? Do you picture Him that way when you pray. I do, sometimes."

"I do, too, Stevie. I do, too. But He's in nature, too."

233

Alison nodded, agreeing.

"But what if He is a she?" I countered.

Jillian replied, "I can only turn to the best source I know, to the Bible and what the biblical historians say, and they seem to all agree that God is a he, that He created us in His own image."

"I can go with that," I said, "but another question I've wondered about… How much input do you think women had in writing the Bible?"

Silence for the next several steps, except for the wind and the rustling of branches.

Alison's turn.

"That will be a good question to ask at my next Bible study group. I'm thinking they had some input, don't you?" she said, eyeing Jillian.

Jillian, eyes blinking, thinking, said nothing.

I turned toward Alison.

"My mom says that God knows when a sparrow falls."

She nodded, then said, "We want to go to the Western Wall in Jerusalem and put our prayers in the cracks. Maybe when we're in college in a couple years. I've been thinking what I want to write, my prayers. I want to know what it feels like to be there. It's called 'The shortest route to God's ear.'"

We walked on. I continued to seek answers to religion's eternal truths.

"I have another question. So, do you think we'll get rewarded for our faith?"

Jillian said, "Depends on how you define 'reward.' What I think is that the more good you do toward your fellow man the more good you receive. You'll be rewarded for your deeds, not just your faith. Will you go to Heaven? Will you attain everlasting life? Well, I think the more good you do the more it increases your chances, don't you? I highly doubt we were put on Earth just for ourselves, to try to accumulate the most money, the biggest this and most that, solely for selfish reasons. And I have no doubt at all, none, that helping others gives you so much back in return that it's your own reward."

"You know, Coach Arnold said something like that, only he was talking about basketball. He said the more you help your teammates out the more rewarding it is for you. Like if you set a screen for your teammate, often you'll be the one wide open for a pass and an easy lay-up when you roll to the basket. And if you pass to your teammates when they're open, the more likely they're going to pass to you when you're open and everyone benefits, and that if you help your teammates on defense they'll help you, that the more unselfish you are, the more good will come your way."

Alison again nodded, brushing away wind-blown hair from her face.

"I think you'll be rewarded for your faith in your coach's advice if you follow it. You have to believe to achieve. Kind of like Coach as The Deity as far as basketball is concerned."

"That's not always been my nature, though. Like when I score the most points in a game and the newspaper sports page mentions my name first or sometimes only my name in their game capsules because I was the leading scorer. Most of the time they don't mention the other guys' assists or how well they played on defense. And they don't mention how many shots I took when I'm the leading scorer, that I scored the most because I shot the most. And if I was the leading scorer, say I scored twenty points but my man scored twenty-five, the paper never mentions that. I'm the one who gets the publicity, the headline, the mention, the props, the reward, instead of my teammates when they should get as much as I do or more. And it's all because I scored the most points. But I can't say that I don't enjoy seeing my name in print. And when I'm in class the next day I usually get two questions - 'Did you win, and how many points did you score?' My humble self always tells them that I'm not sure. But I know exactly how many I had."

Jillian walked head down, taking it all in.

"But that goes with the value system we have, which is often all screwed up. It's so much based on who has the biggest or most whatever. Who scores the most points, who makes the most money, who has the biggest house, who sells the most albums. But a lot of times the people who have the most aren't satisfied because they keep wanting more. But when you help someone, your reward is intrinsic, within you. It's not tangible, doesn't have to be to be a reward."

"My value system needs a little tweaking," I said. "I like when I'm the leading scorer."

The dogs had stopped to look at a squirrel who had been scampering across the red needles on the forest floor, the squirrel pausing to look back at the dogs, on its haunches, nose twitching, then resuming his run back to the den. Fat snowflakes started to fall, twirling downward as the sun set at the edge of the park. A cardinal perched high in a jack pine caught our eyes, his inquisitive eyes searching his landscape, his pale brown colored mate with him, her wings, tail and crest tinged bright red, the pair in a pleasing contrast with the fluffy white flakes. Within a minute, as we came to the end of the trail at the edge of the parking lot, the park resembled a snow globe, the brown grass and green pines coated pillowy white. The snow continued, flakes wind caught, drifting in the cold winter air before touching ground, descending from above, Heaven sent.

Chapter 42

Monday the students of Jackson High School had their prayers answered. Nine inches of snow overnight caused the closing of the school system. Practice had even been canceled, reluctantly, by Coach Arnold, especially because we had league games scheduled for Tuesday and Thursday.

It turned out to be a good week for the Kestrels as we—the players—certainly not the coaches—had anticipated. "This will be an easy win," said no coach ever. We won games on Tuesday and Thursday against Grafton and Lower Sandusky, 60-51 and 59-54, and a non-league game versus Mansfield Malabar on Saturday, 71-51 (Their student section's chant, "We Are - Malabar!" stuck in my head through the road trip home, that night and the next morning). I led the team in scoring against Grafton with nineteen points and with sixteen in the route against Malabar. Of course Coach Arnold had been sparing with his praise, telling me that K.J. had been open in the post several times that I had neglected to see, or selfishly took the outside shot. When coach told me that in the locker room K.J. and I exchanged looks, K.J. nodding, looking pleased and in full agreement with Coach.

Saturday's game also provided a surprise. My dad had made the trip in from Chicago unannounced. He sat with my mom and Benny, Benny in the middle. After the game my mother suggested that my dad stay over and sleep on the couch, and that Benny and Dad and I have a boys' night out. Sounded good to me. I had played pretty well, we won easily, the team tied for first place. Not much fodder for criticism. Dad picked me up when the bus arrived back at Jackson and said we were heading to the Crow Bar to meet Benny. I had only been there once, for lunch with my mom, so this would be an exciting opportunity for a high school kid, to go to a popular bar where college kids and adults hung out - a look into my future.

My father motioned for us to sit at the bar. He and Benny flanked me. I instantly came entranced by bottles of alcohol lining the back of the bar underneath the mirror, backlit on the shelf, inviting contents glowing golden, amber, green, silverish...promising good times if poured, in a shot glass, with friends...1,2,3....tipping glass-to-mouth-to-throat and swallowing...life is better…instantly.

I worked on a glass of pop while my dad and Benny drank craft beers. I looked up and around at the myriad of HD televisions, all turned to sports stations while contemporary pop, new country music and rock oldies pumped from the juke box. Neon beer signs glowed from the walls advertising their brands. Mostly thirty-and-under young adults stood talking in groups, or sat with friends at the large wooden tables, the bar dimly lit with pendant lights hanging from the ceiling, an alluring appeal for college guys and co-eds seeking romantic connections. Several middle-aged men were seated at the long mahogany wood bar, pints in hand, chatting with the bartenders and watching Big Ten and NBA basketball games. Benny greeted friends as they came near to order shots and beers. Some received the combo hand clasp/bro hug, some bumped knuckles with Benny. Benny on his home turf, a minor celebrity. My thought at the sights and sounds of the Crow Bar: This is pretty cool. I can't wait till I'll be old enough!

I hadn't talked much with my father since calling him to say I had decided to play basketball again. (All that did was start him back up on questioning how could I have quit in the first place. Dad endearingly ended the short conversation with, "I hope you can pull this off after you screwed up.") But just maybe, I thought, maybe he'd start calling or texting me with positive comments when I'd had a good game or two. But those came sparingly. I had hoped he'd change. But nope, he hadn't changed.

After some commentary about the Cavs' game overhead, Dad ordered his second beer, then turned and looked at me for four or five seconds. Here it comes, I thought.

"What the hell happened in the Deshler game? Those guys really stink. They're a bag of hammers. I saw you scored two points. Were you sick?"

I sighed.

"No Dad. My karma wasn't right. It happens."

"Your what?"

"Karma. The sum total of my actions in this and my previous states of existence, viewed as deciding my fate in future existences. It's part of Buddhist philosophy. Learned it from the Twitchell's dad."

Benny scowled. Dad didn't quite know what to do with that answer.

"Well, I hope you can get your damn karma right for the rest of the season. And don't be telling any of the newspaper reporters you had a bad game because your karma wasn't right.

"I already did. He didn't include it in the article," I said. "And I'm also working on mindfulness when I shoot my free throws."

Dad screwed up his face and said to Benny.

"Benny, will you talk to him?"

"I try Dad. Are you sure he's really my brother?"

Dad took another drink, drummed his fingers on the bar.

"Ask your mother."

Ouch. I didn't think I needed to hear that. I put my letter jacket back on, my signal that I wanted to leave and pushed back my chair.

"Sit down, son. Let's go over your game tonight. There were a few things I saw that I didn't like. When you take the ball to the basket, why are you looking to pass more than shoot?"

I recognized that my dad was just getting warmed up. An hour and a half later we headed home, near closing time, after having my game skewered by my dad. Benny made an attempt to defend me then eased off his stool with Dad in the middle of a diatribe about my free throw shooting. At one point he stood up and tossed balled-up napkins into the trash can sitting about eight feet away behind the bar. He hit five in a row. I put my head down after that. Dad kept talking. And drinking.

"You make it too hard with all that thinking you do, that karma stuff and that mindfulness crap. Benny just thought about his form and his follow through. Always made the big ones at the end of the game.

My head still down, I turned sideways and said to my dad, "Except for the one that would have tied the game down at state."

Dad tilted his pint beer glass, looked into it, then turned his head back to me.

"Well, that wasn't his fault. The other team asked for the sweat to be wiped off the ball and the chicken-shit referees stopped the game for about five minutes while they got a clean towel. Froze him. The refs knew that it was a ploy by the other team. Not Benny's fault."

Dad looked straight ahead, that moment in time frozen in his mind, Benny's potential game tying free throw rolling off the rim, a Canton McKinley player rebounding, getting fouled, and making the freebies, sealing the win. Dad had to be restrained from launching himself at the refs from over the railing as they ran off the court to their locker room.

He stood up, a slight stagger, almost knocking his barstool over. "Let's go, Stevie. Damn referees. Hate 'em. What a bunch of jackwagons. It's just a part-time job for them and they go screw up your life. But I still don't get what your problem is with making 'em. Did I ever tell you what a great free throw shooter Uncle

Steve was? I taught him how. He never got to play much because of the idiot coach he had, but he could make thirty, forty in a row, just like that."

"Yes, Dad. You've told me. And told me."

I looked over at Benny, standing at the end of the bar with a group of his buddies conversing and drinking near the machine that offered a stuffed animal if you grabbed one right, secured a giraffe's or teddy bear's arm, leg, or head by manipulating the crane claws through the glass enclosure. I felt like one of those fuzzy prizes, trying to escape my dad's critical commentary. My chances of getting free were less than the giraffe and teddy bear.

Chapter 43

Justin Tedrow, a football player, offensive lineman, a tackle of considerable girth and Robin's boyfriend, sat in front of me in Geometry. I couldn't see around him. We sat in the fifth row from the classroom door that led to the hallway, by the windows, the last row to the left as we faced the front board in the classroom (Miss Genovesee's desk directly in front of our row). Those of us in the fifth row, especially those of us who sat in the seats at the back - Justin and me - had an unencumbered view of the main entrance whenever the blinds were open, which was almost always; who came and went, got to school late, left early, what "suits" - the superintendent, the principal - arrived or departed, when the police or rescue squad were called, what parents appeared, coming to conferences or to pick up sick kids, or brought lunch money to some dork who had forgotten theirs or forgotten their Homecoming bid money and their mom had to bring it. For the fifth row it provided High Entertainment, especially when we got bored with the laggards at the board, those with addled minds who Miss G. patiently helped solve area and volume problems after the rest of us had finished and returned to our seats.

A good natured, playful big 'ol boy is how Justin could have been described. An apt description if you'd also include as big as a small planet. A gaseous one, to my regret. When Justin would pass gas a predictable sequence always followed. After letting one out his routine consisted of accompanying it with a small gutteral "mmm" as he put his face into the armpit of his sleeve, turning around the torso of his cruise ship shaped body toward my desk. I could tell that he was smiling as he feigned to be inconspicuous. Kate Berubee sat in the seat across the aisle from Justin. When she got a whiff of Justin's emissions she always reacted as if she had been maced.

"Jesus, Justin!" And she'd fan the air, hold her nose and gasp for air. Justin's act and Kate's response never failed to get a laugh, though by week four of the trimester I think Miss G. had gotten more than a little tired of it disrupting class. I had to give her credit, though. She was a good-natured soul. After one such silent but deadly eruption she engaged Justin in a conversation about his "activity" that assaulted our olfactory glands.

"Justin. Is that necessary?"

"Is what necessary, Miss G?"

"You know what I'm talking about."

"Honest to God I don't Miss G."

"I'm talking about flatulence, passing gas, tooting, cutting the cheese, *farting*, Justin. I didn't want to say those crude terms, but I assume you're the guilty party by the reactions of your classmates. They all seem to be leaning downwind from you."

Robin, working head-down at her desk, without looking up made a passive defense of her BF.

"He can't help it, Miss G."

Justin looked at Robin, then back at Miss Genovesee.

"Oh, those. Yes Ma'am. That was me."

"Is there anything you can do about not doing that in the classroom, Justin?"

"I kinda can't help it. They sneak up on me. They're creepers. I eat a big breakfast before I come to school. It's the most important meal of the day, you know. That's what the coaches tell us."

"What...I'm hesitant to ask, Justin, but what do you have for breakfast?"

"Well, usually three or four eggs, some ham slices or bacon or both, two pieces of toast, some fruit, like oranges or apple pieces my mom cuts up for me, and some cereal or oatmeal with granola. And sometimes a stack of pancakes with blueberry syrup. And another granola bar on the way to school if I'm still hungry. Fiber is an important part of your diet, helps clean you out so you can get on with your day at optimal efficiency."

"That last part is the part I'm concerned about, Justin."

"Getting my day on with optimal efficiency?"

"Nooo, the fiber. Could we just agree that you take the pass when you need to, um, pass gas and go to the restroom? I'll log you out, you just go."

"Okay. Miss Genovesee. I can try, but like I said, they're creepers, they just creep up on me. They skulk. They're covert, stealthy, until they detonate without warning. I wouldn't eat so much in the morning, but I'm a growing boy. I'm filling out my frame. My dad and my coaches want me lean and mean, but they also think I can carry about three hundred pounds, maybe three oh five and still be able to run a 5.1 forty and hit with velocity and precision. I'm getting letters from Big Ten schools. The Wisconsin coaches came to see me play."

Miss Genovesee took this all in. She started to interrupt a couple times but stopped herself, seemed mesmerized at a world that she could not quite comprehend, that of the high school football lineman. The class silent, all of us paying attention to Justin's dietary, digestion, speed, agility, and college recruitment personal details.

Slowly shaking her head Miss G. said, "And for lunch I'm assuming that you eat a similar amount?"

"Oh no, more usually. Fuel for practice. Did you ever get hungry on the practice field, Miss G?"

Miss G. didn't answer right away. Practice field and Miss G. did not compute. Jumping rope as a little girl came briefly to mind, but that was pretty much it as far as her athletic endeavors were concerned. No Big Ten schools sent her letters offering scholarships for her rope jumping skill.

"Are you OK for now, Justin? We OK on going whenever you feel the, uh, urge, need, whatever?"

Justin was good at paying attention. He looked directly at Miss G.

"Sure. I'll give it my best effort, the ol' college try."

"Just the old high school try should be sufficient, Justin."

Class got going again. All of us working, quiet, nothing to be heard except the shuffling of notebook paper, turning of the geometry book pages and clicking of pens and mechanical pencils. We had crossed the Rubicon. Or so we thought.

"Jesus, Justin!"

Kate Berubee once again. Justin once again. Class ended with Miss Genovesee moving Justin to the seat next to the classroom door, the pass resting in the side whiteboard eraser tray, placed next to his seat, within reaching distance. I could see the board now.

Chapter 44

The Monday of the week of the Valentine's Day dance I went with Kyle to Mrs. Huffington's office to ask if Rabbits In The Living Room could perform at the Valentine's Day dance. I think originally it had been Smalls' idea at lunch, but I couldn't be sure because Smalls rarely had original ideas unless it came to food, and occasionally video games. Food and video games took up most of his active thinking time, the two balancing out sleeping on Smalls' personal twenty-four hour activities pie chart. Weighing in at 3.1 x 10 to the second power, Smalls had been recruited by most all of the school football coaches since fifth grade. Along with Justin Tedrow, they were the biggest kids in our grade. The coaches coaxed Smalls to try out in seventh grade, having to fit him with practice gear from the high school team. Smalls got through the first couple days, even seemed to enjoy practice as the coaches continually encouraged and applauded him. On day three hitting began. On day three, halfway through practice Smalls quit, walking off the field, calling his mother, and talked her into stopping at the Dairy Queen on the way home. Any video game original thoughts usually involved yet another way to blow up those annoying aliens and their spacecraft. Smalls' passive thinking time regarded obeying Kayellen's suggestions and directives.

Never-the-less whose idea it had been, Kyle and I were the Chosen Ones from our lunch table to present the idea to the administration. I wondered why I had been chosen, not being a member of the Rabbits. Maybe my tablemates considered me to be the table captain. In English class Mr. O'Donnell referred to whoever sat in the first seat of every row to be the row captain, the ones to pick up the handouts or books from the book cart to be passed down their row. As per usual I asked to be a row captain on the first day of class, embellishing the role, but as my enthusiasm waned throughout the trimester, as per usual, I drifted to the back of the class to the unused seats, Mr. O'Donnell not objecting.

The next day Kyle and I took our petitioning argument to the office during lunch. We batted around ideas of what to say to convince the administration that it would indeed, be a good idea to let a garage heavy metal band appear at the Valentine's Day dance. We had to decide who would talk first. Kyle had no compunction about starting the conversation. But then, Kyle had no compunction about anything that I knew of. What bespoke well about Kyle is that he didn't spend a lot of time worrying. About anything. A lot to be said for that. So, since Kyle had been a bonafide member of the Rabbits since their inception, and since my roll consisted of being a hanger-on, we decided that Kyle would initiate the conversation. My role would be to gain access to the administrators for the two of us.

Getting to the office during lunch without a pass from a teacher equated to going through the Stations of the Cross, replete with an inquisition at each stop. First we had to convince Mr. South of the legitimacy of our visit. Mr. South would then have to write a pass for us. When we finished delivering our spiel to him, he acted as if writing a pass would be pretty much the same for him as going in for a root canal. A gross imposition of his time. He had to find his passes that he had stashed behind the snack counter and borrow a pen from one of the lunch ladies. That would take much effort, for him to walk from one side of the lunch room to the desk behind the snack counter and to have to bother one of the cashiers for a pen. But he agreed to do so after a sigh and a push off the cafeteria wall where he had been leaning, on guard near the odious freshman tables. We followed behind him across the cafeteria like paddling ducklings, aware of the questioning eyes of our classmates. I think it helped that Mr. South knew me from basketball. It wasn't lost on me that it doesn't hurt to have connections.

Next we had to get by the hall guard, Jolene Henry. We submitted our pass to her. She eyed the pass, eyed us suspiciously. Eyed the pass, eyed us suspiciously again. Checked the signature to determine it hadn't been forged. Reluctantly she handed it back to us.

"Make sure you have it signed and a time put on it when you come back."

Kyle saluted her.

"Yes sir."

Mrs. Henry raised her eyebrows at Kyle's lack of proper respect for someone with the prominent rank of high school hall guard. I took the pass from her hand and thanked her.

"We certainly will. Thank you so much Mrs. Henry."

Walking away, she eyed me with what I interpreted as disdain as I gave Kyle a questionable "What the hell is wrong with you?" look. We walked the short distance to the office door, Kyle marching on, oblivious to his lack of social skills. Oh, this is going to go well, I thought.

Entering the office, the next hurdle, the office secretary Ms. Schnitzel, sat at her desk, turned away from us looking at herself in a small hand mirror, teasing her hair, brushing it this way and that, checking it from different angles as she moved the mirror from left to right then right to left. We waited patiently, taking a seat by the office windows where the parents, textbook salesmen, office runners and students faking illnesses waiting for their parents to pick them up usually sat. We finally got Ms. Schnitzel's attention.

"May I help you?"

"We'd like to talk with Mr. Kleindienst. It's about the Valentine's Day dance," I said.

"Did he send for you?"

"Nooo. We just have something to ask him."

Ms. Schnitzel contemplated. Then, picking up the phone, looking at us skeptically, she buzzed Mr. Kleindienst on the intercom. She asked us our names, gave them to Mr. Kleindienst, told him we had asked to see him, then waved us to go to his office.

Mr. Kleindienst, Assistant Principal. In charge of activities and instruction. Tall and slim, he favored gray suits and sport coats, beige sweaters and always wore a white shirt that accentuated his constant tan - did he go to a tanning salon, use spray-on, take weekend trips to Florida? We were afraid to ask. Usually his tie had been loosened by lunch time unless he expected the superintendent to make an appearance in the building or had an upcoming contentious meeting with a parent.

Lanky, lean, Mr. Kleindienst moved smoothly through the halls like a former athlete. I knew he played a lot of golf. His brownish straight hair slanted smoothly at an angle, never moved, looked like a fifty dollar haircut. The look of a rich college frat boy. He maintained an ever-present appearance of coolness, of being cool, in control, not overbearing, kinda hip, approachable but above the madness where others may have become stressed. He preferred to be out in the halls, visiting teachers, talking with students, wandering through the kitchen talking with the cafeteria workers, taking bus duty outside the main entrance before and after school, chatting with the custodians, anything rather than sitting behind a desk. The opposite of Mrs. Huffington's style. She preferred being the CEO, giving commands to her staff through emails, over the intercoms and room phones connected to the office and classrooms, and through walkie talkies that the other Jackson

High School administrators and building engineer, building and grounds supervisor, and cafeteria food director and lunchroom supervisor were required to have on their persons at all times. Mrs. H. preferred a land-locked domain. Mr. Kleindienst preferred sailing the high seas.

Normally Mr. Kleindienst handled all school activities except for sports, Mr. Goldsbee's bailiwick. Mr. Kleindienst would give the OK, and hand out the forms with the school's approval and legal disclaimers to be signed for the parties' request to use the school facilities. But he said he had already hired a DJ as he always did for the Valentine's Day dance.

"This one's over my pay grade, boys."

He motioned across the hall with his thumb.

"You're going to have to talk to the boss."

We thanked him and went back out to talk with Ms. Schnitzel.

Holding her compact mirror to her face trying to tame her rebellious curls, her back to us, she noticed us annoyingly standing behind her reflection, and swung her seat around. We stood at her desk, obvious that we wanted something more from her.

"What?"

"We need to talk to Mrs. Huffington. That's what Mr. Kleindienst said."

Ms. Schnitzel did not look happy, for a variety of reasons. Her obstreperous curls, having to deal with two boys on a dubious mission, and that this might delay Mrs. Huffington's eagerly awaited lunch. She pressed the intercom button to buzz Mrs. Huffington's office, not taking her gaze off us, lest we make a run for Mrs. H.'s office without going through official office protocol, getting by the border patrol unabated.

"WHAT?"

"I've got two boys here that want to see you about the Valentines' dance."

"Tell them to see Mr. Kleindienst."

"They did. Mr. Kleindienst said they have to talk to you."

"What do they WANT?"

We could hear Mrs. Huffington's voice from her office around the corner in the office hallway. Intercom not needed. "They have an idea that they'd like you to consider."

A delay. Nothing for about forty-five seconds. Ms. Schnitzel drummed her fingers. Kyle picked up the photo frame of Ms. Schnitzels's children on the front edge of her desk, looked at it, then put it back down. Ms. Schnitzel frowned at Kyle. I wanted to slap his hand.

"Oh alright. Send them in."

Mrs. Schnitzel wiggled her index finger at us, the motion to come over so she could whisper to us.

"I just want to tell you that she's hangry."

I shook my head a little.

"Hung...ang...she's what?"

"Hungry and angry. The superintendent just left her office before you boys came in. He was not happy. So she can't be happy."

Mrs. Schnitzel pointed toward Mrs. H's office.

"And she's hungry, too. The delivery guy is late with her lunch."

Kyle asked, "What is she having delivered, pizza?"

Mrs. Schnitzel shook her head.

"Oh no. Lobster rolls, French onion soup, toasted baguettes drizzled with olive oil and topped with artichoke hearts, and caramelized apples for dessert. She has some vanilla ice cream in the freezer in the fridge in her office that she'll top the apples with."

"That's what we're having in the cafeteria too," I said.

Kyle looked at me, wondering if I was serious. Ms. Schnitzel smirked and shook her head, dismissing my attempt at humor.

251

She had had it with smart ass kids.

Ms. Schitzel's intercom buzzed. Mrs. H.

"Well, where are they. And has my lunch come yet?

"The boys are coming right away."

Mrs. Schnitzel gave us a shooing motion toward Mrs. Huffington's office.

"And I'll call the deli again."

Mrs. Schnitzel's right hand index finger instantly knew where to go on the oft-traveled route to an oft-used button on the desk office phone. Romanoff's Deli, on speed dial.

"I don't want the lobster rolls to be cold! You tell them that!"

"Yes, Mrs. Huffington. I'm calling right now."

Mrs. Huffington had cleaned off her desk, clearing space for the forthcoming delivery, breaking her morning fast from breakfast - except for the empty bag of Funions lying on top of the waste basket papers that Mrs. Huffington had thrown in sometime during the morning.

Mrs. Huffington became a different animal when there didn't happen to be any involvement with food. In the lunch line and at the Food and Fitness holiday fest, and when I saw her with her friends at the mall food court, Mrs. Huffington's brainy transmitter friends, serotonin and dopamine, kicked in, the neural transmitters sending their food love to Mrs. Huffington's cerebrum, jumpstarting her food mood attitude. Food not involved, her mood quickly deteriorated. *Delaying* her food, well, do so at your own risk.

We walked in. She sat at her desk, unsmiling, hands folded together in front of her. She looked bigger than usual.

"How can I help you boys?" she asked.

"Yo, Mrs. H." said Kyle.

"Pardon me?"

I quickly nudged Kyle aside.

"Hi Mrs. Huffington. Do you have a few minutes that you

could spare to talk with us about an idea we have for the Valentine's Day dance?"

"I have *just* a couple minutes. That's why my secretary said you could come in. Didn't she tell you that? Now what is it?"

She took a deep breath, hesitant in whether she wanted to listen to our idea.

"We were wondering, just wondering, if Kyle's band could perform at the Valentine's dance. You may have heard of them. Most of the kids around school know who they are. 'Rabbits In The Living Room'?"

No sign of recognition on Mrs. H.'s unsmiling face.

"The Twitchells are in the band along with Darby Senna, who's a sophomore here, along with Kyle."

I side-nodded my head at Kyle to indicate that the kid standing next to me on my left was Kyle. Just so she knew.

"They're really good. And they don't want any money. It'd be for free. You know, for exposure."

"Are you in the band, too?" asked Mrs. Huffington, trying to figure out why I had been delivering the band pitch to her if I wasn't, why I had said "they" instead of "we."

"No. I'm kind of, sort of their publicity guy. Doesn't pay much but I don't do much."

Kyle nodded incessantly, like a bobble-head doll, as if his incessant nodding would somehow convince Mrs. H. Mrs. H. leaned back in her swivel chair, turning it to face the windows looking out over the courtyard. She couldn't both look at us and think at the same time.

"We brought a CD our band made," offered Kyle.

The chair pivoted back around, transporting Mrs. H. like a twirling ride at a church festival. Mrs. Huffington reached out her hand. Kyle placed the CD gently in her palm, being careful with wording that he thought would not affront her again in any way, shape, form. Ixnay on any hip teen talk.

"They're the songs of my people."

"Who…who are your people, Kyle?" said Mrs. Huffington with a puzzled look.

I looked at Kyle. I recalled that it hadn't been that long ago when he hardly said anything. I liked THAT Kyle.

"A bunch of guys that I play within the band."

Mrs. H. looked up at Kyle for what seemed like a half minute, looking puzzled by Kyle's reply. I took a deep breath.

Then, Mrs. H turned the Rabbits' CD in her hand, rotated it around, her index finger on her right hand serving as the hub, poking through the center hole.

"My first inclination is to say no. How do I know you won't play something with suggestive lyrics or profanity? I'm really leery of doing this boys. Besides, we already have a DJ."

Kyle turned to me. I looked at Kyle. I didn't think Kyle had gotten the message about the manner in which he should address Mrs. H. so I quickly jumped in, resuming the job of being the band's spokesman.

"They'll only play the songs on the CD. And if you'd just let them play one set, maybe twenty minutes. They're all fast songs. Nothing offensive. No profanity. The kids can rock out, get their energy out. The DJ plays, you know, songs that are pretty lame. I mean, how many Taylor Swift songs can you listen to? The kids, the students would really like it if you'd let the Rabbits play."

Mrs. Huffington, to her credit, listened intently. I should have upped the chances by offering her a food tray, snack items, a steamer plate with spaghetti and meatballs. The smell would tantalize her taste buds, and Mrs. H.'s taste buds dominated her thinking process.

"If I let Kyle's band play, I'll have to be there, just in case, you know, something, something *untoward* might happen when they play. Normally Mr. Kleindienst and some teachers chaperone the dances. I have another commitment, but I might be able to change

254

my plans and be there. Come back and see me tomorrow, boys, at this same time. I'll listen to your CD, Kyle. I'll give you two my decision then. My secretary will write you a pass to go back to the cafeteria."

Mrs. H. turned her chair back around, slowly twirled Kyle's CD on her finger, just above her head, inspecting it, her eyes following the rotation, as if she could hear the music, her hand a human turntable.

Kyle backed out of the office, nodding. We asked Ms. Schnitzel for a pass and went back to lunch, opening the office door for the Romanoff Deli delivery guy holding three carry-out bags.

Optimistic one minute, pessimistic the next about the chances of RITLR getting to play, the lunchroom visionaries at our lunch table proffered their opinions. Smalls said yes, because Mrs. H., knowing she would have to be in attendance if she made the decision to allow the Rabbits to play, would be swayed by the thought of the traditional Valentine's Day all-you-can-eat servings of pizza and Valentine heart-shaped sugar cookies with pink frosting. (Because of Smalls' copious appetite, he knew how Mrs. Huffington's thought process worked. Small's gastronomy also looked forward to the all-you-can eat pizza and fistfuls of cookies.) Kate Berubee said no way. Too much to lose, not enough to gain. That's the way Mrs. Huffington would look at it. Hobie said he hoped she'd come just to see her shake her groove thing. We visualized Mrs. Huffington shaking her groove thing. Philco wondered if her kankles could take much shaking.

"She probably dances like this," said Philco, twisting the top half of his torso back and forth, shoulders taut, arms straight out at three and nine, fists clenched, as if he - imitating Mrs. Huffington - had her hands on the steering wheel, maneuvering through traffic, avoiding the potholes. Philco wiped imaginary sweat away from his forehead, then reached down with a pretending grimace to rub his ankle-kankles, his groove thing finished being shook in simulated Huffington fashion.

The next day, armed with an office pass and not having to run the gauntlet again, we dutifully reported to Mrs. Huffington to listen to her verdict. We entered her office hesitantly after Ms. Schnitzel buzzed Mrs. H. on the intercom.

"Come in, come in, boys. Have a seat."

We obediently sat.

"I'll cut to the chase right away. Kyle, I'm letting your band play. The DJ will be playing three sets, one at the start of the dance, then one after the pizzas are delivered. That's when the Rabbits can play. You'll come on about 10:00 and play until 10:30. Then the DJ will follow you, ending the night with slow songs to wind it down. You'll have to get together with Mr. Danks, the building engineer, to discuss the setup, the extensions cords, outlets, whatever that you'll need."

Kyle's eyes and his smile became bigger the more Mrs. Huffington talked.

I have to tell you boys something, but I hope you'll keep it to yourselves.

We both nodded enthusiastically.

"Sure, Mrs. H," I said. Kyle nodded some more.

"When I was a little older than you boys I was a big heavy metal fan, a bonafide metalhead. I saw AC-DC play three times in concert."

Mrs. H. raised three fingers. Kyle and I stared at them as she held them for us to see and process the implications.

"I still have their LPs. And Deep Purple was my second favorite. Only saw them once, at the old Olympia Stadium in Detroit with my girlfriends. That was quite a show. We still talk about it. Rushed the stage. Still have my concert t-shirt."

We didn't know what to say. How, I mean, why, I mean what...I had pictured Mrs. Huffington, when she listened to music, putting on a Frank Sinatra or Mills Brothers CD, drinking a mint julep or a gin fizz on her patio late at night.

"I'm looking forward to hearing your band play, Kyle. I'll have it put on the announcements starting tomorrow that you'll be appearing. See Mr. Danks, the building engineer after school and tell him what you'll need for your band to set up, the electrical cords and microphones. He's usually in the boiler room after school making out the second shift's schedule. I'll call him on his walkie-talkie to tell him to expect you and that I gave your band approval to play. I'll see you boys Saturday night."

It took us a few seconds to process what we had heard. Then Kyle took a few steps toward Mrs. Huffington's desk and put his hand up for a high-five from Mrs. H. Mrs. H. leaned her chair forward, bent slightly over the desk, the chair's front wheels starting to tip and roll backward, and returned Kyle's high-five with a gentle slap-grasp of his fingers. Mrs. H. high-fived Kyle… Mrs. H. high-fived Kyle. I remember thinking, "Did that just happen?" As she repositioned herself back into her rolling chair with a back sliding thump, she turned to me, smiling, knowing she had surprised us with her answer and tale about her rock and roll groupie past.

"Thank you, Mrs. H," I said. Then stumbling over each other, Kyle hurried out the door first, wanting to tell his lunch mates, and me wondering if I should offer a handshake, a high-five, knuckles? to cement the verbal contract with Principal Huffington. Brain-locked, I gave Mrs. H. a little side-to-side wave instead, along with a vapid smile. She smiled back. Whoda thought…

Chapter 45

The standings in the Lake Erie North Coast Athletic League at the middle of February read like this in the *Jackson Times-Courier*:

	LENCAL	OVERALL
Jackson	11-2	16-4
Midlothian	11-2	18-3
Lower Sandusky	9-4	13-7
Crane Creek	8-5	10-9
Sun Prairie	7-6	10-11
Port Monroe	3-10	5-16
Grafton	2-11	4-16
Deshler	1-12	3-18

One game remaining on the league schedule. Coach said if we didn't beat Sun Prairie, the last team on our league schedule, on Thursday, that there would be no tomorrow. This briefly bummed me out, Friday usually being the only school day I bought my lunch, choices being macaroni and cheese or pizza (cheese, pepperoni, or mushroom - I always went with the 'shrooms) and tater tots. Accompanied by a salad, of course, with my new found health conscious eating choices. Alison and Jillian ate A Lunch and I had B Lunch, so they weren't present to supervise my lunch line choices. I felt slightly guilty whenever I chose the artery clogging mac and cheese. A and J would certainly not approve. But no tomorrow, Coach? A harsh punishment ensuing for the loss of a high school basketball game.

Game Day. Excitement built throughout the day. Coach Arnold often talked to us about playing with a sense of urgency. *That* we had today. As I passed our lockers in the junior wing I shouted out to Jose', Hobie and Kenny over the hall traffic noise.

"Ballz to the wallz today, boys!"

Jose' turned from his locker and yelled back, "We're in it to win it!"

"Dogs goin' down, bro!" Hobie's retort, punctuated by a fist pump.

I crossed oncoming hall traffic to high-five my teammates.

"Up top!" I yelled, extending my hand as high as I could.

Kenny, Jose', then Hobie accommodated my demand with arm-slinging wind-ups, hand-smacking high-fiving, our palms left pulsating, throbbing. Accompanied by macho grins. I U-turned and abruptly crossed back across the hall to my hall cruising lane, causing a couple freshmen girls to brake hard.

Hobie cupped his non-throbbing hand and yelled, "Bound and determined!"

I shouted back, "I'm determined, but why do I have to be bound?"

Hobie shook his head and laughed. He appreciated my taking words literally language schtick.

A pep assembly had been scheduled for last period. We ran on pep assembly schedule with shortened periods during the school day. The team sat together at the end of the bleachers near where the microphone had been set up at the south end of the gym. All other students sat by class, seniors and juniors on the west side, sophomores and freshmen on the east. Laughing, excited students filed in, many wearing Kestrel red and black. The pep band, situated across from the team, blared out the school fight song, *"Onward Kestrels!"* Some—mostly seniors—wore red fuzzy wigs. They referred to themselves as *"The Redheads."* About ten or so juniors carried cardboard signs reading *"The Jack Attack!"* Mr.

Hoolihan signaled with his baton for the pep band to finish. Robin, in her cheerleader outfit, took the microphone. But just as she started to speak a voluminous cheer broke out from the seniors, hands cupped around mouths to megaphy the sound:

Senior Rah!
Senior Rah!
Rah Rah Seniors!

The same class cheer went round in turn, seniors to juniors to sophomores to freshmen. As per usual, the freshmen, caught off guard, answered wimpily, being shouted down by the other classes at the beginning of their limp response, many of the frosh looking confused, stunned looks on their faces as the other classes booed them for their naivete. And this being their fourth pep assembly of the year. Freshmen.

After the castigating of the ninth graders, Robin, clutching the microphone, tried to reverse the venomous beginning.

"OK, guys. Everybody! We're going to start out with the Victory cheer."

The cheerleaders scattered around the gym and yelled in unison:

We want a VIC-TORY!
(Followed by rhythmic in sync clapping)
We want a VIC-TORY!
(More in sync clapping)

After about seven or eight repetitions, ad nauseam of that same line voiced by sixty or seventy percent of the student body, it had been determined that a quorum of Jackson students desired a victorious outcome for the boys basketball team. The other thirty percent or so of the student body didn't partake in the cheer, many of those the shop kids, the Goths, the skaters, the nerds, the geeks, the misfits, the uninterested—those that had a gripe with the jocks, those that thought sports a fool's undertaking, those who found the gym and any gym related activities distasteful, repugnant, and those that resisted the herd mentality. My eyeball estimate came up with the result that about sixty-eight percent of Jackson students wanted us to win, seventeen percent wished upon the varsity a crushing, demoralizing defeat, and fifteen percent didn't give a rat's ass who won.

Most of them were easy to spot. The outliers on the Bell Curve, those that resisted being infused with indoctrinated emotionalism. They sat in groups of two to about six or seven, dissidents, usually sitting at the top of the bleachers, a passive aggressive defiance at having to attend, distancing themselves from the believers, students who believed in the idea of school spirit, an ideology, a brain-warping instilled in their unguarded minds starting on Day 1 in pre-school in the Jackson school district. I have to admit that the past two years on my self-imposed exile from the basketball program that I hadn't drummed up much if any enthusiasm for the team and mostly sat on my hands at the pep rallies and games. I occasionally would give a polite clapping, four or five light claps, sort of like what they do at tennis matches for a decent, but not spectacular shot. I lightly applauded mostly for those players I still considered friends on the team. When I went to the games I didn't root for them to lose, but if they struggled, that was fine by me. I just wanted to be missed.

Next followed class competitions, competing against each other and a faculty team. Tricycle races and bobbing for apples started the activities on the gym floor. In between the cheerleaders did their darnedest to keep the pep assembled throng in at least a semi-engaged state. To the Seniors and Juniors - *"You yell Red!"* To the Sophomores and Freshmen: *"You yell Black!"* They motioned for the upperclassmen to start the acclamation of the school colors.

261

"Red!" They yelled. One wondered what else they would have yelled if prompted. *"Black!"* followed the sophomore and freshmen classes after a short instructional by the cheerleaders in front of their sections. Those students responding did a remarkably adequate job at yelling the one word response.

"Red! Black! Red! Black!"

That tribute to coloration continued for two or three minutes. The competitions resumed, true and false questions asked of faculty members and kids chosen at random from each class by student council members. Wrong answers followed by a pie in the face (faculty given arcane questions such as, "Wally Pip is best known for inventing the Hokey-Pokey." Students questions along the lines of, "During the Civil War there was a North-South All Star game."). Then a dance contest featuring pre-determined students, the known good dancers, versus a faculty member, the winner judged by a panel holding 1-through-10 judging cards, then, musical chairs, and for a final, Mr. Kleindienst with a decibel meter measuring how loud each class could shriek, scream, yell. Seniors won. Seniors always won.

After the cheerleaders quickly cleaned the floor, wiping up the pie-in-the-face shaving cream and water from the bobbing-for-apple contest, Robin brought out Mr. Goldsbee to introduce Coach Arnold. But before Robin could finish introducing Mr. Goldsbee, he wrested the microphone away from her.

"HEEEEEY JACKSON HIGH SCHOOL! WHO'S GOING TO THE GAME TONIGHT! SHOW ME SOME HANDS!" was what he tried to ask the students, though what came out of the microphone consisted of a piercing ultra high-pitched screech that stunned and pained our eardrums as Mr. Goldsbee swallowed the microphone. Flummoxed by students yelling and holding their hands over their ears and a few discreetly showing their middle fingers indicating their displeasure for his lack of microphone etiquette, Mr. Goldsbee willingly handed the offending

262

microphone back to Robin as if it were a snake trying to bite him, who then brought up Coach Arnold.

Coach Arnold looked slightly embarrassed at the applause given by the students. He rubbed the top of his balding head, as if composing what to say. He gave a slight chuckle, the one he always gave our team before he began imparting a bit of his wisdom.

"I want everyone to look at the banner up there on the wall," Coach said, pointing to the banner heading "Boys Basketball Conference Champions."

Everyone looked.

"The last time we put the years for a conference championship up there was twenty-two years ago. I was a young man then."

We laughed. Coach must have been around forty at that time. Nobody forty years old could consider themselves young, we thought.

"I want Mr. Goldsbee to be pulling down that banner on Monday morning and adding this year to it. But in this life I believe that you almost always get what you deserve. And these boys," Coach gestured at us—the team—seated together in the stands to his left, "These boys will get you a conference championship tonight at Sun Prairie, IF they deserve it."

Then he handed the microphone back to Robin and trudged back toward the coaches' office where Mr. Goldsbee and Mr. Kleindienst stood, expressionless. Not really a whoop-the-crowd-into-a-frenzy speech, but that was so Coach, the way he usually talked, not prone to superlatives, compliments, exaggeration, platitudes, hyperbole. Expecting that the student body would be in an uproar following Coach's talk, the cheerleaders stood on the sidelines, hands on hips, looking at each other, caught off guard by the silence in the gym, waiting for Robin to decide the cheer that would re-invigorate the assembled student body. Robin went with the "You Say Red! You Say Black!" But the students, looking at the clock, determining that the bell to dismiss for the day would be ringing in two or three minutes, were more interested in putting on jackets and backpacks. The cheerleaders gave a few half-hearted Red (!) and Black (!) then headed toward the center of the court to talk about whatever cheerleaders talk about, probably congratulating themselves for a semi-well planned pep rally and summing up the students' laggard efforts to do their part in the last cheer as, "oh well." The pep band played the fight song, ushering the students out the doors to their lockers, buses, and cars. I waited for Mindy to depart the cheerleaders pow wow.

"Good job, Derosiers," I said, offering her a mid-high five.

"Thanks, I guess. Kind of crash and burn at the end."

Mindy rolled her eyes in disgust. I listened, acted concerned.

"I was going to do my somersaults - handsprings and cartwheels followed by backflips, from one end to the other while the band played and everyone watched me and cheered me and yelled my name but your stupid coach's talk was such a downer the stupid kids just wanted to go home so I didn't."

"Nobody cares," I said, "It's just a pep assembly."

Whoops. Wrong choice of words.

Mindy gave me a steamed look, and said in a creaky, low slow voice, copping her usual hands-on-hips posturing, "And yours…is just…a game tonight."

My bad. Game, set, match to Mindy on that one. She turned and walked away.

"Yup. *That* might have been the wrong thing to say," I had thought. Just what I needed, more drama, self-inflicted, to think about heading into tonight's game.

Chapter 46

The route to Sun Prairie wound around the lake after exiting the turnpike. An hour and fifteen minute trip, our view from the frosted side windows of the yellow Jackson City Schools bus consisted of watching drifting snow blowing and piling up against the farmers' snow fences along Route 80, the mile markers going past, then by a lake covered by a sheet of crystallized ice as we headed into town on the Sun Prairie Beltline, then an uphill drive to Rimrock Road, home of Sun Prairie High School.

A spanking new high school, opened the past August. As we entered, the school, shaking snow off our knit hats and travel bags, we noticed they had closed circuit TVs to beam the game in the gym into the cafeteria on the walls by the tables near the concession stands. The gym featured huge downward pointing triangular shaped windows over the bleachers on each side. Snow had begun to fall at a faster rate, coming down hard, through the windows above and behind the fans on the scarlet hard plastic bleachers emblazoned with a gray "SP" across the mid-section. Prairie dog cut-out black silhouettes adorned the end walls of the brightly lit gym with the names and numbers of the boys and girls basketball players.

The Prairie Dogs starting line-up featured three sophomores, a freshman and a senior. They had started out slowly, losing six of their first seven, but as the sophs and the freshman matured they had gotten it together, their record now standing at ten and ten. The ten wins featured the improbable upset of Midlothian—at

Midlothian! The Tarblooders also played away on this, the last night of the season for league play before the state tournament started next week. The schedule had Midlothian at Deshler, an almost certain win for the Tarblooders. Our task looked to be considerably more formidable.

I took my Kestrels uniform out of my bag, felt, inspected the red cloth and cast a thought toward the journey we, I, had been through since tryouts began in late October. Black letters accented with white backing spelled out "Kestrels" in block letters, as did my number 22 on the back. The dark red shorts had thin white-black-white stripes on each side. Our Kestrel logo graced the left front of my shorts.

The pre-game festivities started with Sun Prairie's Senior Awards Night. We sat and listened while the announcer regaled the activities and accomplishments of Nick Barcus, read Nick's statements of his favorite basketball moments — "Goofing around in the dorms at summer camp at Michigan State" — and read his thank you's, to his coaches, teammates, and to his little sister Katie for rebounding for him in his driveway while he practiced his shot. Nick had added, "Of course I gave her a dollar for every time she did," which drew a laugh from the crowd.

Mr. and Mrs. Barcus beamed, Mrs. Barcus' black dress displaying the corsage that Nick nervously pinned on her at center court at the start of the festivities. The spectators clapped when Nick accomplished the task, Nick's face a bright red, matching his mom's corsage. Our seniors had played against Nick since junior high, and they and us—the rest of the team and coaches—politely applauded his accomplishments, which included a 3.5 Grade Point Average and an athletic scholarship to Tiffin University where Nick would continue his basketball career and major in Cyber Defense and Information Assurance. Photos finished being taken after Nick's teammates and the Sun Prairie cheerleaders presented him with small gifts, a balloon in school colors with his name on it—how exciting!

Several of Nick's teammates had names of towns in Texas—Houston, Dallas, Tyler, Austin, Irving, Garland, and even one named Laredo. His sisters—Abilene and Odessa. One of our JV players that had grown up in Sun Prairie and moved to Jackson, Jamir Boutros, who we called "J-Booty," held a program and pointed down the Sun Prairie roster, stopping at each player with a given name of a city, town, or municipality in Texas and read it aloud for us as we sat watching the pre-game festivities. But J-Booty had been at a loss as to the reason why. Something must have been going on sixteen, seventeen years ago that influenced Sun Prairians to give their progeny names from the Lone Star state. Maybe a Texas-themed restaurant franchise opening had excited the populace.

Some cheerleader thought the balloons would make a worthwhile parting gift—and they would have, if you were six years old, but they also nicely presented Nick with a framed collage of photos showing him shooting, dribbling, rebounding, at attention for the National Anthem, in the team huddle, flashing a "V" for victory sign after a win. The standard senior night stuff. I sat at the end of the bleachers by our locker room with the other players, lost in thought, hand under my chin, thinking about next year, my senior night, walking out with my dad and mom. Should I ask my dad not to come? With his volatile personality anything could happen. It had the potential to be highly embarrassing. Maybe I could pretend I was an orphan and have the Kestrel mascot as an escort. Instead of getting a handshake from my father and a kiss on the cheek from my mother I'd get a - literal - peck on the cheek.

Warm-ups started. A bigger than usual contingent of our fans had made the road trip including a hundred or more of our students, realizing the importance of our potential conference clinching win and, because of a teacher work day, there would be no school tomorrow.

Mindy and the cheerleaders had brought their pompons, shiny red, clutched against their hips, one saddle-shoed foot out, one back, readying for action. Then rolling their poms in cyclical motion, yelling, they exhorted our students.

Florida oranges, Texas cactus
We play Prairie Dogs just for practice
Put em in a high chair, feed 'em with a spoon
We'll beat your team any afternoon
Put em in a bathtub, pull out the plug
There goes your Prairie Dogs, blub, blub, blub!

A stomp cheer followed, a fan favorite. Jackson's student section exaggeratedly stomped the bleachers as the cheer girls' shoes thumped the floor, pompons shimmering in their hands-on-hips posture, elbows out.

R-O-W-D-I-E!
R-O-W-D-I-E!
That's the way we spell ROW-DY!
(Stomp-Stomp-Stomp-Stomp)
(Stomp-Stomp-Stomp-Stomp)
R-O-W-D-I-E!
Let's get ROWDY!

The cheerleaders each thrusted a single pompom into their air after the last "ROWDY," then clapped both poms together, quite pleased at choosing a cheer that the students participated in. They had had the experience earlier in the season where their cheers went ignored by the student body. Too lame. A cheer fail. Mindy brought along new cheers from her old school, some which didn't jive with political correctness. Mrs. Huffington thought she wanted one in particular banned the first she heard it, but Mr. Kleindienst insisted it was all in fun, just as long none of the girls didn't find it offensive.

Like yeah, for sure
I just got a manicure
The sun I swear is bleaching out my hair
Like 44 or 34?
I don't even know the score
Go go, fight fight
Gee I hope I look alright!!
Go Kestrels!!

The Prairie Dogs played an up tempo game, running and pressing at every opportunity, trying to get shots off as quickly as they could off their fast break, then diving into their full court press when they scored. They prided themselves on being in better shape than their opponents. Their coach, Paul Weston, insisted that any player not playing a fall sport run on the cross country team. Their practices, we heard, consisted of full go, up and down court drills and scrimmaging for two hours, with only occasional breaks for drinks and free throws. They also ran a quick break after the other team scored. Coach Arnold told us that they used "loose nets," nets pulled as wide as possible so that when the opponent did score, the ball came through the net quickly so they could get out and go. Their center had been coached to grab the ball before it hit the floor, inbound the ball to their point guard as quickly as possible while their 2 guard and small forward ran the floor down the sideline looking for the long pass from the point guard for a quick scoring layup before we could back on defense.

At the beginning of the season they had difficulty with the new system, Coach Weston, like Coach Arnold, being newly hired before the school year. But their players believed in the system, cut down their turnovers, started making shots, and being in peak physical condition wore down their opponents in the second half. Coach Arnold told us that Sun Prairie ran Midlothian off the floor in the fourth quarter, that the Tarblooder players had their tongues hanging out, grabbing their shorts, gasping for air. Sun Prairie had trailed by fourteen points in the second quarter, but won by sixteen, 76-60, scoring the last seventeen points of the game. Once they went ahead, 61-60, Coach Arnold said that Midlothian quit, their players gassed, knowing they had nothing left in the tank with which to compete.

But Coach Arnold, as always, had a game plan. And he always said, "If you do exactly what I say, we will win." We believed him.

It turned into one of the best high school games of the season. Two opposite forces, game strategies going at one another. Sun Prairie running at every opportunity, trying to increase the tempo while we tried to slow the game down.

Our coaches had us prepared. We used our 1-2-2 zone defense to slow the Prairie Dogs' fast break, with my assignment to play the left wing on defense and Kenny the right wing, getting back on defense ASAP on every one of our possessions, whether a make or a miss, to stop long passes their point guard would launch to their guards running the sidelines. If those passes connected, their guards would either shoot a quick three, drive to the basket, or hit their post player running down the middle of the floor, looking for easy lay-ups. Our two bigs, K.J. and Tommy, jammed the shoulders of their rebounders to prevent quick outlet passes. We threw in the occasional 2-2-1 fallback press to delay their quick upcourt passes.

Coach told us, "With teams that want to pass the ball upcourt, make 'em dribble. With teams that like to dribble it up, make 'em pass. If you can make them walk the ball up the floor you know you've done your job."

The lead changed hands a dozen times or more. Kenny had his best game of the year, scoring 22 points, his last two giving us the lead at 60-59 with fifteen seconds to play. A Prairie Dog errant shot, a rebound by K.J. and we were into our stall when they double-teamed me and as I pivoted looking for an open man, hacked my arm with 6.6 seconds to go. Their scouting report probably had it underlined in red that I was the one to foul at the end if the game was close.

"Time out, Red!" shouted one of the zebras (as the radio sports announcer on JAX 97.6, Bobby Harrelson, often referred to the referees). No one talked to me during the time-out. Coach Arnold said to stay with the defensive plan we had been using. When we broke the huddle a couple of my teammates whacked me on the butt. I shook my arms to get loose - no need really, my body in full sweat mode. I went through my shooting motion a few times before the referee handed me the ball. I had a brief vision of my dad shooting paper napkin wads at the bar.

"Double bonus. Two shots," the referee said as he handed me the ball. "Relax on the first one," he said to the players readying to rebound on both sides of the lane.

I lined my right foot up with the middle of the rim. Dribbled two times, put the ball in my shooting pocket, planned the release over my right toe, right hip, right shoulder, right eye. The ball hit the back iron, bounced almost straight up, came down, caught the lip of the rim and dropped out. I hadn't heard the crowd, so used to hearing during games now that it seemed like background white noise. But now I heard it, took a brief look at the Sun Prairie students up and screaming, some yelling my name. Nick Barcus offered his sentiment, hands on knees, lined up at the third free throw lane spot, a few feet away, head turned in my direction.

"Brick another one, Buddy."

Another miss and we'd have to worry about defending the

whole court. If I had made the one I had just missed, plus this one, we could have led by three and only would have to defend the perimeter, the three point line. Now, make or miss, we had to defend the whole half court at the defensive end. I knew that Barcus would run the right lane, or if I missed, get the rebound and bring it up. And I knew he'd be hell-bent on getting to the basket, either score the game winner game tying basket or get fouled and win or tie it at the line.

I missed it. Rimmed and fell off to the left. Barcus rebounded and took off on a speed dribble. He used his crossover dribble to get by Jose' near half court, Jose' not wanting to foul, but it slowed Barcus just a touch as he headed toward our basket. I chased Barcus down from behind, trying to beat him to a spot to stop his drive as I had been taught, ingrained in us with our constant diet of zig zag 1-on-1 defensive drills.

Watching the video later, I saw myself plant upright, protecting myself about two steps on the basket side of the foul line. Barcus launched himself into me, thinking he could draw a foul as he threw his shot up on the backboard. The clock read 0:03. I watched myself hit the floor, Barcus falling on top of me, looking up and seeing the ball ricochet off the opposite rim, then the ref underneath the basket putting his hand behind his head and running upcourt signaling a charge against Barcus. I can't say I remember much about the aftermath because I had been knocked out, and spent the next two days in Sun Prairie Hospital.

Chapter 47

Back at school on Tuesday morning, my teammates and coaches greeted me at the front door of the school, carrying the LENCAL championship trophy, clapping as I entered. Looking back, it had to have been one of the best moments of my life. Coach Arnold told me only someone who was a real team player would have done that for his team. I had rarely been accused of being a team player before. I had gone through the multiple tests and the concussion protocol at the hospital, and they released me Monday night for Mom and Benny to take home. Benny, of course, had filled me in on the last 6.6 seconds in my hospital room. He briefly, albeit subtly and quickly, mentioned the Missing Of The Free Throws. But he rained praise, in his own left-handed compliment way, on drawing The Charge. The fact that we were co-champs, that Midlothian had beaten Deshler, didn't matter. We'd still have our team photo in the trophy case, our championship year on the list of championship teams on a red and black banner on the wall inside the gym.

"Not many guys would have had the guts to do that. I've got to give that to you. That's something a team player does, nothing you've ever accused of being. Isn't that the first charge you've ever taken? You could have been called for a foul, lost the game and never been able to show your face around Jackson again."

Mom frowned at Benny when he said that.

"A concussion won't hurt you because you're half crazy anyway."

Mom said, "That's enough, Benny. If you can't compliment your brother don't say anything. He's been through a lot."

"OK. So he's totally crazy. What? That's not a compliment?"

We all laughed at that one. I do know how I summoned the courage for The Charge. It went back to a game Benny and I played in the back yard, where we had to man up. And not solely on the basketball court. My brother and I played a game where we stood about twenty feet apart and heaved balls at each other - tennis balls, hard rubber balls, mini-footballs, and one time, baseballs. It started in the house, in our bedroom, with little plastic golf balls then progressed to outside so that we could throw harder and not worry about breaking anything or Mom hearing us yell what boys yell when a hard cylindrical object propelled from twelve feet away makes an impact on a fleshy part. My brother, being five years older, had about five inches and thirty pounds on me. He said this would make me tougher. Usually I gave in first. We played without gloves and our rules stated that you couldn't move more than a few inches - you had to keep a pivot foot on the ground.

Every once in a while I got my brother good. Aiming for the head usually didn't work because you could avoid the head-high airborne rockets by a quick head turn. But what usually worked for me were rockets at my brother's ankles, knees. I'd get him with a shin burger and he'd yelp and explete an expletive or two, then tell me not to say what he just said. When that happened, when you got blasted, you were expected to keep your pivot foot, no hopping around allowed or you were the double loser and the thrower got a free penalty throw in another attempt to maim a family member in a show of brotherly love. Also, if you said a profanity the thrower was awarded a penalty shot. We often had arguments involving whether the one who had been hit said a no-no under his breath. My usual exclamation was "Sugar!" repeated several times along with a "Crap crap crap." And appeals to our heavenly father - any cries such as "God that hurt!" warranted a freebie. And oh yeah, if you rubbed the appendage, torso or head part where you were hit, guess what? Your loving brother got a free penalty shot for that, too. And of course if you nailed your brother in say, the left forearm, you kept aiming at that same area for maximum damage. Sometimes we'd play for something - the last ice cream bar in the freezer or who got to pick that night's TV shows, but usually we played just because we enjoyed it.

The hard part had been explaining the welts and bluish bruises to our mom.

"Bad hop," we'd say. (My dad always valued toughness in a player, especially when we watched football and hockey games and guys would get hurt, get stitched up and go back in.) But the one time we played with a baseball my brother nailed me in the sconce, a shot to the cranium and knocked me out. I put my hand up to deflect his heater but it must have been a slider. Our rules had evolved over time. Head feints were allowed by the target as well as ducking. Faking a throw by the thrower was not. I think I had been in the process of making a head feint to the right when Benny's sidewinder missile struck pay dirt. Benny let out a big "Oooohhh," like he knew it hurt but that he was downright pleased with himself. That's what I heard as I looked at the sky on my back before passing out. Luckily Mom had been at work, and after the ice bags were taken off I wore my Indians' baseball cap all night so she couldn't see my wound, which was right at the hair-line. Benny and I decided to give up using a baseball after that until I came up with the idea that we could still play with a hardball, but we had to throw left-handed. That lasted one time; Benny hit me just below the left knee on a bad hop and I honest-to-goodness couldn't walk two steps without limping. We decided to tell mom right away.

" Mom, Stevie's kinda hurt. We were playing catch and one of my throws kinda got him in the knee," Benny said to Mom as we came in through the kitchen screen door as she was peeling red potatoes.

I gave him a look when he said, "Playing catch."

Mom immediately went to the door, opened it and saw me dragging my leg as I came in the house.

"Benny, get an ice pack for Stevie."

Then Mom said, "Where are your gloves?"

Benny said, "Uh, we were practicing without them. You know, we think it will make us better. If we can field without a glove, imagine how good we'd be with a glove."

Even though I didn't blame Benny I enjoyed Mom giving it to him.

"That's crazy," Mom said. "You could kill your little brother!"

I grinned at Benny. He didn't have anything to say. I sat down at the kitchen table while Benny went into his bedroom, trying to distance himself from Mom. I could tell that he wanted to explain to Mom about the toughness aspect, but thought better of it. After about a half hour, while convalescing at the kitchen table with a fresh bag of ice on my knee, Mom having asked to see it two or three times, Benny came in, went to the refrigerator and got a popsicle. On his way back to his room he bent down and said quietly in my ear, with Mom's back to him at the stove checking on the boiling potatoes,

"I won."

Chapter 48

"Hit me on my hip," I told Hobie, patting my cell phone. The between class discussion had involved meeting for pizza and watching the Ohio State game at Lonnie's later that night after practice. I told Hobie to text me if he could go. Kyle stood with his back to his locker, half listening, waiting for Josie to go by on schedule on her way to her last period class, transversing her way from the far end from her first floor art class. And there she went, as always, flying by—except for the times she had thought of a put down to direct at me, weaving in and out of hall traffic. Kyle yelled at Josie as she looked back at him, giddy with love eyes, laughing as she headed around the corner, social studies class awaiting, a different kind of social studies on her mind. This as Mindy came running down the hall from the opposite direction, intent on getting around the same corner at the same time, then down the stairs to her fifth period English class, on time for a change. From opposite directions they came, both making a tight turn, both hugging the corner, in the same lane.

Ca-rash! Ouch. Books, make-up, lip gloss, cell phones flying, hitting the hallway floor. Both on their knees, gathering their scattered items.

"You bitch!" Mindy screamed.

"You stupid whore! You stupid whore!" Josie yelled. Twice to get her point across.

Hobie, observing from a few feet away, stated the obvious, "Two objects may not occupy the same space at the same time. The Pauli Exclusion Principle of Physics."

Mindy continued her objection to Josie attempting to occupy the same space as she did at the same time.

"You asshole! You asshole!"

Josie countered. "You're the asshole, bitch!"

"This conversation may be recorded for quality assurance," I said as Mindy and Josie continued to cast aspersions upon one another I observed that Mindy had a gymnast's body, in shape, definition in her musculature, but not nearly with the toughness of Josie. I gave credit to Mindy for bringing her down in the open field.

To Kyle I said, "I believe that's a violation listed in the student handbook," and to Hobie, "Mindy probably should have taken the charge."

Hobie put his hand behind his head, referee's signal for a charge, a ball handler running down a defender that had established defensive position.

Kyle read from a dog-eared page of his student handbook, a page that he had frequently referenced to Josie when Josie animatedly recounted to him a conversation with another student in which her locution contained words prohibited from usage at Jackson High School. "Section four, article two. No student should use profane or demeaning language directed at another student in a harmful manner. Violators will receive a minimum of three demerits for the first offense. Repeat offenses will earn the offender a minimum of six demerits which may result in an in or out of school suspension of up to ten days."

I stepped in. Kyle of no help, watching. Mindy called Josie a dyke. More specifically, "You damn dyke!" It was on. I took Josie's punch, deflecting it with my forearm. Mindy went for her hair, yanked a handful, Josie flailing as her head was being pulled. She worked a hand loose and delivered a right-handed sidewinder that landed just under Mindy's left eye. Mindy fell backward. Josie breathing hard, her chest heaving.

"How'd that feel, bitch?"

In retrospect, much of the dialogue exchange between Mindy and Josie lacked subtlety and had a repetitious quality to it. But insofar as getting their points across, I gave that a "Yes."

Tears filled Mindy's eyes, the swelling under her left eye reddening, enlarging.

Several students, hearing the commotion, came out into the hall and now stood, taking in the scene, regretting they had missed the action. Josie excitedly explained to Kyle her version of who and what had caused the donnybrook. She mentioned the "B" word when referring to her antagonist several times in the telling.

"Better get some ice on that," I said as I inspected the mouse beneath Mindy's eye. Mindy had grabbed her mirror out of her purse, surveying the damage. She alternately wailed then swore, the "B" word now being her, as it was Josie's, choice of descriptions to identify her adversary in the fracas. Arms out, I stood between Mindy and Josie, but the immediate threat had died down, though an adrenalin-rushed Josie repeatedly demonstrated The Punch to Kyle and the onlookers. Mr. Danksmeller and Mrs. Whoobee, whose classrooms bordered the hallway-turned-Octagon, entered the scene and took custody of the girls, leading them down to Mr. Pettaway's. Kyle looked at me and shrugged.

"That's going to put a crimp into our double date plans," I offered.

We followed behind, ready to detail the event to Mr. Pettaway, promising to tell the truth and nothing but the truth, so help us God. I had served as the referee, Kyle in the dual role as the ring announcer and second in Josie's corner.

Both received in-school suspensions. Mr. Pettaway said it wasn't a fight with forethought. After calling their parents he made the girls shake hands before they left his office, Mindy holding a baggie filled with ice up to her ever reddening, ever

279

swelling left eye, glaring as best she could at Josie, Josie giving Mindy a condescending smile, quite happy with herself for the haymaker that would add to her resume' and reputation.

Chapter 49

Mindy and I sat in the back seat of Hobie's Plymouth, driving to the dance, Hobie's date - the senior snack bar girl, Cheyenne.

On Wednesday and Thursday before the dance Student Council offered roses for a dollar, to be delivered to the recipients in their classrooms. Deciding to do something special, I went to a flower shop a few blocks from my house, bought and gave Mindy a bouquet, roses and carnations, after school at her locker. She took them, reached up and placed them on the top shelf with several other single roses delivered to her during her classes from other guys that weren't me, saying, "Thank Kyoooo."

Further adventures in Mindyland, I thought. Why am I subjecting myself to this? Then my thought process changed to my hormonal process. Hormones won out. Not even close.

Small talk in the front seat, Hobie and Cheyenne both excited, Cheyenne wearing the corsage Hobie gave her. Mindy leaned forward, arm on the top of Hobie's seat and interrupted.

"Have you seen Piper lately? I thought maybe you had talked with her. Maybe she'll be at the dance."

Hobie's eyes shot an "If looks could kill" look at her.

"No, not in a long time," Hobie lied.

Cheyenne looked at Hobie with an inquisitive, serious face, eyebrows down. Turning, she gave Mindy the same look, but said nothing. Hobie turned the music on the radio up. Mindy tapped my leg and winked.

"I was juuust curious."

Her voice had an affectation, the low creaky-growly voice that she heard her favorite starlets use. Her comment... Who does that?, I thought, but said nothing, thinking that at some point I should.

The dance started slowly, students filing in, exchanging greetings while the DJ kept the music down. But for me, anyway, things quickly heated up. I was with Mindy. Of course things heated up. Mindy made her way over to a classmate she recognized from a class, with me in tow. Mindy asked John Pignatano, who she knew from art class, about his date, Sandy Appelbaum.

"Where did you get her, at a scratch and dent sale?"

Sandy had her back to Mindy, but Mindy knew that Sandy could hear what she said. What was Mindy's motivation? To tear someone down because she thought it lifted her up? Knowing that her comment had registered, she didn't hesitate to wait for a response from John and moved on. I stood not knowing what to do, follow Mindy or stay and apologize for something I didn't do.

Sandy sat sobbing, head down on the white linen table cloth, her purple wrist corsage dampened from her tears, and asked,

"Why does your slutty girlfriend have to be so mean? I'd like to punch that skank."

Well, we're off to a good start, I thought. I had no response to give to Sandy, no defense for Mindy's remark. A blank look crossed my face. Why indeed?

I followed Mindy to her next destination, a group of four girls, a few that I knew, wondering if she was in the process of dropping yet another grenade. Alicia Kaye, with me standing next to Mindy, asked her, "How's the boy?" Mindy answered, "Which one?" and elbow-poked me in the ribs. I didn't feel like smiling. I couldn't keep it in and asked her,

"Why did you say that about Sandy?"

"It was just a joke. Those are just words."

"Words hurt. She didn't do anything to you."

"It wasn't like I hit her. I don't like the way she looks at me in the hall. So words speak louder than actions?"

"Sometimes they do, Min. Sometimes they do."

"Oh well."

Mindy quickly changed the subject. She pulled me out on the dance floor as the lights dimmed and Justin Bieber sang a teen slop-pop song.

"I like the way you care about people. And know what?" Mindy whispered in my ear, as we slow danced. "I think you're really cute. I think I might keep you."

"Don't I have a say?"

"You'll get a lot more than a say, a LOT more," she replied, putting her head on my shoulder. "And I have a question."

I smiled, gave a quick roll of my eyes and asked, "What's that?"

"Which one of your senses loves me the most?"

The music, her smell, the nearness, my heartbeat, her arms linked around my neck, her face against mine - mesmerizing. My adrenalin surged. I felt confident, thought I looked good in my dark gray tux with matching vest and red bow tie. Dancing with the hottest girl in school. Me.

As the night went on Mindy showed off her dance moves, her steps smooth, side-to-side, forward, back, flowing in rhythm, showing off, knowing she looked good, knowing her classmates couldn't help but watch, girls envious, guys admiring. I gave her room, distancing myself, doing a nondescript bad white guy kind of in-place shuffle, my hands doing a slow imitation of boxing, shoulders trying to move with the beat. Some really, really bad dancing on my part.

I walked Mindy back to her seat during a break, but before we got there she motioned to Robin to go with her to the girls' restroom. She turned and pointed in that direction to let me know. Genesis and Eddieking walked by me, and with Mindy out of listening range Genesis leaned and said in my ear,

"Looks like you got yourself a hoochie mama."

I took a deep breath. "Yeaaah."

"I asked her yesterday if you guys were coming together, if she was still going with you."

Afraid to ask, I asked anyway.

"What did she say?"

"She said you're still in the mix."

Eddieking added, "I think she's playin' ya, brotha."

I hadn't quite absorbed those comments when K.J. walked over, dressed in white on black, white tuxedo jacket, black bow tie, white shirt, black slacks, his demeanor exuding the usual confidence.

"Way to get down, Steven. Way to get FUN-key with your bad self."

K.J. couldn't contain himself, doubled over, giggling, one hand on my shoulder the other holding his convulsing stomach. I shrugged.

I wandered over to Kyle, hands in my pockets, as he stood air drumming with his drumsticks.

"You look a little wound up, Buddy."

Kyle kept drumming, hands up near his head, then with a flourish, banged an imaginary cymbal three times. Sweat showed through his t-shirt.

"Sounds good," I said.

The DJ announced that we would be given a break from the pop schlock that he had been playing - my words, not his - and that Rabbits In the Living Room would begin their performance in fifteen minutes. Mrs. Huffington walked up as Kyle stuffed his drumsticks into his back pockets.

"Break a leg, Kyle."

Kyle gave her a quizzical look.

"I just meant that I'm sure you're going to rock the house,

Kyle."

Kyle smiled. He knew that term, even used it himself.

"Thanks Mrs. H. And your hair looks really nice tonight."

Her short gray hair did look nice that night. Kind of a side swept pixie bob-do thing. My powers of description failed to describe it accurately.

"I was going to go for the spiky look, you know, to look hip for your concert, but my hairdresser Mr. Robert said it wouldn't look principally enough, that I guess you'd say it would look unprincipled."

She patted her hair on one side, then the other, just in case a strand of her new do had strayed. She needn't have worried. The amount of hairspray she had used would have kept the Titanic from sinking if applied to the hole the iceberg had caused.

Mrs. Huffington had told a joke. We both laughed, knowing it was good for business if we did.

"That's a good one, Mrs. H.," said Kyle.

Mrs. Huffington gave Kyle a wink, then wheeled and headed toward the pizza and punch table.

The Rabbits rocked it out, as expected, starting off their set with Metallica's *Harvester of Sorrow*. Josie sat next to Kyle and watered him from time to time and toweled off his face and forehead. I watched from the back, declined an invitation from Mindy to dance as she waved at me to join her on the dance floor. I stood with Smalls, Philco, Jose' and Eddieking at the back, eating sugar cookies, sweating, shirts stuck to our backs, watching the girls dance under the strobe lights illuminating them in white, blue and red streams, making it look as if they moved frame-by-frame in a 1920s movie. Eddieking's girlfriend Genesis rocked it out with her basketball teammates. Eddie had some moves, but the fact that he wore his red high top basketball shoes with his suit limited his dancing dynamics. Hobie and Cheyenne bounced from groups of Juniors to groups of Seniors, dancing group style with both. Alison and Jillian danced with each other, with their boyfriends—K.J. had silky-sweet dance moves—and also with a clutch of their senior girl friends. Lots of head and shoulder shaking along with showing off their dance moves for each other, accompanied by laughter.

At the start of the Rabbits' third and final number, the Scorpions' *Rock You Like a Hurricane*, we heard a commotion behind us. Clapping, whistling, pointing, and more than a few Oh-My-God's! from the girls. Mrs. Huffington and Mr. Kleindienst had made their way to the middle of the dance floor, the students surrounding them. Mrs. H. did a lot of circling movements with a hand on one hip, the other in the air with a wagging Number One index finger pointing up. Despite her girth, Mrs. Huffington had a tight turning radius. I think her ballast helped as she twirled around the floor.

Shouting into Smalls' ear, I said, "There are forces at work here beyond our capacity to understand."

Smalls responded, "Mrs. H. is looking good. She must have given up lunch today to get down to her playing weight."

Though not acceptable to clamor vociferously at an administrator so loudly under normal circumstances, Smalls took advantage of the situation.

"Go crazy, Mrs. H! Go crazy!"

Mr. Kleindienst mostly looked down at his feet, but did a burst of what looked like the Electric Slide as the kids shouted and howled.

"Do it. Mr. Kleindienst, do it! Yeah, Baby!"

Not exactly slam or mosh pit dancing, but still highly exhilarating for those assembled, and an image makeover for Mrs. H.

The Rabbits finished their twenty minute set and thanked Mrs. Huffington, all the members pointing, then bowing in her direction. When the lights came on again, a communal sigh could be heard, a come down from the Rabbits' and the higher-ups' dance performance. We started looking for our jackets, girls their purses, ready to hit the door, not interested in the DJ's last set.

Hobie drove us home, dropping Mindy off first. We had little to say on the ride, but Mindy had her head on my shoulder, tuckered out from her dance-a-thon. I put my arm around her, as I thought protocol called for.

When we pulled up in the driveway Mindy whispered, "I'd invite you in, but you-know-who is waiting up for me."

A quick kiss and Mindy slid out of the car, pulled her dress down, and hurried up the sidewalk and inside her house. The porch light winked off. Not exactly how I wished the night had ended. My summation of my night: 50/50. Still a jump ball. On the dividing line between our relationship going strong or crashing and burning, the needle remained smack in the middle.

Chapter 50

Tournament week. Opening game Wednesday, with the winner advancing to the sectional final on Saturday night. The progression being sectional, district, regional, then state.

"Two wins at each, eight in all and you're state champions," said Coach Arnold. "Dream big, fellas."

Only my tournament dreams had come thudding to a temporary halt. The doctors said no competition for a week. I could practice light, take part in shooting drills, walk through dummy offense, but nothing where contact would be involved. I felt like an outcast, shooting at the side baskets, then stopping to watch my teammates go through drills, plays, then scrimmaging, their reversible jerseys damp from sweat, mine dry. I listened to Coach go over strategy, my name not being mentioned.

"Coach won't even remember who you are after Hobie scores about thirty on Tuesday,' K.J. told me in the locker room after practice. "When's the last time he mentioned your name? Yeah, Hobie's fired up. He's a great 2 guard, that little guy is. He's like a power chord, gives off a vibe, gives his teammates energy."

I listened, not knowing to laugh or frown.

"Oh yeah. 2 guard. That's your position, isn't it? Or WAS your position."

K.J. followed with a high pitched hee-hee-hee.

"Very amusing. I'm very amused. Thanks for sharing. Thanks for caring."

"Just a brotha tryin' to be real with anotha' brotha.' Don't be poutin' now. In fact, don't even think about it, bro."

Instead of going home I went back out in the gym and took a hundred more shots. I'd be ready when Coach decided to play me again. I wondered... Would he let me start if we played into next week, or had my season ended with my decision to be a living sacrifice?

At lunch the next day Mr. South handed Hobie an office pass to the counselor's office. Probably something about his next trimester's schedule we thought. Five minutes later, Mr. South came over with a pass for me. Probably have to make a choice of an elective, choose between a media class or sports medicine, something like that.

My counselor and Hobie's were the same, Mr. Pickwick. He had been a counselor at Jackson for over thirty years. My dad had him as a counselor as well as Benny. His office door open, Mr. Pickwick shuffled papers at his desk as Hobie sat across from him. Hobie looked slightly nervous as he glanced up at me as I entered. As I sat down, Mr. Pickwick took off his glasses, and said,

"Stevie, as I just told Hobie, Mrs. Huffington asked me to investigate this—what's it called?"

He turned back to look at his emails, putting his glasses back on.

"Student Fantasy League," said Hobie.

"Student Fantasy League," echoed Mr. Pickwick.

"Hobie has told me that it was his idea. I have to admit that it is a novel idea. Mrs. Huffington said that, too. We appreciate originality. We can see that it took some thought to come up with it. But of course we're concerned about the money changing hands. I called you in because Hobie said your team is winning right now and we wanted to know how much of an incentive this thing, this Student Fantasy thing, has motivated you. Actually, Mrs. H. and I were thinking about doing something similar next year, but without the students having to pay anything. But putting kids on teams, and providing rewards. Everybody gets something, of course, even the last place teams. You know, everybody gets something just for playing."

"Wait," I said. "MY team's winning? I thought we were in, like tenth place."

Mr. Pickwick looked back at his papers.

"As of this morning. Looking at the info Hobie gave me plus checking the grades of the other students on your team from the teachers' on-line grade book that I have access to, your team…wait, it's not your team, it's the team you're on, Josie's team, the…the…Serpent's Teeth is winning. By a pretty large margin."

Great. This is…just great. More ammunition for Josie.

Mr. Pickwick went on.

"What I want to ask you Stevie, is this league, is it an incentive to do better in your classes?"

My thoughts conflicted, thinking about the derisive comments that little scamp Josie would be making, but kind of proud that I'd be on the winning team. I had to take Josie out of the equation. I said,

"Yeah. It does."

Mr. Pickwick nodded. "We thought about making Hobie return all the money he collected to the kids that are playing, but that would cause a nightmare for us. But we are notifying Hobie's parents and there will be something in the student handbook next year about not allowing students to collect money from other students for anything not school approved. Fundraisers, that kind of thing is OK, but this does cross the line. Don't even think about doing this for the third trimester. But as I said, Mrs. Huffington, Mr. Kleindienst, the other counselors and I might come up with something like your league for next year without students having to pay, but being on teams and going for rewards. It is a very bright idea, Hobie."

When Mr. Pickwick complimented Hobie, Hobie's face brightened and his mood changed.

"When you call my parents would you add that last part, about it being a bright idea?"

"Sure, Hobie. Will do," said Mr. Pickwick.

I had to ask Mr. Pickwick a question.

"Would you still let the kids have a draft? That's what creates a lot of the intrigue, who drafts you, who your teammates will be. And if you're an owner of a team, there's the tension of making the right pick for you team."

"We'd probably place kids on teams. Make the teams fair, make them even. We don't want to hurt anyone's feelings."

"But that's a huge part of the fun, being able to taunt kids on losing teams. We love that. One of your buddies flunking a test that costs his team big-time provides primo fodder for some hellacious put-downs."

"I don't think we want to have that…aspect, Stevie."

"So it's going to be like everyone gets a sticker? There's no risk. And what would be the rewards?"

"We'd probably get the local businesses to donate movie passes, fast food coupons, that kind of thing."

"I like it better when I get some crisp twenties put into my hand."

Mr. Pickwick drummed his pencil on the desk.

"We have a lot more thinking to put into it, Stevie. But congratulations on your team looking as if it's going to win. Josie did a great job with her picks."

And guess who did win the SFL? Josie. I had one of my best trimesters, a 3.6 GPA. And every time I received a test back in class with an "A" on it, my jubilation would turn to aggravation, knowing that while I helped the Abberant Academians, I also helped Josie's team.

We shook hands and left his office.

"That damn Josie," I said.

"She got you good, bro. The girl is one bad-ass schemer, maybe

291

worse, or make that better, than me."

"Yeah," I sighed. But you're legendary. Your idea is causing a change in the student handbook. And that they might use your idea—you should have had it copyrighted."

"I'll think of something else."

"No doubt, dude. No doubt."

Chapter 51

The tournament sectional games went as expected, beating league foes Grafton 59-41 and Crane Creek 64-50. Hobie had six points against Grafton and seven against Crane Creek, along with several steals. Team player that I was, I became the champion towel waver, butt slapper, high fiver, leader of cheers from the bench. More than once Coach Arnold and Coach Pettaway looked at me curiously. I wasn't about to let them forget me.

"Lock em' down, Hobie, lock 'em down!" I yelled when he played on the ball on defense, guarding point guards that couldn't get by their own mothers, dribbling with their heads down. "Yeah-yuh! That's you!" when Hobie made a couple uncontested layups after dribbling through the inept defenses whose defenders' skills resembled orange traffic cones.

Both Grafton and Crane Creek's players played as if they wanted their seasons to be over, and both got their wish.

District play started the following Thursday at Lexington High School, with the finals to be played on Saturday night. By some quirk of the tournament draw we'd have to play Lexington, the Minutemen, on their home court if we beat Marion Local on Thursday. Coach alternated me with Hobie in practice after I came off the DL.

"Stevie," Coach Arnold said before Monday's practice, the day I returned to practice full go, "if you experience anything like dizziness or nausea, just stop right there. Understand?"

I'd have to have experienced cataclysmic tremors of several large organs before I'd admit to that.

293

Marion Local gave us a battle. They had upset Midlothian in their sectional final game, the Tarblooders unable to get their mojo back after the brawl with Upper Sandusky. Midlothian came away co-champs with us, but had limped to the finish. An amped-up Hobie got the start against Marion Local, then committed two fouls three minutes in — a little too amped — and coach called my name. I didn't take a shot until the middle of the second quarter, then hit threes on successive trips down the floor. Marion Local, with only a .500 record, scrapped to the very end. Their kids played loose, as the coaches warned us they would, because they had been expected to lose both of their first two tournament games.

"Those boys be playin' with God's money, fellas," Coach Pettaway warned us.

"You best not over underestimate them."

We promised not to over underestimate them.

As my luck would have it, Hobie played his worst game of the season, committing his third and fourth fouls early in the third quarter, the fourth while I kneeled at the scorer's table, ready to go in for him. (Coach started Hobie the second half; I had the look on my face that I expected that before we took the floor for the second half, but hoped Coach would go with me in place of Hobie.) Coach relegated him to the bench for the rest of the game while I played with a newfound zeal. So my attributes then consisted of: shooting threes, occasional drives to the basket, taking desperation charges, and zeal. (When Channel 47's sports guy interviewed me and asked what I thought I brought to the team, I answered, "Zeal." My dad, after watching the video of the station's interview with me on-line, texted the link to me with a question, beginning with the same question he often asked me. **What the hell is wrong with you? Can't you just say you play hard?** I thought about sending my dad a reply accusing him of being a slave to the vernacular, but that would have stirred him

294

up even more.)

Our press gradually wore down the Flyers, who had little depth, and when we scored the first basket of the fourth quarter we led by thirteen. Our defense had done well up to that point both defending their three point shooters as well as their posts. Another of Coach Arnold's adages: "Good defenses can both expand and contract."

With a little less than eight minutes to play it looked as if the game verged on a blowout as we led 49 to 36. Two minutes later tension was building with each bounce of the ball. Our lead cut to four points at 49-45 as K.J. and Tommy missed power lay-ups on consecutive trips down the floor followed each time by a Marion Local three pointer and two free throws when Tommy was flagged for an intentional foul, grabbing the arms of the Flyers' center as he went around Tommy, beating him to the basket.

Marion Local added one more, hitting the front end of a one-and-one when Kenny fouled on the side out in-bounds play to make the score 49-46. Coach Arnold called time out after K.J. rebounded the missed second free throw and Jose' had brought the ball over half court.

A white knuckler when we had already put the game away in our minds.

"Stevie, we're going to run the elevator screen for you." He tapped his program on my knee. I nodded, wiping the sweat on my face away with a towel.

Time back in, dancing on the baseline setting up the downscreen from Tommy, I sliced off his pick to the top of the circle and took the wing pass from Jose', quickly squared and shot it from a couple inches past the three point line. Looked good. For a second. But shot it short.

"Airball! Airball!" The Generals' fans taunted me on my way back downcourt. A few of them grabbed their throats, giving me the "You choked" sign.

2:45 to play. But in a matter of seconds the game turned back our way. Their point guard threw an errant pass to an open post, three feet over his head out of bounds, then seconds later fouled out when we went into our four-corner stall. Jose' made both ends of the one-and-one, then stripped their back-up point guard of the ball and we escaped with the nerve-wracking win.

Coach addressed us in the locker room.

"Fellas, I'm happy with the way you played tonight, even though some of you didn't play your best game."

We all looked at Hobie, sitting on the bench studying his shoes.

"But we better be ready for Saturday. I don't understand why the Ohio Athletic Association is allowing Lexington to play on their home court, but they are. I'm telling you that we're the better team. They say home court is worth ten points, so we better be eleven points better on Saturday or it's 'Hello, baseball' for you baseball players on Monday. You track and tennis guys, too."

Hobie and I glanced at each other. Hobie played second base with me on the JV team last year, and both varsity starters from those positions last year graduated. He knew that I knew that he knew what I was thinking.

Lexington's field house seated about five thousand. SRO signs hung on the entrance doors an hour before the game. Jackson's fans made up about one-fourth of the crowd, the Minutemen rooters the rest (except for the few crazy neutral high school basketball fans that drove two hours to see a tournament game with a big buildup).

Given thirty minutes to warm-up versus the normal twenty in a regular season game, Coach told us to go out and stretch a little, take a few shots, then when the clock hit twenty minutes to go before game time, go into our normal pre-game routine.

Many of Lexington's fans came dressed in their colors of purple and gold, but the students, standing floor level on up to the second deck, came decked out as the Village People. Native Americans, sailors, policemen, construction workers, nurses, cowboys, leather clad bikers, and of course, Minutemen. And they came to not only party, but do what they could to get us off our game. Sitting on the floor stretching our hamstrings, calves, groins, arms, and shoulders, we couldn't help but look at the festive Lexington students, in our warm-up end, all standing, a few feet onto the floor, whooping, whistling, chanting, "Minute-Men! Minute-Men!"

Hobie stood up, took a ball from the ball rack at half court and casually dribbled over and put up a ten footer that missed, hitting the rim and bouncing to the side.

"CLANK!" yelled five or six hundred Village People. Sounded more like five or six thousand.

Hobie and the rest of the team turned their heads to the unexpected razing.

"What the…" I said, holding a ball standing next to Jose'.

Jose's eyes: huge.

An ear-splitting "CLANK!" followed every missed shot.

Some of us - not saying who - acted afraid to shoot. Our coaches stood at our bench at the other end, arms folded, saying little, alternately watching us, then Lexington's students. Our fans that had made the trip tried a few cheers but were immediately drowned out, outnumbered by the Minutemen fans. Alison and Jillian wore worried expressions on their faces though they had come prepared, game-ready as usual, wearing lamp back stickies under their eyes. Even though several of the Village People stood and danced and high-fived five or six feet out on the floor on our end, the referees acted if they saw nothing, standing at mid-court opposite the Lexington student section, black warmup jackets on, arms folded, leaning toward each others' ears to make themselves heard with their comments.

When the clock hit 20:00 we started our pre-game warm-up

routine. The Village People changed tactics. No more CLANKS, but now they counted our misses. We started with layups, so only a few missed ones prompted their shouts.

"ONE!" Then about fifteen seconds later, "TWO!"

But when we moved farther out to take jumpers the People had a heyday, hands cupped to their mouths, "TWENTY-SEVEN! TWENTY-EIGHT! Our free shooting did not go well, either, as they all-too-eagerly noted to both our team and the assembled throng. "FORTY-FOUR! FORTY-FIVE!"

I turned to Hobie.

"I'm not saying that their act is really rattling us, but it, it has us rattled."

"A minor, but significant distinction," Hobie responded.

Gratefully, the buzzer sounded signaling the teams to come to their benches and line up for the National Anthem.

As soon as it ended K.J. grabbed us one-by-one before the coaches could talk.

"I'm pissed. I mean REALLY pissed. Are you going to let those jokers get to you? Are we playing their team or playing those asshole students? I better not see one of you back down the whole game or you'll deal with me afterward."

The coaches listened to K.J., then looked at each other, and whatever what they had planned to say they now thought what K.J. had said had been better. Coach Arnold put his arms out in a "There it is, boys" gesture.

K.J. tore their center a new one. Thirty-one points, twenty-one rebounds. 35-17 at the half. We scored the first six points of the second half, K.J. hitting an uncharacteristic three pointer from three feet past the top of the key as he came downcourt as the trailer. I followed twenty seconds later with another and the Lexington coach called time-out. The Village People were now sitting, and some headed for the exit, carrying headdresses, cowboy hats, construction helmets, nurse's, sailor's, coonskin hats and old Marlon Brando style motorcycle biker caps. Our fans more than once pointed in their direction and jeered, "WE CAN'T HEAR YOU!," our cheerleaders joining in. Good sportsmanship be damned.

Game over. 75-51, Jackson. We hoisted the district championship trophy and cut down the nets as our fans surrounded us on the floor. In the locker room after the celebrating died down Coach Arnold gave us a salient piece of information.

"Mobey Tech beat East Liverpool tonight. We play them Thursday in the regionals. Let's come in at five tomorrow and watch the video of the holiday tournament game. Now get in here," he said, signaling for us to put our hands together for our team cheer.

"We beat 'em once, we can beat 'em again."

"TEAM!" we shouted, then showered and tiredly dressed our weary bodies, and filed out of the locker room for the long bus ride home.

Chapter 52

Sunday evening after the film session Alison and Jillian and I met at the coffee shop. They talked as I half listened, looking around the cafe, turned away, my thoughts to myself, then turning back to them as they paused in their conversation.

Jillian asked, "What's wrong, Stevie? Is it Mindy again?"

"No, not Mindy. I mean yes and no with Mindy but right now I'm thinking about why I can't make my free throws. They could make the difference in a close game, maybe into whether we go to State or not."

Alison said, "I told you why. It's your brain and your breathing."

I told them what Josie had told me, about singing her birthday song and reciting rhyme to herself that she attributed her success to at making her foul shots.

"Don't you get it, Stevie? That's her mantra. That's how she relaxes, puts her mind at rest, how she achieves mindfulness. You don't have to say 'Ommm,' or the traditional phrases or chants. It's whatever works for you. That's one of the beauties of yoga."

I nodded. But I had to think about whether I'd be singing "Happy Birthday" or nursery rhymes to myself or phrases constructed to provide simpletons with a reminder on how to tighten screws in order to make my free throws. More reflection needed to be applied to the task, I thought.

Chapter 53

At Monday's practice preparing for the district semi-final game against Chones' team, the rematch against the Mobey Tech Craftsmen, Coach Pettaway started off the scouting report with a warning.

"Don't want any of that jaw-jacking again," Coach Pettaway told K.J. Pointing his finger at us in a sweeping motion left to right, he added, "And that goes for all of you."

The crux of good coaching, besides teaching fundamentals, is making game plans. Two schools of thought: Some coaches think that if you beat an opponent earlier in the season, stick with what worked, use the same game plan. Other coaches are paranoid, thinking that even if they were victorious they had better be ready to adjust, even make major tweaks, have something different in their pocket to use. Mobey's coach had neither philosophy. He had lost to us the first time, had blown a huge lead because of Coach Arnold's and Coach Pettaway's half-time adjustments. His offensive game plan against man or zone defenses consisted of passing to the wing and passing it into Chones. Passing to the other wing and passing it into Chones. Passing to either wing, back to the point and passing it into Chones. We were afraid that their coach would use their point guard Belisario more as an offensive weapon. The guy could play. But nope, he didn't. Belisario spent most of the game standing around the perimeter after he passed the ball to someone else to pass it to Chones. Nary a high pick and roll with Chones which we had anticipated, as our coaches told us we may have to play some man-to-man if they figured out something that worked against our 1-2-2 zone.

Coach Arnold had a few tricks up his sleeve, or somewhere, maybe back in his almost bald head that he brought forward.

"Stevie, against their man-to-man D we're going to use you on the pick and roll with K.J. Chones plays the 'Shaquille O'Neal Defense.' He won't come out to trap, hedge, or double you at the top of the key when K.J. screens for you. He'll just rely on number 21 - what's his name—Corky Belisario, the guy that will probably guard you—to get through the screen. If you set it up right, K.J. can set a solid screen and you can pop three's off the dribble all night. The second thing we're doing against their man-to-man is having K.J. play high in our 2-1-2 offense. Chones doesn't like to come up that high. If he doesn't, K.J., you'll be shooting fifteen footers from the foul line all night. If he comes out on you you're quicker than he is and you can drive past him and get scored or get fouled. And Stevie, here's another thing. You're taller and stronger than Belisario, though he's quick. We'll use you to post on him. But remember, they might go zone, though I haven't heard that they have all year."

They didn't that night, either. Though Chones had twenty-seven points even though we doubled and triple teamed him, no one else stepped up. Chones had added two impressive tattoos on his huge biceps, though, the one on his right bicep reading *ADONIS* and the one on his left, *ZEUS*. Very nice.

I had twenty-one points, twelve coming on posts on Belisario as their coach screamed and yelled at him not to let me get the ball. His adjustment late in the game had been to have their bigger 2 guard, Ramon Harkness, guard me. Then Jose' posted against Belisario while Chones looked ponderously between the foul line where K.J. positioned himself, and the block, not knowing whether to drop down and help the guards who were tearing it up against Belisario under the basket or to stay with K.J.

"Keep posting up," Coach Arnold told me at half-time.

302

"You mean just 'posting,'" I said. "Post *UP* is superfluous, Coach. Post means the same as 'post up.' No need for the *'up.'*"

Coach took off his glasses, lowered his head and rubbed his eyes. He could have been back in New Jersey, retired, playing gin rummy with his buddies tonight instead of trying to coach teenage smart asses in Ohio. He turned to Coach Pettaway and said something. Coach Pettaway, head down, closed his eyes and slightly shook his head.

Coach Arnold took a deep breath and turned back toward me. "Just keep doing what you're doing, Stevie. Just keep doing that. Was that sentence to your satisfaction? Do I need to change the syntax, or is that OK?"

"You're good, Coach," I said.

Point proven for no good reason.

The final: 66-56, though it wasn't that close. We cleared the bench with an eighteen point lead with a minute and a half to go.

Chapter 54

The regional final. Winner goes to Columbus to play at the Schottenstein Center on The Ohio State University Campus. The regional games for the northern region of the state, were played near Lima at the Elida Field House. Our opponent: the Lima Senior Spartans, ranked in the top five in the state the entire year, record 25-2, a perennial state power and a state semifinalist last season. Led by their Senior center Kent McAvoy, 6'10," could run the floor like a deer, long levers for arms and legs, quicksilver moves to the basket. Blonde hair down to his shoulders, headband an integral part of his look.

Suffice that our game plan planned to limit McAvoy. None of this "Let him have his points and shut down everyone else" theory. Not part of Coach Arnold's personality.

"K.J., get back on defense, give McAvoy room on the dribble when he brings it upcourt. He loves grab a rebound rebound and take off on the dribble. He's not going to pitch it to the point guard, not gonna want to give it up, and when he posts get your hip to the side he turns. Don't let him turn. And you better be quick about doing it. When he posts when somebody else brings the ball up the best defense is to not even let him get the ball. Move on the post pass, get position, get a deflection. But nobody's been able to do that all year. The guy's just too quick."

Yes he was. My recollection of game, the movie that ran in my head for years showed McAvoy, at six-friggin' ten feet tall— dribbling through our team and laying the ball in at our end, our defenders helpless and hopeless, K.J. frustrated. But as good as

304

their offense was, Lima's defense showed holes. A team that beat teams with their offense.

The game took a twist near the end of the third quarter. McAvoy drew his fourth foul trying to defend my drive to the basket on a block-charge call (part of the game plan that Coach Arnold drew up - drive on McAvoy and maybe he'll foul you. That I drove one more time surprised even me. In the second quarter I had a steal, ahead of the pack, laying the ball up and in— but no! McAvoy came flying from behind, timed his jump, and wound up as a volleyball hitter might do starting her or his spike motion—and blasted my layup, the ball rocketing off the wall with McAvoy's roundhouse swat, ricocheting to half court, the crowd letting out a gasping "Ooooh" that filled the field house).

Clawing desperately from behind with McAvoy on the bench we closed a twelve point half-time deficit to four with a minute and a half to go when McAvoy re-entered the game. After Lima missed a free throw, we ran the back screen play for me - we called it "Princeton" - to shoot a three from the wing after I passed to K.J. trailing the play, a play we had practiced a few hundred times throughout the season. I hit it. 55-54 Lima Senior. Lima went into their four corner stall as the Elida Field House crowd roared, the fans pleading, screaming. The clock ticked down to twenty seconds. We fouled, sending them to the line. A miss! But McAvoy tipped the rebound out to their point guard. Fifteen seconds to go.

Jose' and Kenny trapped the point guard, and Hobie, a defensive replacement for Tommy Hurlburt, came up with the ball on the pass Jose' deflected out of the trap and fed it to me running ahead of the play. Driving in for the game-tying layup I saw McAvoy in my rear view mirror. As I hit the second lane marker I jump stopped and pumped faked. McAvoy bit, went flying by but another Spartan hammered me to the floor, coming down hard across my arm and shoulder. Teammates helped me up as I winced and rotated my shoulder, checking for damage.

Nothing appreciable. The tow truck stayed in the garage.

Time-outs called by both teams. Other than a whack on the butt from Hobie the others ignored me, unsure whether their words would aid or harm my karma. My head down, wiping sweat from my hands with a towel from Trainer Mike, coaches' words loud but not registering. I looked to my left. Cheerleaders on their knees or kneeling, Mindy no more than twenty feet from me a few steps beyond the baseline near the corner, her hands clasped, yelling to be heard.

"You got this, Stevie! You got this!"

Time back in. Stepping to the line, again wiping the perspiration from my fingers and palms, a voice came into my head.

Happy Birthday to Me
Happy Birthday to Me

I drilled the first one. Tie game. The players on the lane trying to get an edge in case I missed the second, jostling for position, putting arms over arms. The second one—Good! I could hear the announcer on 97.6 yelling.

"It's good! It's good! Kalkannes' two free throws puts the Kestrels ahead! We may be state bound! Jackson leads 56-55 with five seconds to go!"

As we scrambled back to play defense, pumping my fist, Lima, out of time-outs, quickly inbounded the ball. Instead of giving it to the point guard the in-bounder hit McAvoy on the fly as he arced across the lane from his rebounding position. He took three dribbles and hoisted one a good fifteen feet from the other side of half court. Hobie had made a token effort to guard him, making sure not to foul. Near midcourt we stood, turned and watched the ball's trajectory, arc and descent, our ticket punched to Columbus unless a miracle ensued.

A miracle ensued.

"Hello baseball," said Hobie. Lima Senior players piling in a heap, celebrating. Kent McAvoy already legendary, always would be a legend, at the bottom.

The framed photo now residing in the trophy case of the gym lobby at Jackson High School is of our regional final team, front row kneeling, back row standing at half court in the Elida Fieldhouse, our backs to the basket where McCoy sank THE SHOT, as it became known in Ohio high school basketball lore. (The *Jackson-Courier Times* sports page headline the next day read "THE SHOT Sends Spartans To THE SCHOTT." And the sub-headline, accompanied by a head-on photo of McAvoy releasing the ball, Hobie and I both with heads turned watching its flight, "Kestrels Clipped By Fifty Footer At Buzzer.") Our players are pictured with dejected faces, hair and unis sweaty, coaches unsmiling, the runner-up trophy sitting unwanted on the floor in front of the team. Behind, barely visible in the distance, the red scoreboard in the far end still read:

LIMA SR. 58 JACKSON 56

Chapter 55

The bus pulled into the school parking lot. Rolling slowly around the square that fronted school, two to three hundred of our fans applauded us. I spotted my dad and my brother at the back of the crowd, both clapping. My mother stood curbside with other parents, yelling, cheering, joining in as the cheerleaders led their chant.

We are the Kestrels
Mighty mighty Kestrels
And everywhere we go
People want to know
Sooo we tell them
Whoo we are
We are the Kestrels
Mighty mighty Kestrels
We are the Kestrellls!

We departed the bus, coaches leading the way, shaking hands. The team followed behind, equipment bags over our shoulders as we made our way down the aisle of the bus, a last solemn congratulation given to fellow teammates with a clap on the letter jacket shoulder, a fist bump, a soft high five. We thanked Jim, our season long bus driver, then stepped down, eyeing friends, family, school administrators who sustained their clapping until the last of us were off the bus.

Well-wishers clapped our shoulders. Hugs from Mom and Mrs.

Huffington. A handshake from Mr. Kleindienst and Mr. Goldsbee. My mom waited with other moms while I made my way through the throng to Benny and my dad. I put down my bag, not certain what to expect, criticism or congratulations.

"You did OK," Benny said. Hands in his pockets. A slight smile, then a whack on the side of my face and a bigger smile. I looked my dad in the eye, bracing for a critical remark or a commentary of what we should have done to stop the fifty foot heave that beat us. Instead, a bear hug followed by tears streaming down his face.

"I'm so proud of you, Stevie. Just so proud."

Mindy took my arm. In something that took me months to process, why she picked that moment, Mindy said to me,

"My dad says we're moving to Florida, St. Augustine, over spring break. Right by the ocean. I can't wait."

I stopped and stood looking at her. She drifted back into the crowd, mixing in with the other cheerleaders.

Hobie overheard, leaned over to me, and said, "Thanks for playing. Please take our survey. How would you rate your dating experience - Highly satisfactory, satisfactory, average, unsatisfactory, highly unsatisfactory. Please add any comments and submit for your chance to win another dating escapade. We hope to make your next romantic attachment even more exciting. Your feedback is important to us."

Multiple thoughts rolled through my head. How… when… why…WHAT?! My dad and Benny and Mom gave me a little discretionary space, then followed me walking through the parking lot. Josie surprised me, grabbing my arm as I walked by the Jimenez family and Kyle, standing by their van.

"I thought you had it won for us, Stevie. Just wanted you to know I was yelling for you to make those free throws. Imagine, me rooting for you."

Josie laughed as Jose' looked at me and shrugged.

"Thanks, Ms. Jimenez. Maybe next year we can root for each

309

other."

Josie, still laughing, turned away, taking only a second as usual to quip from her insult arsenal and said over her shoulder, "Don't count on it!"

Then she added her usual parting warm wish.

"See ya. Wouldn't wanna be ya!"

Kyle looked at me, hands in the pockets of his jean jacket. He gave a what-can-you-do look at me, raising his eyebrows, then shook his head as his beloved walked away from us. A momentary silence as we looked at each other, not knowing what to say. Then, Kyle smiled, gave me a bro-hug and sighed.

"Rock on, man. Rock on."

I nodded.

"Yeah. You, too. See ya at lunch. Keep it steady."

And that's the way we rolled. Boats in dry dock. Season: Over.

JACKSON KESTRELS BOYS VARSITY

NUMBER	PLAYER	HEIGHT	POSITION	YEAR
5	Jose' Jimenez	5'10"	Guard	Junior
10	Hobie Gajun	5'7"	Guard	Junior
11	Punky Schmidt	5'10"	Guard	Sophomore
12	Eddie King, Jr.	6'0"	Gd. - Fd.	Junior
15	Gary Vergiels	5'9"	Guard	Sophomore
20	Jamil Boutros	5'9"	Gd. - Fd.	Junior
22	Stevie Kalkannes	5'11"	Guard	Junior
30	Jonnie Lomax	6'2"	Forward	Junior
35	Kenny Brown	6'1"	Forward	Senior
40	Tommy Hurlburt	5'9"	Forward	Sophomore
45	Jason Lonsway	6'3"	Forward	Senior
50	Jamey Watson	6'5"	C. - Fd.	Junior
51	K'wame Jordan	6'4"	Center	Senior
52	Tyrone Latimore	6'2"	Center	Sophomore
55	Larry Whippington	6'2"	Center	Senior

Varsity Head Coach - Pete Arnold
Varsity Assistant - Tucker Pettaway
Junior Varsity Coach - Luke Kopastynski
Freshman Coach - Tyrell South
Trainer - Mike Swoboda
Athletic Director - Wally Goldsbee
Principal - Edith Huffington
Assistant Principal - Phillip Kleindienst
Dean - Tucker Pettaway

311